TESTING TIDES

Testing Tides

S. Howard

Testing Tides

the second volume of the Mayflower Trilogy

Published by Hodgers Books.

First print edition.

To my friends

Flow and ebb.
Skim these testing tides, and travel
Beyond.

T.R.S. Hayward

Testing Tides (Verse 4)

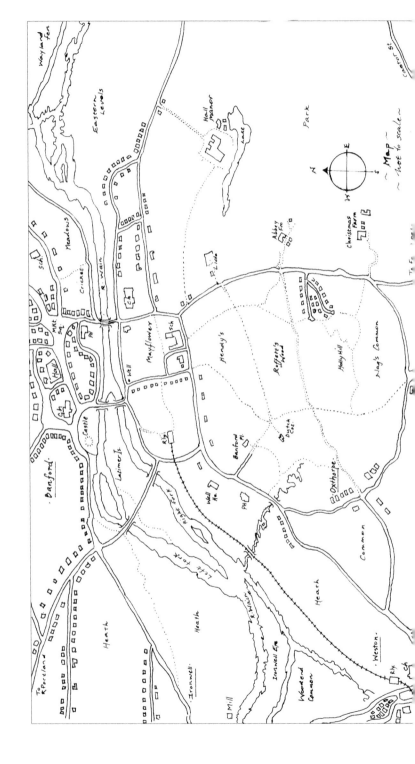

1.

Mayflower

Max

"Honey, is everything OK?" called Chloe.

She had heard a slight thump and came up the stairs cautiously to where Max had been on a step-ladder returning their suitcases to the loft.

He lay in a heap on the floor.

Chloe's heart constricted as she slid down to his side. Without even touching him, she knew he was gone.

"Max, Max!" she cried. "No, no, no. Don't…. Honey, wake up!"

She tilted his face, felt his throat. He was waxen – a lifelike, deathlike, doll.

She shook him, she kissed him, she performed artificial respiration for what seemed like hours. She sobbed and shivered and screamed.

A friend called by on the off-chance of a cup of tea and to welcome them home. Finding no one in the kitchen, she too climbed the stairs. It was she who phoned for the ambulance, which arrived post-haste.

Max was lifted from the arms of his loving wife by strangers, and driven away.

Chloe and her friend Dora sat together holding hands, side by side at the kitchen table, in a house of uncharacteristic silence.

Shock

"I'll have to cancel New York."

"What?"

"We were flying to New York at Christmas. Shane's coming down from Maine. He's going up there to lead dog-sledding trips this winter."

"Where is he now?"

"Colorado somewhere. I have his address in my little book." Chloe found half her brain was still unaccountably able to use words and make rational deductions while the other half was drifting somewhere entirely different – as if two movies were running simultaneously inside her head, both out of her control. She stared at yet another mug of tea without knowing what to do with it.

Dora fetched a pencil and paper, seeking to bring comfort with her own small attempt at taking control. Her hand shook as she made random notes from Chloe's remarks. It was all Dora could think to do. When there were no more odd words to be written, she wrapped Chloe in a coat and took her home to White Cottage where she broke the news to Skipper, her daughter.

Dora ran their friend a bath and put out the fluffiest towels she could find in the airing cupboard. She made up the spare bed, smoothing the sheets with the tenderest of motherly touches. She set two hot water bottles deep down in its snowy depths.

How does one show sympathy, she asked herself. I want to make this nightmare go away, but all I can do is cocoon her with trivialities. However will she cope? How will she survive?

Dora took the batteries out of the little bedside clock and thrust the thing into a drawer. Time didn't underwrite life today. Time was irrelevant, it made no sense. Time was unfair. It never got it right. It either made life cruelly long or brutally short. From the split-second of germination life lay at time's whim ready to be switched off without reason. Babies either grew strong or they withered and died before even feeling the sun's warmth or tasting the air. Old women dragged through yet another day of pain, old men cried out in misery. Where was the order, the progression and the justice? Where was the *compassion*?

Max Shaw is gone, Dora cried in her heart. That sweet, kind man who had finally found the love of his life in our American friend. Two gentle decent people who had only just begun to assemble a life together, had had it all blown away in a missed heartbeat. As if existence were no more than a dandelion clock.

Dora stood at her window and sobbed.

Skipper, as usual when she was angry and upset, wanted to kick something, chop down a tree or swim out into the ocean. The world had abruptly spun out of whack, and people – her people – were hurt. Lost. Chloe had been self-assured that morning, half a happy pair. She had been a wife with a loving husband who together shared a future full of serenity and peace. Now her life was ripped to shreds. Skipper wanted to scream at something, but instead she picked up her little cat and wept into his fur. Dora discovered them together in the garage. The cat leapt down and rushed outside while mother and daughter clung miserably together.

Gradually their storm waned.

"Where is she?" sniffed Dora.

"In the sitting room. She wanted to be on her own for a bit. I'll go back now and light the fire and pour us all a drink. She needs something stronger than tea. Oh Mum!"

"I know, darling. I know."

The doctor called in. He was not only the local GP and Mayflower School's medical officer, but had also become a personal friend. With Chloe Dr Granger was distantly kind and gentle, aware that the warm touch of his hands could bring her no solace today. His heart broke as he watched the beautiful woman drowning before his eyes. He yearned to pull her close and make everything, everything alright again. Instead he checked her over carefully, tenderly, and left medicine on the sideboard.

"Give her two in half an hour, and insist she goes straight to bed," he quietly instructed Skipper. He couldn't look the headmistress in the eye as, even to Granger, the shock was much too raw. Max Shaw had been hale and hearty last time they met – and happier than Joe Granger had ever known him.

He noted Skip was actually wringing her hands as she escorted him to the front door. He paused.

"I'll deal with the cottage hospital and the undertaker for now. Have you phoned Shane?"

"Yes. Left a message. He's out on some trail or other. I suppose he'll fly back over."

Dr Granger nodded. He leaned forward and impulsively kissed her cheek, a daring action but one he hoped would jolt her into paying attention.

"Not quite the moment to say this, but I've accepted a job in Scotland. Starts September first. Sorry."

"What? Scotland? You can't …"

"My replacement …"

"Joe, you *can't* go!" Skipper felt this second blow almost as hard as the earlier one. Dr Granger was as central to her life and her school as Max Shaw had been. As every single person in Mayflower's world was to her. She burst into tears again.

Joe Granger let himself out.

Reg takes charge

"No, that's not right," cried Mrs Bailey, the school secretary. She gazed at the headmistress, stupefied.

Mrs Clark was explaining that Max Shaw had suddenly collapsed and passed away yesterday afternoon. "You've made a mistake. I only spoke to him Friday. He was here sitting on my desk and telling me about….. You're wrong, he's fine."

"Nevertheless, Peggy. I'm so sorry. I'm as shocked as you. We all are. I have to break it to everyone today."

"Oh my god, poor Chloe." Peggy burst into tears. "They've only just got married! How can he be dead?" She wasn't the crying type, but today she howled.

Cathy Duke came in only to be told the same story and react with similar disbelief.

"Why? Why would he die? He isn't ill. He's *happy* for the first time for ages. He loves Chloe. They are going to be happy together, finally. That's not *fair*."

It wasn't fair – there was no doubt about that. Whatever force managed the universe it did not include fairness in its kaleidoscope of qualities.

The teaching and cleaning staff came into school later to prepare for the Autumn Term, and all were met with the appalling news.

"Where's Chloe now?" asked May Fisher. She was as white as a sheet. Jean had her arm around her. Everybody was in the staffroom, feeling the need to have their friends around them.

"My place, with Mum," said Skip, her mind adrift. "I don't know who to speak to, really. What should I be doing?"

Nobody had any suggestions other than to engage some undertakers. Such a sudden tragedy had never happened to any of the tightly knit personnel at Mayflower School. The death of its former headmistress, three years previously, had been entirely expected and occurred at the local cottage hospital. Miss Broadstock had been a difficult old lady – more respected than actually loved. None of the present staff had been especially close to her. After she died the school had run itself for a year before Skipper Clark and Chloe Owen arrived from America to take it over.

The teachers stared at each other, unable to suggest anything.

Reg Green, the caretaker, unexpectedly took command.

"You'd better leave this to me, Miss," he said kindly. He was not unused to dramatic situations and knew very well how to cope with death however suddenly it arrived. He abandoned work for the day to use the phone, talk to the vicar, and make several visits.

The staff sat on in school, talking everything over. They tried to think of ways to support Chloe however they could. Eventually Guy, Mike and Charlie walked round to Well House and cleared away the suitcases and step-ladder. They tidied up, cleaned and locked the house securely, calling in at White

Cottage on their way back to school to hand Chloe the door keys.

She was sitting with Dora in the lounge looking out at the beautiful summer garden but seeing nothing. She was grey and limp and her head ached. She stared at the house keys as they lay in her lap, and wondered who they belonged to.

Shane

Shane arrived within the week. He had only been back in the States briefly, and now here he was again. It felt all wrong.

Attending his mother's wedding just after school broke up for the summer vacation and moving her into Max's home, had been the whole happy, hopeful reason for his first visit to England. Now here he was again trying to hold onto her as her life spun out of control. To Shane it was unwelcome déjà vu. This was how it had been when Sam, his father, had left home all those years ago. Then, barely an adolescent, Shane had put his own misery aside in order to stop his devastated mother falling to pieces. He watched the wheels of the plane touch down on the tarmac and felt very old – old and weary. Life was a series of repeats, like the chorus of a song. It wore you out.

Ernest Chivers the school librarian, and Mike Paton who taught the fourth form, met him at the airport, and they had a long, long talk on the train ride home to Banford. Ernest had arranged to put Shane up at his home, Garratt's Hall, where there were plenty of spare bedrooms. Ernest had recently started to rent Dutch Cottage, a charming house a few miles away, but a week into his summer visit to a cousin in Portofino, his father had sent instructions that Ernest was to move back to the Hall while he himself went abroad for an extended visit.

As Ernest had always found life much calmer when he did not argue with his father, he shook off his disappointment and did as he was told. But he was finding Garratt's Hall dreary and lonesome now. He privately welcomed Shane's company.

The three clattered in through the front door and Mike threw Shane's haversack down on the floor. He looked around.

"Where's Sir Hugo?" he asked.

"Canada," said Ernest shortly. "Ottawa, I think. Won't be home until November apparently. I spoke to him on the phone last night. That's right isn't it, Bunting?"

Mrs and Mrs Bunting were Sir Hugo Chivers' live-in housekeepers.

"That's correct, Mr Ernest, November." Bunting knew it would not be November and it certainly was not Canada, but he did not enlighten Mr Ernest. He took the haversack upstairs while Mrs Bunting poured three cold beers.

Mike walked Shane down the street to find his mother. He came back in low spirits.

"That poor lady," Mike sighed and sank down heavily onto the sofa. "She's a mess."

Ernest nodded. He had been brooding on the international nature of Chloe and Max's relationship. She was American, he English. They had become engaged in Paris last Easter, and their honeymoon had been spent in Venice.

"Paris and Venice. Two beautiful places she'll never want to return to," he commented and poured another drink for them both.

Shane returned after a few hours, and ate some dinner with them. He was very different from the effervescent cowboy Mike and Ernest had come to know barely a month before.

Mike cycled home about nine to his own mother. It was a relief, after all the emotional exhaustion of the day, to be riding along in the fresh air. It gave him time to think and appreciate everything he had, especially his darling, dotty, irritating old mama and his own tediously predictable schoolmaster life. He gave thanks in his heart for all things reliably ordinary.

Max's funeral took place the following week. The church of St Andrew was packed, and many local ladies found themselves weeping afresh at the loss of such a charming, romantic and attractive local figure. Only now there was room in their broken fantasies for poor Chloe too. They had almost hated her for marrying Max and scooping the most desirable man in town from right under their noses. Now she was a tragic, shattered heroine, for whom no one had anything but genuine sympathy. The fairy tale courtship, the wedding, had been dreamlike. The happy-ever-after had lasted precisely a month.

Rev Bill, the vicar, was kindness itself. His words were sincere and his professionally delicate handling of the formalities impressive. There was comfort, Chloe found, in the gravity of the old Anglican service and in the dignity the vicar accorded to the ceremonials. He had known Max well, and spoke from his heart.

The next day Chloe and Skipper, Dora and Shane and her husband's niece, scattered Max's ashes beneath the huge willow tree in the garden of Well House, where he had lived his entire adult life. The glorious evening sun lowered itself beyond the river in a final salutation. His rites of passage were done.

Chloe reorganises her life

"I can't live there, Skip, not in that house. Not now."

"What do you want to do? You can stay here at White Cottage with us for ever if you want," said Skipper. It was time to reopen school and her mind was trying to focus on all that that entailed while also giving as much attention as she could to her grieving friend's needs.

"I've called the landlord of my old place in Church Road. It's still empty, so I can go back there. That wasn't ever Max's home, so I'll be fine. I'll take Cassius. It's best."

"What will you do with Well House?"

"Lock it up. Sell it, maybe. I don't know yet. I have a little money – Max's money – but I don't want to stop working. I wouldn't know what to do if I did. Look, if you're OK with me staying at your place for now, that'd be great, then I can move back to Church Road once school has settled down again. Is that OK? I may be a little tardy and less energetic at first though. I'm sorry."

"Sweetie, I'm OK with whatever you want to do, and I'll help any way I can. You stay with Mum and me as long as ever you want. But, actually, I think Church Road is a very good idea. As you say, it was your own home, nothing to do with Max. It's pleasant and just right for you. Will Shane be staying on?"

"For a little while. Until he thinks I'm OK again, I guess. Yes, Church Road will be better for me. I have Cass to take care of, too." Max's dog was now her responsibility and Skip privately hoped caring for the animal would prove therapeutic. "Poor old boy. He keeps looking for Max and pining. We both need a change."

This move sounded like a step in the right direction. Skipper wanted Chloe's innate practicality to kick in now that a little time had passed. In her view, making such a definite choice was a healthy start.

Shane helped relocate his mother. On moving day Charlie Tuttle drove a borrowed pick-up truck with her few sticks of furniture in, which Terry Green and his mate Olly placed back in the house under Skipper's direction. Mike, Ernest, Ben and Betty Nesbit all mucked-in, and Chloe's home was cleaned and set up again in only a few short hours. May and Jean dropped by with some fresh groceries and Rev Bill and June brought a casserole. Dora helped by taking Cassius for the day. The place looked like home in no time. Even the curtains Max had hung for Chloe the very first morning he had walked past her front door were back on their familiar hooks.

As for Well House, it was locked up, shuttered, bolted and abandoned. Chloe secretly hoped she would never have to walk through its gate again. Gradually, hour by hour, day by day – just as she had done when Sam had walked out on her all those years ago – she locked all her hopes and dreams away behind a steel door in her mind, and threw away that key too.

Shane returned to Colorado. Life went on.

Despite her predictions and her shaky state of mind, Chloe Shaw was standing ready on the playground the morning Mayflower school reopened for its new academic year.

School opens again

"What are we to call her then?" asked Pru Davidson, the cleaner, on the first day of the Autumn Term.

"'Ow d'you mean?" asked Reg Green.

"Mrs Owen or Mrs Shaw?" This was a hot topic of conjecture in Pru's world.

"Shaw. She's Mrs Shaw. If she was Owen still, it'd be like Mr Max never 'appened, wouldn't it?"

"I suppose so. Alright, Shaw it is." Pru trundled off, slopping water on the step. She turned and added, "Did she kill him with too much sex then?"

"Gawd's sake, Pru! Don't go saying such things. O' course not. 'Eart attack. Some kind of weak bit they said, what 'e never knew nothing about." Reg had never thought of the possibility of having too much sex, and now he couldn't stop thinking about it.

"Oh," said Pru, scornfully. A heart attack was far less sensational, a bit hum-drum. "Should have had a medical examination before getting married. They do on the films." She poured her dirty water down the outside drain by the wisteria. "Should have checked."

Reg scratched his head. Too much sex?

Three children crunched up the drive. They were neat and tidy for now, with new uniforms and brightly polished leather satchels and home-made shoe-bags.

"Morning Mr Green," they chorused. "Morning Mrs Davidson. What's for lunch?"

"Never you mind lunch, just get through the morning without muckin' up my clean floors," growled the caretaker. Pru Davidson almost smiled. It was nice to be back to normal.

Joe Latimer and his friends, Keith and Samantha, hurried around the side of the building into the playground. It would never do to be late, today of all days. They swung their shoe-bags like the other children, confident they were fully equipped and completely ready for their new school term.

The whistle blew. Every child stood still and silent. Mrs Clark addressed them, hoping they had had a good break and wishing them a very happy school year. She blew it again and they walked over to their new teachers.

Keith smiled at Mr Tuttle. He had loved and adored Miss Fisher last year, but a man teacher was what he was looking forward to. There'd be no more old lady stuff now. Mr T would teach them boy things and not worry so much about neat writing and good spelling. At least that's what Keith hoped.

Samantha and Joey were to be in Mike Paton's form. They already knew he expected a lot of work from his pupils, and they hoped they were up to it. Joe was well-aware his reading and writing were not as good as everyone else's but he had vowed to try really hard this year to please Mr Paton. Mrs Raina would be there to help-out sometimes of course, which was a massive relief. Joe liked his additional learning support teacher very much. She was never cross if he forgot how to do something.

Mrs Sandi Raina, the invaluable learning support teacher, was already in her quiet study room up in the attic. It was a gorgeous morning and the window was wide open letting in some much needed fresh air. It also allowed the scent of the roses that grew against the school wall to waft by. She looked around her. The room was clean, welcoming and orderly – exactly how she liked it. Lots of books, lots of games, lots of specialised activities, all neatly labelled and stored. Sandi was very much looking forward to getting down to work again. The summer had been far too short, and she and her husband Jamal had taken their two children back to boarding school only a few days previously. Home already felt empty and was much too quiet without the sound of their voices.

Peggy and Cathy were busy in the office, answering the usual queries about lunch money and the anxieties of parents whose children had begun kindergarten that morning.

"He'll be just *fine*, I promise you. There's no need to cry, Mrs Jones, have a tissue. I'll double check in an hour and give you a ring. How would that be?"

"Yes, I realise she's not used to having it plaited. How about you giving me a new packet of rubber bands and I'll keep them in this drawer, so that if they *do* come undone I'm ready?"

"You leave those with me Mrs Gordon, then if he *should* have an accident we can pop a fresh pair on. No, I'll bag the wet ones up and put them in his satchel, so make sure you double-check every afternoon."

"And if he needs a little encouragement to eat all his veggies up, I'm sure Mrs Moore – the kindergarten aide, you know – will be there to give him a gentle nudge. Please try not to worry."

Gradually the tide receded. Cathy put the kettle on before she settled down to checking the first lot of dinner money and figuring out the savings stamps, feeling the need of a brew. It was nice to be back but she hated dealing with Post Office savings stamps. Collecting the extra cash each week was a time-wasting chore for the teachers and a nightmare for her. She decided to remind Mrs Clark to review the desirability of continuing with the dratted things.

Cathy caught a glimpse of herself in the little mirror over the filing cabinet. Her twin-set today was grey. She wore pink on a Monday, blue on Tuesday, yellow on Wednesday, grey on Thursday and Friday was always her favourite – lilac. A single strand of pearls elegantly completed her smooth look, and a black Alice band graced her hair. It pleased her sense of efficiency to be colour-coded. On this first day of term one needed to be extra smart and calm, so cool grey was today's perfect choice. She glanced at her colleague. Peggy Bailey was a vision in Autumn tints of orange and brown which went well with her fiery red hair, not to say volatile temper that this morning was showing a few signs of warming up. Coffee and a digestive might help.

The ladies sipped their drinks, talking in subdued tones mostly about Chloe.

"Who's taken over Dutch Cottage – do you know?" asked Cathy, relieved to see Peggy's irritation gradually subsiding.

"No, I don't. It's a shame Ernest didn't get to live there for very long. Trust Sir Hugo to stir things up for the poor man again," said Peggy. Sir Hugo had vanished and Ernest was clearly browned off by being summoned home like a naughty child. Nothing seemed to be turning out as they expected this term.

Alf Rose, the milkman who delivered the crates of school milk each day, popped his head around the door at that point. He took his cap off, though whether in deference to the ladies or the fact that he was indoors was unclear.

"Mrs Bailey, Mrs Duke. Is it true?"

"Unfortunately it is, Alf. Three weeks of happy married life. Not fair is it?"

"That it ent Mrs Bailey. How's she holding up?"

"Mrs Shaw? She's in school. I suppose she's trying to carry on, like you would. Says she wants to work, not stay at home. And she's moved back into Church Road so will probably want the milk delivered there as before. You'd better go and check. She's upstairs in her study."

"I'll take you," offered Cathy, seeing Alf's eyes roll at the thought of having to find his way deeper into the school. "It's assembly, so you won't get trampled in the rush."

They found Chloe in her study, trying to concentrate on drafting an agenda for the first governors' meeting. Mrs Scott, a retired teacher, was to be acting chairman while Sir Hugo Chivers was elsewhere.

Alf shifted from foot to foot as he mumbled his condolences and asked about future milk and egg requirements.

He was glad to get his orders straightened out, and virtually hopped back down the stairs. Grieving customers – especially attractive American women – were not common, and he felt embarrassed on several fronts.

His horse and cart were a comforting sight. Horace twitched his ears as he munched away inside his nosebag, eager to be off. He had not appreciated being made to wait so long, nor being tied up to the school gatepost like a wild beast. He rolled his eyes at a black cat that emerged from under the hedge and came prancing towards him sideways. One long snuffly harrumph was enough to send the feline scooting away. Alf took the horse's nosebag off and ruffled his ears. He climbed onto the seat for the short ride over to St Andrew's.

"Giddup." he said, clicking his tongue and unwinding the reins from their tether.

Horace was surprised at being asked to trot, but complied all the same. He knew the quiet churchyard with its sweet summer grass was waiting. It was worth a little extra effort.

Class

"I thought we were getting the one with the big hair," whispered Susie Brown, looking askance at Mr Tuttle who was walking round the room, dropping a Beta maths book onto each desk.

"Miss Major's not coming back," Crystal reminded her. "She had that baby – Dylan, remember? We got *him* now, Mr Tuttle. It'll be all singin', 'cos he dooz music."

Susie sighed. Third form was going to be awful – unless you liked music. She was very unsure about male teachers too. She opened her book and wrote her name carefully inside on the special label. She would try her best not to upset Mr Tuttle, but anxiety always went straight to what her mum called her waterworks.

"Please may I be excused?" she asked, her hand waving in the air.

"That aunt of yours needing an early visit?" smiled her teacher.

"Yes, Sir."

"Go on then." Mr Tuttle knew all about Susie and her frequent need for the lavatory. He made a mental note to chat to the new doctor about her when he got the chance.

Crystal carried on laboriously writing her own name inside the new maths text book and hoped Mrs Moore or Mrs Raina would hurry up and come and help her, like they had in Form 2. Remembering how to make each letter-shape was still a problem for Crystal, and she guiltily remembered she had not practised at all over the holidays, as Miss Fisher had advised she should. Crystal wished it was still last year. She looked up as two tears slid down her round cheek and splashed onto her arm.

Mr Tuttle took a folded strip of cardboard he had prepared from his jacket pocket and placed it on her desk. Crystal opened it and saw it had the alphabet and numbers neatly printed on a black line, with a red dot at the starting point of each. This could help.

"There you are," said her teacher softly. "That might come in handy when Mrs Raina can't be here. What do you think? We can stick it down above the pencil channel later. But don't tell everybody or they'll all want one." And he winked his twinkly eye at her, causing Crystal to become instantly devoted to him. She nodded, and decided to tell Susie life in the third form might not be so bad after all.

Dr Legg makes an early start

The new school doctor turned out to be a woman.

Her name was Afra Legg, and she was from the West Indies. She had taken the lease of Dutch Cottage, and had moved in already. She was parking her Austin at the school's front gate one morning, when a cocky-looking terrier trotted up. It was Stringer, the school dog nominally owned by the caretaker.

"Hello, boy," cried the doctor, patting his head. "Take me to your leader."

Stringer obediently led her to the wide front door, which stood open. A horse-faced woman in a cross-over pinny was buffing up its brass letter-box.

"Good mornin'. I'm Dr Legg. Could you direct me to the office, please?"

Pru Davidson sniffed. She wiped her hands down her floral front and led the way across the entrance hall into the school office. Stringer turned and resumed his constitutional.

"Antihistamine," Dr Legg informed Pru, wagging a finger. "One a day will stop that sniff. Ask in Boots. Buy a box of tissues while you're there." She stepped around an astonished Pru and grinned jovially at the two secretaries.

"Good mornin'. Legg, Afra Legg. I believe you're expecting me?"

"Ah, yes indeed," smiled Peggy. "How do you do? I'm Peggy Bailey and this is Cathy Duke. The headmistress will be along after assembly, which should be in about five minutes or so. Your little medical room is through here. Yes, all the records are locked in that filing cabinet – the key's in Cathy's drawer. Now then, coffee or tea?"

"That's very kind. Tea please, if I've a few moments." Dr Legg sat down at the desk. The chair was just about big enough. She beamed at the women.

"I can see everything is nice and orderly here. That will make my visits so much easier. Some of my Ledgely schools were *total* chaos. *Total* chaos, you know!" She roared with laughter. "I didn't bother with breakfast today, though you'd never think it to look at me would you? Tea is most welcome, thank you. I'm hoping to lose a little weight now I live closer to where I work. Maybe I'll walk here across those fields next time."

Mrs Clark bustled in and welcomed her all over again.

"It's so nice to see a lady doctor. Not that we didn't love Dr Granger, of course," she chattered.

Some more than others, thought Peggy.

"Are we all set for the little ones' medicals Cathy? Oh good, I knew you would be. Yes, the mothers will be waiting in the lower corridor. Reg has put a few chairs out. We don't mind if the toddlers come in too. It's a family school, is Mayflower."

"Grand, that's grand. So, thank you for that cuppa tea, Miss Cathy. You can wheel the first client in, I'm quite ready." Dr Legg handed back her cup and waved the women out. Time was pressing and there were other schools to visit today.

Before she left, two hours later, she put her head round Skipper's study door

"Sorry to butt in. I was wondering how your Mrs Shaw is doing? Dr Granger left very strict notes for me to keep an eye on her. What a terrible tragedy."

Mrs Clark was glad this lady was showing sympathy. Skip felt immensely protective towards her American friend and couldn't have tolerated anyone who suggested she should simply pull herself together.

"Chloe's putting on a brave face. Yes, it was an awful, unexpected business, Doctor. They were only married in July, you know. Three weeks. But I think that the routine of school is helping. It's when she's alone she'll be feeling it most. Max and she had spent practically every weekend and evening together since she arrived from America last year. It's been a real whirlwind for her."

"I see," said Dr Legg.

"She's with the Infants now, or I'd say pop in and have a word. Maybe come back later when you have more time. How are you settling in to that lovely house, Dutch Cottage? And how's Dr Granger doing in Scotland? Where's he gone exactly?"

"Oh I'm fine, thank you. He's fine too. He has taken a temporary post in Edinburgh, which includes teaching a class in the university. It's quite a prestigious thing, I believe. I've only stepped in *pro-tem*. I'm not sure what my future will be. I was rather glad to be able to move on from Ledgely as my husband and I have recently separated."

"Oh, I'm sorry to hear that," said Skipper, unsure whether it was the right thing to say.

Dr Legg chuckled. "Well, I'm not. Our lives were impossible. He's an orthopaedic surgeon and I'm a GP so we haven't exactly seen much of each other for about ten years. It makes sense for us to live our own lives, and we are each going to feel much less grumpy now the other is out of orbit. Banford Surgery seems friendly and efficient, and Dutch Cottage is the perfect rural home for me. Do you know it?"

"Yes, the house is lovely. Lady Longmont, your landlady, is one of our governors. Our school librarian, Mr Chivers, lived there for a short while, and before him an artist for several years. It's in a lovely spot and, as you say, very rural."

"But I'm learnin' the birds wake up extremely early around there," laughed Dr Legg. "No rest for the wicked is their motto! And the garden is so overgrown it's like a jungle. Well, I'll pop back sometime and meet your Mrs Shaw. Now I must ride like the wind. Which is the best way to Dane Street Primary?"

She drove off with a toot-toot of the Austin's horn in a blue cloud of exhaust fumes.

*   *   *

2.

Riding home

Playtime for all

Somewhere a child was singing. "Nelly the elephant, back to front, and trumpled back to the jumble…"

I suppose I should really go and put her right, thought Skip Clark wearily. Why do I always have to do everything?

Because you're the headmistress. It's you duty to educate the pupils properly. Off you go, ordered her bossy inner voice.

Let her sing it wrong, retorted her own rebellious inner child. That version is much more fun.

Skipper strolled on, looking for conkers under the trees. It was breaktime and being on playground duty was no chore.

The little ones were happily playing 'houses' in the wilderness. The majority of the school's acreage had returned to nature decades ago, hence the nickname. Within its stout perimeter lay uninhabited Longmont Lodge, a recently restored grass tennis court, and some allotment squares where her pupils grew and harvested their own choice of produce during the year.

Skipper Clark loved all Mayflower's acres, wild or semi-tamed. She and Chloe had been the driving force behind such modest reclamation as had been achieved after decades of neglect. The wilderness was a miniature world where one could wander and dream and regenerate. Where one could pretend to be anything – even a runaway circus elephant.

The youngest children grew very intense when clambering around the roots of the various trees. They had several very specific and traditional 'residences' set up – some large, some small. The Long House, Tiny Corner, Grandma's Tree, Round Robin were the names previous generations had christened these dusty dwellings. Inside, the children defined bedrooms, kitchens, cupboards, beds, chairs and tables. They collected twigs for cutlery and leaves for crockery. Acorn cases could be cups and pebbles might form a hearth. The kindergarteners themselves were the mothers and fathers and babies who dwelt therein. It was the very best playtime fun and competition was fierce for the most popular houses. Shoes and hands might be caked in grime, but imaginations ran as clear and free as mountain streams.

The older children played different games. 'Horses' was very popular. One girl (it was always girls) would be a spirited nag made to jump over the line of bedraggled old box bushes on a complicated circuit, with a friend as her jockey hanging onto the back of her belt. Sometimes the horses were paraded around on a leading rein made from two ties, and encouraged to change speed with the help of a long switch of grass. Sometimes the horses were harnessed together to take a party of four for an imaginary carriage journey. The boys also galloped about, although generally without a friend acting as a horse. They preferred cowboys or spacemen or TV scenarios to dressage. They also liked anything competitive such as tag, a special form of football involving an obstacle course, or sword-fighting with the long leaves of iris plucked from what had once been a vast herbaceous border. Some children spent their time as explorers, creeping around looking for tigers, while others genuinely watched the wildlife, which was plentiful. Others simply enjoyed walking around with their friends chatting and enjoying the open air. Playtime in the wilderness always managed to refresh everybody's spirits.

The whistle went, and a hundred and fifty sweaty children trooped reluctantly back indoors for the hour before lunch. Hands were washed, socks inspected for grass stickers, and jumpers brushed down.

Carol Moore, the kindergarten aide, was a dab-hand at cleaning the babies up and re-tying hair ribbons. Mrs Nesbit, their teacher, looked around at her latest little brood of chicks.

"Now then, before our story, we are going to listen to Kelly's news. Yes, we heard yours, Jason. That's right Kelly, stand here next to me. Now, what's your news?"

Kelly stood up. She squirmed her toe into the side of the teacher's chair and whispered something.

"Use your big-girl's voice, please, so everybody can hear."

"I got two daddies now. My mummy says we're very lucky. I got one in the army what's coming home Christmas, and we got another new one last week. He's got blue pyjamas."

Mrs Nesbit, to the slight annoyance of several little boys who would have liked to know how one went about acquiring additional daddies, quickly closed the session by explaining that it was, surprisingly, already time for 'My Naughty Little Sister'.

Lifebelts

The weekends of the new term were proving tough for Chloe, so she distracted herself by spending them in her study at school gathering assessment data and updating details in the children's dossiers.

These files recorded each pupil's progress together with their equivalent reading and spelling 'ages'. They also included reasoning levels and formal intelligence quotients. This year Chloe wanted to make sure each one included any relevant health or other background detail that might suggest why any particular child was struggling to learn. Not that there were more than a handful of these at Mayflower. Keen to avoid burdening the form teachers with the collation of all this information, she took it upon herself to record and analyse everything, which was a lengthy procedure despite there being only a hundred and fifty children in Mayflower. She and Skipper had been used to managing considerably more at Cedar Street, the American elementary school they had run together.

As she filled in the details of the three new pupils in the top class – two boys and a girl – she thought about each one. The girl – Lizzie Timms – seemed to be settling down nicely and doing well, although she was very young compared to the others in her class. The boys were quite another matter. Ryan Hale was in need of a great deal of extra support since Mr Denny had quickly discovered the child could barely read. He was a large and clumsy lad, who verged on the bellicose. The other child, Gregory Price, was a confrontational and disruptive boy – not the usual type of Mayflower pupil at all. He was bright enough, but his behaviour was atrocious. Greg had a contemptuous attitude towards authority and every adult in the place found him a real problem. The other children were intimidated by him, not least because of his unpleasant habit of spitting everywhere. After only a few days of term no one could stand him. Chloe shook her head and sincerely hoped some blessed Mayflower magic would soon rub off on both lads. She didn't want any unsavoury role models leading others astray.

"You going home any time soon?" Reg Green knocked and peeped around her door. He was limping about the place, checking doors and windows for the night. Stringer came in and licked her hand encouragingly.

"Oh hello Reg. Yes, I'm just off. How's your hip been today? Arthritis is such a beast isn't it? My knuckles are sore too, this damp weather. OK, no, I won't be long. Dora's made a casserole for dinner and promised me something called savoury dumplings."

Reg chuckled. "Soul food, you'd call it," he suggested. "Nice and meaty and nourishing. I expect Mrs York's trying to build you up a bit. You're still a mite pasty-looking, if you don't mind my saying."

Chloe pulled a face. Her friends meant well, she knew, but it was proving hard to be the focus of constant kindness. She shook herself. That sort of ingratitude would never do.

"So how *is* your hip today?" she said, diverting the conversation back to the beginning. Reg's hip had been causing him a great deal of pain lately.

"Hip rhymes with gyp, don't it? Gives me fair old gyp sometimes. Not too bad today though. Must be because it's Sunday – the better the day and all that. I managed to turn me veggies over alright this a'rtnoon."

Chloe's mind raced a little as she figured Reg simply meant he had been able to dig the earth over in his vegetable garden after lunch. Her English translation skills were improving.

"Well that's good," she said, locking the filing cabinet and switching off the light. She bade him goodnight, went down the stairs and outside into the early evening where the church bell was already tolling for evensong. It had grown cool and she was glad of her wool wrap for the short walk over to White Cottage.

How strange it was to be walking alone once more. No warm hand to hold, no muted intimate conversation about nothing at all. Had it been only a year since she had arrived in England? Chloe had not uprooted her life in America with any thought of finding romance – far from it. But then Max Shaw had walked into her life and swept her away like a force of nature. Chloe's astonished heart had soared so very high – like a new-fledged Icarus – higher than she had imagined possible, bright and glittering and free for a few heady happy months, only to plummet down and down, straight through the earth's crust and on into the very bowels of the cold dark earth. And here she remained transfixed, silently screaming through each suffocating subterranean moment. Above her pressed an intolerable weight – beneath her lay circular infinity. She had no strength to change. She could never, ever, claw her way back to the light again. She had no will, nor any desire to even communicate. Nothing mattered any longer. And yet, despite all that, she continued to rise from her bed each day and drag one heavy boot after the other. Why was that? Who was responsible? Tick and tock, step by mechanical step she plodded on. Time was shoving her, time was pulling her. The present moment flared briefly, then its relentless hands dragged her forward against her will. She felt she was being constantly forced down a darksome trail away from 'then'. She had no say in the matter. Tick, tock, tick, tock, tick. Time slammed its heavy minutes down behind her in a wake, with its two callous careless hands. Like so many concrete slabs.

Yet still, every day, from somewhere high above, she was being thrown generous lifebelts from the world she had left. They arrived in the form of a pile of laundry to wash, a dog to feed, a stack of assessment folders to alphabetise. Such kindly-meant life-preservers distracted and carried her on for a while, but she understood what they were and resented them. How dare anyone try and rescue her? How could she leave him behind?

Hearing the doleful church bell tolling like a terrible tocsin, Chloe struggled back to the present, and recalled that today's lifebelt took the form of a casserole with savoury dumplings. Unhungry, unwilling and unconnected, she forced her mind and manners into a semblance of gratitude.

She paused at Skipper's front gate and glanced up at the ancient moon rising out of eerie threads of mist, its lonely face gawping like a huge circular yellow mirror. It too rose and set, rose and set, waxing and waning just as she did. So be it. If the moon could put on a face when everyone knew its heart was dust and ashes, so would she. Another twenty-four hours had tick-tocked away and here she was – still alive, still being forced reluctantly forward.

Still angry.

Trouble in Form 6

Ryan Hale and Gregory Price sat together at the front of Guy's class. They did not know each other and barely spoke, but they shared a similar opinion about the school. It was a stinking dump.

Neither of them liked their teacher. He was tall and bossy and the rest of the class seemed to idolise him. He was always on his feet engaging them in discussions instead of writing what to do on the board and leaving them to it. He knew every one of his pupil's likes and dislikes, their academic strengths and weaknesses, who to gently encourage and who to crack a silly joke with. He knew heaps and heaps of factual information about anything and everything. And (what was worse) he expected you to keep up with him. Every lesson was a headache. You couldn't spend your days on autopilot any more, drifting along under the radar. The new boys also discovered, to their mutual dismay, that Mr Denny was not taken in by any whiningly tearful appeal for sympathy. Women teachers were a much softer touch in both their views. They both unreservedly preferred women teachers. Sitting at the front, being new, having a man teacher who watched them like a hawk and who expected them to behave like the other kids, absolutely stank.

Mr Denny did, indeed, watch the pair closely. From the first day of term he realised this year was not going to be easy.

Greg was from Ledgely and Ryan from some tiny village east of Banford. Each family had moved house during August – Ryan to the hamlet of Ironwell, and Greg to a council house in Trafalgar Road. Even though Mayflower was a particularly friendly and welcoming place, Guy knew it wasn't easy for any child to settle into the top-end of junior school. The work was hard for all the children. They were no longer developing basic skills, they were learning to use them in increasingly sophisticated ways. Friendships were already well-established, and kids arriving from outside could easily be isolated if they made no special effort to be friendly or to join in. Neither of these boys seemed to be at all interested in making friends and were both, alas, very poor influences. Ryan used his fists too frequently and could barely read, while Greg was constantly looking for ways to disrupt the class, undermine the teacher's authority and attract attention. Every day was a battle of wills with Greg. In the playground he spat and swore, in class he was crude and insolent. Interestingly, Form 6 had not taken at all kindly to Greg's continual diversionary provocations and were already ostracising him. They stopped asking him to play, and after the first few days did not join in his attempts to subvert their lessons. Ryan they tolerated slightly better, but rapidly learned to stay out of his reach, as if he were an unpredictable giant. Mr Denny was annoyed that his attention was constantly being hijacked by the two newcomers.

Sandi Raina quietly entered Mr Denny's maths lesson one day, to sit alongside Gemma who found anything involving numbers gave her a stomach-ache. The child looked gratefully at the aide who cheered her up with an encouraging smile. Guy nodded at Sandi. He had asked her to include Ryan in her little extra help group.

He glanced over at the boy. Ryan was large and awkward and barely fitted into his seat. He was currently ramming his pencil into a groove on the desktop and rocking it back and forth. His textbook was on the floor under his shoe, which was too small, unlaced, and very muddy. Guy scooped the book up and slapped it down hard to wake the boy from his reverie.

"Problem?"

Ryan stared back as if from a great depth. He shook his head and slowly bent forward. He held up his broken pencil in mute application for a replacement.

"No more till after Christmas, old son. No, sit still, I will sharpen what's left of it myself. Give it here."

The task was impossible. Guy grudgingly dug out a replacement stub from his drawer and passed it over.

Sandi drifted over to Mr Denny's side.

"Would you mind very much if I took Gemma and Ryan for a short extra session this morning in the Study? Thank you, Mr Denny."

Guy could have hugged her. He caught Gemma's eye and nodded it was OK. She and Ryan bundled out after Mrs Raina and the whole class breathed a sigh of relief.

"Fat thicko," muttered Greg audibly, already on the final section of the maths page. His academic skills were surprisingly good. "He stinks of pee."

"That will do, Mr Price," barked Mr Denny crisply. "Any more rude remarks from you and I will wash your mouth out with soap."

That will only make him spit and swear more, thought Trudy wearily. Her desk was directly behind Greg's and he was constantly annoying her. But it would be interesting to watch Mr Denny try.

Unwelcome news

Mrs Clark hurried out for a breath of fresh air along the dewy paths to Longmont Lodge after opening her morning mail. Mr Watson, the postman, had delivered a huge sackful that had been held up in the sorting office for some reason, and slitting open all the envelopes and scrutinising everything had taken ages. Most of it went straight in the bin, but one delayed communication was stiffly formal and augured nothing good. The more she re-read it, the more it took her breath away.

It was the notice of a school inspection by the Local Education Authority. This formal inspection was due to be undertaken the second week in October. Skip, her mind racing, stared at her calendar in dismay. Only three weeks in which to prepare! The staff would have a melt-down.

She had never undergone a school inspection before. How should they prepare? She flipped through the accompanying sheets of paper but could find no helpful advice. Would they want to look at fancy stuff like special gym displays and needlework? Would they talk to anyone or just watch everything? There was barely time to ensure there were enough textbooks to go round, and that all the lavatories were in full working order. The further Skipper walked, the more panic-stricken she became.

She found Reg in his mower storage room in Longmont's old stable block. He was puffing happily at his pipe as he sanded down one of the playground gates he was preparing to repaint. Stringer, the intelligent little terrier, sat beside him as usual.

"Oh, Mr Green," she cried.

Reg didn't like the sound of that. Use of his surname normally meant he was going to be given another tricky job. He stared at her as Stringer rolled his eyes.

"What's up, Miss?" he asked. He put his sandpaper on top of the paint tin and gave her his full attention.

"There's to be a formal school inspection. It's in a few weeks."

Reg took his pipe out and whistled. "Never 'ad one of them before. Well, not since nineteen sixty-something. Damn." He started packing his paint things away. This was a real nuisance. Stringer noticed the signs, yawned, and cantered off to hunt for rats.

Reg and Skipper walked back to the main building together, deep in discussions about what might need seeing-to around the place. Reg couldn't remember any details of what had come up back in nineteen sixty-something, so Mrs Clark dug around in the cupboard containing Miss Broadstock's records until she found a solitary relevant document. She took it in to Peggy in the office.

"We'll have to have a proper long staff meeting," she fussed. "Cathy, can you see everyone knows? Yes, this lunchtime will be fine – if Sandi and Carol don't mind doing the extra playground duty. I think we have to give the teachers as much notice as possible don't you?"

Peggy concurred. She could well recall the teachers' anxiety when the inspectors had arrived before, and although the school had passed muster then, it might not be so fortunate this time. Standards changed.

The staff heard the news with sinking hearts.

"Why such short notice? What do they actually *do*, Skip?" asked Heather. "Are they inspecting us, or the children or the books or the building or what?"

"No idea, really. This letter doesn't provide much more than an arrival date. It's late because mail isn't delivered to school during the Summer holidays. They should have sent it sooner so we'd have more warning." Skip's mind was racing. "I suppose they'll want to see everything – lesson plans, books, equipment, spending. That's my guess. I suppose they will talk to us all. Children too, maybe. Look, I'll have Reg put up a notice board in here, on that wall, and pin everything I get from the Education Office on it. I've booked a call to Mr Morton, Max's replacement, for tomorrow morning."

"Will they want to know about outside things, like swimming or field trips?"

"I suppose so."

"What about parents? What about the governors?"

"No idea."

"How long will it all take? Is it one day or more?"

"I'm simply not sure, Mike. Last time, apparently, it was a single day and they sent two inspectors. A man for the Juniors, and a lady who observed the Infants doing PE. She asked the children some questions, ignored the teacher and went away."

"Well let's hope it's the same low key event again. I think I could cope with that," said Jean faintly.

"And what if we don't pass muster?" enquired Chloe, voicing everyone's fear.

"I guess they give us time to correct things and come back again later to see we've done it. Or, if it's all terrible, they close us down. I honestly don't know." Mrs Clark was wringing her hands and feeling hot. Why was being a headmistress so harrowing? All she wanted was a quiet life. Then she glanced at the faces of her stalwart staff again and pulled herself together. Showing fear would never do. It was her job to lead. She stood taller and smiled.

"Look. It's a challenge I know, but we'll be fine. We all know Mayflower is a wonderful little school and its staff is the very best by anybody's standards. Let's each of us endeavour to make sure our own little corner of the world is as good as it can be between now and October 13th. Chloe and Peggy and I will cope with the administration side of things, Reg will deal with the buildings, and you folks with the teaching. It's a bore, but we will be fine, never fear."

The governors are told

Skip called an extra-ordinary governors' meeting to inform them of the school inspection. Luckily all were able to attend, even at short notice. It felt strangely lopsided being without either Max or Sir Hugo, but Mrs Scott quickly brought the session to order.

"I'd like to welcome Mr Pelham as our new neighbourhood representative this year, and Mrs Lara as parent governor," she began.

The two new members smiled self-consciously.

Mrs Scott suggested some flowers and a card of condolence be sent to Mrs Shaw, then Skip was asked to explain why she had called them together.

"Lordy-loo, what a to-do," cried Lady Longmont, once she got the drift. She had been unwillingly co-opted onto the board by Sir Hugo, but now found she adored everything to do with the school and would rather be boiled alive than not give it her all in its hour of need. She definitely saw the inspection as an hour of need. "But nil despers, folks. We'll get through this invasion of the body snatchers… " She stopped herself, suddenly realising what a tasteless remark that was. "We'll pull together, Mrs Clark – tally-ho and all that. Don't worry about a thing. What do you want us to do?"

Skipper had had a good think about that following her conversation with Mr Morton at the LEA. He had explained, rather curtly, that no area would be off limits. The inspectors would want to see it all, basement to belfry, kindergarten to top juniors. Before answering Lady Longmont she asked Julia Scott for hints from her experience, as Julia had been a primary school teacher for many years prior to retiring. Skip had high hopes she would have some helpful insights.

"No idea, sorry," shrugged Julia, disappointingly. "Never suffered any inspection other than some woman in horn-rimmed glasses wandering round one morning looking at scripture books. Oh, and some vicar asking about PT. PE you call it today. Sorry."

Daunted, but not entirely surprised, Mrs Clark got back to Lady Longmont. "Well, unless anyone has a better idea, Mrs Shaw and I would be most grateful if a few of you would mind drafting some comments for the inspector to read when he comes. About activities you've been included in, or seen, or think are going well. Or things you dislike, of course, or want changed. We both consider your insights would be most helpful. And maybe you would like to drop by for lunch the day of the inspection and have a word with him. Or her. Just let the kitchen know in advance, if you would." She smiled wanly, hoping they all still loved the place.

The group nodded and agreed enthusiastically. So enthusiastically, in fact, that Mrs Clark knew in her heart they would certainly not show up, let alone write any helpful letters. She was seeing them today as a bunch of well-meaning amateurs, but only in the job for the kudos. She could hardly blame them. Governors were always a random collection.

No one had anything else remotely helpful to say, making Mrs Clark cross she had wasted an hour of her time.

"Well, that's all I wanted to say. I will let you go. If any additional details drop through my letter-box I will make sure you're informed," she said crisply. "I think I will telephone a few other local headteachers and ask about their experiences. Do please keep an eye on this noticeboard for updates whenever you drop in. Thank you for your time."

Rev Bill talked to her afterwards. He could see she was peeved by the governors' lack of practical advice or suggestions. He helped her empty the tea urn and wiped up the cups.

"I don't suppose there's anything much to worry yourself with, you know," he said, trying to be supportive but fearing he only sounded like one of Job's comforters. "He's probably only coming to see what's changed since old Miss Broadstock's day.

Have a bit of a chinwag with the new management and so forth. It'll be fine, you see. This is a splendid little school. It'll be over in no time, and then you can press on with your own ideas for school improvements, can't you? You're always full of bright ideas. Is there anything particular on this year's wish list?"

Mrs Clark stared at him. She had spent weeks last term talking to staff and drafting a long list of suggestions for school improvements, and had handed copies to the governors before the Summer break – but clearly Rev Bill hadn't read his. Had any of them?

She reeled off a few items she was aching for – a little bus, a modest greenhouse, a new shed and some of that double-glazing she had read about for the upstairs windows. She wanted every room painted. She wanted wooden cubby-holes for the children's shoes and some lino to cover the attic floorboards. Reg needed a modern ride-on mower. Ivy could do with some new baking pans. There was the duplicator, the boiler, the skylight, and the staff lavatory. Her list was endless.

Now she was probably going to be forced to hold off on everything by a bunch of official busy-bodies who would like the playground carpeted or the children to study nuclear physics. She stood at the sink sulking.

"Well, you're always energetic," said Bill again, a little taken aback. "You won't have to postpone your ideas for long, I'm sure. Try not to anticipate trouble, my dear." He sounded like a fussy old maid, even to his own ears. He hung up his tea towel and left her to it.

The weather was turning. The wind was rising and the trees beside the road were thrashing madly, sending brown leaves into the sky to get mixed up with the jumble of birds that had been feeding on the harvested grain residue in the local fields. If he had been wearing his cassock Bill could have set sail and been blown all the way home.

"Evening Rev," called Mike Paton, pushing his bike through the front gate and bending down to slip on his bicycle clips. "Better not put that brolly up or you'll turn into Mary Poppins."

"I was just imagining something like that," grinned Rev Bill. "Nasty weather's coming. Wind's in the north – not our usual quarter. It should push you home quickly, of course, you living where you do. If I had a land-yacht I could sail it back to the vicarage."

Mike laughed. "Yes you could. Well, see you soon. Good night!"

"Good night, Mike."

The vicar held his hat on and began his windswept walk home. What a nice fellow that Mike Paton is, he thought. He would have made a good clergyman.

Mike has an idea

Mike hardly had to pedal his bike at all that evening, the wind blew so steadily. He fairly zoomed up the main road past the farms to his junction. Turning east onto Caster Street was quite another matter, however, as the gale was now trying to shove him sideways over the hedge. He was breathless by the time he finally wrangled his bike into the woodshed and went indoors.

"Home again, home again!" he called from the scullery.

"Jiggety-jig!" answered his mother, as she always did every day. Glenda might be growing more forgetful in her old age, but she remembered that. Mike kissed the top of her head as she sat in her chair by the fire. Tilda, their cat, was sprawled out on the sofa beside her.

"Good day?"

"So so. It's very windy. The vicar said he wanted to put a sail up so he could get home quicker."

Glenda chuckled.

"Dinner's in the oven. Just put a match to the gas under those potatoes, dear. They won't take a minute."

Mike washed his hands in the kitchen and looked in vain for the saucepan full of potatoes. There was a nice piece of brisket roasting in gravy in the oven, but the spuds were nowhere to be seen. Glenda was probably remembering those she had prepared the day before. It didn't take long to rectify the situation, and the pair were soon sitting down to a warming supper. Mike wondered again why he remained so skinny. He consumed two good dinners every day.

"You used to like sailing," his mother informed him as she dished out their dessert peaches and custard. "Your dad used to take you over to Benning Water in the summer, when you were about nine or ten. Do you remember?"

Mike did. He had loved standing on the reservoir's sandy beach, because preparing the little sailing boat had been something he and his father had done together. His dad, although morally opposed to fighting, had been drafted into the army pay corps and was therefore mostly absent during Mike's childhood. Right before the end of wartime hostilities he had been posted to Palestine where he immediately died of dysentery. Sailing with him on Benning Water was one of Mike's very few memories of his father.

As he marked books that evening, the idea of teaching children to sail kept intruding on Mike's thoughts. Maybe he and Ernest and Guy, or Charlie, or possibly even Heather, could rustle up a little group of boating enthusiasts. Would Skipper permit it? Would she buy them a boat? How about if they *built* a boat? They might be able to find a kit. Reg Green had served in the navy, hadn't he, so he might help. Mike lay in bed and hoped Ernest would agree to join in. It would do his friend good to be outside in the fresh air and have some proper fun. It would do them *both* good. Mike reined his thoughts sharply back at that point. It served no purpose trying to make other people interested in what you decided was good for them. That was the way to lose chums – and the last person Mike Paton wanted to lose was Ernest. He turned over and punched the pillow with his fist. Tomorrow he would talk to Skipper.

Tempers flare

There was an urgent tooting of a car horn and the grinding of gears as a white Morris Minor rounded the corner into Mellow Close and bumped through its deep puddles to the school's side gate.

"Slow down!" called Reg Green, who was cutting back the hedge at the time. "Ruddy women drivers."

The driver wound down the window. It was Nurse Presley, come to follow up on Dr Legg's visit a couple of weeks earlier. She was more than a little flustered.

"Where shall I park, Mr Green? Yon wee car park has a very tight turn into it and I'm mortal wary of my new bumpers," she cried.

Reg closed his mouth but the scowl barely lifted from his brow. Nurse Presley's bumpers didn't look that pristine to him.

"Where's your old bike?" Obviously the nurse's black bicycle was a thing of the past, but he had to ask.

"I know, I know. I miss Tilly terribly, but the doctors insist I now use this wee car, so I can run out into the highways and byways with all my equipment. I passed my driving test this summer you know, but it was a trial, Mr Green, a sore trial. Luckily my test was on market day in the town with many a cattle truck, so I didn't have to change gear very often. Well, twice. Now then, parking?"

"Leave it 'ere in the lane, Miss. I'll keep an eye on it. Give me the key so's I can move it if a delivery comes. I don't want Ivy kicking up."

Nurse Presley gratefully handed over the keys, and hurried into school with her bag. She wasn't sure about that new car at all. It made her flurried in a way Tilly the Bicycle never had. She pulled her hat straight and braced her shoulders as she entered the school office. Appearances were important.

Cathy was explaining something complicated to Chloe while Peggy dealt with a sobbing first former whose knee was bleeding profusely.

"Och deary deary me, a great deal of blood there, Mrs Bailey. Will I take over? Come, child."

So saying, she whisked the hiccupping infant into the tiny medical room and closed the door.

Peggy stared after her. "And good morning to you, Nurse," she seethed. "I had that perfectly under control." She glared at Chloe and Cathy who visibly shrank.

"I'll just go and…" Chloe abandoned Cathy without looking back. Cathy puffed out her cheeks. This term wasn't getting any easier.

"It's because Dr Granger's gone, I expect," she suggested to Peg. The nurse had a decided crush on their former GP. "She'll be missing him."

Peg snorted. "Hmph. That's no excuse. My guess is he's done a runner just to get away from her."

Cathy smiled. "I wouldn't be surprised. Or else he's in Edinburgh learning the language so he can come back and woo her in perfect Scotch. What do you bet?"

That lightened the mood. "Now that *is* bonkers!" Peggy chuckled. They thought they knew who the doctor was romantically interested in, and it wasn't his nurse.

Having calmed down, Peggy turned her attention to the pile of moth-eaten documents she had spent the morning gathering from old archive boxes stacked in the attic. She scooped them up and carried them into Mrs Clark who had erected a trestle-legged dinner table in her study. Here she and Chloe pored over anything that might relate to school inspections. The log books had yielded some pointed observations, and a few pages of additional paperwork had finally come through from the LEA, but none of it really explained the details. Skip took Peggy's armful gratefully.

"Is there anything in this lot, do you think?" she asked. "I can't find much here."

"No, I wouldn't say so, but you might want to… " Peggy had just begun to speak when the door burst open and a furious Guy Denny stormed in holding Greg Price by the scruff of his collar. The boy's eyes were blazing and he was trying his best to kick Guy on the shins. The ladies looked up in alarm.

"Would you please take this boy for a while, Mrs Clark?" snarled Mr Denny. "I've had just about all I can stand for one morning. First he rips out two pages of his geography textbook, then he swears at three kindergarteners for running across the area he wants to play kickball in, and then he spits in the face of one of my girls! Little Lizzie Timms, who wouldn't say boo to a goose. Spat in her actual face!"

"I weren't aiming for her *face*, you fuckin' dipshit!" yelled the boy.

"You shouldn't spit at *anyone*! It's filthy and disgusting you little… "

"Thank you, Mr Denny. I will deal with this. Come over here, Gregory."

Skipper hated this kind of thing. It was the worst part of being a headmistress, dispensing disciplinary punishment. But even though she loathed it, she didn't shirk it. As Chloe said, it was why she was paid the big bucks. Guy and Peggy disappeared out of the room, closing the door firmly.

"Fuckin' stupid prat!" shouted Greg and set about kicking Skipper's desk.

"That will be quite enough of that," said the headmistress sternly. "I suggest you sit down on that chair and calm down."

Seeing his enemy gone and only a stringy middle-aged woman in front of him, Greg made a bid for freedom. He pulled open the study door, hurtled across the hall, through the front door, and straight into the arms of Reg Green who had finished his hedge and was coming in for lunch. Reg was nimble-witted and possessed a grip of steel.

"Oi you, not so fast. Hold on, 'old on! You looking for this?" Reg asked Skipper, who had hurried after the escapee. "Suspect acts guilty to me, boss, and was caught doin' a runner. Can't have that now, can we? Calm down, son. Why would you want to run away from a nice little school like this, eh? Now now, none of that filthy behaviour. Resistin' arrest, 'e is, Mrs Clark. Shall I clap him in irons and throw him in the brig?"

Greg was swinging punches and kicking again, and doing his best to spit in Reg's eye. Stringer was barking and getting ready to bite Greg's socks. The lad writhed and twisted but it was no use. Reg's big hands were like steel clamps round his arms. Finally realising he was vanquished, Greg fell to melodramatic sobbing and screaming about being hurt.

Skipper Clark, frustrated and angrier than she had been for a very long time, thanked her caretaker formally and followed as Reg frogmarched the boy briskly back into her office, where she locked the door and telephoned his mother.

As she dialled, she couldn't help thinking about Reg clapping people in irons and locking them up. It was chilling to remember how close to Mayflower's commonplace school life an alternative and unpredictably dangerous other-world lurked.

*   *   *

3.

Plumbers

Christmas Farm

"Are we nearly there yet?" puffed Mungo James. His mother had volunteered as one of the kindergarten helpers this afternoon, so Mungo felt he was entitled to complain a little.

"Yes we are, so you can turn your whiner off. Look, there's Mr Dawkins coming to meet us. Hasn't he got a big umbrella?"

Simon Dawkins was the tenant farmer at nearby Christmas Farm. He greeted the children warmly and ushered them into his smallest barn. It was set out with some old bales of hay to sit on, and a few temporary pens which contained four piglets, a calf and some hens. He also had a milk churn, some beakers and a plate of biscuits on a table. Mrs Dawkins was there too, smiling fondly at the youthful visitors. She loved seeing the children's enthralled faces as every year a new class learned where their food came from.

Mrs Nesbit, Miss Jackson and the parent helpers sat down gratefully on the bales. It had been a long walk from school on such a damp and windy day.

Mr Dawkins, eighteen stone and rosy as a ripe apple, welcomed them all again – explaining the farm was one of Lord Dexter's estate properties. They all knew where Lord Dexter lived, in Hall Manor, the huge mansion set in its own sweeping grounds nearby.

"I bin there," Sarah Snell informed him. "My mum took me. It's got a lake with ducks."

"So it has," agreed the farmer. "And sheep. What are baby sheep called?"

The time wore on. The questions kept coming as the children were first shown the creatures indoors and then went outside to see others in the nearby fields. All the children were soon thoroughly absorbed with the novelty and wonder of the afternoon's experience, sipping fresh milk and nibbling oaty biscuits. Questions abounded.

They were on the point of leaving when Mrs Nesbit's husband Ben, Lord Dexter's gamekeeper, dropped in to say hello and help walk the group back to school. He had two of his working dogs with him, Fly a sheepdog and Hades the Jack Russell terrier. Ben was already a familiar figure to the children as he dropped by their classroom whenever he could. Betty was delighted to see him, and thought bringing the dogs was a nice touch. They could herd everyone together very efficiently.

The children waved to Mr and Mrs Dawkins, and those who hadn't been collected by parents in their cars began the long trek back down the bridle paths.

"So, can you remember what you saw today?" Ben asked little Bronwen Dyson, a pretty child with a huge bow in her hair.

He pulled her hood up over her head for her as rain was threatening the floppy top-knot.

She beckoned him to lean down so she could whisper in his ear.

"It was really quite a lot of big poo," she told him conspiratorially. "But don't tell your mum 'cos it's rude."

Ben nodded gravely. "OK," he whispered back, glancing over at his wife. "Not a word to Mrs Nesbit."

Making a start with Ryan

Guy grew slightly more hopeful about Ryan's learning and behaviour after the first few weeks, particularly when help came from Sandi Raina.

She was always patient, and took Ryan to her quiet study every morning without fail, in order to focus on teaching him to read. There, for an hour, he ploughed doggedly through flashcards and memory games, through book after simple book, gaining coloured stars to stick on a chart when he read a word in one book and then recognised it again in another. Anything to boost his visual memory and engage his interest. However, even Sandi agreed it was uphill work. One week Ryan advanced quite well and then another he forgot everything. He appeared to be trying hard, but neither phonic decoding nor identifying whole words helped him sustain his fluency. When faced with a sentence longer than five words, he lost the meaning. The boy was perfectly compliant in a one-to-one situation – not lazy, simply un-inquisitive. Sandi tried every motivational strategy she knew and some she invented. She tried every appropriate teaching technique. She formally tested his intelligence, which turned out to be average, and then his current levels of achievement, which only confirmed he was functionally illiterate and almost innumerate. He could laboriously copy words from a book, but not read back what he had copied. He could not compose a sentence more sophisticated than 'I went to the shop'. He could draw a little. He liked colouring-in. He could add, perform simple subtraction and multiplication with a chart to help, but could not divide numbers. The squares on a page of his arithmetic exercise book and lines in a composition book meant nothing. Numbers and words were scattered randomly across his pages. After his hour of intensive tuition he would return to the form-room where he would sit passively awaiting help whenever he was stumped – which was almost all the time. He continually broke pencils and gouged pieces out of his desk. He rocked on his chair and dropped everything. Trying to figure any problem out for himself was not a strategy he employed. At least after a few weeks he stopped punching other children at playtime, which Guy took as a positive. Sandi, Skipper and Chloe were as worried as he was about Ryan's academic future.

"Where's he *been* all this time? What's he actually been *doing* in school?" queried Chloe.

"Not much, is my guess. Where was he?" Skipper flipped open the boy's notes. "Last school – Sorburn C of E. That's out in the countryside somewhere, isn't it?"

"I think so," said Sandi. "It's only a tiny place. I think they are amalgamating the schools in that area as the villages don't have enough children to make each one viable. I read it in the local paper."

"Yes, so did I," said Chloe. "I don't expect jobs are easy to find around there either, for the parents. I guess his dad moved them into Banford for work."

"Mmm. Has Ryan had a medical lately? What did the doctor say?"

"Can't see any record of one. Would you ask Peggy to put him on Dr Legg's urgent list, please, Sandi? Give him the full works. There's nothing here from his mother or any useful comment from his previous teacher. It's very frustrating." Skip closed the file and put it in her pending tray. "You know, it's astonishing to me how some children *don't* learn to read, given the amount of writing we're surrounded by these days."

Ryan had his medical with Dr Legg a few days later. Afterwards, she climbed all the stairs to Mrs Raina's eyrie on the top floor.

"Oh my god," gasped the doctor, and subsided onto the squishy old sofa by the window. "It's a climb up here, isn't it? That awful iron staircase really takes it out of ya! Whew, let me get my breath. Goodness, what a view. I can almost see the Tower of London. You get all the sun up here, don't you, Mrs Raina? My, what a lovely welcomin' room."

Sandi beamed. She was proud of her little world.

"Now then, Ryan Hale." Dr Legg put her specs on and looked at her notes. "Adenoids and tonsils. I've referred him to the cottage hospital, so we'll wait to hear when they can operate. He's the tallest boy in school and also somewhat overweight, much as I am myself. Eyesight is poor, so I've recommended his mother take him to the optician's as I think glasses may be in order. Hearin' is way down in both ears, though whether that's because of wax or sinuses or that horrible snotty nose, it's currently hard to tell. I should say he always gets very congested after a cold, which means he's probably had an intermittent hearin' loss since he was born. Glue ear. Balance isn't good. The tonsil and adenoid op should help, and possibly grommets. He certainly needs to bathe more and learn to take greater responsibility for his appearance in general. Other than that he's not too bad – strong. I'll certainly keep him on my watch list. Oh, and there's some residual enuresis – bed wettin'. His mother says he sleeps very deeply, which may account for that. It may clear up once he's lost a bit of weight. I've already told Mrs Clark all this and I've seen his mother. Mrs Clark says she'll inform Mr Denny and Mrs Shaw of my findings – I can't go traipsin' about this buildin' all day long. Basically your Ryan's a big clumsy boy whose not too keen on personal daintiness, eatin' right or changin' his clothes, but there's hope, Mrs Raina, there's definitely hope. He's goin' to be a very large fellow when he's grown up, you know. Have you met his dad?"

"No, I haven't. Well, thank you so much Doctor Legg, that's very interesting and hopeful and extremely helpful to me. I appreciate your coming up our horrible stairs to tell me."

There was a thump on the door and Ryan himself shambled in and crashed exhaustedly onto a chair. His morning with the doctor had obviously been enervating. He tipped out the coloured pencils from their pot and started sharpening them onto the tabletop, hardly appearing to notice the two astonished ladies.

"Bin sent out," he informed the room. "When's lunch?"

Greg's point of view

It was Friday afternoon. Greg had been back in school only a few days since being sent home for spitting at Lizzie, and was already angry with everyone again. He had punched one of the girls he fancied on the arm, and she'd gone howling to the teacher who had made him move his desk over by the cupboard away from everybody else – even stinky Ryan. It was all stupid.

She was stupid. Mr Denny was very stupid. Greg hadn't been allowed to eat his lunch with the other children either, because he'd purposely kicked over the bench and the fat lady cook had yelled at him. She was boring and ugly and *criminally* stupid.

The trouble with this school, thought Greg, is there's no getting away with anything because the teachers always catch you. Life was only fun when he got away with stuff right under people's noses, because that proved he was smarter than everybody else. They were suckers and losers for letting him upset them. These namby-pamby Mayflower kids always whined and grizzled and told on him, and the stupid interfering teachers always believed *them*. And yet – astonishingly – they kept giving him second chances. Why? It was all topsy-turvy and too stupid for words. They should expel him.

He sat at his desk and glowered. It was art, and he was carefully drawing the imagined interior of a human brain, complete with rooms full of ideas and functions and intricate little trapdoors and staircases leading up and down. It afforded him time to think.

He and his mum and five brothers, one of whom was currently serving time in Ledgely Prison, were back in the Banford neighbourhood after a break of a few years. None of them liked the quiet little town, although their mum had a decent job at the jam factory. Banford was a lame, tame sort of dump in his brothers' view. The whole place was full of irritatingly weedy goody-goodies. Every anoraky one of them was just asking to be ripped off, have their things pinched or smashed up. One railwayman down at the station this morning had been especially annoying. He had yelled at Greg just as he was going to spray-paint his own graffiti tag next to Weasel's on the level-crossing gates. Greg spent all morning plotting his retaliation.

The afternoon eventually ended. Greg, still in a surly mood, pulled his bicycle out of the storage rack in the bike-shed and rode it across the playground, weaving closely in and out of the smaller children. Let the teachers say you weren't to ride bikes on the playground, he didn't care. Riding full speed towards some dumb little kid and then jamming his brakes on hard really scared the pants off them.

He was accelerating towards a group of third form girls to repeat this amusing effect, when he suddenly found himself yanked forcibly by the arm and stood up on the ground. His bike tumbled over.

"Here, you've broke my bloody bike!" he cried, wriggling like an eel. "Let go!" The grip on his arm increased. Mr Denny was on exit duty today and had pounced.

"It's fine. I'll just help you off the premises, Gregory."

Guy lifted the bike with his left hand and frogmarched the lad out into the lane, well beyond the school's gate. "There you go. Now you can ride safely home. Try not to be late on Monday morning, there's a good boy." He turned back before Greg could utter another searing comment.

The boy grabbed up his bicycle and pedalled off, spitting in contempt at he did so. He bumped it angrily over the uneven lane surface and crashed down heavily into each chalky puddle. Stupid interfering teacher! He'd be *really* late on Monday – that would show Denny the Nazi. He cycled down Fen Lane, along the footpath in and out of groups of children walking home, and veered off to the railway station. Weasel's nice blue graffiti tag was gone, and the level crossing gates had been patched with fresh white paint. Greg snarled in renewed fury. Now they would have to do it all over again.

The younger of the two station employees, who was standing watching the children go home, spotted him.

"Hey, are you the boy I saw vandalising station property this morning? Well don't bloody do it again, you little 'ooligan. I'll call the police next time." Kevin, the young porter, was still very annoyed. It had taken all morning to erase the blue paint. "What's your name? Where d'you live? Here come back!"

Not bloody likely, thought Greg. Call the police? See if I care. He cycled off, waving two fingers above his head and shouting abuse over his shoulder at Kevin.

Kevin shook his fist. He recognised Greg as one of his new next-door neighbours.

"Well, I may not know his name yet, Mr Coker," he told his boss. "But I certainly know where he lives."

Dreamboats

"A sailing club? Now that's an idea." said Guy.

Ernest was less sure. "We'd obviously have to transport the kids over to the reservoir somehow, so we'd need some kind of minibus, and a trailer for the boat. Where would we get those? We'd also need proper insurance and some safety and first aid certificates." He was trying not to sound too discouraging despite his misgivings.

"Yes, well, we'd have to see it was all done correctly, obviously. Safety first and all that. It won't be like 'Swallows and Amazons'," said Guy defensively. He had loved those stories as a child and already had visions of a little school dinghy bobbing on a blue lake, himself at the tiller and the wind at his back.

"Maybe we'd need more than one boat," added Charlie enthusiastically. He was a very competent amateur yachtsman himself, although the others weren't aware of it. He had spent many a summer sailing around the rocky Welsh coast as a teenager. "Have you talked to Skip yet?"

"Yes, I mentioned it, but she's very distracted by this blessed inspection. I can't really get through. She keeps rambling on about plumbing and buying Reg a new mower or something. I couldn't really get a word in. I doubt there'll be anything left over for boats," sighed Mike.

"You know what she's like," said Guy, lighting a small cheroot. "She's already gone and pledged all the left-over maintenance money from last year to replacing the old lead water-pipe system. It really needs doing too. Should have been done last summer, but it wasn't. Now the plumbers say they're able to start right before the inspection week and if she puts them off they can't reschedule until next April. I can see why she's all of a tiz-woz."

The others nodded sympathetically. Their headmistress was certainly preoccupied at the moment. And the deputy head was still in shock, as she struggled to come to terms with her loss. No one had the heart to bother her with anything more than superficial matters. On the face of it, Mike's sailing project did not seem likely to be undertaken any time soon, no matter how enthusiastic the four men were.

"This inspection can't be as bad as all that can it?" asked Charlie.

"Don't honestly know," answered Guy. "They'll probably come in, take a look around, say 'how nice' and flit off again. No, I think it'll mostly likely consist of a retired headmaster whose only aim is to glean a few numbers from Peggy and then scuttle back to his nice quiet desk for a cocktail before lunch. We're in the wrong job, you know!"

Mike and Charlie laughed.

"I hope you're right," said Ernest. He had a much more cautious nature.

"Don't worry," sighed Mike. "It will come, it will go. Let's hope it's plain sailing."

Wallflowers and fried bread

"What's them, then – cabbages?" asked John Mason, as he dug over his allotment square like a professional. He nodded towards the plants Veronica Moon was gently easing out of a seed-tray with her fingers.

"Wallflowers," she replied. "My dad says they'll make a nice border and flower early, if I put them in now. I've already got tulips in and some nar… nar.. somethings."

"Narcissi?" suggested John. "They're like daffs ent they?"

"S'posed to be white with orange middles. Like fried eggs."

John nodded approvingly. He liked fried eggs. "Pity there isn't a bacon plant," he commented.

Veronica got the joke. "Or a sausage plant. Or a fried bread plant! Mrs Hewitt, is there a fried bread plant?"

Jean clomped over.

Her boots were heavy with mud and she was not enjoying the afternoon at all. Her son John, who worked in Holland, had written to ask if he could bring his fiancée to meet her this Christmas. Jean hadn't been aware he was even seeing anyone, let alone planning marriage. What a dark horse. It would be lovely to see him, or course, but entertaining a strange female over the winter holiday, when she was always exhausted after the madness of pantomimes and carol services, would be decidedly challenging. Then Jean forced herself into a more Christian frame of mind – after all, she remembered, it was the season of goodwill and the welcoming of strangers from foreign lands ought to be top of the agenda. But somehow, this afternoon, the future was looking complicated. Life was a struggle. The chin elastic on her hat had broken and there was a big hole in the thumb of her new glove. Her boots were caked in mud and she had forgotten to buy Sweep's dogfood.

"Fried what? Bread? No, of course not. Don't be silly, Veronica."

Veronica looked at John and then down at the earth. The fun had gone right out of planting her baby wallflowers. Mrs Hewitt saw immediately that she had spoken too harshly.

"Come on, hurry up you two. It's starting to rain again. Let's see if we can get everyone's digging done quickly and go inside for a game of Pirates in the hall, shall we? Veronica you can be the captain first."

Veronica immediately cheered up. She loved Pirates, a glorified game of tag played over the randomly spaced gym equipment. If a foot touched the floor you were eaten by sharks.

"Lucky!" muttered John.

The plumbers arrive

As expected by Peggy, but much to Reg's cynical amazement, three plumbers from Voysey's Pipeworks arrived on the first day of October. They were to start replacing the water pipes in the Great Aunt, leaving the upstairs toilets still usable. When finished downstairs, they would proceed to the Upper Aunt and finally the Attic Aunt in sequence. By proceeding in stages thus, Mr Voysey told Mrs Clark, there would always be enough working lavatories available for use. He would keep any disruption to a minimum. He would be well out of her hair by the inspection on the thirteenth, no question.

Mrs Clark bit her lip and nodded. This work could not wait. Who knew how many children were being slowly poisoned by the lead-laden water they drank daily from Mayflower's taps?

The replacement copper and plastic piping was stacked alongside the railings just inside the wilderness out of the reach of interested little hands, and another area was cordoned off to store the old leadwork. It took all morning for Voysey's men to unload their gear, and half the afternoon to rearrange it to their satisfaction.

"I should have been a plumber," sighed Peggy, toiling over the scribbled receipts and notes Mr Voysey had picked out of his waistcoat pocket and left in a pile on her blotter.

"Earning a fortune and knocking off at 3 o'clock you mean?" asked Cathy. The secretaries never left school until 4.30 at the earliest.

"Yes. How do they justify it? Come in!" Someone had knocked loudly on the door.

"There's a boy out 'ere. Says he's been sent by 'is teacher," said Pru Davidson putting her head round. "Looks like trouble to me. I caught 'im trying to open the display cabinet."

This was where the silver trophies and cups for various achievements were shown off in the entrance hall.

Pru called back over her shoulder, "Wossyer name? Price, I think 'e's saying." She looked with satisfaction upon the irritation her words were causing Peg and Cathy. "Oy you, I said 'ands *orf*. I don't need all them fingerprints on my glass. Anyway, that's all locked shut."

Peggy bustled out.

"Why are you down here Greg? Leave that alone and stand still. No, you didn't just want to see the cups – don't give me that. Put your hands behind your back and stand up straight when I'm talking to you. Now then… Mr Denny said to go to Mrs Clark. What for? You were flicking ink pellets at who? Don't know. Why were you doing that? Don't know. Well, let's see what Mrs Clark knows, shall we?"

Greg Price spent the final twenty minutes of that afternoon finishing his work in the head's office, and covertly gleaning a great deal of information about the plumbers and what they were doing in school. Over the next few days, by careful listening, he learned even more. On Friday night he told some of his brothers about where the stripped-out lead piping was being piled, and for how long it would probably be there before it was removed by the salvage company.

By that Friday a substantial heap of metal pipework had accumulated. At ten o'clock Monday morning all of it was found to be missing. Arthur Voysey scratched his head as he stared at his men, Kieran, Algy and Roddy.

"Where the blazes did all that go?" he asked. His men shook their heads in bewilderment.

"Gyppos nicked it, prob'ly," shrugged Algy. He didn't care.

A boy cycled through the playground gate. For once Greg wasn't more than an hour late for morning school. He dismounted and walked sedately over to the bike shed, took out his cap and placed it correctly on his head.

"Good morning," he called politely.

Roddy was the only one who paid him any attention. "Wotcher," he responded gloomily.

The boy smirked and went jauntily into the school office to report his arrival.

A bit of a mess

Cathy looked at the stockroom shelves in despair. What a mess! She had stacked everything tidily at the start of term and now it looked like the aftermath of the January sales. The teachers had obviously rummaged about at will, never mind her little labels and logical piles. Some of the stationery was spilling out of the door.

Rick Hodges, from Miss Fisher's class, ambled up. He had been sent for ten sheets of sugar paper as his teacher was busy taking down 'Our Summer' art work ready for a new seasonal display. The blue would make a nice background, she said. This afternoon in art they were painting bunches of conkers and autumn leaves. Rick quite liked painting. He bent down and helped Mrs Duke collect some of the escaping paper.

"Cor, that's a bit of a rat's nest. Like under my bed. Mum says it's a tip."

"It *is* awful. I wish people were more careful. I must tidy up or this tide of exercise books will end up at the front door. Oh, thank you Rick. Now, what were you after, dear? You know you're not allowed in this cupboard alone don't you?"

"Yes, Mrs Duke. I went to the office but Mrs Bailey said you were here so I was to come down. I need ten sheets of sugar paper, blue if possible, please." Rick repeated Miss Fisher's words precisely, which was why he was always sent on messages. "It's for our display. Miss Fisher says it's going to be 'Nature in Autumn'. I'm going to do some conkers."

"Sounds lovely. Alright, here you are." Cathy rolled the paper and handed it to him. "Not too heavy? Alright, now mind how you go up the stairs."

Cathy watched him start the ascent. What a helpful little boy he was.

Rick climbed slowly, wondering why Mrs Duke had made such a mess of her stock cupboard.

A birthday gathering

Dora had the bright idea of hosting her birthday party to include Charlie and his family. Their birthdays were on consecutive days so a joint celebration made sense. She cooked a grand roast dinner and pulled out the dining table to its maximum.

"I've just seen Brenda Kirk and that Dick Perry from Manor Lodge in a clinch," announced Skipper arriving back from shopping in town, where she had been sent for some last minute items. "They were by the war memorial at that bus shelter. Canoodling."

"A clinch? Canoodling? Whatever have you been reading?"

"I'd have made a good writer. No, there's no mistake. I don't suppose they thought anybody could see them." Skip put the her shopping bags down on the table. "Poor old Len."

Len was the local farmer who collected the school's food left-overs every Friday afternoon for his pigs.

"Poor Len indeed," said Dora, who had no time for cheats. Brenda Kirk had three small children at home and no business openly kissing other men. "Whatever can she be thinking?"

"Well, maybe she's unhappy or something."

The subject came up at the birthday dinner and was a brief topic of conversation. Jean had decided views on Brenda's morals although May was less quick to judge, having experienced quite enough spiteful finger-pointing to last a lifetime. Charlie and Fiona were agog at the seedy goings-on as they had hitherto assumed Banford was quiet to the point of boredom. Ernest and Chloe didn't actively care one way or the other, each privately feeling the era of free love had somehow slipped past without them noticing.

"Are you coming to church in the morning?" Dora asked Fiona later as they sipped coffee and sampled some slim mint chocolates.

"Oh yes. Charlie's playing the organ and Tim's now in the choir so it's pretty much compulsory. I love the harvest festival tunes even though I'm chapel really."

"I've often thought of turning Methodist myself, just for all those splendid Wesleyan hymns," smiled Dora. Having lived a long time in a rural Cornish village she had found a great deal of friendly rivalry between its two main places of worship. "I daresay Charlie will persuade Rev Bill to include a few now he's taken over as organist, and Mr Timms the choirmaster is open to anything catchy and jolly. I like him."

Fiona nodded and agreed. Banford was turning out to be a very acceptable place to live, she thought. She had a good job at the local hospital, Tim was settled in his school, and her husband was more than content working at Mayflower. Now, if only they could find a more permanent home they could afford to buy. She glanced around the spacious living room with its wide fireplace and french windows. It would never be as lovely as this, but they might get a lucky break.

Busy busy

Every classroom had been subjected to an extra spruce-up prior to the imminent inspection and every teacher wanted fresh displays of the children's work on their walls. Ernest was beset by requests for book-boxes containing historical or geographical reference volumes, and Cathy's stockroom was constantly being raided for drawing pins and art supplies. The teachers checked and rechecked the children's exercise books for errors, brought every record and every written comment up to date, and followed up on remarks such as 'see me'. The children caught the seriousness and diligence of their teachers and tidied their desks until they were all in apple-pie order. They helped with everything, from weeding their allotments to seeking owners for every wayward piece of lost property. All their exercise books had fresh brown-paper covers and neatly written titles. In the top two classes, each inkwell was washed, dried and carefully refilled. New blotting paper pieces were cut and distributed. Coloured pencils were sharpened, rubber erasers taken outside and wiped on a flagstone in order to freshen them up. Every blackboard wiper was banged hard against a tree deep inside the wilderness so the resulting dust cloud did not sully Mr Green's newly painted railings. Stringer scampered around delivering items here and there, as busy as everyone else.

Miss Fisher sent for Ryan on the Friday afternoon before the inspection was due. He came in with a look of surprise on his face.

"Ah, there you are, dear. I was wondering whether you would be kind enough to put these rolls of Binca and those boxes of embroidery silks into that top cupboard for me?" She indicated which one she meant. It took Ryan a minute to catch on – he was tall, the cupboard was high. He nodded and smiled.

"Cor, he's really tall when he stretches isn't he?" commented Helen. She lived next door to Ryan and was rather in awe of him.

Her friend Chrissie agreed. "You put him next to our Jimmy Birch, you'd think they was a TV act or something."

"The winkle and the walrus," suggested Helen, wittily. The girls giggled hysterically. Then Helen caught her teacher's eye and stopped abruptly. Miss Fisher was not in any mood for levity.

Jimmy was handing drawing pins to his teacher. He knew his goddess was under pressure and was doing all he could to help, keeping a constant eye on her movements. She was not a young person after all.

"Thank you, Jimmy. Now then, would you go and see whether Mr Green has any new waste-paper baskets in his store cupboard please? That old one of ours is decidedly past its best. Remember to knock and wait for his come-in. If he's not there…"

"He might be doing sweeping or painting outside somewhere," suggested Jimmy and skipped off.

"Miss Fisher! Miss," cried Poppy. "Ryan's stood his foot on my maths book, Miss. Get off you flippin' lump!"

"Now then, Poppy, kinder words please. I'm sure he didn't mean to. Ryan is helping us, and I must say he's done a very good job. Ryan – *Ryan*! Come over here a minute would you please?"

The tall lad ambled over, glad to be out of his own class and doing something useful for once.

"Now then, reach up and push that pin into the corner of this paper. My thumbs aren't quite up to the task today. Yes, it's hard isn't it? There, good boy. Well, you *are* strong. That's almost straight! Now the next one."

Gradually the autumn paintings went up on the display board and the classroom resumed its tidy, fresh look. Even the box of old newspapers, kept for covering the desks on art afternoons, had been refolded and neatly stacked. Gillian and Lulu wiped the window panes to crystal clarity. The nature table's exhibits would have done credit to the town museum. Every storage box and cupboard was immaculate. The jam jars and paint brushes, mixing trays and plasticine box, looked almost new. Andy gave the floor a final thorough sweep before he and Carl took the waste-paper baskets – one old, one new – down to Mr Green's big bin and emptied them one last time. Ryan was thanked and went back reluctantly to his own classroom. Miss Fisher insisted everybody wash their hands and tidy themselves up before sitting quietly at their desks for the story before home-time. It had been a very long day.

"No homework this weekend," she told them. The weary children felt refreshed in an instant. "Everybody has helped enormously today. Our classroom is quite ready for anyone to inspect it, I think. Well done, and thank you very much for your help. Please don't forget what we talked about if the inspectors ask you questions when they visit on Monday morning. Make sure you come to school especially neat and tidy. Good, now we will have our story. Who can remember where Alice had arrived?"

Hands shot up. Miss Fisher opened the book and held it up so they could see the next illustration. The children sighed with contentment and lay their heads on their arms to listen, in well-earned peace, to the funny, silly story of one little girl's adventure in Wonderland.

*   *   *

4.

Halloween

The inspectors call

It was a Monday morning almost halfway through a wet and windy October, and the day of the LEA inspection arrived. Mrs Clark had been up for hours by the time breakfast was ready. Her mother set a plate of scrambled eggs and some toasty soldiers on the table, and commanded Skipper to eat every bit.

"You'll need your strength if these people are as picky as you think they'll be," she observed. "Come on now, don't let it get cold. Here's your coffee. You've got a little time, surely? They won't be on the blessed doorstep, now will they? Just act confident."

Skipper did her best, but nerves were jangling in every part of her and it was a struggle to eat. Today a harsh public spotlight was going to illuminate her perfect little private world. She donned her mac and took an umbrella against the steady drizzle before hurrying over to school.

A strange car was parked outside the front gate, its windows steamed up. She felt her breakfast settle like a ball of lead, even as heat rose into her pounding head. Why was she so scared of these officials? They were probably perfectly nice. Act confident, Dora had said.

Two people got out.

"Good morning. You must be the school inspectors. I'm so sorry to have kept you. Have you been waiting long?" Mrs Clark chattered, extending her hand and smiling to put them at ease.

Her hand was shaken by the man, a scrawny-looking type in a long, unfashionable overcoat. He could have been mistaken for an undertaker. The woman was quite another matter. She stared directly into Skip's eyes with a piercing, unblinking gaze. Even this early in the day her wavy hair was glossy brown and perfect, her lips a shiny crimson. She wore an elegant square-shouldered camel coat, and her bright blue patent leather three inch high-heeled shoes were brand new. She removed one immaculate glove and gripped it like a weapon. She did not shake hands.

"We'd like to begin as soon as possible, Mrs Clark. That's if you're *quite* ready."

Skipper, her mind racing like a high-speed movie, felt anything but ready. Her wits scattered, unable to determine the school's current state of readiness. No one was ready. The office, the classrooms, outside, inside, no one. Had Peggy finished the lost property box? Would Reg remember to keep Stringer at home? The plumbers, if they actually turned up today, would have to continue working in the upstairs lavatories, as they were still far from being finished. The morning rain would be seeping down the staircase wall. Polished floors would be wet with dirty footprints and the windows all shut against the rain, making classrooms stuffy. Had she reminded staff about fresh air? The pain in Reg's hip would mean his temper would be short, which would affect his ability to remain civil. All the teachers were already on edge, and the children would be particularly crazy from being cooped up indoors by the weather today, all last week, and probably over the weekend too. There would be wet-day lunch, and indoor playtime. Ivy would be flustered and duty staff cross. What else had she forgotten?

Mrs Clark gazed dolefully at Mrs Alicia Busterd and Mr Colin Phillips, as they perched in her office on the embarrassingly shabby dining room chairs, like aliens from a superior universe. Mrs Clark folded her quivering hands in front of her and forced herself to wait. That was as much 'acting confident' as she could manage. From their expensive briefcases the two simultaneously took out clipboards prepared with multiple pristine forms. They clicked their silver ball-point pens and began explaining their requirements.

Today there would be a general walk around, then they would separately visit each classroom, sitting in on lessons, and questioning the staff and students afterwards. Tomorrow there would be a perusal of all paperwork, the school accounts, plans and records. They would then depart to their Fenchester offices and write Mayflower's report, a copy of which she would receive in due course, although an education officer might be in touch earlier should preliminary findings suggest any urgent action was required. The report would comment on the school's current educational proficiency, its state of physical suitability and repair, and point out areas that would require improvement. Their findings would be delivered first to the local authority and then to the school governors and herself. Was that quite clear? Here was their letter of authority. Did she have initial questions?

"Would you like some coffee before you make a start, and meet the teachers in the staffroom?" Skip asked faintly. At least now she knew how long the scary pair would be there, and the scope of their remit.

"No, thank you. We have already breakfasted at the Yeoman. We'd like to begin at once as we are already late, Mrs Clark."

It was, indeed, a very long morning.

The initial walk-through occasioned some pursing of lips and some definite grunting from Mr Phillips as the two inspectors climbed ever-higher up the dribbling iron staircase. Trying to see the premises through their eyes Skipper realised it was probably not the most convenient building in which to house a modern primary school. What she regarded as charming original features – the tall stained glass windows, the quirky room arrangements, the wide floorboards, the open fireplaces – had Mr Phillips shaking his head and scribbling furiously on paper after paper.

Assembly went well. The choir sang, and everybody behaved impeccably. Morning lessons followed quietly and studiously. The kindergarten children were observed learning to read, the first form practised subtraction, and Jean's class showed off their PE skills in the hall. Everyone made a huge effort at breaktime to keep reasonably quiet.

Mr Denny dispatched Greg down to Mrs Clark's office halfway through the period after break. The child brought a sealed note which asked her to keep him busy for twenty minutes if she could. She duly sent him first on an errand to Ernest in the library, then to Peggy with a complicated message, and finally back to his classroom with six reference books. Unfortunately, Greg bumped into Dean Underwood on his slow climb back up the Iron Duke. Greg nudged the top book off his pile with his chin so that it fell in a wet patch on the floor just as Dean was edging past.

"Now look what you made me do, you pillock. Pick it up."
Surprised, Dean obliged and placed it back on top.

"There you go, mate," he said. "Need a hand?"

It was Greg's turn to be surprised. He hadn't expected an offer of help.

"And exactly where are *you* two boys going? You should not be out of class at this time." Alicia Busterd swooped like a vulture on the boys. "Why are you carrying all those, child? This floor is extremely wet. You – you help him. Take some of the load. Who gave you this great heavy pile to carry?"

Greg was perfectly able to manage six modest books. He hesitated briefly, undecided about whether to appear a martyr to child slavery or reply with something snarky. This woman clearly had power, so he chose the former. He sniffed, swallowed and looked at her dolefully.

Dean took three of the books off the pile and said nothing.

"What class are you? Form 6? I have just come from there."

"Mr Denny made me go and get them for him," whined Greg, squeezing an easy tear out. "He's always giving me jobs that takes ages. Just when I'm working. He says he's going to wash my mouth with soap. He don't like me. He lifted me up by the collar once, and broke my bike. I'm scared of him – and I'm the newest boy."

Dean's mouth dropped open.

Mrs Busterd marched both boys upstairs to Guy's room where the class was breathing a quiet sigh of relief that the inspector had finally departed. She opened the door with a crash and strode back in.

"This pupil has missed a great deal of his lesson time, Mr Denny," she cried. "He is struggling to carry books *far* too heavy for him up some very dangerous stairs. He says he is terrified of you assaulting him. Go and sit down, little one. Why is your desk not in line with everyone else's? Arrange it."

She glared at Guy who was, for once, lost for words.

Dean Underwood dumped his three books on the teacher's desk and fled.

Form 6 bent their heads over their writing and became suddenly deeply engrossed, thoroughly uncomfortable that their teacher was being yelled at. Guy listened to a further tirade, then finally found his tongue and quietly suggested he discuss his classroom management with Mrs Busterd later, in private.

She was not about to be diverted.

"I will want to see this child after he has eaten lunch, and again at the end of the afternoon. Then I will want to speak to you and Mrs Clark together at 4 pm, without fail." She glanced at Greg who was back in his place writing copiously. "Now, I believe one of your *other* pupils requires your attention," snarled Alicia Busterd through her glossy white teeth.

Guy glanced over her shoulder to see Ryan rocking back on two chair legs and waving yet another broken pencil in the air.

Mrs Busterd spun crisply on her high heel and exited the room, closing the door with a loud click.

At which point Ryan fell off his chair backwards and Trudy Hilder was sick.

At the conclusion of a very trying day the teachers staggered into the staffroom. Chloe knew they would want to let off some steam and share the frustrations of trying to teach under such critical scrutiny. Each stressed countenance looked tired, except for May Fisher who was, as usual, calmly composed. She took out her perpetual knitting and listened, nodding, as the others shared tales ending with Guy's description of Ryan falling off his chair.

"I think that kid might have finally made a few friends today," said Guy hopefully.

The door was flung open without a knock.

"I will see you in the headmistress's office, Mr Denny. At once," announced Mrs Busterd briskly. She enjoyed combining surprise, loudness and orders as an intimidatory tactic. This approach was particularly effective when it came to shaking the superior complacency of arrogant men, she found. A woman these days must be aggressive, not just assertive, if she wanted to make her way in a man's world. Play them at their own game. Alicia relished the air of personal perfection and power she radiated, and was proud of the looks of envy, fear and awe she attracted from lesser women.

"I have spoken with the boy Gregory Rice, and noted his multiple comments and complaints against you, Mr Denny" she continued for all to hear. "I've given him a letter for his parents. I fully expect them to take the matter to the Chief Education Officer. Come!"

The staff could only stare as Guy puffed out his chest and went to take what was coming. He looked like Sydney Carton heading for the scaffold.

"Price! His name's Gregory Price with a P!" Ernest yelled angrily after them.

Day two

The following day was less stressful for some, but rather more so for others. The weather did not let up, which helped nobody.

Reg Green, as spick and span as a sailor on parade, escorted the two LEA inspectors on a visit to Longmont Lodge before morning school began, and explained its unique significance in Mayflower's educational firmament. He had the visitors peer out of the upstairs windows at the dripping wilderness as the rain rendered it far too sodden to actually set foot out there. The pair did little to hide their abhorrence of so many wasted resources, within and without. As they picked their way back to the main building they cast a perfunctory glance at the children's allotments from beneath matching golf umbrellas. Reg was cynical about either inspector ever truly understanding why other people valued gardening or owning the empty lodge with its many impenetrable acres. You didn't have to be an old sea-dog to see which way the wind was blowing.

Ivy Green and Sally Turk had a terrible shock when Mr Phillips entered the school kitchen, clipboard and biro in hand, later that morning. They had not expected to be included in the general inspection and were decidedly 'put out' by him, as they complained to Mrs Clark later. His scrutiny and questioning delayed them, so they were late pushing the lunch trolley over, which resulted in the gym hall rapidly becoming even noisier than usual on a wet day, as the children had to sit and wait.

Unlike the cooks, Peggy and Cathy were geared-up for their visitation. They had been instructed to dig out every account book they had ever stored and all current records. The ladies' personal certificates for first aid, typing, and general office competence were peered at, as were all the classroom registers and personnel files. The medical records were inspected, a finger run along the shelves and the children's health folders examined. Emergency procedures were scrutinised in particular detail, the Broadstock trust details and all budgets picked apart. Not an area of management was overlooked. Peg and Cathy hovered around hoping their explanations were satisfactory, while the investigators turned pages and made notes, indifferent to the discomfort they were causing and making no comments.

During the afternoon, Mrs Clark and Mrs Shaw were cross-examined. What were their policies on punishment, testing, improving literacy levels? What was their long-term plan regarding the wilderness? What did the governors have in mind for the Lodge? How many parents came in regularly? How much were their various private trust fund totals? Skipper had been advised to be evasive about the latter – the governors did not think it necessary to share too much of this information – so she only provided a broad figure, despite Alicia Busterd's relentless grilling on the specifics. Phillips joined in. When would the current plumbing work be concluded? Was she aware open fires in schools were completely banned? Had there been accidents on that slippery iron staircase? Complaints from parents? What local goodwill was there towards the school? Did Mayflower have a waiting list? And so on. Skip and Chloe answered as carefully as they could, but several topics were so beyond anything they had expected they were stumped. Did they ever ask parents to sponsor events? Had they thought of selling off the playing field? Would they ever amalgamate with Dane Street? The interview went on and on.

Relief eventually arrived in the form of three school governors. Daylight was fading fast when Julia Scott, Lady Edwardia Longmont and Bob Pelham knocked on the study door and bustled in, wreathed in smiles and oozing *bonhomie*. Having been rapidly updated by Peggy as they hung their raincoats on the hatstand in the hall, they immediately pitched in with fulsome praise for the wonderful little family school, its brilliant staff and well-educated happy pupils, even before being asked a single opinion by the hawk-like duo. Mayflower was a hidden gem, they gushed. It was the envy of all other local schools, they added. Mayflower not only taught traditional values, it fostered *kindliness*. It really was top notch. Best in the county.

Mr Phillips pursed his lips and jotted down one extra note as the three gabbled on, but Mrs Busterd sat impervious – her shapely legs elegantly crossed at the ankle and her immaculate face completely expressionless. The governors eventually stopped chattering and sat back, well satisfied with their hearty positive input. That's the stuff to give 'em, thought Lady Longmont smiling to herself. A full broadside.

Which was when Skip and Chloe concluded the school was definitely doomed. Well-meaning amateurs held no sway with these remote professionals who so obviously despised the place. Mayflower might be a perfect wonderland to its two starry-eyed principals, but after this inspection it would certainly be branded out of date and unsuitable by modern standards, and no amount of well-intentioned 'jolly hockey-stick' rhetoric from the governors could save them. Skipper felt the guillotine blade was already descending.

With two days of turbulence satisfactorily completed, Mr Phillips and Mrs Busterd finally drove away, leaving Mrs Clark and Mrs Shaw to turn off the lights and lock the front door.

Chloe was firmly hung onto by Skip and taken home to White Cottage. Dora had demanded she bring her, no-matter what the hour, as they would both need to unwind, she said. They would need feeding. Dora was right, but unprepared for the utter despondency of the two women who sank exhaustedly at her kitchen table and watched her ladle out hearty chicken soup and butter chunks of freshly baked bread. They ate slowly, in silence.

"There's nothing to be done," sighed Skipper. "Mayflower was nice while it lasted."

Chloe agreed. "Those guys were just *horrible*, Dora. How come they get to be so nasty? They never had one good or encouraging word to say. They think our school's hopeless. Worse – they think it's *ridiculous*."

Dora's reassuring motherly presence and comforting food eventually began to soothe their jangled emotions, leaving only deep weariness. Maybe Dora was right – maybe they had it all out of perspective. At least the two days of humiliating forensic scrutiny were finally over. Perhaps the eventual report wouldn't be as damning as all that – surely someone at the LEA still thought the school was valuable?

Skip got up and fetched the whisky bottle, feeling the weighty responsibility of keeping her vulnerable little ship afloat more than ever, but grateful for a moment's calm after the storm.

Doughnuts don't even come close

On Wednesday the general disruption subsided. The children relaxed, the teachers stopped fretting and lessons returned to normal. Peggy and Cathy put away all the files in the cupboards, Reg and Stringer went back to painting railings and checking the boiler, and Ivy served lunch on time. The febrile atmosphere stabilised and normal service resumed. Even the weather improved. The rain eased enough to allow the pent-up children outside to play, and they spent their breaktimes whirling round the playground like spinning tops.

Old-fashioned skipping was back in favour with the girls, as was something new called 'Lastic' – a game that was a cross between jumping a rope and cat's cradle. It involved a long loop of knicker elastic stretched between two girls' ankles while another hopped and wove it into patterns using only her feet. Most boys preferred more movement and simply hurtled around like wild things or kicked tennis balls into makeshift goals. The smallest children returned to their favourite 'mothers-and-fathers' and tag, while those feeling less energetic simply hung on to the duty-teacher's hands and shared tales from home.

Lunch that day was everyone's favourite – sausage, peas and chips – and in the afternoon every class was indulged with a free-choice art lesson. The children could paint or draw whatever they wished, and even the teachers joined in the fun by painting a picture of 'A Fabulous Bird' of their own imagining. It was as much a relief to the adults as the children to leave school that day feeling relaxed and happy with life once again.

By the time the staff met together for a brief tea-time chat on Friday afternoon, even Mrs Clark was slightly more optimistic about their future. She gazed at her wonderful colleagues with real gratitude and affection. What a super bunch they were. They had pulled out all the stops this week and no mistake. Chloe undid a large box of fresh doughnuts, ordered specially from Mrs Lara's cake shop, and handed them round.

"So, how did we *really* fare with the dynamic duo, do you think?" asked Mike, passing May the bun with white icing, which was her favourite.

"Have you had any formal feedback?" added Heather, anxiously.

"Well yes, some. Mr Morton from the education office rang earlier and I jotted down a few things. He has eased my mind a bit, though I'm afraid it's not all good news."

There was a collective sigh. Not all good? What now?

Skip studied her scribbled notes. There were two pages, some of which need not concern them at the moment.

She read aloud. "Main findings. School building in need of improvements. Various hazards and dangers, unfortunately. That's the fireplaces and iron staircase and so on. Workers on site – that's the blasted plumbers. Funds and resources, see further comments. Development plans, ditto. Children mainly articulate and knowledgeable, thank heaven. Teaching and discipline all fine except Form 6, which apparently has both management *and* discipline issues. Sorry Guy."

"That's Gregory Price, the little..."

Guy's stomach cramped. He put down his cup and thought back over his handling of the boy the day Mrs Busterd had intercepted him carrying six library books upstairs. Was it only last Monday? Alright, so Guy had sent him off with a needless message, but only to get the kid out of the way during the formal observation session. It had been as much for Greg's own benefit as the rest of the class. The child had no concept of respectful behaviour – he simply couldn't be trusted not to say something designed to set the others off. It had been dreadfully bad luck he had encountered the blue witch on the stairs, thought Guy. Now I'm Wackford Squeers and he's a terrorised tot. He sank lower in his chair. Teacher-baiting was a winning sport for Greg. Defence was impossible.

He glanced at May Fisher, who understood only too well what he was feeling. She leaned across and held his hand.

Mike said, "Well you can't have a kid like that constantly disrupting perfectly good lessons. He's just the same obnoxious little trouble-maker when any of the rest of us take him too, Skip. Guy's done a sterling job of keeping Greg in class, we all know that. You'd have to be a saint to do any better, and keep the class up to speed. Ryan, for all his problems, hasn't been anything like such a nightmare, now has he? And he's just as new. So's little Lizzie Timms. She's a sweetheart, but Greg Price he's, well he's… ."

"Subversive," chipped in Betty, whole-heartedly on Guy's side, as they all were. "Underhand. Unpleasant. Monstrous."

"Yes, that's right," added Heather vehemently. Poor Guy, he looked awful. "Greg's an absolute … *pip*."

Guy smiled wanly, feeling very grateful for their understanding. "He's certainly something. I guess I will just have to take the inevitable reprimand when it comes. Sorry Skip. I didn't mean to add to your concerns. Did Mr Morton mention anything else?"

"Oh, lots. Mostly about the site, which is what I now think Morton's primarily interested in. Phillips has written reams, apparently, on the state of the inadequate buildings, and about the wretched bally plumbers clattering around with hazardous equipment during school-time. Anyone would think I'd booked them to work those days on purpose! I'm afraid Phillips and Busterd have been every bit as witheringly critical as we expected. I have the feeling there is nothing the Education Office would like better than to force us to close shop. Then they could dispose of our assets."

"What, sell us off?"

"Exactly."

"They can't do that, can they? I know they're closing little village schools and flogging off everyone's playing fields for housing estates and whatnot, but not ours, surely?" cried Charlie. "Seems a very unsound policy, educationally speaking, to me. Small schools with a long tradition like ours are where kids always do well. The fact that they are small is often the key. It's what parents say they want, too, smaller classes."

"The LEA is more interested in making a profit than providing quality education, if you ask me," said Jean. This conversation was so depressing. "Mayflower is on prime land – near the station and the town. They could knock us down, build a state-of-the-art primary with all mod cons, and still make money from the deal. Even if they just got their grubby little hands on the wilderness they'd be quids in."

"Skip, we won't *have* to sell our back-forty will we?" asked Chloe. "Or the Donkey Field?"

"No, I don't think even they can actually force us to do that, but they might have a case for selling Longmont Lodge."

"No! It's ours. They can't have it," squawked Heather.

"But it's empty, and it's huge. What *should* we do with it? It's a drain on our finances every time something needs fixing."

Skipper looked over at Reg Green. They were both only too aware of one reason Longmont had been left neglected for so long. Unlikely as it was, Sir Hugo Chivers had previously shielded it from official interest for decades by pulling strings somewhere in Whitehall. He had used it as an occasional covert safe-house, with Reg Green as his on-site minder-in-chief. Their occasional 'guests' had been kept perfectly secret, away from everybody except Skipper, who had been overly inquisitive when she first arrived and had therefore to be let into the official secret. She had unwillingly agreed to remain silent about any of MI6's further activities provided these posed no threat to anyone in her school. However, now Sir Hugo had, he told her, transferred his operation elsewhere, the lodge was vulnerable once again.

"Why does *anything* have to be done with it," argued Jean defiantly, "Apart from us keeping it watertight and safe? It's great having it there. It was Sir Garnet's home. And anyway we have used it, occasionally."

"True. But you can see their point. It would bring in a small fortune if it were sold for office development or a hotel or something. I suppose if we made it usable we could double the size of this school. Personally, I think it could be made into a wonderful annexe. We could take weekly boarders, or create a nursery, or a senior school department with a science lab." Skipper was winding herself up with her dreams again. "I don't really see how they can *force* us to flog it off, if we don't agree – although they might be able to strong-arm us into making better use of it. I think I'll phone Jamal for some legal advice."

The staff breathed a moderate sigh of relief while the headmistress scanned her notes again, sipping cold tea. That was at least a sensible suggestion.

Skipper continued. "After the official written report comes through, Chloe and I will have to meet with Mr Morton and his chums down at the Education Office to go through their findings formally. Maybe that's when we get a chance to challenge anything. You know, I feel we've been properly put through the wringer."

They all felt exactly the same. Especially Guy, who grew more silent and pale as the meeting ticked by. He might be formally reprimanded. What would that do to his career? He drove slowly home convinced his reputation was in tatters and that he would be handed his cards before Christmas. His stomach churned and his mind raced like a runaway bus. Confrontation and injustice were bad enough. Being thought incompetent as an educator cut him to the quick.

The following Monday morning Beth telephoned Skip to say Guy was in bed and very unwell. She had no idea when he might return to school.

Mrs Clark put the receiver down with a sad shake of her head. Nothing was going right this term. Nothing at all. How she wished Max were there.

Halloween bazaar

Guy was not the only member of Mayflower's staff feeling distinctly rattled. Skipper felt very shaky after the Friday staff meeting – so much so that Dora gave her a dose of what she called 'jollop' and sent her to bed with a hot-water bottle. Of what the jollop consisted Skip had no idea, but she slept until ten the next morning. When she finally arose she felt marginally less battered and slightly more optimistic. Life's struggle had to go on.

She and Dora called for Chloe on their way to the St Andrew's Harvest and Halloween Bazaar after lunch. They knocked on her front door, admiring a carved jack o' lantern pumpkin on the front doorstep. Next to it was a witch's broomstick and a black cat cut out of cardboard.

"You can borrow Nicky anytime you want," Skip informed her. Nicky was a year old now, and very independent. "He's a tad more authentic-looking than that."

"No thanks. Cassius might have something to say. He's not impressed by felines." Chloe patted the lurcher's head as he settled down by the window to wait for her return.

They made their way across the road to the church hall. It was pleasantly busy, the opening tidal-wave of bargain-hunters having receded. Dora elbowed her way to the cake stall and grabbed a gingerbread loaf and some madeleines while Skip and Chloe made for the bric-a-brac where June, the vicar's wife, was presiding. She had a bargain set aside for Skip.

"What is that? Ooh, an electric pencil sharpener! Does it work? No, well I can try it out later. How much? Gosh, thanks June," said Skip. It felt like finding gold. She had been wanting a good desk-top sharpener for ages.

"Hey look, a Rolodex," cried Chloe, also on the scout for anything interesting. "I didn't think you used such things over here."

The Rolodex was a set of blank cards on a pivot. The idea was to write names and addresses in an alphabetical sequence then rotate it to select what you wanted. It apparently saved looking things up in an address book.

"Yes well, clearly we do," commented Skip. There was no point in a Rolodex in her view. "Are you actually buying that? What else is there?"

Handbags, ornaments, a hideous vase with a clown on it, some cutlery tied up with string, two oil lamps and sundry dishes and plates lay on June's table-top. Dora came over, her shopping bag bulging and her eyes glinting with the thrill of the hunt.

"Oh, I like those oil lamps," she cried.

"Mum, they're filthy and so old. Look, no wicks. What would you want them for?"

"Well, there might be a power cut, you never know. We had that awful storm last winter and it was horrible having to poke about with a torch. I'm sure you can still buy the wicks. Let's have them."

So they bought the lamps, which reserved in a cardboard box under the table until they were ready to leave.

The book stall yielded further amusement.

"Here's a nice boxed set of Peter Cottontail," Chloe said with delight. "I love these. Peter Rabbit, you call him? I'll buy them and keep them in my study for any little person who comes in. They all like bunnies. What's that big book?"

"It's a thirty-year-old Rupert annual. My absolute favourite. The artwork is brilliant. Oh Chloe, here's an old reading primer. Now this'll be a revelation for you. Royal Readers – just look how thoughtfully they designed it. Funny how some books never date isn't it?" Mrs Clark was in her element.

"I bet Alicia Busterd would have something pithy to say if she saw those on our shelves," chuckled Chloe.

"Please, don't remind me. I cannot believe that woman's attitude. The undertaker-man wasn't so bad, but she was perfectly frightful. I suppose I simply don't expect glamorous-looking femme-fatales to behave so nastily. She was more like a man than a woman, when you think about it."

"Maybe," said Chloe, not at all sure about *that* observation. Sharks came in either gender. "The world has changed, I'm sorry to say. She seemed to positively relish cutting poor Guy down to size."

"Maybe she gets a kick out of being mean to good-looking men. Oooh look, comics! I'll buy this bundle to reinforce the wet-playtime boxes. Beano, Dandy, Eagle, and Beezers, Toppers and a few Twinkles. All good. Can these go in the lamp-box please, June? Come on, let's have a cup of tea and some of that iced flapjack at the little cafe. My treat."

The afternoon was pleasantly normal and restorative. Skipper found it comforting to sit for a while with those she loved and chat about nothing very much. Rev Bill discovered the three ladies nattering over a second cup of tea and thought they looked more relaxed than he had seen them in a very long a while.

"Hey there," he said, pulling up a chair. "Sorry I couldn't get over to meet your inspectors. How did it go?"

Skipper and Chloe looked at each other.

"Not wonderful," Chloe told him. "There were two. The man looked like a ghoul and the woman like a catwalk model. I don't think they were very impressed with Mayflower."

"Good lord, why ever not? A model, you say? Pity I missed her. And a ghoul? That's a little weird and halloweeny. Let's hope they don't send us all to hellfire, eh?"

"Hmm," interrupted Dora. "They were unnecessarily hard critics, from what I've been hearing. And not very impartial." She smiled at Chloe and Skipper proudly, which amused the vicar. "But my girls here won't be beaten or demoralised for long, will you darlings?"

She laid a loving hand on each of their shoulders, and they both felt a sudden surge of encouragement from the gesture.

"I'm sure they won't, Dora, not with you in their corner," grinned Rev Bill. He glanced across the room to see Charlie Tuttle and his wife heading their way. Tim was also with them, his arms full of toys.

"Hi," called Charlie. "Mind if we join you? Tim's been buying Action Man stuff and – what's that inflatable thing? A space-hopper, that's right. I can't see how he's ever going to use it, mind, because I think it's got a puncture. And we haven't any garden for him to bounce around in anyway where we're living."

"That's a shame, Tim," commiserated Chloe, making room for the lad and his bulky purchases. "Do you prefer playing outside?"

"Oh yes," said Tim. Football was his thing, he said. He didn't much care for animals and birds. Cricket was good too, and cycling and motor racing and model aircraft.

Chloe looked at the jolly little family, an idea stirring in the back of her mind. If she wasn't going to live at Well House and enjoy its sweeping lawns, airy rooms and happy atmosphere, maybe the Tuttles should have it. It was worth thinking about.

Charlie squinted at her, his eyes sparkling.

"You're up to something, Mrs Shaw," he said softly. "Don't tell me you're not, because I recognise the signs."

"Ha! Busted," laughed Chloe.

"Oh lord, not that ruddy woman again – please!" cried Charlie.

A Sunday trip

Rev Bill carried Dora's box of purchases home to White Cottage that evening and stayed a short while to hear more about the inspection. He didn't like the effect it appeared to have had. His old friend Guy had taken some unwarranted criticism very much to heart, which wasn't like him at all. Bill walked home thinking he had better make a point of looking in on him next week and suggest a drink and a chat down the Yeoman.

Dora spread an old newspaper on the kitchen table and set about cleaning her Victorian oil lamps that evening. She was very happy with them, and soon had the pair washed and polished ready for their new wicks which she would go and buy in town on Monday. Mrs Bicknell will appreciate these, she thought, happily. Their charlady liked nothing better than to polish objects to a lustrous finish. Since Bick's advent, all the household wood, brass and copper-work of their arts-and-crafts house gleamed as never before. Such a household goddess as Ada Bicknell should continually be offered new items to buff-up.

Ernest Chivers arrived on Sunday for lunch. Dora hadn't attended Matins as the weather had turned damp again, and her back was a little tender after all the gardening she had done during the week – cutting back shrubs and wheeling the barrow over to the bonfire patch. Soon it would be Guy Fawkes Night, she remembered. Ernest was only too delighted to be invited round. He loved Dora's home-cooked roast dinners. He hung his coat in the hall and gave her a hug.

"How are you, dear?" asked Dora, as they settled in front of the fire before lunch with a glass of sherry. She did not like the idea of him dwelling alone with only a couple of reclusive housekeepers, and made a point of inviting him most weekends.

Ernest stretched out in the chair enjoying the sensation of home as he chatted. Having spent most of his life in either boarding school or university study-rooms, and having a father who often travelled abroad, he felt very grateful to be included in this comforting little domestic world. It had been a lucky day for him when Skip and Dora moved to Banford, he thought. Nicky jumped on to his lap and sniffed at the sherry glass, but sweet wine wasn't to his taste. He snuggled down comfortably on Ernest's tweedy knees.

"Hey puss, you just wait. There'll be a little taste of roast pork coming your way in a moment if you're good."

The front door bell rang and Skipper went to answer it.

"Chloe!" cried Skipper in genuine delight, then grew instantly concerned as her chum looked completely washed out.

"I know I said I'd be OK on my own today, but it turns out I'm not exactly. Can I come in? I won't eat anything and I'll sit quiet in a corner if you're busy. Sorry – I think I just need a little company. Is that alright?"

Skipper hugged her. "Of course, sweetie, any time. There's plenty of dinner too – you know what Mum's Sunday roast is like. Ernest's here."

Last year Chloe would have suspected Skip of having romantic designs on Ernest, but now she knew better. "What kind friends you are," she said in a shaky voice, and took off her coat.

"Look who it is. There's plenty of lunch, isn't there, Mum? Here, sit down by the fire and hoover up some sherry. Yes, I know you don't like it, but this is medicinal."

Dora brimmed with happiness. It was as if she suddenly had two additional children in her family. She fussed over them all, making Ernest carve the joint and Chloe sprinkle parsley on the mashed potatoes. Skipper was handed the task of chopping up a tiny piece of meat for the cat, who sat expectantly on the sideboard. Dora winked at Skipper.

"Nothing like a Sunday roast to bring our family together, is there?"

After lunch the drizzle let up, so they packed into Skip's car and drove to Benning Water, the large reservoir Mike had mentioned when he had explained his sailing club idea. Ernest knew the area quite well, and pointed out the pretty stone villages and odd landmarks along the way. It was not a long journey, and they soon came to the woodlands and neat meadows which framed the little beach where a deserted boat club crouched beside the rumpled grey water. A pumping station of grandly pseudo-classical appearance crowned a tiny headland nearby, turning its shoulder to the south-west wind.

"Is this where you want your sailing group to come?" asked Dora. "It's very picturesque. Is it safe?"

"Well, no stretch of water can be deemed entirely risk-free," said Ernest, seriously. "But we'll do everything we can to minimise danger, obviously. I know our kids are young, but that's the best time to begin to learn to sail, Mike says. They need to take a few moderate risks, or how else will they learn what they're capable of? Isn't it lovely?"

It certainly was, even on a grey day. However, Skip was not yet convinced the parents would be all that eager to permit their precious angels to bob about on the cold water with only a little plywood, canvas and rope between them and eternity. She said she would think carefully about the project for a while longer.

They turned for home, just as the driving rain began again. The annoying trickle of water that oozed from some undiscoverable spot around the car's windscreen returned. It wetted Skip's knee and gradually ran down into her shoe. Although she stuffed as many dusters around the dashboard as she could, it did not diminish. By the time they turned into the drive and everyone got out, her shoe was soaked.

Water, water everywhere, she thought, irritably. From angry tears to rising damp, there was no escape.

* * *

5.

Guitar

Stinkers

Mrs Clark phoned around for an especially resilient supply teacher that Monday morning. Not everyone was robust enough to handle a class of the oldest children – especially when this one included Greg and Ryan. She was fortunate enough to engage the services of a Mrs Wheatley, a battle-hardened veteran of many a local classroom. Peace reigned in Form 6 all day.

On Tuesday morning, Skip had Reg Green light the study fires, leaving only the main classrooms to be warmed by the feeble central heating. It was a very cold day, and a sly little wind came whining across the flat countryside like an eel, slinking under the old doors and window frames. Reg grumbled, but obliged – Stringer politely carrying the box of matches after him as he coaxed each fire into life.

It wasn't many minutes before the library chimney started to smoke badly. Billows of eye-stinging fumes puffed lazily out into the room, driving Ernest to seek some breathable air in the office.

"God, it smells," he complained. Peggy lifted an eyebrow.

"I thought you used wood on there, not coal. It's the coal that usually makes it smelly. Or have you been burning old socks again?"

"Might be a dead squirrel blocking up the flue or some nesting bats I suppose. Is that possible?"

"Shouldn't think so," said Cathy. She could smell the smoke even though Ernest had closed the doors behind him. "I don't understand it. We had all the chimneys swept in the summer, as usual. I'll go and check if the others are doing it."

She looked in on Skip who was deep in money talks with Chloe. The fires in the head's study and staffroom were drawing nicely, no problem. Chloe's modest one was fine, its sturdy fireguard clipped safely in place. The stove in the extra study workroom in the attic was also doing well and Sandi Raina reported no problems. Apparently it was only Ernest's library hearth that was causing trouble.

Ernest opened some of the library's tall windows as wide as he could. There was a rope and pulley system for the topmost and a boathook pole for the others. The air was slowly, slowly clearing. Cathy wedged open the front and the library doors in order to get a through-draught.

"I don't want all my books smelling of smoke," fussed Ernest. "Nothing worse. D'you know, some books I've lent out have come back suffering quite horribly from parents' cigarette smoke. People don't look after them at all. The worst I ever had returned had bacon rind as a book mark. Yeah, still inside! Can you believe it?"

Cathy couldn't. She had not even imagined such a disgusting possibility.

Greg Price suddenly appeared in the library doorway. Mrs Wheatley had coped with him until ten o'clock, but had finally had enough of his insolence and sent him down to Mr Chivers in order to give the class and herself some much-needed relief. Ernest had been warned he might turn up.

"That Widdley woman sent me. I'm to do my maths here. Bloody hell, what a smeech!"

"Language, Gregory!" cried Mr Chivers sternly. "Sit down over there and get on with your work. I'll want it all completed *neatly* by breaktime. If it isn't, you don't go out."

"Your *fire's* gone out," the boy commented. What a weird school this was, with fireplaces and pets everywhere. None of his other schools had been like it. He wished he was far away from Mayflower, fixing cars like his brother Phil, but his mother insisted he get an education. She didn't want him ending up in jail like Jason, or like Malcolm out on probation. Ian and Weasel both hated school too. They were at Portland Secondary and kicked up a hullabaloo every day. It was annoying their mum still insisted an education was worth having.

"Want me to rake that out for you?"

Never having heard Greg offer to do anything remotely helpful before, Ernest rapidly decided to swallow his instinctive refusal and let him. Cathy retreated to report the phenomenon to Peg.

Greg grabbed the dustpan and bucket and set-to with a will. He made a good deal of extra dust and mess, but at least something positive had emerged from the morning. And Mrs Wheatley's maths problems could always be completed later.

The power of music

Mrs Wheatley nobly tried to cope with Greg again that afternoon, but his interruptions and rude comments got under her skin to such an extent that she eventually sent a pleading note to Mr Tuttle, asking if he would take the boy for the final hour of the day. Charlie's eight-year-olds might shame him into silence, she thought. Charlie Tuttle had been kind enough to commiserate with her during the lunch hour and had offered to take him if she reached the end of her tether. Charlie knew only too well how tough life could be for a supply teacher, remembering that even normally docile children often went for the jugular when a substitute was in charge.

Mr Tuttle was ending his afternoon in the gym hall. Form 3 had been good all day and he usually rewarded them with a grand old sing-song around the hall piano. His boys and girls were currently learning traditional songs by heart, so no books were required. He stood them against the wall bars and shifted the big piano slightly to allow the weak daylight to illuminate his keyboard. He grinned around at their happy faces.

"OK, Greg, just stand on the end of that line of boys. There you go. Now, come on everyone, let's do our warm up."

They ran through some simple la-la-las and mm-mm-mms, up and down the scales. Then he let rip with one of their favourites, 'The Keeper'.

"A keeper did a-shooting go, and under his coat he carried a bow; All for to shoot at a merry little doe – among the leaves so green-o!" they sang.

Wow, thought Greg. Shooting songs. Guns and killing. He stood silently, wondering who he could report this celebration of criminal behaviour to, and who might end up in the most hot water with the police if he did – the silly-looking Welsh berk with the mad crinkly hair, or the frumpy old headmistress? Singing was stupid. Greg wasn't going to do it. Only maybe it would be quite funny to join in and sing loudly off-key. That would upset the little babies.

They began learning a new song – the one they were to memorise today – section by section. Mr Tuttle sang a line, then the children repeated it, joined it all together from the beginning and proceeded. The system worked well and the class learned fast. Charlie irritated Greg by pointedly requesting him to sing-up a bit louder. Greg disliked being singled out when he had not invited attention. He grew even more annoyed when some of the kids nudged each other and smirked at his croaky mutterings. He raised his head and let fly.

"That's better!" cried Mr Tuttle, approvingly. "Very good! Now, everyone – give it a bit of gusto, like Greg."

Like Greg. No one had ever, in his eleven years of life-experience, ever, ever, ever been required to copy anything Greg did. This singing lark might not be so bad after all.

"La di doo, la di doo da day; la di doo, la di aidy. He whistled and sang 'til the greenwood rang, and he won the heart of a la-a-ady," warbled Greg in his very clear, pleasant voice. It didn't actually matter that he was singing rubbish about what his brothers called 'lerve'. It was quite exhilarating singing along with everyone else.

Next day, Mrs Wheatley sent him back to Mr Tuttle before lunch to complete his morning's poorly-presented work, but Greg didn't object any more. He sat and did what he had to at the back of the room, hoping there might be a little more music on offer before they ate. Charlie realised this was what the boy was waiting for, and as Greg behaved reasonably during the remainder of maths and English, he decided to let the children use the percussion instruments for half an hour.

Bells, tambourines, castanets, chime blocks, triangles and scrapers of various designs were distributed. Greg, to his secret delight, was handed the coveted drum and a stick. This was the best instrument of the lot. He could whack it hard and break it if he felt like it. Only today he didn't feel like it. He awaited instructions.

They played together, they sang. They played solos one after the other and sang again. Greg's job was to keep time, not too fast, not too slow, following Mr Tuttle's hand movements. It was a very responsible job, and Greg was excellent at it. He handed the drum back reluctantly when the lunch bell rang.

"You did a first class job with that drum," commented Mr Tuttle, putting it in the box. "It's not as easy as everyone thinks. Thank you. You have a real talent for music Greg."

"Do I?" Greg was surprised. Then he scowled at the teacher, suspecting he was being teased. Only Charlie wasn't teasing.

"Yeah, you do. Ever thought of taking up an instrument? A guitar, maybe?"

"A guitar?" Charlie might as well have said a Chinese gong. The thought had never crossed Greg's mind. "What, like a fol-de-rol one? Classical?"

"No, an electric guitar. Look, I'll bring in my old one tomorrow, if I can find it. You can have a try and see if you like it." Charlie was amused he had managed to engage Greg in some kind of normal conversation.

"I won't be able to play it. It's like for pop stars and bands. You gotta get lessons and I ent doing stupid lessons."

"You think all band players had formal music training? Far from it. Most of them just picked it up as they went along. They make a mint of money too, some of them," said Charlie. "No training, just a good ear and a few years of practice."

Greg approved of that. He'd never really thought about how much the Rolling Stones made, but it interested him. It interested him a lot. He quite liked the idea of starting his own group, maybe with Ian and Weasel. Possibly even Phil. Be less bother than nicking lead off church roofs, like Malcolm.

New aunts for old

The plumbers finally completed the pipe refurbishment. They had removed all the old leadwork in the various sinks and lavatories and replaced them with bright white plastic. They had also fixed corroded ballcocks and wonky toilet seats. Even Pru Davidson was modestly impressed at the amount of effort Voysey's men had taken and how tidy the results were, even if they had taken twice as long as predicted.

"I never expected them old bogs to look as sanit'ry as that," she remarked to Chloe. Chloe nodded wisely, catching up on her meaning after the usual slight delay.

"Yes, oh yes. I will make sure the children are reminded to use them respectfully," she said.

That made Pru shake her shoulders. Chloe thought she was having some kind of seizure until she realised Pru was merely amused.

"Respectful? That ent what kids are. Them boys pee up the wall and the girls clog everything up with too much torlet paper. But remind them anyway, why don't you? Respectful!" She went off down the hallway making more odd sounds Chloe took to be laughter.

"It's a pity those bathrooms couldn't have been finished before the inspectors came," Chloe said to Skipper, later on. "Before they paid us a visit, so to speak."

"Bigger job than they expected, you mean," chuckled Skip. "Oh dear, it's good to be able to joke again. Did you get back to those costings we were looking at?"

"I did, but you're not going to like them any better this time around," Chloe sighed. She pulled out the various estimates for a range of items they had talked about while Skipper slit open an envelope containing Voysey's final bill. She almost fell off her chair. Skip gazed at the total amount dumbfounded, and slid it across the desk to her deputy.

"Whoa," gasped Chloe. "That's double what they quoted. How can that be?"

"Gosh, I hope it's wrong. Let's see. Well, there are various things here they never mentioned before. Let's go and see Peggy."

Peg pointed out that among other items, such as new timber and bags of cement and plaster to fix unexpected holes, there was also overtime added on. She did not view the final costings as altogether unreasonable. Cathy checked the original estimate and pointed out its wording stated there would definitely be variable additional items. No, it really wasn't too outrageous.

Chloe and Skipper retired to talk privately again.

"I really hadn't bargained on this huge extra amount," Skipper whined despondently. "Money's disappearing so fast."

"That's what I was thinking," Chloe agreed. "Do you suppose some of the parents might possibly lend a hand? Not dig in their pockets to supplement the bricks and mortar, obviously, we can't ask that. But they might give us practical help with other things – like donating gardening implements say, or paying for a bus trip somewhere, or painting the cricket pavilion or something. It's all I can think of."

Skipper was dubious.

"Well, we can but ask I suppose," she said. Parental voluntary labour would fall into the 'improve parent involvement' category of the LEA's inspection suggestions, after all. The notion at least had the merit of ticking one thing off Mrs Blasted Busted's 'Must Do A Whole Lot Better' list, Skip thought.

Ryan has a shock

Miss Fisher's form usually created the Guy Fawkes figure to burn on the school's annual bonfire on November 5th. This year it had been constructed from some very jazzy striped jeans and a silky blouse sewn together and stuffed with old newspapers. The children *papier mâchéd* a balloon-sized head on top, complete with cotton-wool whiskers and fierce painted eyebrows. It looked crazily sinister as one eye was slightly larger than the other, but everyone agreed that this only added to its impact. From some hidden repository Miss Fisher dug out a very moth-eaten old felt hat and stuck a long feather in its brim. The result was a fancy paper-stuffed traitor who satisfied the whole class.

"He's brilliant," sighed Poppy ecstatically.

"He ought to have some boots," suggested Peter Bailey.

"But they'd take for ever to burn, wouldn't they, Miss?" said Lulu. Her own feet were rather flat, and as she had been given exercises to do by Nurse Presley she felt she was the class expert on anything foot-related.

Miss Fisher said no one would want to hand any boots over for burning anyway, as they were expensive. The guy would have to do without.

Peter and Rick placed the figure on a spare chair at the back of the room until he was required. It made the children smile to pretend he was joining in their lessons.

Ryan Hale was sent in to borrow a picture book one afternoon. Mrs Wheatley was struggling to find any reference material he could make sense of, his reading skills being so far below the class average. He shambled up to the teacher's desk.

He really is a slummocky child, Miss Fisher sighed to herself. Plenty of bulk but no muscle tone. She directed him to the bookshelf at the back.

"Andy, will you please help Ryan find a book on… "

"*Chrrrrrist*!" yelled Ryan, jumping out of his skin at the sight of the lifelike mannequin slumped at the desk next to the bookcase. Everyone gasped at such profanity.

"Ryan! Mind your words!" called Miss Fisher, seriously annoyed. She marched over and stood beside the lad who had gone as white as a sheet. "It's alright, it's alright, it's not real. It's for Guy Fawkes night, you know." She did her best to calm him down.

"It's not alive, mate," added Andy, kindly. "It's only paper and old clothes. Didn't you ever make one? Me and Rick do penny-for-the-guy every year."

"What? Cor!" breathed Ryan, realising his mistake and grinning at Andy. "That give me a proper turn that did. What you say?"

"Come on, let's find that book on Australia, shall we?" said Miss Fisher loudly. "Australia, Ryan. Book. Are you coming to the school's bonfire night?"

"When is it?" he asked.

"November 5th," chorused the children. Of course, Bonfire Night.

"Two weeks time," added Miss Fisher. The boy seemed to have no idea about anything. He could usefully borrow a few other books, she thought. They might bring his grasp of everyday life up to speed.

"Have you ever had glasses, Ryan?"

"What?"

"Say pardon, not what. Have you ever had a proper eye test? Or a hearing test?"

The lad nodded his head. The cottage hospital wanted him for his adenoid and tonsil operation next week, during half term. But he didn't feel like explaining all that to this old lady in front of these nosey kids. Telling stuff wasn't his best thing.

The teacher handed him three books. One on Australia, one on Superman and one about dogs. Without uttering another word he sloped back to class and drew pictures of kangaroos for the rest of the afternoon. The book on dogs he took home. Superman stayed in his desk for quiet reading time.

The governors get the picture

Lady Longmont knocked at the office door and slid in while Peggy was opening her less-important stack of mail. Gibb held a bunch of rather ragged roses from her garden wrapped in a piece of newspaper and tied with string.

"What ho! Thought you might like the last knockings of my yellow rambler. How's tricks?" She came in and sat on the visitor's chair. Peggy grinned and voiced her thanks. She had grown very fond of the eccentric old lady.

"Any news?" asked Lady Longmont. She liked Peggy, who was as forthright as she was herself. Peg had no time for humbug, and was the fount of all knowledge when it came to Banford.

"Lots. 'Though I can't speak about the inspectors' final report which came in the post this morning. That's for your governors' meeting later on. Typical sneaky official trick to send it out the Friday before half term. What else? The plumbers have finished the loos and are asking a king's ransom. Half the old lead pipes they ripped out have gone missing. Nicked by a gang, the police say. Jimmy Birch has been sent home with scabies again. Guy Denny is still out sick. Mrs Shaw isn't doing well – I don't know what's to become of her. Reg's hip is worse. One new boy in the top form is a proper dunce, but he's having an operation on his tonsils today to see if that helps. And another lad in that class is a nasty uncouth trouble-maker who's making himself a real nuisance. The iron stairs are still dripping. The nurse is pining for Dr Granger and can't be civil. And our last order of composition books arrived with all their covers stapled on upside down. So we're trying to deal with all that."

This was meat and drink to Lady Longmont, who lapped up every detail. She was often lonesome at home, and her garden in winter didn't provide sufficient distraction to help her through the short dark days. She watched the telly most evenings, but there was nothing much good on until the nine o'clock news.

"I feel very sorry for Mrs Shaw," she remarked. "Have the children made Mr Denny sick or was it something else? He's such a charming man and always comes across as so confident."

"Well he is, usually. Here, have a biscuit. I keep them in my drawer so I can sneak one when Cathy's not looking. She worries about my waistline. No, he's usually fine, but that blasted Mrs Busterd – one of the inspectors – really got under his skin when she was here. Made him doubt himself, I think. Can't see why. He's a marvellous teacher by every other account."

"Bullies again," nodded Lady Longmont, munching her custard cream. "Wasn't there some silly business last year about somebody saying Miss Fisher was too old to do her job? Utter tosh. Guy Denny should remember that. At least Mrs Clark gives bullies what-for, doesn't she?"

"She did then, it's true, but that's water under the bridge now. I think Mr Denny will be alright. His wife's very sensible and will help him buck up. Now, I'd better go and ring that bell, and get this place on track for the afternoon. Why don't we meet up for a coffee in town tomorrow morning?"

There was a full complement for the governor's meeting, despite none of them really wanting to be there. They listened to Mrs Clark's explanation of the inspectors' formal conclusions, wishing none of this upset had occurred on their watch. Where was Sir Hugo Chivers when you needed him, wondered Julia Scott.

There followed a long silence as the governors took it all in.

"Yes, so, well, the bottom line – as you see it then, Mrs Clark – is the LEA would like us to sell up, and give them at least half the resulting proceeds. Then they will build a modern school with all mod cons next to a bloody great housing estate built on the wilderness which they will have flogged off to some developer. Is that right?" asked the cynical vicar. He was shocked.

"Swines!" growled Lady Longmont.

Skip nodded. "Pretty much," she said. "Apart from that, we're doing an adequate job."

Lady Longmont felt she was choking with rage. Her heart raced and she wanted to go out and shoot something. How could two measly little here-today inspectors have so much impact on a perfectly decent little school that had been happily piddling along and minding its own business for decades? Was this how the Ministry of British Public Education was operating these days? Sending bully-boys in and forcing them to sell off their assets? Gibb stared at her fellow governors wishing they would say something – anything – that would encourage the headmistress, put some heart back into her. Unfortunately, they all looked more like cringing curs than bulldogs ready for a fight.

"Damned fascists. Isn't there some kind of appeal procedure? What can we do?"

"I don't know, Gibb, but I have an appointment with Mr Raina, our solicitor, to see what he has to say."

Skipper locked her study door that night and went around the block, the long way home. Everywhere, within herself and without, was dreary and dark. The repetitive act of walking provided no comfort but it gave the illusion of adding space between her defined areas of overwhelming worry.

Last year had been a roller-coaster ride, tough but exhilarating – with everyone around her travelling in the same direction. This year she was slogging it out alone as if in some kind of hellish boxing ring. Chloe was out of action, there was no Max, no Hugo, no Dr Granger even. No Guy Denny. No solidly dependable supporters cheering her on. No one with any practical advice to offer, or influence they could bring to bear. Everybody either had other priorities, no time to spare, or no genuine interest in helping. Skip trudged slowly down the dark and slippery footpaths with rain seeping through the shoulders of her coat. Only half a term had elapsed and she already felt beaten to her knees.

Guitar

While the long governors' meeting had been in progress, Greg was completing his day's schoolwork in Mr Tuttle's room. He didn't mind being sent to the younger form any more. The class was well-aware he was trouble – bigger, older, and unpredictable. They eyed him as if he were some kind of dangerous animal.

As usual, Charlie ended the afternoon with music. The children were growing quite accomplished, and he was proud of them. They could sing rounds and part-songs, and various individuals could be called upon to perform a reasonable solo without being too overcome with embarrassment.

"Let's have the percussion out, please Philip. That's it. You and Billy can decide who has what today. Mix it up a bit, though. Everyone needs to have a try at everything sometime this term. We must be ready for our Christmas concert."

"And the plays, Sir?" asked Poppy.

"Yes, Poppy. What did you perform last year?"

"The Night Visitors. Mrs Fisher wrote it."

"I expect Miss Fisher adapted it. We don't know what it will be this year yet, though do we? Who decides?"

"Mr Denny. His lot done Cinderella. It was brilliant."

"Yes, I heard that was really good."

"What would you like? A Nativity Play?"

"No! The kinders do that, and Form 1. It's good, but it's very important and serious," Tania told him. "It's got Jesus in it."

"Oh, OK. So – something fun?"

"Yes! Like the top forms' pantomime."

Charlie bore that in mind as they sang their way through a medley of their usual favourites. Greg was handed a tambourine today. He was not best pleased, and shook it in all the wrong places at first, just to make a din, but no one laughed or complained so he stopped. Eventually he decided it was quite an interesting instrument as it definitely added drama to a number.

At home time, he showed his exercise books to Mr Tuttle, who stacked them on his desk ready to hand back to Mrs Wheatley.

"I finally found that old guitar of mine, Greg. It was at the back of our loft space. My son doesn't want to learn, so I brought it in for you to try. Take a look."

Greg was thrilled. No one expected him home for a few hours, so he decided he could stay on at school instead of kicking cans into the river as he usually did.

The guitar was shiny and red with a place for an electric cord to plug in. Charlie showed him how to set it up and where to place the amplifier so there wasn't an awful whine. He showed him the various parts of the instrument and how to tune it. He sat Greg opposite him with the guitar on his knee, then picked up his own acoustic instrument and demonstrated a few basic chords. Greg had strong nimble fingers and was a quick study. He soon got the hang of the chords and how to play a scale. He looked up and grinned.

"That's brilliant," he said, enthusiastically. "Can I take it home? I won't bust it."

That was a step further than Charlie wanted to go. It was quite a good instrument and he didn't trust Greg or his rowdy brothers.

"Sorry, no. School doesn't permit us to lend instruments. But you can practise any break or lunchtime, when I'm around. And you can borrow this book on guitars if you like over the half term. How would that be?"

Greg scowled. He was disappointed and felt like throwing the thing across the room. Instead he grabbed the book and picked up his bag.

"Alright. I'll come back after half term." So saying he departed, leaping down the main stairs two at a time and whacking his bag against the wall at each turn.

"And thank you so much, Mr T, for letting me play your guitar and showing me the fundamentals," said Charlie softly to himself. "Charmless. Utterly charmless."

He locked the instruments away and went home.

His mood lifted as he crossed the bridge and hurried up the town street. There was something important he wanted to talk over with Fiona tonight. He forgot all about Gregory Price.

Fall back

"Have you done all the clocks?" called Dora.

Skipper had been turning each of the household clocks back an hour. Spring forward, Fall back she remembered. "Yes!" she yelled down the stairs.

"I wonder how your little boy's got on with that surgery," chatted Dora, handing Skip a cup of coffee later on. They took their morning drink over to the table by the window which faced the back garden. Everywhere was very trim now that Dora and Terry Green had completed what Dora called 'a good old Autumn tidy up'.

"Who? Oh, you mean Big Ryan. Yes, I suppose he'll be back next Monday, all done."

"How's the other one doing?"

"Gregory? Spending most afternoons with Charlie Tuttle, thank heaven. He seems to have settled the boy down a bit with some music lessons or something."

"Clever. Was it Ryan's adenoids as well as tonsils?" asked Dora.

"Yep. The poor kid must have had a rotten sore throat most of his life, I should think." Skip was suddenly quite sorry for the lad. "I ought to ring his mum and see how he is."

"Good idea," said Dora. "And after you've done that, how about dropping by to see how Chloe's doing? Bring her home for dinner. I've made plenty. Cassius too, if Nicky's out of the way. They're not too keen on each other, are they? You should tell her you've been talking to Jamal."

Dora knew Mr Raina, the school's lawyer, was the only other professional her daughter considered to be genuinely interested enough in keeping Mayflower the way it was. He knew all about the school's complicated foundation and trust funds. Skip had taken the inspectors' report and a copy of the governors' draft response plan into town and handed it over for him to see. Mrs Milligan, sitting at a neat desk in front of a massive new photocopier, had smiled and thanked her. Skipper wondered how much that glittering machine had cost.

Jamal came out of his office and shook her hand. He asked the secretary to copy the report immediately.

"It won't take a moment," he said. "I'll take a good look at everything – maybe talk to your Mr Morton, if I have your permission, and discuss the LEA's position. I do understand your anxieties, Mrs Clark, I really do, but don't worry, there must be a precedent somewhere. I will do what I can and let you know."

They sat down while she reiterated her most pressing concerns and hopes.

"Ah, here we are. Thank you Mrs Milligan. Now, leave this with me, Mrs Clark, and I'll give you a ring next week and drop by school for a chat, if that's OK?"

It was very much OK. Skipper left feeling much more hopeful.

She strolled home, glad of the exercise and fresh air. Half-term was an annoying hiatus in some ways, but it was also provided an opportunity for her to calm down and re-assess the situation. Already there was the sting of winter in the air. Skipper looked at her surroundings and gave thanks that she had a solid home for herself and her mother, and food on the table.

As Dora had suggested, Skipper winkled Chloe out of her shell and brought her over to White Cottage for dinner. The American was paler and thinner, and very quiet. She had spent two days alone in London over half-term, which Dora prayed was a good sign. Some shopping and a show away from Banford might help her feel more like her old self, but they waited in vain for Chloe to tell them what she had actually been doing. She showed no interest in Skip's visit to Jamal.

The headmistress looked across the table at her dearest friend. It was as if forces beyond Skip's control were pulling her friend away. Every day she drifted a little further out of reach.

Dora watched them both, and her kind heart ached.

Building fires

The days at the end of half-term were sunny and bright. Reg opened the school's delivery gate onto the main road and various parents carted wheelbarrows full of garden rubbish in to add to the bonfire pile that was accumulating in the usual corner of the Donkey Field. Most council allotment holders burned their own debris, but some liked to add to the children's fun with old pea sticks and other bits and pieces. This Firework Night there was to be a proper roped-off area for the spectators.

Ernest walked over and admired the bonfire mountain.

"That's looking magnificent," he said to Reg, who agreed. It was coming on nicely.

Distantly, the school bell could be heard ringing. It meant a visitor had arrived.

The sweep, Mr Bracegirdle, had arrived in his ancient van to clean out the library chimney for the second time that year. He had fortunately had a cancellation.

"Don't understand it, Mr Chivers. I swep' it in August, like I were asked. What it's thinkin' of, kipperin' your books like that, I can't say. Well… here… goes… " Mr Bracegirdle shoved the flexible rods hard upwards, screwing another onto the end and shoving again, before bringing the whole paraphernalia sharply back down. A collection of dirty twigs and mess avalanched into the cloths he had placed in the hearth.

"Whoa! Looks like you've had jackdaws nesting!" he coughed.

Ernest was horrified. The library's chimney flue was the straightest in the building. He did not want a dead or half-kippered bird falling directly into his grate. Luckily no cooked corpse was found in the mess Mr Bracegirdle shovelled into his bucket.

"Can't you put something on the top to stop them?" asked Mr Chivers, vaguely. "A top knot of some kind?"

"A cowl, you mean?"

"Yes, a cowl. A hat on top of the chimney pot. To stop them nesting."

"Well, I could. I could do all of them if Mrs Clark likes. Bit pricey, of course."

"I'll put it to her," said Ernest determinedly. In his view, a cowl fell into the urgent and necessary category of spending, and he would make sure she agreed with him. Even if he had to have a whip-round he would get that chimney cowl. Nobody wanted a pile of smoked jackdaw in their fireplace.

* * *

6.

Fireworks

A damp walk

Jean Hewitt opened her front door.

"Happy birthday!" cried Chloe and Skipper in unison.

Her spaniel emerged, wagging his plumey tail with joy at the sight of the visitors. Cassius wagged his in reply, and snuffled round. Maybe they would be going for a walk together.

Skipper presented Jean with a lavender plant in a pot and some birthday cards.

"It's no fun having a Sunday birthday is it? No mailman staggering up the road with a ton of parcels," smiled Chloe. "Only us."

Jean grinned at them both. "How kind you both are," she said. "Thank you. Come on in, or are you off for a walk?"

"Well we were, so we won't come in, thanks. Would you like to come too? Or shall we just take Sweep?" Skipper was well buttoned-up against the misty morning and sported a new pair of tall leather boots she had bought in Fenchester.

"Right, I'll come. Hang on a tick while I find my coat. Can you clip his lead on? It's hanging by the door. Thanks. How lovely."

It wasn't much of a birthday outing, but it would have to do. To make up, there would be a cake in the staffroom later in the week for all to share. Skipper put Sweep's lead on.

"How old is she?" whispered Chloe while they waited, holding on tightly to the dogs who were eager to be off.

"Fifty-five I think. Or fifty-six. Can't remember," muttered Skipper. Not that it mattered.

They strolled to the end of Fen Lane and looked across the river at the castle on the far side. Only its topmost tower and a crumbling rampart could be seen through the mist that lay heavily on the water. The path in front of them, known as Stokes' Steps, led directly to it, touching the tip of Latimer Island halfway across. It was usually a pretty way for pedestrians and cyclists to reach the town, and a fine walk for dogs as the island was a grassy recreation area, although today very little was visible.

"I'm not groping over the Steps through that fog," Skip said firmly, and the others agreed. "Let's head the other way – down past the railway station and back up Dutch Lane, shall we?"

It was fun for the dogs to explore the verge beside the quiet road as it curved between the station yard and the right fork of the river. Sweep was always searching for ducks, so spent most of his time off the lead wading through mud on the boggy bank. Cassius was far daintier in his investigations and loped along beside them in the grass. He would have preferred considerably drier conditions.

"So what's the latest on the library chimney? Did Bracegirdle sort it out like he said he would?"

"He did. It's all clear now. It was a nest or something causing a blockage," said Chloe. "He's going to put little hat things on top of all the chimneys to stop it happening again, apparently."

"And what about Ryan's operation? Have we heard?"

"Nothing. I rang his mother but I got no answer. I suppose he'll be back on Monday. Is your son coming over for Christmas?" Skip asked Jean. "John, isn't it?"

"Yes he is, and bringing his fiancée. I haven't met her yet. I didn't even know he had a girlfriend." Jean was miffed at her son.

A short young man in a railway cap and coat was just closing the level crossing gates as they reached the station, so they stopped and clipped the dogs back onto their leads for safety. He smiled at them.

"Hello, Kevin," called Mrs Shaw. She had come to know him during her waits for the London train earlier in the year when she and Max had so often travelled together.

"How are you, Mrs Shaw?" he greeted her and came over. His cigarette dangled from his lip and his teeth were crooked, but Kevin's smile was warm and friendly. "Up to no good again?"

"Walking the dogs. This is Cass and this one is Sweep."

"Oh I know them alright. We're old friends, ent we boys?" Kevin ruffled Sweep's ears.

The old-fashioned steam train ground heavily over the crossing and sighed to a halt in the little terminus. It was like an exhausted dragon puffing home for a sleep after a long quest, its smoke mingling with the Autumn fog. Chloe loved English trains, especially this local one, but today it made her think of Max, and she grew quiet.

Kevin unlocked the white gates and pushed them back. They were heavy old things, but well balanced as he kept them greased. They clanked loudly into place with a wobble. He waved the ladies a cheery farewell as they resumed their walk.

Turning right, Skipper belatedly realised they now had to pass Chloe and Max's marital home, Well House. She glanced at her chum and took her arm. She was looking sad, but brightened up at the contact, and smiled back. Jean caught on, muttering something encouraging to the dogs.

"It's OK. I'm OK. We can't *not* walk past places, can we?" said Chloe. "Look, that maple tree Max planted has turned some really pretty colours this Fall, hasn't it? I think the sun's finally coming through this awful fog now. See how nice it all looks? And that… what is that?"

"Hawthorn," said Skipper. "The birds love the berries. And our kids eat the new green leaves in the Spring."

"They do *not*!"

Jean laughed. "They do. Bread-and-cheese they call it, though it tastes nothing like either."

The trio crossed the road and turned up a paved track that shortly deteriorated into an unadopted lane, beside the tangled hedges of Banford Place. There was no sign of Lady Longmont, although her front gates stood wide open. They continued up the steep hill and finally onto the footpath across Hendy's fields towards home. Once they were over the stile the dogs galloped off to play freely and the women scuffed along through the damp tussocky grass.

Chloe told Jean that Skipper had been to see Jamal Raina.

"That's the most sensible idea I've heard in ages," Jean said warmly. "He has a good head on his shoulders that one."

"You know, it's no use," moaned Skipper, starting to limp. "I'm going to have to wear my wellies and some thicker socks next time we come this way. These boots are pinching terribly and they're rubbing my bunion. Yow!"

"Not far now, Limpy Lou," chuckled Jean. "Here, hang on to my arm. If you *will* buy kinky boots instead of sensible rubber wellies, you've only yourself to blame. Look, the mist is clearing away at long last, so cheer up do. It's my birthday!"

Christmas scripts

Much to everyone's relief, Guy Denny was back at school the Monday morning after half-term, but he was still very sensitive about the inspector's scathing criticism. His wife, Beth, had suffered a difficult couple of weeks with him at home, but now at least he felt able to face his colleagues once more, for which they were all heartily glad. It hadn't been the same in the staffroom without him.

Mike eyed the two bundles of typed manuscript Guy pulled out of his briefcase and set down on the staffroom table.

"What's all that?"

"Panto. And a new play for the middle ones," said Guy. "Who's been buying this coffee?"

"Mrs Shaw. She said the other tasted like cat's wee or something. What panto?"

"Well it's jolly strong. But not bad, not bad. Yes, I've murdered Aladdin this year. Rhyming couplets as usual. I had to focus on something positive while I was off." Guy smiled at his friend.

"Oh thank heavens! I thought we'd have to re-cycle that awful Babes in the Wood from three years ago. What's the other?"

"The Gingerbread Man, original author yours truly. I hope they like it."

Mike flipped through a few pages with his thumb. "Looks fine. Who do you like for the lead role?"

"Well, Philip Barnes or Bobby Sykes sprang to mind. They're smart little chaps." Guy mentioned two of Charlie Tuttle's boys.

Mike thought about them. "Mmm. Bobby's grown very tall. What about that shrimp Carl Goodman in May's class? He's a funny little lad."

"What's that about my Carl?" asked May coming in and catching the end of their conversation. "Oh good morning, Guy. Lovely to have you back."

"Guy's been writing pantos," grinned Mike.

"Oh no he hasn't," cried Charlie following May in. "Lord, who brewed this coffee? It looks a bit strong. Do you want some May?"

"Yes, but more diluted please. Oh, it's quite nice once you get used to it. What's our play?"

"Gingerbread Man," said Mike and Guy, handing out scripts.

Heather and Betty joined them and they soon had an audition schedule drawn up. The normally quiet playtime period after lunch would work best. Charlie said he would look out some suitable music, Betty and Heather would draft a begging letter to the parents for some help with costumes, and Mike took on the organisation of various bits of scenery painting. Jean was always their expert stage manager, and Guy the director of both plays. He loved this theatrical period of year, and felt much less apprehensive about work by the time the first bell rang. He made his way up to his classroom.

The children trooped in and sat down. Greg was there. Ryan was there. Guy stared pointedly at them both, and nodded.

"Welcome back, Ryan, hope you're feeling better. Nice to see you again, Greg. I hear you've taken up the guitar? I'd like to hear more about that later on – maybe we can have a chat. OK everyone, find your hymn books and line up by the door, please. Gregory, you're leader. Ryan, you're tail-end Charlie. Try to make sure the classroom door is *properly* closed after you, please, to keep the heat in. Come on."

Guy and Skip share a view

"Well, Ryan seems like a different boy," said Mrs Clark to Guy, at lunchtime. "It's like a miracle. Look at him."

Ryan was loping about the playground with a few of the other boys from his class in a game of tag. He was well muffled up but uncharacteristically active.

"I know," commented Guy. "Like a whole new kid. Still big and awkward but not as distracted as he was. I think he can breathe much better now his adenoids have been taken out. He is certainly less bunged up."

"Dr Legg told me they put grommets in both ears while they were giving him the full MOT service. They will certainly help his hearing for a while, until they drop out in a few weeks. I noticed Ivy had done him some custard and jelly for his dessert today. She's such a kind heart. His throat must still be sore from the operation."

"Did she? That was sweet of her. But if she keeps on doing that he'll be bigger than one of Farmer Kirk's pigs!" laughed Guy.

It was good to hear the man laugh, thought Skipper. I'm so glad he's back.

They wandered over to the railings and looked across the field at the bonfire stack. It was getting to be just the right size for the celebratory blaze on Wednesday evening. Reg and some of the boys had been piling more branches on it, but the mist and drizzle threatened to keep the heap disappointingly damp.

"I hope that bonfire burns through," fussed Skip, "Or we'll have a mountain of bits to shovel out of the way before your football match next week." She turned back to watch the playground again. "When do you want to start play rehearsals? Are you feeling up to it?"

"I'm fine Skip, thanks. You know I don't know why I let that bloody woman rattle me as much as she did. Thanks for understanding." Guy was embarrassed to acknowledge his own frailty, but she was his boss after all. No one else was within earshot, which made speaking slightly easier.

"Well, she completely rattled me too," admitted Skipper angrily. "Blasted woman. I hope she gets promoted a very long way beyond the point where she pokes her nose into hard-working schools again, and slings her ill-considered remarks about. Give her some nice desk job in a hermetically sealed office far, far away."

That made Guy chuckle. "Wall her in, like a vampire, you mean? Clamp her in a coffin somewhere? Let's stake her to the top of our bonfire and have done!"

Skipper laughed and spilt her tea down her coat front.

"Oh stop," she said. "Let's concentrate on Christmas and finding a foolproof way of including Ryan and that wretched Greg in the festivities. I'm sure you're brimful of ideas."

Bonfire night

The colourful guy with the scary eyes, made by Miss Fisher's class, was lifted up and tied into its ceremonial position on the top of the bonfire pile on Wednesday afternoon. Mr Paton had organised the modest firework display, and Reg would monitor the bonfire itself. Children could only attend the fun if accompanied by a parent. If the weather stayed dry it should go well.

It was rapidly growing dark when Mike put his coat back on and headed outside. He was glad he had his bicycle lamp to light the way as he walked down the gloomy path to the Donkey Field. It was so muddy underfoot he had been obliged to borrow Reg's second best wellingtons. The fire would be lit at five-thirty, and the handful of fireworks Mrs Clark had sanctioned would be let off at a quarter-to-six. Time enough after the end of school for the kids to get home, have a bite of something, lock their pets safely in a dark bedroom, and come back to school with their dads or mums. Mike hoped there wouldn't be too many infant brothers or sisters in tow as it scared him to think of unpredictable little ones running about when he was lighting roman candles and rockets. Fireworks were notoriously dangerous.

Ernest joined him in their little roped-off corner where they had previously set up some milk bottle holders for the rockets and nailed two large catherine wheels to a goalpost. He was wearing a flat tweed cap with earflaps.

"Blimey, it's freezing," grumbled Ernest, beating his arms against his sides.

"Soft-living librarian," commented his friend genially. "You need to get out more. Toughen you up."

"I don't want to be a backwoods-man, like Shane," Ernest replied, remembering Chloe's mountain ranger son. "Give me a deck-chair and a martini on the Riviera any day. What's my job here?"

"Er, hand the sparklers around at the end. They're in that bucket and I'm bound to forget them. If you light this catherine wheel, I'll do the other, then we stand well clear. There's your set of rockets and roman candles. I've given you the volcano too. I'll tell you when to light the blue touch-paper and retire. The whole display will probably take all of ten minutes, is my guess."

Ernest hoped Mike was right. It really was perishing cold.

"Plenty of kids and their parents are here already. Look, Reg is lighting the fire. I hope he's put some firelighters in it, or it will never catch. Ah! There it goes. He didn't have to chuck a gallon of petrol over it after all. I can see Heather and Betty and, who's that? Oh, Ben Nesbit's come along too. May's standing with Charlie and Tim. I think she might adopt those Tuttles."

"Charlie adores her. Reminds him of his Auntie Gwladys, apparently – the one who knitted every article of clothing he ever wore. Yes, and Jean has a swarm of kids around her as usual. Nearly time for our first catherine wheel."

Just then, thee boys rode their bicycles in through the field gate. They had no lights on their bikes and were dressed in dark hooded parkas. They whooped loudly and zoomed about intent on riding round and round the bonfire. One of them threw a banger at the blaze, just as the guy was catching fire. It exploded and everyone yelled. Fathers scooped up their toddlers while bigger children clutched their mums' coats.

"Oi, you three!" yelled Reg waving his arms and trying to block their progress. "Clear orf out of it! Is that you Gregory

Price? Them your brothers? Well, clear orf I tell you! We don't want none o' you louts in 'ere."

"You can't stop us," yelled one of the three. "We got a right to be here!"

"We're not scared of a fat old gimpy man!"

"You ent got no rights at all, you little 'ooligans! Not when you frightens young kids and create a danger to the general public. Get them bikes out o' my field, and take them bangers with yer. You Price boys are a bloody nuisance. Go on, 'op it, or I'll call the law on yer!"

"Yah! Come on then, where are they?"

"Already here, boys. Do like the man says and get going, or I'll charge you with disturbing the peace and public endangerment, not to mention riding bicycles without proper illumination." Everyone turned as Ben Nesbit stepped forward, an official-looking card held out in his hand. "Special Police Augmentative Service. I'm on Banford's bonfire patrol tonight. One of our busiest, is Guy Fawkes Night. Move along there now, unless you want your collars felt. That's right, that's right. Close the gate quickly, Mr Green. We don't want them back."

Mrs Clark was near enough to Ben to catch his eye. "You're a special constable, Ben? Well I never knew that."

Mr Nesbit grinned and nodded at her. "There's probably quite a lot you don't know about me Miss," he said, sounding like Dixon of Dock Green. "One thing is – I'm not actually a special or any other kind of copper. Another thing is I joined the Allotment Association at the weekend, where they give you a very nice, posh-looking membership card."

Skipper burst out laughing.

"Well, three cheers for Mr Nesbit!" she cried.

Art day

Last Autumn a local artist had visited the school, and given a printing lesson to selected classes. He had united two forms so that as many children as possible had been able to join in. But now he had moved away to London, leaving Skipper to wonder whom she might prevail upon to provide a little creative inspiration in the dark days of November. She talked it over with Peggy who knew almost everybody in the neighbourhood.

"Why don't you ask that woman who's taken over the old watermill at Ironwell?" she suggested.

"Why? What does she do?"

"Not sure, but it's something arty crafty. Painting, printing, posters – something. I heard she has a gypsy caravan parked out front. All very hippie."

So Skip and Dora had driven to the nearby hamlet one evening, and knocked on the door of what had once been a rambling old brick watermill that stood beside the Wain. An interesting-looking woman answered it, all multi-coloured clothing, chipped fingernails and wild hair. She peered at them through thick spectacles and, when she realised some actual remuneration might be in her future, warmly invited them in. She was a textile artist, she said, specialising in weaving, printing and fabric-work of all kinds. She had been an art teacher at a private school until recently, and was now starting up her own business and gallery.

The upshot was that she agreed to spend a whole day at Mayflower, working with pairs of classes on simple fabric-based projects with a Christmas theme. The teachers, when they heard, were delighted.

"If she rolls up in that gypsy wagon, let me know," said Betty. "I'd like a photo."

When the day came, Fay Winstanley did not roll up in her caravan but on an ancient Triumph motorbike with a large side-car attached. It was packed with fabrics, ribbons and threads of all types. She left the machine to drip oil onto Reg's clean gravel outside the front door and staggered down the corridor to the gym hall clasping two massive bags of off-cuts.

Mr Denny dispatched two sensible boys, Christopher and Basil, to help her prepare. They were amazed at the amount of items she had managed to squeeze into the sidecar.

"That's a nice old motorbike," commented Basil. "Here, help me yank this contraption out. What is it? A loom? What's a loom?"

"It weaves things. Like blankets I think. I'd like a go on that, but it must take ages to set up," said Christopher. "My mum'd love a little blanket for Christmas."

"So would my new puppy. We'll ask her if we can have a try at it, shall we?"

The hall was soon buzzing with children cutting shapes, gluing, glittering, sewing and tying knots in everything from felt and strips of cotton to string and wool. They attended with their teachers, two classes at a time, for an hour. The aides, Carol and Sandi, stayed all day to assist and maintain a semblance of order. It was a slightly hectic experience, but everyone managed to end up with a unique handmade gift for a loved-one to unwrap on Christmas morning. There were cards, gift labels, bunting, table runners, and place mats, egg cosies, finger puppets and hairbands. Basil and Christopher each managed to weave a simple mat out of strands of ribbon and wool. They were delighted with their handiwork. Some children even fabricated little bags with a button-down flap and a strap. They had previously benefited from craft lessons with Mrs Major, a former Mayflower teacher.

"Golly," sighed Miss Winstanley, once the last of the clean-up team had disappeared and she was gratefully sipping a strong cup of tea. "I'm pooped."

"You did splendidly," said Mike. "It was really, *really* good. They loved it, didn't they?"

"They did," agreed Jean. "Even I managed to create a masterpiece for John's Christmas present." She proudly held up a table mat she had made out of felt and wool off-cuts. It showed a crooked robin on a snowy bough, with golden ric-rac braid glued around the edges. Everybody admired it.

"And lunch went well in the individual classrooms?" asked Miss Winstanley. As an ex-teacher she knew how much extra planning *that* logistical exercise must have required.

"Well, we've never tried it before," said May. "But our children always rise to an occasion. Ivy and Sally planned it like a military campaign, and I don't think anyone went hungry. No, there weren't any great disasters. Not after we found the custard."

They all helped Miss Winstanley load the sidecar up again and waved as she roared out of the gate in a huge puff of smoke.

"She needs to spend some of the cash she earned this a'rt'noon on that ruddy exhaust," observed Reg, sweeping bits of wool and cotton off the doorstep and switching on the porch light.

"Gosh, it's gone jolly gloomy again," commented Jean as they made their way back inside to finish putting the hall chairs away. "I hope the weather perks up for tomorrow's matches."

Mr Denny makes his selection

Mr Denny clapped his hands. "Alright, everybody, I know we're a little late starting. But ever onwards and upwards."

"Why does he say that?" Trudy asked her friend Annie. Sometimes their teacher said the strangest things.

"Over here. Come a bit closer. Sit down. Ryan, tuck your legs back a bit, please. Now then."

Guy looked around at two attentive classes – his and Jean's. The children were agog to find out who was to play what in the pantomime. It was a Mayflower tradition that the two top classes joined together for this theatrical delight which was considered the year's most fun event. Last year, Cinderella had been a resounding hit and they were all eager to repeat the success this time. Guy drew a deep breath and hoped there would be no tears of disappointment.

Jean busied herself with a clipboard and the script, taking pencilled notes as Guy explained the story and where the various scenes took place as he gave out the parts. She had already booked the two extra spotlights from the lighting shop in town. All she had to do now was make sure there were some pretty coloured filters for each, and some vaguely eastern music to add an exotic flavour to the production. Hand props and cues, and maybe some green smoke, would all come later.

Malcolm Dale was to be Aladdin – a good choice, as his extravagantly affected posturing as Dandini last year brought the house down. Malcolm was thrilled and already foresaw his future career in Hollywood. Yulissa Fielding was chosen as his Princess Song. She was an elegant child with the longest, shiniest dark hair that hung in a plaited rope down her back. All the boys admired her. Freddy was to be the genie of the lamp, and Leo Lara would make a brilliant Widow Twanky. He seemed destined for cross-dressing parts as he had been cast as a stout Ugly Sister the previous year. Wishy-Washy was Teddy Swift who had played the other Ugly Sister. He loved slapstick comedy.

Ryan listened hard to all this. He was amazed at how much actually went on in a school day now he could hear what was being said, and it was alarming to suddenly find out everything he was supposed to know and do in Form 6. Before his recent operation he had thought school terribly boring, but now he was discovering every moment held something interesting. Luckily Mrs Raina was finally teaching him to read properly so it wasn't too late. He was getting there. He was making connections. He listened attentively and watched Mr Denny much more now he knew the teacher would be expecting something back from him. He sat and watched it all through his new glasses. The scripts were handed out one by one. He desperately hoped he would be included. Finally he heard his name.

"Ryan. I'd like you to be Soldier Number One. Is that OK?"

It was more than OK. Ryan's smile grew wider and wider. He was to be in the panto! And as a soldier, of all wonderful things. He really, really, *really* wanted to join the army when he grew up. How did Mr Denny know?

"Yes Sir," he said brightly. Guy grinned and saluted him.

The only person left sulking was Greg. Not that he had expected to be chosen for anything in the stupid kiddy pantomime. Although he would have been really good, if Mr Denny had bothered to find out. It was another way of punishing him for telling tales to that inspector, Greg decided. He slid over to the vaulting box and sat on top drumming his heels. No one took the least notice.

Then suddenly, after everyone else's name had been called, he heard his own.

"And Greg – you will be helping Mrs Hewitt with the stage managing. This job needs a first rate memory, and quick-thinking should something go wrong. She and I consider you're exactly the right man for this vital job. Alright?"

Greg stopped thumping the box and nodded.

"Sure," he agreed with a shrug.

Match-time natter

"Hello! Here we are at last," called Sandra Elbridge, the headmistress of Dane Street Primary. She led her netball and football teams into Mayflower's muddy field, having walked the mile distance from their school. "Sorry we're late. Gavin dropped the ball into the river."

Gavin looked anything but abashed. "Sorry Miss," he said.

Guy and Jean warmly welcomed her and the two other members of Dane Street staff. It was always nice to see their local colleagues, even on a chilly afternoon like this.

The matches rapidly got underway. Miss Phelps and Mr Lomax, Dane Street's games teachers, were today's referees – which allowed Guy the pleasure of yelling encouraging advice to his team and Jean and Sandra the fun of a long chat while supposedly egging-on the netball girls.

"How's your Chloe doing?"

"Sad. Very sad still."

"It'll take more than a few months to get over Max. Such a tragedy. He was a lovely man."

"I know. We all miss him. He used to pop in all the time you know, even before he met Chloe." Max Shaw had been a big fan of Mayflower. He had worked as a deputy officer at the local education department and adopted Mayflower as his pet school because he lived nearby.

"I bet they miss him at the Fenchester office. I doubt we would have had that ghastly pair of LEA inspectors let loose on us recently if Max had been around." Jean was still livid at the amount of upset they had caused.

"Oh, who was it? Don't tell me you had that awful Busterd woman and Worzel Gummidge." Sandra brought her friend quickly up to speed on the pair's terrifying county-wide reputation.

"Well, they weren't exactly terrifying," said Jean, trying to be reasonable. "But they undermined our Guy enough to make him stay home for two weeks."

"No! Guy Denny? Two weeks? You sure he wasn't just playing golf somewhere? No, but I am surprised. I'd have thought he was tough as old boots."

"Not when it comes to people criticising his management of a particularly difficult child and then taking the child's lies as gospel." Jean reckoned that was what it boiled down to.

"Who's the kid?" Sandra asked. "Get up, Gillian, please. Now pass it on, pass it on. That's better."

"A new boy called Gregory Price."

"Oh, you haven't got *them* have you? Poor old Guy, if he's got Gregory. The Prices lived near my school a few years ago and I had the pleasure of the two older brothers, Ian and William – known to all as Weasel. They'd be at secondary school by now, I suppose. Sneaky little pair. The littlest, Gregory, was a right terror, even as a toddler."

"What's their home like? Can you remember?" asked Jean, stamping her feet in boots which seemed to do little to protect her from the rising cold. "Goal! Well done, Lizzie! Good shot. Let's have another one."

"Very – what's the latest expression? *Unstructured*. That's it. Means chaotic." Sandra frowned as she tried to remember more about the Prices' domestic arrangements. "The older lad went to jail for burglary, I think. The next one down wasn't too bad – Bill or Phil. Phil I think. He must be out at work by now. Malcolm was awful. Ian and Weasel were the bane of my life for a couple of terms, then they moved to Portland. Where are they living?"

"The council houses in Trafalgar Road. You're right about Greg. He seems to spend every moment of the day being sarcastic and disruptive – although Charlie Tuttle has managed to find a connection."

"God, what?" Sandra could not imagine any of the Price boys being interested in anything more normal than torturing small animals.

Jean smiled at her. "Music. He's teaching him the electric guitar."

"No!" said Sandra. "Well, I'll be blowed. Music? Is he aiming to be some kind of Beatle? It would suit him, all that limelight and mayhem."

Jean found that very amusing. "No, I don't think he's quite up to that standard yet. Charlie tutors him at lunchtimes – says he's not bad. We all feel like clubbing together and buying Charlie a bottle of champagne. The boy isn't quite so obnoxious since he started playing, but it comes and goes. Don't know what he gets up to at home with those brothers, mind you."

"Didn't you have some old lead piping go missing when your water pipes were being renewed?"

"You don't think the Prices took it do you?"

"Well, I wouldn't put it past them," answered Sandra, darkly. "You should check with PC Pink. Now, that's *walking*, Margaret.

Give the ball to Deirdre. And there's the whistle! Well done, Dane Street. Well done Mayflower!"

Jamal finally brings order

Jamal Raina loved visiting Mayflower. It was his idea of a picture-perfect English school, which was one reason he was happy to be its legal advisor. The other reason was that his wife was working there.

He found the headmistress and her deputy in the library one morning, sitting with the librarian, Mrs Julia Scott and Peggy Bailey at a refectory table. It was a lofty room, and the overhead lights did little to dispel the slightly smoky murk of the place. All this wasted space, thought Jamal, glancing up at the distant ceiling with its fancy plasterwork. If it weren't for the children's books and cheerful posters it could be a film set for Dracula. He took a seat and opened his briefcase.

He did not bore them by relating all the dead-ends he had met with during his several conversations with Mr Morton, but definitely gave the impression he had left no stone unturned. He had gone through the detailed findings with the deputy administrator one by one, starting with those pertaining to the quality of education on offer, and had cynically come to agree with Mrs Clark that the LEA was far more interested in the potential value of the property than in its provision of good basic educational skills. He believed Mr Morton was, in fact, rather irritated the place was so successful, and so universally loved. Results were excellent, parents were happy. Mayflower served the town's children very well, the man had grudgingly admitted. What he and his colleagues did *not* care for was the fact that it possessed its own trust funds and was therefore neither fish nor fowl. It was an administrative anomaly. The Authority was having to subsidise an essentially private educational foundation without having any control over its considerable assets.

"I rapidly put him right on several points, Mrs Clark," Jamal assured her. "I explained that Mayflower School was here long before the education authority. I reminded him of the legal strictures in our foundation, one of which states the education on offer must conform to government standards. I also pointed out the Local Authority derives direct and particular benefits from Mayflower, not least of which is the considerably smaller amount of funding the county has to provide it with. He was not comfortable being reminded of those things." Jamal allowed himself a sudden smile as he remembered Mr Morton's huffiness.

The result was, Jamal went on, that the LEA agreed to stump up a very tiny extra amount of cash this academic year, which absolutely must be assigned to fixing the top half-a-dozen critical issues. Mayflower would have to supplement this cash itself if it did not wish to incur future financial penalties. Mrs Clark had until the end of August to complete this list to Mr Morton's satisfaction.

Mrs Clark mulled that over. It was no less than she had feared.

"And what about Guy Denny?" she asked.

Jamal shook his head. "They have no on-going concerns about the singular incident regarding discipline. There was no complaint made from any parents."

"After all that?" gasped Skipper. "After wilfully… ? Well that's rich!" She stood up and marched around the room, her head in a spin.

Jamal peered over his glasses. "Yes," he said, "I know. One feels the unpleasant manner in which your inquisition was conducted was ultimately little more than smoke and mirrors."

"Coming in all guns blazing, and stirring up discord, while trying to camouflage their desire to make a grab for our resources, you mean?" Chloe's eye's darted, briefly full of their old vigour. "It's like a land rush. They're nothing more than opportunists!"

"Yes. I think that was it. Grabber and Grabber are not just to be found in the Molesworth books, Mrs Shaw. But I believe I helped Mr Morton to see some reason. And now, of course, you are no longer at the top of the county's inspection programme. Mayflower School can look forward to a few years of relative peace from that quarter."

Mrs Clark stared at Jamal in admiration. He was a quite an advocate.

"And Longmont?" she continued. "There's no way they will drop that particular bone, is there?"

Jamal sighed. "Not that I can see. Longmont and the wilderness land will always constitute a separate, thornier issue. I think it would be wise for you to begin to draw up your own plans for any possible future educational use you might wish for it with Sir Hugo, when he returns. So that you have something on paper. This will give you a leg to stand on in any future battle. But for now – with their unfortunately inescapable imperatives in mind – I have taken the liberty of drafting this." He handed out a paper to each. "In this column you will see I have listed Mr Morton's priority requirements. Here, I suggest approximate costs, based on local estimates. Here, what the LEA would contribute. Cash will be exceptionally tight this year for you, no question, Mrs Clark. Maybe next year too. I hope it helps to clarify things a little."

They thumbed through the papers in silence.

"You've been very thorough," commented Ernest, wondering how much school was having to pay him for what must have taken hours and hours.

"It did take a little while," admitted Jamal.

Mrs Clark thanked him warmly. Jamal's methodical, unemotional handling of the situation had been exactly what she needed. Now all she had to do was make a start.

"I honestly don't know what we'd do without you, Jamal. Thank you," said Skip.

"No problem," he replied with a dazzling smile. "I've included my bill on page five."

* * *

7.

Left, right

Greg cracks a joke

Play rehearsals continued every afternoon as the weeks raced towards Christmas. Fitting the on-stage rehearsals around regular lessons, lunch, PE and educational broadcasts on TV made a complete shambles of the regular hall schedule.

The kindergarten and first formers struggled through the traditional nativity play with much help from Betty, Carol and Chloe. Any parent helpers who turned up were put to work hunting out props, fixing scenery or sewing costumes. Making the shepherds' crooks caused heaps of trouble as the hook parts kept falling off. Reg had to construct a brand new manger this year as the old one was found to be mysteriously missing two legs.

"How that 'appened I couldn't tell yer," he said to Ivy. He yelled across the playground to Greg, who was doing his best to annoy the second form girls by running into their skipping-rope game and messing it up. "Oi there, Gregory! Come over 'ere."

The lad slunk over, expecting the familiar ticking-off.

"Can you 'old a bit of wood steady if I was to saw it?"

"What?"

"Can you help my husband fix some new legs onto this thing?" explained Ivy.

" 'Course," said Greg. What a dumb question.

Help fix a baby bed? Greg wasn't fooled. Everybody at this stupid school was taking a crack at trying to keep him out of mischief by having him do little jobs for them. Mr Paton had had him label all the cricket equipment. Mrs Clark got him to help her organise the tool shed. Mr Chivers wanted a load of books unpacking and another lot packing up. And he was constantly on call to Mrs Hewitt to help with the lighting and props backstage. It was as if proper lessons didn't matter any more. Being kept permanently busy was simultaneously annoying and flattering. Here he was, doing his best to get sent home, or expelled forever, while every adult in the place was equally determined to thwart him.

He picked up the broken manger legs and looked at Mr Green, the old sailor with the limp.

"I could make you a wooden leg, too," he offered cheekily.

That made Reg laugh so much he had to find a hanky and wipe his eyes. "You young varmint," he chuckled. "Git along with yer."

Greg grinned – a rare occurrence. He hadn't meant it as a joke, but it had turned out to be one. He tried not to enjoy the sudden surge of happiness that rose in his chest.

Greg mistrusted happiness. He had learned that when you showed any delight you were immediately ridiculed and called unkind names. As a toddler, when any toy or storybook had made him happy it would soon be snatched away and derided by his five brothers. Finding anything fun usually led to being beaten-up. There was no one around to stand up for him, no one more mature to model himself on. Mum was always at work and Greg had no memory of his father. His brothers had grown up enjoying the feeling of superiority they gained by humiliating anyone different to themselves, and loved nothing more than to make someone else cry or lose their temper. Greg's only option had been to adopt his brothers opinions, copy their arrogance and cynicism, and modify his friendly instincts. Because he was smart he learned fast. After ten-and-a-half years, he had developed a very tough shell.

But Greg enjoyed making Mr Green laugh. Mr Green was impressive. He was a man's man, who saw right through people. Greg respected Mr Green and found he wanted the old boy to like him. So he picked up the broken manger and followed the caretaker without another word.

A flying visit

"I sorely miss him," sighed Nurse Presley to Heather Jackson. She had been inspecting Form 1 for head lice and found none, which disappointed her.

"Who? Oh, you mean Dr Granger. How's he getting on, have you heard?" asked Heather politely even though she was not terribly interested.

"Och, the dear man's slaving like never before. He phoned a week ago to have us forward something when it arrived at the surgery. He told Mrs Drysdale, our receptionist, the teaching role he has with the university is *very* important and enjoyable work."

Heather muttered something she hoped was appropriate, and made her escape. Nurse Presley smoothed her apron, adjusted her trilby hat and was pulling on her raincoat when the door of the medical room opened and a head appeared.

"Dr Granger!"

The nurse sat down in her chair with a thump, face scarlet and heart racing. "Oh my, I was only saying a minute ago… "

Joe Granger smiled broadly at her astonishment.

"Good morning Hilary," he said. "Here you are at Mayflower, as usual."

"Yes, oh yes, here I am! And all satisfactory – quite *wonderful*, Doctor. Oh my, but you gave me a turn!"

"Sorry," he said. "I only looked in briefly. Are you heading off?"

"I am. There, that's me packed away now. I have a nice little car these days, you know."

"So I saw. Here, let me get the door for you. I'm calling by the surgery very briefly this afternoon, about two. Hope I catch you again." He knew he would. Wild horses wouldn't stop her being there.

Dr Granger waved as the nurse drove off and returned inside. Skipper met him, thrilled he was paying some kind of flying visit south, and that Mayflower had been included.

"We do miss you," she beamed. "Afra Legg is brilliant and we all love her, but she's not you. Come and tell us about Edinburgh – we're all dying to hear. I'm sure Ivy can squeeze another lunch out for a special guest. Come on, they'll be dishing up."

Happy to be marched off to a lunch of meat pie and cabbage in a hall full of noisy children, the doctor went willingly. There was a very gratifying cheer when he entered and a place was found for him with Chloe and May at Form 2's table. Ivy brought over an extra plate together with some cutlery and a beaker.

"Room for a little one?"

"How lovely to see you," cried both teachers. "Are you back for good?" added May.

"No. Flying visit, I'm afraid. I'm booked on the evening train north again. Lord, that's far too big a slice of pie for me, May, and take off that extra potato. You'll have me the size of a double-decker bus."

"Oh, Sir," grinned David Davies, who was sitting on his other side. The doctor looked at all his former patients.

"Nice to see you, Jimmy," said the doctor to Jimmy Birch, the boy who had always caused him the most concern. Neglect and poor nourishment had led to his being included in Dora's after-school cooking club. Dr Granger ran his professional eye over the lad's slightly improved appearance. Jimmy smiled at his old friend as he scraped the meat out of his piecrust and used his fork as a spoon.

"I'm still in the Nosh Club, Sir," he confided. "It's really good because you get to cook stuff and then take it home. I make stuff for Mum and me at weekends too. Healthy stuff."

May made a mental note to try to extend Jimmy's vocabulary beyond the word 'stuff'.

Dr Granger listened and nodded and ate his way through every particle of his own pie and cabbage, but he declined Chloe's offer of a jam tart and custard for dessert. It was a step too far.

He watched her serve their two tables, glad to see a glimmer of her old charisma as she smiled at the children. Chloe had always appeared so golden and radiant, it was hard to take his eyes off her. Every movement was graceful no matter what lowly task she undertook. Kindness spread around her like a cloak. She was thinner, though, dark circles around her eyes. He glanced at her engagement and wedding rings, so new and shiny, and wanted to touch them.

May Fisher raised her eyebrows and glanced across the room at Mrs Clark who was speaking very brightly and a little too loudly, as she dished out jam tarts at her own table. Well well, thought May. I must have a word with Jean.

The doctor said goodbye after a mug of tea and a chat in the staffroom with the rest of the teachers. They were sad to see him leave again, but he said he would do his best to be back for the Christmas plays, which cheered them up. Nurse Presley would like that, Peggy remarked, and had been advised to go and boil her head.

Dr Granger walked swiftly to the town surgery by way of Stokes' Steps, buying a large bunch of chrysanthemums from the florist on the way. As promised, Hilary Presley was in the reception room, filing and re-filing record cards.

"Happy birthday, Hilary," said Joe, handing her the flowers. She was predictably overwhelmed.

"Och, no! You remembered! Why thank you very much, how gorgeous they are." She would have loved a hug, and a kiss on the cheek, but the doctor was standing the other side of the desk so the moment passed.

Dr Legg breezed in and introduced herself.

"So, now I know when Nurse Presley's birthday is," she said cheerily. "I will write it in my little book for next year."

"You won't be with us that long, surely, will you?" asked Hilary, blissfully unaware of causing offence.

"Oh, I hope so, nurse," returned Dr Legg crisply. "Unless I get sent packing by the returnin' whizz-kid here. I don't rule anythin' out."

She caught Dr Granger's eye and they burst out laughing.

"I suppose we'll have to see," he said.

Drains

Terry came over to help his dad Reg with the school's list of urgent maintenance jobs. He set-to with a will hacking back the worst of the undergrowth along the wilderness paths, burning debris, replacing broken tiles, repairing cracks and even unblocking gutters using a device of his own invention.

"It's a hook on a stick," he explained to Skipper. "It's amazing what you can do with a strong bit of bamboo and a coat hanger."

She admired it. Anything that was both useful and cheap was alright in her book at the moment. She had been forced into purchasing a new step-ladder that week, as the old wooden one had finally given up the ghost despite Reg having replaced several rungs over the years. You couldn't expect much from a twenty-year-old step-ladder, he had said apologetically, not when it was in constant use. There had also been two new dustbins and some extra gallons of floor polish. Her petty cash box was emptying rapidly, as was every other little fund. Skipper pushed down her financial anxieties and reminded herself how lucky school was to be able to rely on such imaginative, inexpensive and talented people like Terry to help out. Steady as you go, she told herself.

"I'm very grateful for everything you both do" she said as she watched them replace a fixing-bolt on one of the netball hoops. "I don't know where we'd be without you. If we didn't have your family to make-do and mend, Reg, we'd never be able to satisfy the wretched LEA."

"You cuttin' our wages then?" Reg said, picking up his bucket. Outpourings of gratitude embarrassed him and were pointless. He was only doing his job. Terry smiled at her. He loved old Mayflower school and was only too happy to help keep it running. He stood the netball hoop back up.

"There. That's good for a few more games," he commented.

Skip disappeared indoors while Reg limped off to get the wire snake, as the staff toilet was reportedly backed up again. He hobbled along slowly and painfully, wishing the damp weather would end and his hip joint cease grinding bone against bone. It was getting beyond a joke. Everything this Autumn seemed to be falling to pieces or seizing up, he thought as he raddled the snake round and up and down through the sludge of tea leaves. And I'm one of them.

Bick checks in

Mrs Ada Bicknell was employed as a cleaning lady in two local houses. There was Mrs Clark's White Cottage, where she cleaned and cooked three afternoons a week, and Mrs Shaw's place in Church Road. Bick had originally been engaged by Mr Shaw early last summer to 'do' for him once a week at Well House. Now he was deceased and that house locked up, she continued honouring the engagement reckoning she had a duty to the grieving widow. Chloe was more than happy to keep Bick on as she had always hated housework. Bick knew, from her days in London during the blitz, how cataclysmic a sudden bereavement could be. Her afternoons in Church Road enabled her to keep a sympathetic eye on poor Mrs Shaw, whom she liked. Bick had always been a kind, watchful sort of person.

Bick's watchfulness had been noted by others, too. She was currently also employed to spy on local comings and goings for Sir Hugo Chivers. She reported anything unusual she saw or overheard either directly to him, or to Mr Green the school caretaker. Always in secret. Sir Hugo informed her the local surveillance was part of a highly important secret service network, vital for national security. She had become a valuable cog in a national machine and had been specially selected for the work, he explained. Astonishing though this information was, Bick trusted and believed Sir Hugo, and took to her surveillance task with patriotic fervour. None of her friends knew what she was up to, but it was for Queen and country so she carried on come rain or shine. Even though Bick would have done the job for nothing, Hugo paid her well.

The trouble was, since the Summer, she was the *only* local lookout. Last term there had also been a schoolboy named Jumbo Ellis – a particularly observant eleven-year-old who could often be found standing by his bicycle, apparently gazing at birds or distant animals through his binoculars. He had been an excellent watcher, supplying detailed reports. However, Jumbo had now moved to Portland.

"Anything?" Reg enquired, as Bick stood at Mayflower's side-gate one day watching a sparrow feed on a fat ball that Cathy Duke had hung in the bushes.

"Not much, Mr Green. Gypsies come through again, heading west. They stopped by the scrap metal place in Ironwell on Tuesday last, and spent a long time talking to that Miss Winstanley about her old caravan. Janey Birch has got a new job cleaning down the Mint. I think the Yeoman was a bit too much for her, she ent strong. Brenda Kirk's having an extra-marital fling. I sees her about the place a good deal more than before. I hear she's paying attention to that Mr Perry what lives in Manor

Lodge and rides one of them scooters. My friend 'Liza Muggeridge's seen Brenda traipsing back 'ome to the farm very late some nights with a smile on 'er face. It don't pay to mess on your own doorstep, I says to Eliza, and she agrees. Len's took to the bottle by all accounts, poor man. Drownin' 'is sorrows, is how 'Liza puts it. He's good reason in my view."

"Len still collects our swill for his pigs of a Friday. Usually drinks down the Yeoman," nodded Reg, remembering. "But if 'e's taken to the sauce reg'lar, 'e won't be able to swing a cricket bat next season." That was a sobering thought. Reg decided to have a word with his old chum – offer some friendly advice.

Ada Bicknell sniffed as she pocketed her cash envelope and stumped off in the direction of home. She looked at all the berries in the hedgerow and then up at the crows circling the tallest elms in the wilderness, and shivered a little. Winter was definitely on its way. Brenda Kirk ought to be grateful she and her three kids had a good warm roof over their heads. It didn't do to go gallivanting with a hard Winter coming on.

Nature ramble

"We will have a final nature walk this afternoon," May Fisher informed her seven year olds. "There is no rehearsal today, and we all need the fresh air."

The children sat up straight and folded their arms, alert to Miss Fisher's every wish.

"The river levels are a little too high today for us to go down to the water meadows," she informed them. Several faces fell, as they had sometimes been allowed to fish for frogs and tiddlers and bring them back from the ponds and creeks. "So we will go up the hill instead. If it is too muddy or starts to rain we will turn around and come home."

The children nodded, trying to appear sensible and thoughtful.

"Now then, Carl, I don't want a repeat of last time." Miss Fisher's gaze bore into the child's very soul. On the last walk he had been caught short and had to pee against a tree in full view of the rest of the group. Carl blushed and grinned nervously.

"Yes Miss. Sorry Miss. May I be excused now?"

"I think that's a wise idea, Carl. And anyone else who needs to spend a penny, go now. Wash your *hands* and return quickly or it will be dark before we even start."

May looked out of the window at the clouds. They were scudding swiftly against a shining sky.

The crocodile of children crossed over Mayflower Road a short while later. They climbed over the stile into the fields where a clear track followed the line of the hedgerow. Today each child had brought a little notebook and a pencil to list as many natural objects as possible, rather than collect things to take back for their nature table. Miss Fisher thought any collection today could only result in some very messy pockets.

"What can you see there on the ground Lulu?" she called to one of her girls.

"It's an old nest, Miss. Can I kick it?"

"No, leave it alone. What else?"

Lulu surreptitiously nudged the tempting nest with her foot and watched it roll into the ditch. "There's a load of red berries. Is it hawthorn?"

"Well done, yes. What else?"

They rambled on over the slightly rising ground. There were ponies grazing as best they could on the tussocky pasture, one of which was a tubby little thing with shaggy legs.

"Look, it's Twitch, Mr Tuttle's pony. He has a nice tartan coat on today. Here boy!" called Sarah Grigg. She and Jimmy Birch tried to entice the fat little horse over. Jimmy was usually quiet and sleepy in school, but grew alert and attentive enough out of doors. He clicked his tongue in an encouraging way.

Twitch ambled over, hoping for a sugar lump. No one had any, so Sarah pulled up a handful of grass for him. Twitch snorted in disdain and rolled his eyes.

"Mind he don't bite yer," warned Alexandra. She affected to like most horses as she had an hour's riding lesson each weekend at Mint Farm Stables, but she had also developed a healthy regard for those that rolled their eyes. Twitch showed his yellow teeth to prove her point.

"Cor, don't horses ever clean their teeth?" asked Chrissie. Her own teeth were often a cause for concern and she hated the dentist.

"It'd have to have a big toothbrush," remarked Jimmy, trying to amuse his teacher. He desperately wanted to hold Miss Fisher's hand, but he knew she wouldn't allow it, so he hopped off to look for something interesting to bring her.

They crossed muddy Dutch Lane with its ruts and puddles and climbed up into the wood where the footpath divided. The terrain changed and there were now holly clumps, pine trees and rank patches of brambles. Nuts were ripening and fungi were thrusting through the fallen leaves. Old Man's Beard wreathed the twiggy bushes in clouds of fluff and bright streaky crab apples festooned ivy-strangled trunks. Hips and haws crusted the bushes indicating a long winter to come. The air smelled rich and damp.

"Blackberries taste rubbish now," commented Carl. He had tried a few of the leftover fruits and concluded they were inedible. "I like it when you can pick 'em and take 'em home and make jam."

"That's my house down there!" called out Sarah. Her family had moved into the newly built homes in Monk's Close. "Ours is number four."

Everyone admired the modern houses. It was an easy walk for Sarah to get to school over the fields in the summertime, but her mother insisted she catch the bus on wet days. It was two stops to school and only cost a few pennies. Riding the bus alone made Sarah feel very grown up.

"Come on Jimmy," cried Miss Fisher. "This is the last bit of the climb. Give me a pull."

Thrilled to the core, Jimmy took Miss Fisher's warm gloved hand in his little cold one, and tugged gently to help her gain the highest point in the beech hangar.

Holly Hill was quite a landmark in the locality. Its summit was pitted with dips and dells and the well-worn paths over it were hazardous with spiky bushes, fallen branches and rocky outcrops. The turf was studded with smooth chalky slides and patches of brushwood, while all around rose the stately grey trunks of ancient beeches like massive dinosaur legs. Today the treetops were clinging to their leaves as if they were clasping golden sovereigns in their skeletal fingers and trying to snag a few demented crows as they pitched and tossed past on the wind.

The children gathered around their teacher.

"Can we play?" asked Rex.

"*May* you play?" Miss Fisher automatically corrected him. "Yes, go and have fun until I call you back."

The children whooped off to scamper up and down the well-worn slides and hollows. The boys pretended they were on scramble motorbikes and the girls on spirited horses. Only

Jimmy remained nearby, picking up stones and leaves, turning them over and bringing them to his teacher to identify.

"Go on, Jimmy, go and play with the boys. Or find Sarah. She'd love to have a game," suggested Miss Fisher.

He looked so forlorn, she hadn't the heart to insist. She recalled how insecure she had felt up here once when life was getting her down, and how comforting it had been to spend time with people who cared.

"Alright then, stay here with me. Let's lay all your pretty stones out in a line and see how many you've got, shall we?" Miss Fisher looked at his skimpy hair, pinched little face and chapped fingers. She felt around in her pocket for a packet of Polo mints and unscrewed the silver paper. The Knit Club at school would be working on cosy mittens next week and she knew where one pair was going to end up.

"Now, that's better. What tree do you suppose this leaf came from?"

Cycling deficiency

Mr Denny and Mrs Hewitt were once again on the playground together, and they were both shivering. PC Pink was chatting happily to them about neighbourhood crimes, while retired policeman Bob Bostock explained the finer points of the cycling proficiency test to the top two classes.

"And when I am com-*pletely* happy with your abilities, you may take the test. If you pass, you get a cer-*tificate*," he bawled like a sergeant-major. The boys and girls stood silently listening, storing up this idiosyncratic delivery for some fun later. "Which means you are then safe to ride your bi-*cycle* on the road. Is that clear?"

"Yes, Mr Bostock" chorused the children.

They were split into groups to practise traveling safely, come to a junction, turn right, turn left, perform hand signals, slow down and stop, mount and dismount. It was all terribly serious. Later, there would be a written test on the highway code.

Mr Denny and Mrs Hewitt checked their clipboards. It was cold and they couldn't wait for the session to be over.

"When are they taking the actual test?" sniffed Jean into her hanky.

"Next Tuesday morning. I hope your Joey Latimer works out which way left is by then," answered Guy. "He could do with a sticker on his handlebars."

Jean agreed. The child was almost in tears this morning. He was trying as hard as he could and really concentrating, but left and right always flipped in his mind, and which-ever direction he was told to go he automatically turned the opposite way.

"Come on, lad – *think*!" cried Mr Bostock. This was entirely the wrong advice. Joe wobbled and fell off.

"Here, here, young Joey," said PC Pink coming forward and picking him and his bike up off the ground. "You come along o' me for a minute. There you go. No harm done."

Joe hiccupped and tried to stop sobbing. Cycling Proficiency was *hard*, and it was obviously very, very important because policemen were here.

"Look," said PC Pink, pulling something out of his tunic pocket. "It don't matter if you're more cycling *de*ficiency than cycling *pro*ficiency. You're just learning, right? Now, if I puts these on yer *right* hand you'll know which way is the *right* way to go – al*right*? There now."

So saying, he clipped a pair of handcuffs onto Joe's right wrist. Joe looked up at the constable in astonishment.

"It's OK, son, I ent arresting yer. It's just to remind you, like. A lend. You have a lend of them for the morning. You'll be alright now, I'll lay money on it." He grinned at the lad.

Joe suddenly understood. He smiled back at the officer, and then burst out laughing. Several of his friends looked over, green with envy.

"You lucky thing, Joe," called Mick McDonald. He would have dearly loved to be really, properly handcuffed. Some people had all the luck.

Joey remounted his bike, and the next time Mr Bostock called 'right turn' there was absolutely no mistake. Clank, went the heavy handcuffs swinging from his wrist.

All *right*, thought Joey.

Parents' evening

The first parents' evening of the academic year arrived.

"Have all your parents signed up?" Betty asked Heather.

"No, I'm two short, but they might just turn up anyway. I'm pinning the list with the names and times to my classroom door. They won't stick to it, but I live in hope."

"Do you want me to lock the bottom door?" There was a door and a private staircase between the kindergarten and first form classroom above, which was very useful most of the time as the two classes often combined activities.

"Oh yes, lock it please. I don't want any parents sneaking up that way when I'm holding forth on somebody else's little darling. That would never do."

Heather passed over a box of plasticine models to her colleague. Betty took out a dinosaur and a sausage-like caveman. She had written labels for all the items as they formed the centre of a display of the children's best work in the gym hall. Already the walls were covered with selected paintings and drawings done by the older classes.

"Who did that lovely blue chicken?" asked Heather.

"Mungo," answered Betty, proudly. "He's a bit of a wild card, but when it comes to painting he really does well."

"Bless him," said Heather.

That was a condescending comment that always irritated Betty. She pointed to a wonderful portrait of Nurse Presley on her bike.

"Is that supposed to be Hilary? It's really good. I can't quite read the signature. Oh, Stanley Scott. He's in Mike's I think. Any relation to Judith Scott?"

"Nephew. And who did that fabulous racing car? It's wheels look almost circular."

"Colin Wright. Hasn't that class just finished their cycling proficiency tests?"

"Yes. All passed, so now they can ride their bikes to school safely. It's a good scheme."

"Did Joe Latimer pass? Sandi wanted him to wear a glove on one hand so as to be able to remember which way was left, or something."

Heather laughed. "Yes he passed too, thanks to a pair of PC Pink's handcuffs. He clipped them on Joe's wrist to remind him."

Betty went back to her classroom chuckling at the idea. It had a lot of merit. Having her five-year-olds learn left from right took quite a chunk of her PE time. Handcuffs for all might be the answer.

The parents began turning up soon after lessons were over for the day. They sat on chairs outside their child's classroom and waited in trepidation, as if at the dentist. When finally invited inside they had ten to minutes to hear about their son or daughter's progress and discuss how they might best help and encourage their child at home. Homework was often a bone of contention, with parents wanting more and teachers preferring less. Marking homework could take up a substantial amount of teaching-time unless staff waded through it at lunchtime, which Skipper was determined should not happen. This year staff were reminding parents to hear their children read aloud, practise their mental arithmetic, multiplication tables and spelling lists, and answer any questions about extra work promptly, without resorting to unhelpful advice such as 'go and look it up'. And they were also encouraged to send a note in if they encountered a particular problem. Most agreed they could manage all that, and left feeling better informed and satisfied.

Chloe and Skipper provided endless cups of tea and sandwiches for all the teachers throughout the parent conference evening. It meant a long and busy day for all, even if parents kept to their scheduled times. Luckily, by nine that night, all the visitors had departed and only Guy was left. His was the largest class, so he always expected to finish slightly later than the others. He finally clumped wearily down the stairs and handed his empty mugs over to Chloe who was doing the dishes at the staffroom sink. He kissed her on the cheek, which surprised her very much, and made her suddenly tremble.

"Thanks for all the tea," he said. "You're a real trooper, Mrs Shaw."

She smiled and pulled herself together. "Does that mean I should wear a red coat and go fight some rebellious colony demanding no taxation without representation?" she asked brightly.

Guy studied her with his head on one side. He'd had such a crisis of confidence recently, it made him very aware that

156

pasting on a brave face every hopeless day required a superhuman effort. He knew how near to uncontrollable tears one could be at any given moment, and how a kindly word could so easily tip one over the edge. Tonight, he clearly saw what a toll was being taken from this particularly gallant lady – yet here she was, still putting one foot in front of the other.

He set down his briefcase and picked up a tea towel.

"You, ma'am, always look wonderful whatever you wear, and are the bravest fighter I know," he said gently. "And the rest of us, floating in our little Mayflower ship full of old-world pilgrims, appreciate our tough colonial sisters, and take our hats off to them. You're amongst friends here, Chloe. Let's both keep bailing a bit longer, shall we?"

She turned back to her washing up bowl and busied herself with its contents.

"Beth is a very lucky girl," she croaked.

*　　*　　*

8.

Ryan makes more friends

Ryan liked dogs. Having often felt disconnected from other children as a little boy, he had grown fond of a neighbours' puppy and played with it every day until the neighbour moved house. He desperately wanted the school dog, Stringer, to like him but the terrier was far too protective of Reg just now to leave his master and scamper off to play ball. Stringer knew Reg was in pain and that he often needed help with a task. The dog wouldn't play while there was work to be done.

Jean noticed Ryan trying to lure Stringer away from guarding a toolbox one breaktime. The boy looked less stout than he had been at the start of term and had certainly grown less belligerent and more personable. It was good to see him enjoying life. She wandered over and started a conversation about dogs and home as they walked together around the playground in the sunshine. Frost dusted the edges of the wilderness weeds that poked through the railings, making the area almost pretty. The boy became quite animated as he chatted.

"I like taking dogs for walks," he informed her. "Mum lets me. You got a dog, Miss?"

"I have. His name is Sweep. You've met him. He likes Latimer Park to run about in. If you come to my house in Fen Lane on Saturday you can take him for a run there, if you like," smiled Jean. Ryan wasn't such a bad kid. "Number 6."

Ryan grinned and nodded. He would do that.

"Mr Paton says I can help with the boat too," he went on happily.

"Oh, the sailing dinghy they're going to build?" Mrs Hewitt hadn't had Ryan pegged as a sailor, so maybe it was the joining-in that appealed. Mike, Ernest and Charlie had finally acquired Skip's permission to fix up a sailing boat sometime after Christmas, and start their little sailing club in the summer term if they managed all the funding themselves. Everybody in school was talking about it.

Dean Underwood came galloping up, kicking a blue plastic football he had brought from home. It had been presented to him by his mother and sister at the end of his first year at Mayflower for doing well. The blue ball was his pride and joy.

"Hi Mrs Hewitt. Hey Ryan, wanna come and play? Miss Clark says we can go on the field if we stick to the edges where the grass is longest."

Ryan loped off after his new mate, clanging the gate hard behind him.

"Mind the gate!" called Jean. It wouldn't stay on its hinges very long if that was how it was treated. "About eleven o'clock, Saturday, Ryan!" She called after the boys in vain. Neither was paying her any attention.

From the roof

Mr Bracegirdle returned to strap the new cowls onto the school's chimney-pots later that week. He had an immense and frighteningly rickety set of ladders that reached to the eaves, and another strange contraption that hooked over the roof-ridge allowing him to climb to the topmost pots. Picking a dry day had been his biggest hurdle, but this morning it was sunny and bright and the roof tiles even felt warm to the touch. He clambered about, digging in his apron pocket for this and that and whistling through the matchstick gripped between his teeth. Finally he took his cap off, scratched his head, and called down to Reg who was, quite pointlessly, holding the bottom of the base ladder.

"Want me to throw this blue football down?"

"Yep!" yelled back Reg. Dean's precious ball had been booted by Ryan higher than the attic windows and had lodged in some netting by a downspout. There had been tears and apologies and sulks. Both lads promised to take more care next time they played. The ball bounced down beside Reg.

"You doing some work on that roof over yonder?" called Mr Bracegirdle, pointing over the trees in the direction of Longmont Lodge.

"No. Why?"

"Looks like you're missing some lead sheeting, from here. Might be slates. You oughta take a look, Reg."

Job done, Bracegirdle began his laborious descent. He was ready for a spot of lunch.

Reg fumed as he hobbled across to Longmont Lodge after the sweep had finished. He felt like booting a blasted football all the way to Ledgely he was so mad. Stringer galloped in front keeping well out of kicking range. Reg was unpredictable at present and he was mighty strong when annoyed.

"If it ent one ruddy thing in this godforsaken place it's suthink else," the caretaker snarled aloud. "I get the damn chimberlies crawsed orf 'er perishin' list and another bloody problem pops up. It 'ad better not be thieves."

His hip throbbed more than ever as he mounted the backdoor steps and unlocked the building. He turned on the low-watted bulbs that lit the length of the ground-floor corridor and began the long painful journey up to the attics. Cold tiles, creaking floors, old carpeted hallways, more brass-bound steps up and down, higher and higher he climbed, following the familiar route that either he or Stringer took every evening to check Longmont's window latches and locks were secure. Finally, man and dog reached the roof-space entry. It was always perishingly cold and draughty up there under the slates, so the door was kept securely bolted and padlocked. Stringer sat waiting while Reg found the right key from the collection he had clipped inside his brown overall coat. Neither of them had actually inspected the interior of the loft since the summertime as there were bats roosting – not Reg's favourite wildlife – and they were best left undisturbed.

An unusually strong breeze blew past Reg's ears once the thick heavy door was finally dragged open. Bright bars of sunlight filtered in where there should have been inky darkness.

"Damn and *blast* the buggers!" seethed Reg.

Longmont's attic dormers had once been closely covered with neatly nailed sheets of stout grey lead, moulded to fit tightly over the boarded wooden frames. Now Reg could see stripes of blue sky between the solid oak boards. The valuable outer metal skin had gone.

How anyone had climbed that high up the outside, prised it all off and lowered it down was not Reg's concern. Right now he wished whoever it was had fallen the four storeys onto the flagstones and broken their thieving necks. He shuffled around the odd-shaped loft-spaces and checked each window to make sure, but alas, every trace of the malleable metal roofing had been stripped from all six dormers. Nothing remained, it was a very thorough job. He swore again, impressed by the audacity and obvious organisation of the robbers, given that the building was so regularly patrolled.

"Can't have 'appened many days ago," Reg informed Stringer. It was sheer chance Mr Bracegirdle had looked over that way. "Maybe last weekend."

Reg locked everything back up and returned to school as fast as he could to find Mrs Clark, thinking gloomily that the school wasn't having much in the way of good fortune so far this year. Whichever way they turned, troubles seemed to rise one behind the other, like waves in a choppy sea.

PC Pink swings by

The local bobby, Police Constable George Pink, licked the end of his pencil and flipped open his notebook. He peered over his reading glasses at Mrs Clark and Reg Green who sat facing him in the head's study.

"When do you think it might have occurred, Reg?"

"Well, I reckon it must'a been last weekend sometime. I usually send the dog round the upper levels, 'cos me leg's been a bit…." He glanced at Skip. She would have every right to complain that he hadn't been doing his job properly by sending the dog to check on things, but so far she had not commented

162

on him delegating this duty. "It were Bracegirdle noticed it, when 'e were putting the cowls on the chimberlies. Noticed it through the trees. We 'ad that other old lead piping took too, don't forget, when the plumbers put in them new water pipes. Proberly the same set of buggers," growled Reg.

"Most likely," agreed the policeman. "They'd be familiar with the layout of the grounds and know your security routine from scouting round before they nicked all that, I don't doubt. It's how they shifted those heavy lead sheets I'm puzzling over. They'd have had to have a van or a truck of some kind. That's a big quantity of lead to shift, that is. Somebody must have sinnem."

Reg jumped as if a pin had been stuck in him. He knew someone he should ask about that.

"Do you have any likely local suspects?" interjected Mrs Clark. She had watched TV detective shows and knew the drill. "A gang?"

PC Pink nodded at her. "Oh yes," he said. "I got a few ideas up me sleeve. Is there anything else gone missing?"

There wasn't, although Mrs Clark privately decided to have a thorough inspection of every part of her school's acreage later on. She should make a proper inventory.

The policeman took off his glasses and stood up, buttoning his notebook back into his tunic pocket and picking his helmet up off the floor.

"Well, I'll get started on this today and let you know how we do, just as soon as there's anything to tell, Mrs Clark. I suggest, in the mean time, you take a look at your insurance policies. Find out what exactly you're covered for and make a claim if you can. I'll give you a case number. Oh, and nail some tarpaulins over them dormers, Reg. I don't think you'll get a builder this side of Christmas, or for quite a few months, and you don't want the snow getting in. I'll keep you informed about my investigation, as I say. Thank you for the tea."

He and Reg and Stringer walked slowly back over to Longmont Lodge for a final look at the crime scene, while Skipper went to update her deputy on the latest calamity.

Well House

Charlie and Fiona Tuttle unlocked the wide front door of Well House and pushed it open.

"Ooh," whispered Fiona, cautiously. "It looks terribly big."

"It *is* big. Come on, in you go." Charlie nudged her over the threshold and into the hall. It was square with pale panelled walls and colourful modern rugs on the stone-flagged floors. Doors stood open showing glimpses of various rooms, and light filtered dustily down from upstairs. Five bedrooms, Mrs Shaw had said. Three bathrooms, a study, a kitchen etc. A morning room. Charlie was in love with anywhere that boasted a morning room.

"We can't afford this!" cried his wife, walking into the sitting room. "Oh look Charlie, an inglenook."

"Come and see the kitchen."

They tiptoed through the place, feeling as if they were intruding, as it still contained Max Shaw's furniture and belongings. There were couches and beds and carpets, tables and chairs – shelves full of neglected books, ornaments.

Fiona pressed her nose against the window and squinted out at the garden which reached down to a long line of willows. The railway line was immediately beyond, then the river and a stretch of open heathland. Trains were infrequent, as the local station was only a single branch line ending in a terminus. Noisy trains would not bother them in any case, as their previous home had been situated right next to a national main line and they had found the comings and goings rather fun. This lovely view seemed to stretch peacefully for mile after country mile.

"Tim will love that garden," commented Charlie. "It's all grass, so he can kick a football to his heart's content. He could wave to the people on the trains, like in the Railway Children. Come on, Fee. What do you think?"

"Isn't it just a little – well, too *grand* for us? It's super-posh. Isn't it too big?"

"No, Mrs Tuttle, it is *not* too big. We could fill it with some pets, or your relatives, or hordes of our own bouncing little babies. We could invite your mother down for Christmas, and my brother and his brood, and *still* have room. It's ideal for us. You love Banford. Tim's happy, *I'm* happy. Come on, Fiona, you know it's perfect. We'll never have another chance like this. Chloe's open to us either renting or buying – she just wants it off her hands. She's not asking a king's ransom either. I vote we buy it before she changes her mind."

Fiona looked at him standing there, so excited and enthusiastic. It had been a long while since she had seen her husband this happy, and her feeble reservations melted completely away in the heat of his eagerness. It was the perfect home for their little family, it really was. So she hugged Charlie and he swung her round and round in the hall.

"Come on, let's go and celebrate next door!" cried Charlie.

"What on earth do you mean?"

"I mean the Mint is right next door! Did I not mention that? No, don't hit me, you can't go back on your decision now! Perfect house, perfect location, perfect wife. And a perfect pub next door. Come on!"

"You!" Fiona laughed, exasperated. Trust Charlie.

Tests and preparations

December was upon them before they knew it.

Exams, the fire drill, the concert and the famous Mayflower Christmas Bazaar are actually the easy things, thought Chloe, as she attempted to cram them all into her diary. Dress rehearsals and the play performances were by far the more demanding events. Mayflower's Christmas season was as stuffed as one of those Victorian plum puddings she had read about.

For three blessedly peaceful mornings there were what her British colleagues called exams, and she called tests. The children were assessed on what they had learned so far that term, which in Chloe's opinion would amount to very little, as there had been harvest festival, halloween, bonfire night, the church bazaar, field trips, bank holidays, half-days and half-terms. Not to mention the dreaded inspection and parent conferences. The list of British celebrations and other interruptions to learning was apparently endless. She sighed and shook her head as she stacked the student dossiers on her desk ready for updating.

The children, naturally, revelled in anything that was not work-related and each afternoon during exam week let themselves go with the all the fun and organised chaos of the play rehearsals.

Aladdin was coming together nicely. A wonderfully exotic lamp had been dug out of storage, and a whole bolt of blue chiffon fabric donated for costume material by Mrs Lara, who had originally purchased it to drape around her shop window but later feared it would only encourage cobwebs. Three mothers and a sewing machine set up camp in the little multi-use room where they had Reg erect some rails upon which to hang the ever-growing line of costumes.

The Gingerbread Man production involved the construction of four animal costumes, two of which had to have four legs. Dean and Oliver were to be the pantomime horse, Martin and Crystal the pantomime cow. Dawn was the pig and Philly was the fox. The children who had to work as a pair spent a great deal of time hanging onto each other and practising co-ordinated walking movements around the playground at breaktime. Soon the horse could perform an excellent, if slow, march. The cow, however, was rather more choreographically challenged and resorted to relying heavily on some bashful eyelid-batting as a distraction from its drunken stumbling.

For the Christmas concert, Charlie and Heather put together a programme of carols and songs, interspersed with solos from any child willing to perform. The school choir, comprising the most able singers, was the core around which they designed their playbill. Some of its members were also church choristers and Charlie suggested they appear at the beginning as a carol-singing group holding a lantern on a pole.

Mr Timms, St Andrews' choirmaster, called by with one they could borrow. He was Lizzie Timms' uncle.

"Oh is that the lantern?" asked Peggy, greeting him at the front door, when he rang the bell. "Does it need a real candle?"

"No," said Mr Timms stamping his feet on the doormat and following her into the office. "It's got a battery and a switch. I made it myself."

"Gosh, aren't you clever? Now, have you bought your extra concert tickets yet? There, that's right. And can I sell you some extras for the pantomime that Lizzie's in?"

"She's really looking forward to being City Woman Number Four. She never had a part in anything at her old school," laughed Mr Timms, forking over some cash.

"Well, I wouldn't say Mayflower is exactly Drury Lane, but you never know – this could be the start of a splendid career," smiled Cathy. "Has she settled down alright?"

"Well, to be honest, I'm glad you asked. For the most part, yes. But she's a bit nervous of that Greg boy in her class. He's quite a ruffian, isn't he?" Mr Timms was glad Cathy had broached the subject. "He tried to spit at her once."

"Oh, I'm very sorry that happened. He's not our usual type of lad, I'm afraid," answered Peggy. "You've spoken to Guy Denny? Well, I'll be sure to remind him to keep a special eye on things, shall I? We don't want Lizzie being upset. Leave it with me."

Gratefully, Mr Timms handed over the light on a pole and went back to St Andrew's vestry. He glanced up at the roof of Longmont Lodge as he strode back to church, where he could see the tarpaulins that were stretched over the dormers flapping in the breeze. He shook his head. Mayflower School was not the place it had been last year, and no mistake.

Fire drill

Peggy rang the old ARP bell vigorously. It clanged urgently through the school's empty corridors and up the shaft of the Iron Duke stairwell. Every child felt a thrill of excitement mixed with fear zip through them. Their teachers grew suddenly serious and intensely brisk.

"Stand. Leave what you are doing and line up. Anyone in the toilet? No running or pushing. You know where we gather? Good. No talking at all. Lead on." They grabbed their registers and closed the form room door firmly behind them.

Every class rapidly and silently exited the building to stand in its designated outdoor muster area, shivering with cold. Mrs Shaw timed the event with her little stopwatch, while Mrs Clark oversaw the whole evacuation regally from the playground steps. She only had to yell a reminder to one child.

"Gregory! Stay in line and watch what you're doing with your feet!"

Everything's gone pretty well this time, she thought, but there's always room for improvement. This assembly area is probably much too near the main building. If the wind were to fan flames from the south we'd be roasted alive. She decided she had better relocate the muster stations further away, in the playing field. That way the fire engine will have unimpeded access to any of the building's exterior doors. She made a note to ask the local fire safety officer about it next time he came to check the extinguishers. Perhaps he would also like to observe their drill.

"Very well done, everybody. Thank you, teachers." They all trooped back indoors, more than ready for lunch.

At least that exercise didn't cost us any money, thought Mrs Clark, gratefully.

Farmer Kirk plays skittles

Len Kirk, the pig farmer from Abbey Farm, now spent his evenings drinking at the Mint public house. He had, until recently, frequented the Yeoman but the old Mint down Mayflower Road was quieter, and trudging through gloomy woods and down a muddy lane to get to it suited his sour mood.

One midweek night in early December he sat in the public bar as always, drinking hard and glowering at the barmaid. Janey watched him, not trusting what she saw and wishing her long day would end. Soon Len's muddled feelings of betrayal and impotence and misery regarding his wife's infidelity were submerged in a sea of bellicosity. By chucking-out time he could have picked a fight with a snowman.

Carefully negotiating the yard's frosted puddles he paused before crossing the road. Roads meant kerb drill, he recalled, trying to focus. He cocked his head to listen. Just as he was about to step out, a motor scooter suddenly appeared. It came screaming along the road like a banshee doing about fifteen miles an hour. Len immediately recognised it as the transportation of his arch enemy, Dick Perry, the very person who had seduced his buxom Brenda away from home and hearth. What were the chances of that?

Seething with furious energy, Len leapt into the road wildly rotating his arms. He caught the scooterist a hefty whack and Dick toppled off onto the soft grass verge. The scooter itself skidded, slithered, spluttered and died.

"You little piece of … Hold still while I bloody kill you!" snarled Len. He yanked Dick up by the scruff of his parka, and whirled him round so he stood facing him. "You pitiful little pipsqueak! You snake in the grass. You wife stealer – take *that*!"

Len whacked Dick another wallop with his meaty right fist and was gratified to see his enemy go down like a skittle. The illusion was enhanced by the fact that Dick was slim-built and wearing his globular white scooter helmet. His head hit the road surface with a satisfying thwack.

"Get up, you puny bastard," cried Len hopping about like a boxer. "Get up and take some more!"

"Here, here, hold on," called a voice from the darkness. Len glowered at the interruption. It was Mr Bunting, Sir Hugo

Chivers' factotum. Bunting had also spent an evening at the Mint, except he had been in the lounge bar.

"Piss off, Bunting, go home to yer missis. This bastard's been luring mine away from home all Summer and needs a bloody good thrashing!" Len pulled Dick Perry up to his feet again and held him by the throat while he delivered two good slaps, left and right.

Suddenly Len felt a searing pain in his neck and his arms went numb. He found he could no longer make his hands grip his enemy's coat. Dick Perry slid gratefully back onto the ground again in a heap while Bunting placed a friendly arm around Len's shoulders.

The landlord of the Mint, hearing the commotion, had by now switched his outside light back on and come hurrying out to see what the fuss was about. He found Mr Bunting holding someone up while another person lay sprawled on the road beside a fallen motor scooter.

"Lor, what's happened?" cried Mr Unwin. "Is it an accident? Shall I call an ambulance?"

"It's alright, Fred, no harm done. Len appears to have collided with this scooter while crossing the road. The rider says he's fine, thank heaven, and will be on his way in a jiffy. I'll see my old pal gets home. Nothing for you to worry about. Good night!"

At that point, Dick Perry rallied and staggered to his feet. He grabbed his scooter's handlebars, yanked the vehicle upright and pushed it off down the road as if the devil himself were on his heels.

Bunting, supporting the bewildered and tingling farmer, waved and turned in the opposite direction. It's going to be a slow walk home, he thought, but Kirk can't manage alone. He felt in Len's pocket for some house keys and slipped them into his own alongside the sharp knife in its tough leather sheath that was always secreted there. Kung Fu wasn't Bunting's only means of disabling a person.

"Come on, old man," he muttered, patting Len lightly around the face. "I didn't incapacitate you permanently. The feeling will come back soon. Let's get you home."

Mr Unwin shook his head and returned indoors, sorry beyond words that Len Kirk should have come to this.

The Christmas season begins

Heather and Charlie strove hard to prepare and rehearse the various parts of the Christmas concert programme meticulously, whilst also trying to keep everything a surprise for the rest of the school. It wasn't easy, especially as the usual coughs and colds of Winter raged on unabated. They were relieved when the day of the event finally dawned.

The french doors in the hall were unlocked at 6pm for the audience to begin shuffling in, eager to be out of the cold. It was a cloudy, moonless night and the BBC weather forecast suggested there might be more than a sprinkling of snow before morning. The place buzzed with anticipation as people took their seats and discussed the hand-printed programme. Christmas had begun at last!

Mrs Clark introduced the little show and Heather took up her position as conductor while Charlie settled himself at the grand piano. Tonight he was resplendent in an evening jacket and bow tie, while Heather wore a long black velvet gown of sixties' vintage, which suited her rather well. The singers arranged themselves on stage, grinning at their friends with embarrassment. Every girl had her hair tied back and every boy had his slicked down. Miss Fisher commented she had never seen the children looking so smart in all her days.

The well-chosen programme was a huge success. After the little band of carol-singers entered singing 'Sleigh Ride' – complete with bells and clip-clopping sound-effects – they launched into 'The Keeper', closely followed by 'The Lincolnshire Poacher', 'The Ash Grove', and 'Frosty the Snowman'. The audience hummed along with all their old favourites and applauded loudly whenever they could. Next came the nervous solo pianists followed by two seasonal pieces from the recorder players. The ensemble of instruments performed a lively modern Mexican piece. Finally, onto the stage walked Greg Price with Charlie's red electric guitar. Mr Tuttle handed the piano over to Miss Jackson and joined him on stage with his own acoustic instrument.

"Our final items tonight come from Gregory Price from Form 6. He has taken up the guitar since he joined Mayflower last September, and we are all eager to hear what he has learned," announced Mrs Clark with a smile, as the two settled themselves down. "Take it away, Greg."

The audience glanced at each other. This was that horrible kid no one liked, right?

Together Greg and Charlie played and sang 'Red River Valley'. It was absolutely excellent, and the applause that followed was genuinely enthusiastic. Greg smirked and nodded, then beckoned Lizzie Timms to join them. Their duet was 'Tie a Yellow Ribbon Round the Old Oak Tree'. They performed so confidently, in such pleasant transatlantic accents, they were forced to give an encore. The choir and the audience joined in the singing too, and ended giving the pair a standing ovation. It was a truly festive and happy evening.

"Wow!" cried Chloe to Skip over the applause. "I didn't think Greg would ever play as well as that! Amazing. Well done Charlie, I say."

"Encore!" yelled Mrs Clark, clapping hard. "Encore!"

Greg Price grinned around the hall, wishing some member of his family were there to witness his success. This felt really, really good. It had been easy enough to learn the guitar and even easier to walk on stage and sing, which surprised him. Maybe he really could be a pop star one day. He nodded to Mr Tuttle and Lizzie.

"Let's give 'em that last verse and chorus one more time, shall we?" he suggested.

Bazaar

Snow had been falling thick and fast during the concert. When the performers finally met up with their parents, they found themselves being bundled up in scarves and gloves and woolly hats brought along for the cold walk home. Reg Green ushered everyone out as fast as he could and closed the doors tight against the perishing weather.

The following day there were long lines of wellington boots standing on newspapers in the downstairs corridor, and umpteen duffle coats and mackintoshes draped on the hat pegs. A musty smell of damp wool and gabardine drifted all the way to the gym hall where Chloe, Skipper and Stringer were watching Reg and his group of helpers set up the tables for the afternoon's Christmas bazaar.

"Ryan! Lift that one out and over to Chris and Basil can you? Then that other one will slot in behind it." Reg was barking orders at the boys as easily as he had once instructed able seamen. He stood, surreptitiously leaning against the wall. Today the cold and damp felt as if they were gnawing right through every nerve in his entire body.

Ryan was rapidly turning into a kind-hearted and gentle giant. Apart from his improved hearing and clearer head, he could now see things properly. His round, National Health glasses had changed his life dramatically. For a start, he could judge distances and see details, which made him much less clumsy. Of course he remained considerably larger than most boys his age, but he was learning this could be an advantage. Mr Green, for instance, usually wanted at least one strong fellow in his group of helpers and Ryan was often chosen. When he was using his strength productively, the boy was in his element – which made him a happy lad and far more tolerant of the world in general. Other kids liked him. He was the person people turned to for help.

Once the stalls were set out and prettied-up with crêpe paper and tinsel, the hall looked lovely. There were cards and cakes and decorations to buy, games to play. Ivy Green put the urn on to boil in one corner and Ryan helped her arrange some chairs and a table for the teas she was serving. She had grown rather fond of the big lad. He was turning out to be both willing and reliable.

Promptly at three o'clock, the hall doors were again flung wide and the mums and dads, brothers and sisters, grannies and grandpas, aunts and uncles arrived in droves. Reg was grumpily resigned to the fact his polished parquet flooring would be ruined. Whenever there was a lull in the stream of buyers, he kept trying to close the doors and slide an old towel over the worst of the puddles with his foot. It never lasted long. Someone would fling the door back again, then neglect to close it or wipe their feet. The constant draught and frustration did little for his temper.

"Can't you leave your umbrella outside, Mrs Latimer?" he complained to one mother. "You'll 'ave someone's eye out. Give it 'ere. I'll stick it in this pot behind the curtain for yer. Now then, the roll-a-penny's good, or are you after some uniform for young Joey?"

Mrs Shaw watched the busy scene with detached amusement. School was fun on days like this with the snow falling like feathers outside and a warm happy hubbub burbled within. She suddenly discovered Greg Price standing next to her.

"Hey, you did great yesterday at the concert," she congratulated him. "I was blown away."

Greg nodded. "Yeah, it was alright." He shrugged his shoulders.

"You should try some other instruments too some day, you're very talented. They can be a little expensive to buy, of course."

Greg nodded. He had already thought about getting hold of his own guitar, and maybe a mandolin or a banjo. He would really like a full-sized drum-kit too, and a proper harmonica or keyboard.

"Perhaps Santa will bring you something in your stocking." Mrs Shaw smiled, then realised too late that this jokey suggestion had been a mistake. Maybe the Prices didn't celebrate Christmas. Maybe they didn't have money to spare for gifts.

Greg gave her a withering look. How old did she think he was?

"Father Christmas is for little kids," he said scathingly. "My brother's buying me a Gibson in the New Year. He might even get two. Then we'll be rockstars and go to America and be in films in Hollywood."

"I'll be sure to watch out for you," said Mrs Shaw politely as the boy lounged moodily away. I've lost my touch, she thought bitterly. I have definitely lost my touch.

Nativity nerves

"One in a taxi, one in a car," sang Victoria Kemp. "One on a scooter blowing his hooter, following yonder star." She loved singing. Funny words made singing even better. 'Yonder' was a very funny word.

"Come along, Victoria, into line please," called Mrs Nesbit. Victoria hopped to it. It didn't do to keep Mrs Nesbit waiting. Victoria was a camel.

"Now then, for the last time kings, walk in looking haughty. Chins up!"

No one knew what 'haughty' meant exactly, but it sounded like 'naughty' – which was obvious enough. The kings did their best to appear mischievous. Teachers were very bossy but they didn't always explain.

"Miss! Mrs *Nesbit*!" hissed Zoe Smith urgently. The townspeople of Bethlehem were arranged on one side of the stage in a large group and Zoe stood at the front.

"Not now, Zoe. That's it – no, yes, walk like *that* kings. Very good. Eyes on the baby in his manger please, Mungo. No waving to people in the audience. Yes, I know Miss Jackson is over there at the piano. She's waiting for us to be ready to sing our next song, isn't she? Whatever is the matter, Zoe?"

Betty Nesbit was getting more exasperated by the second. This final dress rehearsal should be smooth perfection, and it wasn't. For a start she was down to only two shepherds and one stuffed lamb.

The townspeople were all quietly stepping aside and giving Ellen Grover a very wide berth. She was standing in a warm puddle that was growing wider by the second. Thankfully, Mrs Moore swooped.

"Come on, sweetie," she said kindly. She took the child's hand and led her away to the staffroom toilet for a clean up, it being the closest to the hall.

A trail of footsteps gleamed damply on the brown lino. The townspeople eyed their teacher with bated breath, not daring to scream in disgust or feigned horror at this disgusting disaster.

Mrs Nesbit, inveterate nativity play director and altogether perfect kindergarten teacher, drew herself up tall and stately and simply ignored the 'I-told-you-so' look Zoe was giving her.

"Close up that gap, Andy, please. Kay come in a little closer to Michelle. That's right. Thank you, Miss Jackson. Now then everybody, eyes on me! One, two and – 'Little Jesus, sweetly sleep...' Sing gently but *clearly*."

Reg keeps watch by night

Like a biblical herald angel, there was an unexpected visitation at the entrance to Longmont Lodge just as Mr Green and Stringer were finishing their evening security checks.

Tap, tap, tap. Tap tap.

Reg was surprised. He recognised the rhythm of the signal immediately and undid the wicket set within the oaken carriage gates for the visitor to step through. The man was tall and darkly dressed. Once inside he took off his hat and brushed the snow from its brim.

"Wasn't expecting to see you, Sir," murmured Reg. Stringer sniffed the man's shoes and wagged his tail in welcome before retiring under the hedge where it was dry. The two men also retreated out of the fitful moonlight.

"Not really here, Mr Green. Flying visit."

"Aye-aye sir," was Reg's automatic response. "Anything pertickaler?"

"No, not really. Bring me up to date if, you would."

Sir Hugo Chivers, retired international lawyer, absentee chairman of the Mayflower school governors, and also current director of their local MI6 operation, wedged himself against one of the verandah's solid oak pillars and carefully lit a cigar. Reg pocketed the one he was offered, saving it for after his Christmas dinner when the Queen would be on the telly.

As former bosun to the man beside him, Reg knew how to give his report succinctly. There was not a great deal to tell, though, since MI6 had paused its covert activities that Summer, when the latest safe facility at Dutch Cottage had become compromised. Last year two important Russian defectors had been terminated right under their very noses by unknown hands, and Sir Hugo was still desperately trying to stem the subsequent fallout from these disasters. Reg reported nothing especially noteworthy from Mrs Bicknell, other than the expected civilian comings and goings. He went on to update Sir Hugo about the state of the school's personnel, including the misery following the loss of Mr Shaw, the recent inspection and its possible potential for future direct interference from the Local Education Authority. There was the theft of the pipework and roofing, the outbreak of anti-social graffiti vandalism and his own shortage of reliable lookouts. Reg even mentioned his anxiety over Len Kirk's domestic situation. He regretted the fact they had not re-established a safe-house but otherwise judged their security levels to be appropriate. They were most likely unwatched. However, he cautioned, if Sir Hugo re-activated the operation, security ought to be doubled.

Hugo sighed and brooded for a while. Mr Green was never far wrong.

"I'll see what I can do, Reg. Things may be on the move again. I'm working on it. You have the Buntings of course. And my boy's alright?'

"Mr Ernest is fine. Him and Mr Paton and Mr Tuttle are going to build a little sailing dinghy come the better weather. It's keeping them occupied drawing up plans. I'll 'elp too, o' course."

"The headmistress and her mother are well?"

"Fine. The American's still cut up about her 'ubby, but Bick keeps a weather eye out."

"Good. I may have a solution for that particular issue soon. Her ladyship?"

"Potty as ever, but toeing your line, so far as I can make out."

"Don't underestimate her, Reg. She's not as potty as she looks. Remember that brother of hers. Is Granger still in Scotland?"

"Yes Sir."

"Well, that's all satisfactory, Mr Green. I want you to remain vigilant, though." Hugo pinched out his cigar and slipped the stub into a tin which he returned to his pocket. "I won't be stopping to speak to Ernest tonight, so don't mention you've seen me. He'll think it odd, it being Christmas and all, but I have to be elsewhere by tomorrow. You know how it is. Although I will have a quick word with Bunting before I go. Oh, and there's one more thing."

Reg knew it. There was always that important bit extra with Sir Hugo.

"Sir?"

"Keep your eye on the Holt at Nag's Hill, will you? It's an old empty stone cottage out there near the racetrack. Check whether there are any movements, come the New Year, and let me know as soon as possible. Usual channels. Now, my driver will be waiting round the corner so I had better be off. Happy New Year to you and the family, Mr Bosun."

So saying, Sir Hugo stepped nimbly back through the wicket and was gone.

Reg and Stringer listened hard for a few minutes more. A car door clicked softly shut somewhere. An expensive engine purred, then the sound faded, muffled by the thickly falling snow.

"I wonder where 'e's *really* orf to," muttered Reg to his dog. "Back up to the realms of glory or someplace a trifle warmer down south, d'you think?"

With Sir Hugo, either destination was entirely possible.

*　　*　　*

9.

The Star

Good news for Reg

"It's funny your name bein' Legg," commented Reg, "Cos my leg's givin' me gyp today."

"That's not really funny, though, eh?" sympathised the doctor. Reg looked very drawn and a good deal thinner than when she had seen him last month. Even his moustache seemed to have lost its vigour. "But don't give up, Mr Green. I've got good news and bad news today," she said, peering at him over her glasses.

"Go on." Reg was amused despite himself.

"The good news is that the cottage hospital can replace your damaged hip."

"Oh? Well, that's wonderful! I wasn't expecting that. What's the bad news?"

"They can do it Saturday 27th. They've had a last minute cancellation. If that's not convenient it will be at least another eight month wait."

"Eight months? You 'avin a laugh?" Reg was astonished. He would be bedridden and out of two jobs if he had to wait eight months.

"No, I'm not joking. But you should speak to them yourself. Here's the details," smiled Dr Legg. She dug in her bag and handed over a paper and a small pamphlet. "This is the phone number. I suggest you call as soon as possible, or somebody else will beat you to it."

"Right, well thanks Doc," croaked Reg. This was all a bit sudden. He watched the doctor squeeze herself back into her car and wave cheerily as she pulled out of the icy car park.

"What the blazes Ivy's going to say, I dunno. And what Mrs Clark will do — well. It'll be one hip and no ruddy 'ooray as far as she's concerned."

Gingerbread dress-rehearsal

"Oy you — Joey Latimer! Pick them jacks up out of my blessed way. And while you're down there tie my shoelace up, will yer?" asked Reg, as he and Stringer hooked back the playground gate. His leg hurt horribly and bending down to fix his shoe himself was too painful and highly risky. He didn't want to be upended like some turtle.

Joe grinned at the caretaker as he picked up the little metal game pieces and pocketed them. He liked Mr Green and he was good at laces since his uncle had spent a whole day teaching him.

"Tighter," ordered Mr Green. "That's good. Double knot. Thanks Joey."

"You're welcome," responded Joe, just as Mrs Shaw had taught them. Americans liked you to use their style of manners sometimes and Joe always tried to please. "Can I help with the hall chairs?"

"You may," agreed Reg, nodding. "You're big and sensible enough."

Praise indeed. Joey hopped off to help in the hall while Reg finished his slow, never-ending scrape of the playground with the snow shovel. If he didn't keep it clear those light-weight kinders would be base-over-apex, as his mother would have said. They ran everywhere, whatever the conditions, the little varmints.

The hall was noisy and busy when Joey got there. He helped slide the connecting brackets of the metal chairs together in two short rows and two columns, following Mrs Shaw's directions. They didn't need all the chairs today as it was only rehearsals, she said. Joey decided helping indoors was fun, and better than playing jacks outside in the cold. His friend Jonah was there too.

"Jonah, wanna go and see if the pool's iced over on the way home?"

"Yeah alright," answered Jonah. It meant their usual route would include a diversion over the edge of the boggy heath and across the single railway line to the water's edge. Mint Pool was where a small stream entered the River Wain and where local boys liked to fish and swim in the summer. It might be solid enough today to allow them to create a good slide.

Just then, there came a clamouring at the door and down the hall steps tumbled some of the cast of the Gingerbread Man.

"Sit along these front benches, please," called Mr Paton, his hair standing up wildly from his head. It had been a sore trial getting his children ready for this dress rehearsal. Two four-legged animals was proving two too many. "No, I've explained about make-up Edwin, I wish you'd listen. Sit down. All of you just sit down. Well, do the best you can please, Dean."

Mr Tuttle's and Miss Fisher's classes clattered in next, also fully costumed and ready. The air vibrated with excitement. Charlie hurriedly opened the piano and ran through various musical warm-up exercises while Mike and May fussed over the scenery and last-minute hitches. Jean Hewitt and Greg joined the frenzy to manipulate the spotlights and see that the props at least began the afternoon in the right places. Greg was also chief curtain operator, an important assignment, and not as easy as it looked. Joey and Jonah slowed their work with the chairs to watch some of the rehearsal fun.

Eventually, the adults were satisfied and the play's dress rehearsal began. It proceeded far too slowly but relatively correctly, until almost the end.

"Right-o! That was very good, Pig, well done. Let's move on quickly again to the Cow… remember we don't want long gaps after Ginger's done his final run-around, do we? Come on, Cow, where are you?"

The cow hoisted itself awkwardly out of the wings and stared around, batting its eyelids. Then the back-half suddenly started to writhe horribly, emitting growly sounds and wildly thrashing its tail, while the udder swung madly left and right as if trying to detach itself and make a personal bid for freedom.

"Whatever's the matter with him, Crystal?"

"Says he can't breathe, Sir," the front half of the cow calmly informed him. "Shall I undo his belly-buttons?"

Mike stared at Charlie then at May and Jean. He clasped his aching head.

"I suppose so, Crystal, I suppose so. But make it the most *underneath* belly-buttons, please. We don't want his head poking out through the gap and gasping like a codfish for all to see, now do we?" He turned his back on the scene and gazed up at the ceiling in despair. Dear heaven, he thought. Would anyone in the real world believe the things teachers sometimes found themselves saying?

Aladdin havoc

"I am the genie of the lamp!" roared Freddy Dawkins in a voice like his father when he was calling last orders at the Yeoman. "What will you ask of me?" He gave a very camp twirl. "I'm free!"

Let's hope someone laughs there, thought Guy grimly. "Come on Aladdin, a bit louder now."

"Young Washy's meant to work with me, oh how I wish he'd quicker be."

Teddy, as Wishy-Washy, galloped in at full speed and zoomed around the stage like a whirling dervish. Unfortunately, in his enthusiasm, he barged into Kit Grant who was dressed as Father Christmas and awaiting his cue behind the curtain. The result was a sprawling Santa and three flattened kindergarteners in the front row of the audience who had been permitted to watch the final rehearsal as a special treat.

"There, there, never mind," soothed the tireless and ever-comforting Carol Moore. "Father Christmas just arrived a bit early, didn't he? Come and sit by me. You're not hurt Kelly, you're just surprised."

This lurches from Rupert-and-his-Little-Chums to pure Frank Spencer, sighed Guy inwardly. But never mind, the parents will love it.

"It'll all be over by Friday," he muttered to Jean who was wobbling with suppressed laughter. Even Greg Price was grinning.

Jean nodded back to Guy. "You and I are going to need at least one bottle of whisky each before the end of this term," she prophesied. Then she caught Greg's baleful look. "That's a *joke*, Gregory. Teachers never drink."

Greg had the grace to smile back. Not much they don't, he thought.

Tree day

School started relatively quietly the next day.

Terry Green and three big boys – Ryan, Nigel and Kenny – brought in the Christmas tree from the snowy yard and stood its pot on a piece of carpet in the centre of the gym hall. They placed boxes of decorations in a line on the floor and arranged the gym mats for the children to sit on. One by one, each class entered and the children were allowed to hang a decoration on the branches while the biggest boys and girls managed the tinsel and cotton-wool snow. By breaktime the school tree was finished. It looked glorious.

There was a good deal of running about and yelling at morning playtime which expended some of the children's pent-up excitement, then they filed back indoors and sat quietly around the tree to watch some special gifts being handed out. As usual there was something for every Mayflower helper and, most thrilling of all, something for each pet. Dean Underwood had suggested this idea the previous year and it was he who nominated this year's helpful elf. He had thought long and hard about who the honour should fall to and decided it ought to be

Zoe Smith, in the first form. He had heard her sing at last summer's concert and thought she was really fun, with her red hair and round freckled face. And she could really *sing*. Dean admired that, as he was a tuneless growler himself. Zoe was thrilled to have been chosen. She happily handed out wrapped-up bones to Mr Green for Stringer and to Mrs Hewitt for Sweep. There were bags of biscuits for Lady Longmont's two dogs and for Cassius. There were tins of catnip for Nicky and Marigold, and a whole lettuce for Hannibal, Miss Fisher's energetic tortoise. Hammy the hamster in Miss Jackson's room was given a little plastic ball to play with.

Everybody was well-satisfied, especially as lunch arrived early. Today there was real roast chicken on the menu, followed by chocolate sponge and custard. There were even crackers to pull and paper hats to wear. The children loved seeing their familiar guests, the vicar, Terry, Mrs York, Dr Legg and Lady Longmont, laughing at each other in paper hats and reading out silly riddles.

"Let's hope no one regrets that big lunch this afternoon," commented Dr Legg. "I can't wait to see the plays."

Stars

The single performance of the Nativity was directly after lunch. While Reg cleaned the floor up and down with his wide dry mop, the boys set out the rows of chairs like a well-oiled machine. Chloe checked the spotlight, Jean and Greg tidied the wisps of straw escaping from the bale Mary sat on, Heather prepared the music, and Betty and Carol herded the nervous little actors into their starting places. Ben Nesbit had been roped in once more as additional crowd-controller.

"My mummy's coming to see me," shrieked Alice. She was swathed in the traditional Blessed Virgin Mary blue and held a floppy doll wrapped in someone's christening shawl. "Where's Jovis got to?"

"*Joseph* is over there. Do try to say his name right, Alice."

"I do," she replied, a little sharply.

At one o'clock the hall was crammed with the inevitable grandmas and grandpas, aunties and uncles, mums and dads. This year everyone felt particularly Christmassy as the snow outside lay deep and crisp and even, adding immensely to the traditional charm.

The children started nervously, but quickly warmed up to perform splendidly and sang their carols so sweetly even Heather Jackson was pleased with them. No one wet their pants, no one fell off the stage and no one cried. Mary remembered to say Joseph's name correctly, and did not drop the baby – two exceptionally bright points in Betty's opinion.

The only slightly wobbly moment came from the star itself, personified by Sarah Snell, a tall five year old with hair like a halo and a head full of catarrh. She found it troublesome trying to breathe while holding the star vertical on its four-foot bamboo pole. She leaned her prop carefully up against the backcloth of the night sky during the hymn 'We Three Kings of Orient Are', and (as she had recently mastered the art of blowing her own nose) allowed herself a jolly good blast into her hanky.

"Hold the star up *high*," Betty kept hissing at her. "Keep it *still!*"

Reluctantly Sarah grabbed the stick and waved the silver-paper star vigorously around before leaning it back against the wall again for a follow-up wipe. When she eventually came off the stage, Betty asked why she hadn't keep the star motionless over the painted stable roof as directed. It was all to do with Kevin Lang, said the child, the donkey who stood next to her and sang very loudly.

"What do you mean?" asked Betty.

"Well," said Sarah snorting hard to try to unblock her still stuffy nose. "Kevid kep' siggig 'westward leedig'. So I leed it against the wall." It took Betty a good ten minutes to realise what she meant.

"Take me home, Ben," she pleaded.

A real cracker

The first Gingerbread show was as a much more relaxed affair than the nativity play. As soon as the audience started laughing, the actors hammed it up beautifully, much to their teachers' delight. Skipper could not believe the dramatic abilities of her school. The cow clod-hopped its way through the entire thing with its shoe-laces undone and never tripped once. Dean, as the head part of the panto horse performed a complete tap-dance without his rear end apparently knowing anything about it. The costumes were a sensation.

"And this is only the first performance," commented Dora to Chloe. "I just hope they haven't peaked too soon."

"Peaked? Maybe, but the *peke* appears in Aladdin. There's just so much talent – and so many dogs – this year!" Chloe answered, still applauding.

Paper chains

Ben Nesbit, always a glutton for punishment, came to help in kindergarten on Thursday afternoon while the Gingerbread play was on – there being little doing in the gamekeeping world. He left his dogs at home, much to the children's disappointment.

It's nice having him in the classroom while we're making these paper chains, Betty thought. The children looped and pasted the strips of paper their teacher had cut, and soon the room was bright and gay.

"Oh – bingle jells, bingle jells, bingle all the way," sang Ben. He was tall and could reach the ceiling of the classroom to push in the drawing pins which held the paper decorations.

"Mr Nesbit, you're saying it wrong," whispered an earnest little girl called Jessie, tugging his jacket.

"Am I?"

"It's alright, I'll help you. It goes, jingle bells, jingle bells…"

They practised for a while until she was satisfied. Then Ben changed his tune.

"Rudolf, the blue-nosed reindeer, had some very shiny toes," he warbled loudly.

"No!" yelled the class.

"Miss Nesbit," said Mungo confidentially "Your daddy's pretty hopeless at singing."

"I know, Mungo, I know," she sighed. "But what can I do?"

Mungo had a bit of a think. "Well, sometimes you just has to be kind. He don't know no better. At Christmas time you should be specially kind to everybody, you know."

"Who taught you that, Mungo?"

"My Granny Buttons. She says all sorts, but I remember that one."

"Why do you call her Granny Buttons?"

Mungo hesitated, getting the sequence straight in his mind. "Well, when I was a baby I couldn't even do my coat up right. She showed me you start the buttons at the bottom and then go up. So I call her Granny Buttons."

"I like the sound of her. Granny Buttons has very good ideas."

Mungo was pleased she understood. "I agree," he said. "I like her too."

Thursday

Everyone had a low-key Thursday morning, but by a quarter past one the curtain went up again on the second Gingerbread Man show. The children romped through it.

The hall was cleared and clean again by two o'clock when the first Aladdin pantomime was staged. It was a little stilted at first, but as the actors warmed up and the laughter began, they relaxed. Joe Latimer played a very lifelike pekinese dog named Ping-Pong, and Teddy Swift brought the house down as Wishy-Washy. The Banford parents fell everlastingly in love with beautiful Yulissa as Princess Song, and when Father Christmas clomped around with his sack of toys at the end, having been marooned on an island by the genie of the lamp, Superman himself made a surprise appearance in the form of Ryan Hale in a bright red and blue costume complete with cape, to make everything well again.

He grinned down at his mother, tearfully clapping in the second row, and couldn't decide whether he wanted to be a soldier or a cartoon superhero in the future. Both definitely on the cards.

Two for one

"Can I wear my costume home?" pleaded David Lyall, who played Abanazar, for which part he sported a very fluffy black beard. The actors were supposed to be hanging up their costumes ready for the next pantomime performance at 6pm. "I could tuck my beard down inside my duffle coat. It'll keep me much warmer than my scarf, Mum."

"I'm taking Ping-Pong out for a walk. Come on Joey!" Kit caught Joe Latimer's dog lead up and paraded him round the classroom. "Good dog, Ping-Pong. Walkies!"

Stringer came galloping into the room just at that moment and tugged Joey's lead right out of Kit's hand. There's was nothing for Joe to do but be towed helter-skelter after the scampering terrier, all the way out of the classroom and onto the landing, right into the arms of Mrs Clark as she came upstairs to congratulate her actors.

"What, two dogs for the price of one?" she cried. "Stringer! Drop it. Go and find Reg. He needs your help, and I need to get Joey out of this costume before he ends up in lost property. Joe – heel, boy. There's a good puppy!"

A tiring evening

However harassed Mrs Clark might be, the parents loved all the hoop-la and kept congratulating her on the school's wonderful drama tradition as she welcomed them in at the door. Those who could not attend the earlier Aladdin performance, due to work or other commitments, crowded into the gym hall that evening so that it was very quickly packed to the rafters. There were even one or two faces peering through the windows from outside. The noise was deafening even before the show began.

"Have your brothers been to see the show?" Jean asked Greg as they set up their props and adjusted the scenery for the final time. He had enjoyed being this side of the footlights more than he had expected. Mrs Hewitt wasn't such a bad old bag, he decided.

"Nah," he scoffed. "They wouldn't come to this kind of rubbish." No one had ever attended any of his schools for any reason – formal or informal. No parent evening, no jumble sale, no sports day or play. He doubted his mother even knew where Mayflower was. Phil might, but he was always too busy working. "You want me to close the curtains now?"

"Yes, good idea, thanks. That rope is too heavy for me and my rheumaticky shoulder."

Greg pulled the curtains shut, wondering what 'rheumaticky' meant. Must be an old lady thing.

Again, the Mr Denny's panto was a triumph. Malcolm Dale played his heart out in the leading role, and the stunning costumes of the Emperor and Empress (Mick McDonald and Bella Reynolds) gained a round of applause all to themselves. The children belted out the songs with gusto and every corny old joke was welcomed like an old friend. There were, as usual, a few new ones added about members of staff and their little idiosyncrasies. Stringer, dressed as a pierrot, made an appearance as Wishy-Washy's shadow, mimicking his dance steps and finally running off-stage with his cap.

"I don't know when I've had more fun," chortled Lady Longmont as she thumped Charlie on the back afterwards. "You certainly put on a good show, for a little pipsqueak school."

"Brilliant, wasn't it?" laughed Fiona Tuttle, who had come to support her husband's musical directorship. "Whatever next I wonder?"

"Well," said Charlie. "If you can stand it, there's the carol service in the church tomorrow morning at eleven. It will be much more sedate, but well worth coming to. After that we give out the reports and then stagger home for a forty-eight-hour lie-down in a darkened room. And if you want me to do anything at all after that, Mrs Tuttle, you can jolly well think again."

Carol service

The end of term service in St Andrew's on Friday morning was, as Charlie predicted, much more sedate. The children walked through the snow and sat in their coats and hats and boots that dripped gently onto the tiled floor. The choir emerged from the vestry looking like fat snowballs, as most of them had kept their coats on underneath their white cotton surplices. It was not a warm building. Lizzie Timms smiled at her uncle and stood ready at the front for her solo – the opening few lines of 'Once in Royal David's City'. Rev Bill beamed at everyone and began with his usual predictable statements.

"Merry Christmas everybody. Here we are at the end of another term."

Chloe cast her eyes down and sighed. Another term endured, another chunk of her life sent spinning down a bottomless plughole. Skipper nudged her back to reality and nodded her head towards Ryan who was gazing in adoration at Lizzie, for whom he had recently developed the most enormous crush. Chloe's open handbag fell upside down onto the floor at that point and her neighbours had to scramble to retrieve its contents.

After the carols, Rev Bill's words of wisdom, and the final prayer, Mrs Clark and Mrs Shaw stood and wished the school well before reminding them to collect their end of term reports from their teachers before leaving. Then the little church, pretty with modest advent flowers and stonework lit by flickering candles, echoed with children's happy voices as they scuffled away into the grey and white churchyard.

"Merry Christmas, Miss!" called Ryan to Mrs Clark. He barged past Greg Price who stumbled and hit his shoulder against one of the pillars.

"Watch out, you big …" began Greg, just as Rev Bill stretched out a steadying hand and saved a worse catastrophe.

"Oops, no harm done. There you go, young man. A very merry Christmas to you both!"

Winding down

More and more heavy petals of snow tumbled down to earth in the still air. The world was white and growing whiter – monochrome chalk on Victorian slate.

It might look pretty but its beauty soon wore thin, in Jean's view. She swept her step and front path every morning with vigour, and did her best to keep her patch of the public footway free of snowy build-up, but it was a never ending job this year – one which made her puff and blow and come in for her coffee all rosy-cheeked and hot. Sweep encouraged her by watching from the front window and wagging his tail.

Jean's end of Fen Lane was closest to the river, which meant it was often shrouded in mist in the mornings, and sometimes all day. Today, the first of the Christmas holidays, the sun broke the shreds apart fairly rapidly and by ten the world had a far less sombre aspect. She took Sweep for a long walk, then sat and finished writing her Christmas cards and a long shopping list. One day when she retired, she told herself, she would post the cards earlier and be altogether more organised. Today she must make the spare room ready for her son and his fiancée. She had reluctantly decided she absolutely had to embrace the nineteen-seventies and let them sleep together in the same room, even though they weren't married. It went against the grain but these days there were birth control pills, right? So why should she worry about the couple's morals if they did not? In any case, she only had one spare bed.

May arrived for tea just as it was growing dark again. It was very pleasant to be able to spend time with her old friend as they were always too busy at school for a proper chat. Now they could be together and have a comfortably long natter. May settled down and worked on completing the colourful scarf she was knitting, while Jean simply relaxed by the fire stroking Sweep's silky head. Terry had brought some dry logs round and the two women were very cosy indoors listening the wind outside. It had whipped up again and grains of snow were once again being flung at the front windows like shrapnel. They barely heard the whistle of the five o'clock train as it ground into the nearby station.

A short while later, Chloe knocked on Jean's door. She had been down to London on some important business, although she did not immediately enlighten the two ladies as to what. She was cold from her short walk up from the terminus. She presented them each with a bottle of scotch.

"Blow Christmas, I'm opening mine now," said Jean happily, and they all had a tot.

"I've just sold Well House to Charlie Tuttle," Chloe informed them, settling comfortably on a stool. Both ladies grew round-eyed wondering how much she had sold the place for. "I could have rented it to them, but no, they wanted to buy it."

"Won't you miss it?"

"No. It was always Max's home, not mine. It's just a house."

May considered Max's beautiful home was not something she would have dismissed quite so lightly. However, she wasn't in Chloe's position. Well House had never been 'just a house' to anyone in Banford. It was one of the oldest local buildings, and quite a landmark. "I'm sure he and Fiona will love it. It's a grand place to bring up a child."

"Plenty of room to kick a ball about in that big garden," Jean agreed. "How are you managing now you're back in Church Road?"

"Fine. Well, Mrs Bicknell keeps me in order. What a gem she is. She did something called 'bottoming out' when I moved back. I swear she found places in that house that had never seen the light of day before. Oh, listen! What's that?"

Some carol singers were letting rip with 'The Holly and the Ivy' as they crammed together beneath the porch overhang. Jean closed her passageway door so as not to let the cold air invade the house, and opened the front door to find Mr Timms and some St Andrew's choristers together with a couple of extra Mayflower kids carolling loudly in the windy air. Joey Latimer grinned at her as he sang, and Mike Paton rattled the collecting tin invitingly. The three ladies applauded but did not ask the group inside as there were far too many to fit into Jean's little front room. Anyway, their boots looked alarmingly wet.

"Thank you! Merry Christmas," the carollers called and shuffled away, waving, out of the gate. It was cold work but they knew they would get a hot mince pie at Mrs Clark's house, so they pressed on.

"Wasn't that nice?" commented May. "I'm beginning to feel quite festive."

Jean laughed. "That's the effect of the whisky, my dear," she said.

John arrives

John Hewitt and his girlfriend Lisa arrived late in the evening a couple of days later. They walked up from the station with their cases, having flown over from Holland where they lived and worked. Lisa straightened her coat as they stood waiting for the front door to open, and pasted on a smile, feeling tired and quite nervous. This was the first time she had met John's mother.

"Come in, come in! You must be Lisa. How lovely to meet you," gushed Jean in genuine delight.

Lisa smiled and kissed her on both cheeks which Jean found charmingly foreign.

"Darling!" Jean hugged her son, who replied with a single kiss she noticed. He had slimmed down since she had last seen him but still took up the entire hallway.

"Come on through, you must be tired." Jean ushered the travellers into the front room where Sweep wagged his tail and dribbled all over them.

"Oh, I forgot you have a dog. I am not a fan of dogs," said Lisa, pursing her lips.

"Sorry," said Jean and dragged Sweep out to the kitchen where he flopped into his basket under the table.

"Hang your coats in the hall and make yourselves at home," Jean called as she put the kettle on. The house was suddenly full of life and very much more festive. "How was the journey?"

"Fine. Busy, but mercifully trouble-free." John preferred life to be trouble-free.

Lisa sat nervously on the edge of the sofa while John ran the suitcases upstairs and Jean brought in their hot drinks and a plate of warm sausage rolls.

"You must be starving after that long journey," she said, fleetingly wondering what Mary had offered the Magi and shepherds by way of restorative snacks. She passed out plates and seasonal paper napkins.

Lisa welcomed her cup of tea, but flared her sensitive nostrils at the food.

"I do not eat animal products, alas," she said. "I am vegetarian only."

That took her hostess aback.

"Are you? John never mentioned it."

"What didn't I say? Oh, yes Lisa's a veggie – I'm sure I mentioned it, Mother. Not a problem is it?" John bit into a sausage roll like a starved man.

"No dear. Of course it isn't. I'll go and find the biscuit tin and just have a poke at the dinner if you'll excuse me a second. Then we can have a jolly good catch-up, can't we? I'm so looking forward to all your news."

Jean and Chloe take a walk

"How is he?" Chloe asked Jean as they met to take Cassius and Sweep for a walk in the park next day. "I bet it's lovely having him home this Christmas."

200

"Oh John's just the same. Getting more of a fuddy-duddy by the minute, though, I'm sorry to see. Must have his egg boiled just so, and his slippers on properly at all times. She'll have her work cut out with him."

"And what's she like?"

"Well, she's a vegetarian."

"No!"

"Yes. I had to rustle up a cheese omelette for her supper last night, when I'd made a perfectly good lamb stew."

"Hadn't he said?"

"No, I don't think so. I don't remember anyway. Now I've got to re-think most of what I'd planned for Christmas dinner."

"Maybe Mr Hearn has a nut roast or something," suggested Chloe vaguely, thinking of the butcher's window in town. But she wasn't very optimistic. Banford shopkeepers did not seem to go in for exotic fare.

Jean agreed. "I doubt it," she said. "Or I could maybe try that other shop up in Beargate. That new delicatessen. They sometimes have odd things. I should have ordered."

They plodded along in silence, deep in thought.

"Look," said Chloe, suddenly. "Why don't you give me Sweep and I'll finish his walk. You head right on into town over the bridge and nail down some – I don't know – Brussels sprout cutlets or something. The stores are bound to be heaving with people, but today will be your best shot at landing a mushroom pie or whatever. Go on. I've got him. Have you money? OK – you go."

Jean could have hugged the woman.

"Really? Well, alright, I will. Thanks Chloe. You're a brick."

She hurried up the path into town, turning briefly and waving.

"So long!" called Chloe, assuming being called a brick meant something good.

She clicked her tongue to the dogs and turned the other way, into Latimer Park with its pleasant tree-lined trails. It was good to be able to help her friends out, she thought. She had met so many nice people since she had arrived here, even though she had spent most of her leisure-time last year with Max. She feared she may have missed several opportunities to forge new friendships during their whirlwind romance.

"Hello Mrs Shaw," called a voice. A boy on a brand new Chopper bicycle overtook her and circled round.

"Why, hi there, Greg. Nice bike."

"My brother got it for me. It's for rough trails like this. Early Christmas present." He showed off some fancy manoeuvres while Chloe duly admired his expertise.

Bragging was as close to acting friendly as Greg felt like being today. He left Mrs Shaw to her dog-walking and raced away, reaching in his pocket for his cigarettes and lighter. He'd go down to the far end of the island and have a fag. Maybe clear a space in the snow, make a camp and start a little fire, just to see if he could. Lighting fires was a fun hobby. After all, there was no one at home to hang out with. Jason was still in Ledgely jail, Malcolm and Ian and Weasel were out shoplifting in Portland. Phil was at work. Yes, starting a little fire was something to do. He and Weasel shared that particular hobby. It was some kind of bond, he supposed.

Midnight mass

Midnight mass at St Andrew's on Christmas Eve was not to be missed. Ernest called for Chloe next door and escorted her, while Dora, Skipper, Jean and May walked along together, arm in arm against the slippery conditions. They met up and sat in adjacent pews.

The candle-lit church was packed with well-clad worshippers and several party-goers in evening-wear. John and Lisa had elected to stay at home, to Jean's secret disappointment. Ernest looked about, wishing his father were there instead of somewhere in Canada, where he was reportedly snowed in. Bick and her friend Miss Muggeridge were in the front, and Peggy and Albert Bailey sat next to Mrs Dawkins from Christmas Farm, who was on her own. Charlie Tuttle played a soft and slightly religious medley of tunes on the organ. Even Lord and Lady Dexter from Hall Manor had managed to turn out, as for once they were not spending Christmas at their Belgravia flat. Rev Bill warmly welcomed everyone and jokingly hoped they would all wake up early and return in the morning for another festive sing-song.

The congregation hushed. Two distant voices from the choir drifted through the dark like approaching angels. Candle flames bobbed about in the draught and a tiny lantern stood ready to be lit at midnight in the Sunday School's crib scene. It all suddenly became quite magical. The congregation sat and listened to the ancient story. They sang, they waited, watched and prayed. The majestically ticking clock at the back of the nave started to whir and chime.

A peal of eight bells in the belfry clanged out announcing the joyous moment that time itself stepped forward, and the little golden light flickered on over the children's model manger scene.

Skipper felt tears of gratitude well up, and she squeezed her mother's gloved hand. She knew how lucky she was to be spending another Christmas with her beloved mum, and she felt humbly and intensely grateful to be with her.

Dear God, she thought, let our troubles be over. Friends are all around me, and I am happy – right now, in this single moment – I am happy, and at peace.

*   *   *

10.

Swan

Christmas Day lunch

Chloe and the dog arrived with Ernest at White Cottage for Christmas Day lunch. They were well wrapped up as yet more snow was falling, and now it was thicker and whiter than the icing on Dora's fruit cake. Nicky hated it and kept staring through the sitting room window, willing it to disappear. Cassius ignored the black cat and flopped down in front of the big open hearth to watch and listen to the logs as they slowly burned to ash. Little rivers of red dots ran to and fro on their massive sides like fairy lights. His nose twitched. Something good was cooking.

The turkey was appropriately vast and handsomely brown and shiny. The Brussels sprouts were round and very green, the roast potatoes crisp and fluffy. Chloe had not even thought about Thanksgiving this year, having no wish to be seen sobbing her heart out by anyone here. Christmas was a much simpler day to cope with, plus it involved the pleasant activity of presenting little gifts to people who had been kind to her.

"Ooh, socks! Thanks Dora. Did you knit them?"

"I did. If they don't fit I can do some more."

"No, they're lovely. I never had Fair Isle socks before," said Ernest. No one had ever knitted him anything that he could recall.

"Oh, Ernest, Barbara Pym! Thank you very much," cried Skipper.

"What can this be, Cassie? Oh a beautiful new plaid coat. That's exactly what you need on these cold mornings. Thank you, Skip."

Dora slid her feet into her new slippers, well-pleased with her little family. She nipped into the kitchen to put the kettle on as everything she had eaten today made her thirsty. She spooned Kitti-pix into Nicky's dish and wondered how Jean and May were faring with John the humourless, and Lisa the vegetarian. It would be a long day for her friends, she thought, but family was family. You accepted what you were given, or you built from scratch.

The meet

"The hunt is meeting at eleven down at the Yeoman," Jean informed her guests on Boxing morning. She was desperate for some fresh air, having been cooped up all the day before. She was also guiltily beginning to feel the strain of hosting guests in her little two-up two-down house. "We could stretch our legs and go and watch if you like."

John took his nose out of the biography of Pasternak she had given him and yawned.

"Yes, alright. I'll go and see what Lisa wants to do."

Lisa was still in the bathroom. Jean had the immersion heater on permanently as the girl seemed to be constantly soaking herself in hot water. By a lucky chance Jean had given her talcum powder and some fancy soap as a gift, but the constant bathing was something of a strain on the heating system.

"We can catch the hounds as they come over the bridge. Have you brought your camera? The meet is always a colourful sight when it comes up the road from the pub. Or we could stand at the turning down to the manor if you prefer."

By the time Lisa was dressed and ready to go Jean had already walked Sweep down to the school and back. The three of them, Sweep stowed safely at home in his basket, hurried to the end of Fen Lane, along beside the crispy-edged river, and mingled with other family groups waiting near the end of the old stone bridge for the hunt to appear – which it did almost immediately.

First came the hounds in a steaming, noisily excited pack, closely followed by glossy thoroughbreds and cobs, some ridden confidently by pink-coated huntsmen, tall and polished, and then a great many more stout hacks on which perched tweedy county types, flushed and eager for the chase. Lisa was astonished.

"What is the little trumpet-horn for?" she enquired.

"To signal the hounds and the hunters what's happening," answered John politely, though even he considered it obvious. He held Lisa's hand feeling romantically invigorated by the seasonal spectacle.

There were quite a few conventionally dressed foot-followers hurrying behind the busy procession, looking bold and bright in their Christmas hats and scarves as they hurried past. The spectators waved and clapped. When the hunt reached West Lodge it turned through a gate onto Hall Manor lands and abruptly disappeared down the long drive.

"Wasn't that fun! I wonder if they will find today."

"Find what?" asked Lisa.

"A fox, dear. It's a fox hunt."

"They kill them?"

"They usually do."

Lisa turned pale. England might look very pretty with its red-coated horse-riders, its snowy riverside and its quaint buildings, but it was proving to be a horribly primitive country in many other ways. Lisa privately did not care for England at all. It was barbaric. It was bloodthirsty. Everything seemed to be about meat. Meetings. She could imagine only too clearly how a dead fox might look in the snow.

"I think I would like to take a little drink, please," she whispered to her future husband. "May we go to the public house?"

"Of course. Let's have an egg-nog or three," said John, quite jovially. "Come on, Mother."

Under the knife

"What? In *that*? It ent got no back to it!" Ivy was scandalised at what her husband was being asked to wear for his time under the surgeon's knife. "Reginald, pull your skirt over!"

Reg did as he was told. It wouldn't do to show off a grand opening in this kind of theatre, he thought. He was far less concerned than Ivy, but it didn't do to argue when she was in this mood. He lay back decently on the trolley with her help and began to feel decidedly woozy.

"He's going under," said Ivy's voice softly. "I can see his eyes crossing."

Reg couldn't wait to get the day over with, and was only too pleased to be finally on the butcher's slab, as he put it. He fumbled for her hand. "Now, you told Terry where that key is, didn't you?"

"I did. Stop worrying."

"I ent. You've put that fish back in the car? And you remember where we put my will?"

"Stop talking rubbish for gawd's sake, Reg. Nurse, you can wheel him orf now, he's making even less sense than usual. See you later on, Reggie, my old love. I'll be right here, darling, when you wake up."

"Don't fuss, old lady," he slurred. "Always fussin'. Back in a jiffy. Don't forget that potato."

He was pushed away by a crisp-looking nurse who was once more on theatre duty after a Christmas spent trying to keep her in-laws happy. She was relieved to be back in charge of nice compliant patients. She smiled kindly at Ivy over her shoulder. "Don't you fret, me duck. I'll see he's alright."

Ivy's daughter Pat steered her mum to the little tea bar down by the cottage hospital's front door, and bought her a mug of tea and a biscuit. All the Christmas decorations were still up and the desk was ringed around with lopsided cotton wool snow. The receptionist had removed her jolly elf hat – an improvement in Pat's opinion.

"It's just that I'm not used to him being laid out flat on his back, and not everlastingly poking about here and there," explained Ivy as she sniffed into a tissue. "Your dad's always the one working things out and telling me what's what. You wouldn't understand."

"Yes I do, Mum. Dad's going to be fine, just you wait and see. We don't want him in pain any more, now do we?"

"No, love, o' course not. But he is a worry!" Ivy sniffed hard into the tissue.

Pat nodded. She looked up at the clock. It was going to be a long day. "Now, let's think about what you're going to make for his dinner when you get him home in a couple of days." Food was always a good way to distract her mum's mind. "And I'll tell you all about this boy Phil I've met. He works up Chandler's garage servicing the bus engines."

As she had rightly predicted, menu-planning and a little romantic news distracted her mother perfectly.

Joey, Jonah and the swan

Joey Latimer phoned his friend Jonah five days after Christmas.

"Wanna come snowballing over the heath?" asked Joe. He was bored. "Mum says you can stay for lunch if you like."

Jonah's parents and older sister were all back at work after the Christmas break, so he was on his own at home watching telly. Spending the day with Joey would be great.

The boys met and set off across the heath. It was lumpy with snow-covered tussocks of grass and a fun place to play, even though the railway line ran directly through it. The little local train never went more than a few slow miles an hour as it crossed the heath in either direction, as it had to stop at the next village. It was easy and safe to cross over the single track to reach the riverbank.

"This side's froze solid like glass," cried Jonah in amazement. The watercourse was a skein of channels, some wide, some narrow, weaving lazily between low irregular islands. The creeks and streams entering it were all shallow and sandy. Today the surface of the river was almost completely solid.

"Someone's built an igloo over there, look," said Joey, pointing. Ironwell Eye was a large boggy island usually only frequented by wildlife and adventurous children during the summer months. It was clear someone had been trying to make a snow-house on its tip.

"Maybe we could build one too. I've always wanted to try," said Joe. Jonah looked a bit doubtful. He thought you needed a special sort of snow to make the blocks, and a long knife, but he was willing to give it a go.

"Let's see if the pool's solid too, shall we? We could walk across there – save going round by the bridge."

Mint Pool looked very strange today. The usually bubbling water was now firm, clear, dark green ice, all ridges and bumps and sprinkled with a light dusting of white crystals. Twenty yards out a dead swan lay sprawled on the surface, trapped by its legs in the ice. Jonah, who had a tender heart, began to cry.

"Oh look, Joe! He's dead. Probably got stuck tryin' to find food."

"Poor thing," said Joey. He tested the surface with his foot. "It's hard. We could maybe pull him out and get some feathers to make a pillow."

Jonah wasn't interested in pillows, but he did want to release the dead body. It looked so horrible lying there, like a piece of windswept rubbish. He wiped his gloves down his eyes. It was a long way out and the ice might be thin near the middle. He took off his anorak.

"Here, take off yer coat, Joe. Now tie my coat arm to yours. I'll tie this end on the back of my jeans' belt. We can use it like a safety rope, see? You're stronger than me so you stay here and sit down. I know it's muddy, but you'll be like my anchor. I'll lie flat on my belly and worm my way over to it."

Joey sat in the snow and mud and dug his heels in, as instructed. He was surprised Jonah knew what to do, as usually he was the one with the bright ideas. He watched as his friend edged his way like a snake over the ice, tapping carefully as he went to make sure the surface was thick enough to bear his weight. The sun went in and both boys began to shiver.

Just then the local train puffed up the track from Weston and the driver sounded the whistle when he saw two lads on the river bank. The slow old steam engine hissed and stopped dead in a cloud of smoke and steam, much to the surprise of its two passengers.

"Oy! What you think you're up to?" yelled the anxious driver.

"It's alright Mr Polkinghorne, we're just getting a swan!" called back Joey.

Mr Polkinghorne and the two passengers jumped down into the snowy grass and came over as fast as they could to stop the boys before they fell through the ice and drowned.

"Is that you Joey Latimer? What the 'eck d'you think you're playing at? You'll get froze or fall in." Kevin, the porter who worked at Banford station, crouched down next to Joe and put his arm round him. "Who's that out there? Hey – come back! It's too dangerous."

The other passenger, Sir Hugo Chivers, cried out in alarm as Jonah suddenly yelled and jerked away from the enormous bird he had been advancing upon. The swan, terrified and not entirely dead, gave a sudden lurch and beat its huge wings wildly at its rescuer in a vain bid for freedom. But there was no escape – its legs were held fast by the terrible ice.

"I thought you said it were dead," called Joey. "Watch he don't peck yer eyes out, Jonah!"

"Not yet it isn't," said Sir Hugo. "Hey there, whats-your-name, Jonah! Stay clear of it's wings! Let it alone."

Jonah wasn't about to retreat.

"I'm safe enough. It's pretty thick ice here. But he's stuck. His legs is stuck tight. I need something to chip the ice to get him out," explained Jonah patiently. He was the calmest of them all.

The three men looked at each other.

"Hold on," called Mr Polkinghorne, a thought suddenly occurring. He nipped quickly back to his cab where the engine was panting like a tethered animal, and returned with a small hand-axe. He slid it across the ice to Jonah who, by a miracle, managed to pick it up with his half-frozen hand.

"Just chip round it a bit and get him free. Don't cut his legs orf!" yelled Mr Polkinghorne.

"Kid's got guts, I'll say that for him," muttered Sir Hugo. "Well done, lad. Take your jumper off. Can you get an arm round to hold the wings down? That's it, hold tight! Now wrap your sweater round it – good boy. Yes, tie it if you can. Hold its beak shut with your other hand to stop it pecking your face while we pull you back in."

The bird finally came free of its icy shackles, and Jonah held on as instructed. He was hauled back from the middle of the ice like a sack of potatoes. As he slid, the ice began to crack alarmingly under the combined weight of swan and boy. Jonah's clothes were ripped and soaked through with ice and muck and snow by the time he finally he reached the shore.

"He ent dead!" he cried, grinning with delight. "He ent a bit dead. He's cold but he's alive."

"Like you, you little swan-saver," laughed Kevin. He took the frightened bird and tied his own jacket around it like a parcel so that only the head stuck out. With Mr Polkinghorne's help he then tied his red spotted neckerchief over the terrified creature's eyes and bill to quieten it down. "I'll take Swanny here up the station with me and warm 'im up a bit, shall I? You think his legs is broke?"

"I dunno," said Jonah shivering like he had ague. "He might need a vet to see him."

Sir Hugo managed to get the boys' clothing untied and back on the children before they perished from frostbite. He wrapped his own scarf round Jonah's head and ears. The wind was getting up and there was more snow on the way by the look of the sky. "Where do you boys live?" he asked.

"Just over there Sir," answered Joey, pointing. He was surprised to see his mother loping towards them across the heath from their back garden gate. She had arrived home from shopping, noticed the stationary train almost opposite her door and come to find out what was wrong. She clambered around the end of the last carriage and shrieked when she saw Joey and Jonah with three men beside the river.

"Joey!" she cried. "Joey! What on earth are you up to now? Oh my lord, Jonah, look at the state of you. What is that – a swan?" She ran out of words as she gathered the two lads up and hugged them. She was horrified at their recklessness. They might have been drowned. "Whatever are you doing over here? You stay away from this river, I've told you a million times. No, come home. You come home right now, you two. You're getting into a nice hot bath, and no arguments. Lord, whatever will your mother say, Jonah? You'll be the death of me, Joey Latimer. A swan? Well, is it alright? No don't touch it, it might bite. Oh my goodness, you boys."

She hustled them away, leaving Kevin to deal with the swan, Sir Hugo to walk briskly home in order to restore the circulation in his legs, and Mr Polkinghorne to scratch his head and chuckle as he drove the overdue train into Banford railway station. That was a turn-up for the books and no mistake.

Hugo's birthday

Ernest was feeling lonesome and a little gloomy. It was his father's birthday and usually they spent it together, often cooking a simple meal at home to eat later in the dining room, after which they would stoke up the fire, sip some brandy, and actually have a conversation. Some years they spent the day in Fenchester, buying something or other in a department store. Other years they'd be in London at Hugo's club and take in a show. It felt odd today, not having his father around. Ernest went down to the kitchen to ask Mrs Bunting if she had any news.

"No, Mr Ernest, sorry I don't. Why don't you go into the study and read the papers? I've lit the fire."

Ernest wearily plodded through the house to the study where it would at least be warm and snug and he could do the crossword in peace. He opened the door.

"Father!" he cried.

Sir Hugo rose from his wing chair and hugged him, a rare occurrence.

"Ernest, how are you? I thought I'd surprise you. Sorry I couldn't be here for Christmas Day, this is the soonest I could make it. How have you been?" He poured some of Mrs Bunting's scalding coffee from an electric percolator into a cup for his son, and beamed at the little subterfuge he had played. Ernest appeared genuinely delighted to see him.

"How's Canada? When did you get back?" Ernest was in a tizzy of delight.

"Just now," smiled his father. "I'd have been earlier, only I was sidetracked. One of your Mayflower lads was rescuing a trapped swan when the train was halfway between Weston and Banford. The driver stopped and we got out to help."

"Goodness! One of our boys? Where was the swan?"

"Stuck in the ice in the river. Just where you go over that little stream before the pub."

"Goodness," repeated Ernest. "Who was it?"

"Joe? Jonah? Joey? Plucky little pair, I thought."

Ernest shook his head and chuckled. "Joe Latimer's a good kid. And Jonah Webb? He's quite a one for helping animals in distress. I must remember to tell Skip."

"How is she? How's school?" Sir Hugo asked as he threw another log on the fire.

"Fine. The inspection was pretty awful though, and threw Skip into a lather because the final report was so critical. I wrote to you about that. Christmas pantos went well. We made a few quid with the ticket sales, thank goodness. Reg Green's had his hip operation. Jean Hewitt's son and future daughter-in-law are visiting. Or they may have gone back to Holland by now, I'm not sure." Ernest tried to remember the highlights.

"Hip operation? That was a bit sudden."

"Well, I think the local surgeon had a cancellation. It's usually a six month wait, I believe." Ernest didn't know the details. "But he's home tomorrow, Ivy said."

"That's good – all fixed up ready for the New Year. I must remember to pop by. I expect he'd like a box of cigars or a bottle of whisky."

"If Dr Legg permits it," chuckled Ernest. "She's quite a force to be reckoned with. Oh my hat – I just remembered it's your birthday! Many happy returns, Father. Wait a sec while I get your present." He rushed off upstairs to find the gift he had not yet wrapped and the card he had not yet written, feeling ridiculously happy. Finally, finally, *finally* he too had family at home.

Reg has a smoke

Reg returned home on the morning of the last day of the year. Being in his own place again felt ridiculously good.

After supper he limped slowly down to the front gate, leaning on two sticks. Terry had gone out for the evening with Pamela Finn, a girl he'd met at a Christmas party. Pat wasn't coming round to see him until the morning, and Ivy and Stringer were watching something Scottish on the telly. He had been told to exercise little and often, but it was going to be tough, especially in this cold weather. He stuffed and lit his pipe, and stood staring at the shifty-looking moon, glad of his new thick muffler. He'd been looking forward to a quiet smoke and getting back to normal. He had already made a start on building some footlockers that afternoon at the kitchen table, from some old wood Terry had stripped out of a building that was being demolished. Ivy hadn't been best pleased with the mess, but she didn't want him sitting about like a fried egg, she said, so she buttoned her lip and worked around him as best she could as he drew lines on short lengths of old planks. It was a decent bit of pine and he would have Terry saw it up properly tomorrow, ready for screwing together and moving into position next week. In Reg's opinion the kids' shoes would still be all over the floor whatever storage was provided, but the cubbies were a step in the right direction. The headmistress could tick another item off her blessed 'Must Do VerySoon' list.

"You comin' inside for Big Ben?" called Ivy.

Old year, new year, thought Reg. Time and tide waited for no man.

"In a minute," he replied. He took a last look at the familiar silhouette of the conifers, the fruit trees and the copper beech across the road.

"G'd evening," said a voice. Someone was passing by. Not many people used the lane at night as it was un-made-up and un-lit and quite likely to inflict a broken ankle on the unwary with all its potholes. The voice was cultured, warm and pleasant-sounding.

"Evenin'," answered Reg. He stood still and watched the figure detach itself from the gloom. It was wearing a long overcoat and a trilby hat. It wasn't Sir Hugo. Who was he?

"Nice night."

"More snow on the way," commented Reg. "So they say."

"Oh, d'you think so? It is a bit nippy I suppose. I'll better press on, then. Happy New Year to you." The figure touched his hat brim and was gone.

Reg drew on his pipe, and said to Stringer, who had pottered outside when he heard his master's voice, "Well, you didn't earn yer supper did you? Perfect stranger walks by and you don't even bark. What's up? Got a belly-ache?"

Stringer wagged his tail and set about actively sniffing the path as if for clues.

"No use you pretending to be all interested now. Come on – there's no mystery 'ere for you to worry about. It's the last day of the year so I'm going to crack open that bottle of rye whiskey Mrs Shaw give us, and drink to better days to come. Things can't be much worse than they've been this back-end, now can they? We'll have a nice little toast, me boyo, and you can do one of yer party tricks for the missis. She'd like that. She might even find you a mince pie for old lang zine. Come on."

Off to a party

Pat Green hurried into town to meet Phil Price, her boyfriend. He was closing up the garage workshop where he was employed servicing Chandler's buses. They were an ageing fleet, and Phil had his work cut out keeping everything roadworthy, especially at this time of the year. He kissed his girl, who squealed and told him not to mess her hair up. They were off to a New Year party in Portland. She told him to de-grease his hands well when he had a wash, as she hadn't put on her best frock only to have it covered in engine oil, thank you very much. Phil grinned and did as he was told. She was a good-looker was Pat, and he was more than a little smitten.

"Did Mr Chandler say it's alright to borrow the van?" she asked anxiously.

"Yes, course. He don't mind, I told you," called Phil from the toilet. "As long as I fill it back up with petrol," he added. It was fair enough. He liked Mr Chandler and worked hard for him.

"You use it often?"

"Yeah, all the time. I can use the pick-up too, when I want."

"What, the truck? That old thing?"

The pick-up truck stood out in the yard in all weathers — a useful but down-at-heel vehicle. Phil frowned, thinking about it. He remembered he had discovered it almost out of petrol one morning a while back. He was convinced he had filled it up only the day before, and it wasn't leaking or anything. Mr Chandler hadn't driven it, as he'd had a bad bunion at the time. Phil thought someone could only have sneaked in, borrowed it, and returned it without them being aware of it. It would be easy enough to hop over the fence, unbolt the gate and drive it away as the keys were always kept in the ignition. It was useless checking the milometer to see how far it had gone, as it hadn't worked for years. The real question, in Phil and PC Pink's minds, was why it had been returned at all – and the yard then locked back up. It was a complete mystery. Any normal thief would have nicked something better in the first place, or left this one parked in a ditch. It didn't make sense. Phil wanted to talk to his friend Kevin about it again when they met up at the party tonight. Kevin was taking Iris Underwood, and they were going as a foursome.

"Do you wanna go in the pick-up, then?"

"I'll pick you up, Mr Cheeky! I'm not getting in that dirty old heap!" Pat was round-eyed at the idea.

"Well, the van it is then," said Phil, finally ready. He had brushed his wavy hair and looked slick in a long-collared shirt and flared trousers. He had on the patterned tank-top Pat had knitted him for Christmas.

"You been wearing that under your overalls all day?" asked Pat.

"Yeah. And I had a squirt of that aftershave too. I'm not too stinky. Here, cop a beakful!"

Pat giggled and switched off the lights as they stepped out of the workshop. Phil was a lovely fellow. She liked the way he did his hair and how he always paid for her when they went out. It meant a lot, that kind of attention, she thought.

A new year message

Fenchester was as pretty as a picture postcard in the snow. Below the mighty medieval cathedral ancient buildings crusted the steep hill like barnacles on a rock. An icy little river wound between warehouses and wharves looping the walls almost entirely. Frost glittered on the fallen snow.

The January sales season had begun early, only today the narrow lanes were half-empty as none of the buses were running to town from the country villages. Black ice, warned the weatherman, stay home. Trains continued to arrive and depart, but road traffic was very sparse.

Sir Hugo Chivers bumped into Mrs Clark in Treve's, the department store. She had been selecting new underwear and also a birthday present for her sister, when she almost catapulted into him near the gentlemen's outfitters. They went for a cup of tea and a bun in the café.

"It's nice to see you again," smiled Skipper, and meant it. "We've missed your guiding hand at the governors' meetings. Are you home for long?"

"No, I'm afraid not." Hugo sipped the tepid tea and ignored his rock cake. "Sorry I haven't had a chance to drop by. Ernest tells me the inspection was pretty grim. I'm sorry to hear it – although I'm sure you and Mrs Shaw can weather any little storm."

Skipper was nettled by that dismissive remark. It was as if he could care less. He was their chairman of governors after all. She gave him a cold look.

"How is Mrs Shaw coping?" Hugo pressed on.

"She's still very sad, but back on track, I think," Skip answered, more defensively than she meant. "It has taken a while and times have been challenging. We're down several hitherto reliable people this year, one way or another."

Hugo knew she meant him.

"Granger, you mean? Yes, I heard he was in Scotland somewhere. But you have a new school doctor?"

"We do. Afra Legg. She's excellent and we all like her very much. She's moved into Dutch Cottage. So... did you know Reg has a new hip?"

"Yes. I wish I'd time to visit everyone properly, but I have a train and another plane to catch this evening. Please give him, and your mother and everyone else, my best wishes and the season's greetings."

"I will. Well, I must be starting for home. I want to head over the mountains before it is too dark and slippery to even try. Goodbye, Hugo, safe travels and thank you for the tea."

"Goodbye, Skipper. I'll call in when I'm back in Banford more permanently, I promise. Happy New Year to you" He kissed her cheek, which made her blush, and left her to gather her parcels and struggle out to the car park alone.

Hugo stopped at the line of polished wooden telephone bays just inside Treve's front entrance on his way out. He sat in one and scribbled something on a small piece of paper, made a short phone call, and left the paper wedged behind the receiver.

Pulling his collar up, he hurried down the hill to the railway station and collected the suitcase he had temporarily left in lost property. The girl behind the desk smiled at him. He often left a piece of luggage with her while he went shopping. She was more than a little taken with the elegant gentleman in his cashmere overcoat. Hugo rewarded her with a soft smile that sustained her fantasies for months.

A little before the store closed, when Mrs Clark had driven halfway home and Sir Hugo was rattling through the dark night in a near empty train, a man stopped by the telephone bay and picked up the small piece of paper. He tucked it deep into his pocket before departing to the Italian bistro around the corner for a light supper.

*　*　*

11.

Castle

Toby Tremayne

An MG roared up the old Roman road from Fenchester and branched left onto the slippery lane down Nag's Hill before pulling up at the empty dwelling known as The Holt. Holly Hill lay lofty and ancient a mile north on the opposite side of the narrow lane, the tiny hamlet of Oxthorpe another mile west down the same track. It was a remote spot, especially in Winter.

The Holt was probably several hundred years old. It had withstood many a chilly January hunched like a beast against the prevailing east winds. Its roof was steep and high, slated with massive slabs of local stone. The chimney stack rose like a cliff of solid blocks and constituted almost half the entire house. The four ground-floor rooms inside were cramped, but the vast hay grange under the oak roof beams had afforded generations of dormice and bats, beetles and spiders plenty of space in which to spread out and proliferate. Cockroaches and rats lurked in the drains down below, birds gathered on the roof.

Behind, in the backyard, there was an old well – plugged-up through neglect – and a tumbledown bread-oven, a relic of the days when the cottage had been a bakehouse. There was no front garden, but in the half-acre of backyard grew a lichen-covered cherry tree, an apple, a plum and a pear which year after year still yielded enormous quantities of fruit. The grass beneath the fruit trees had not seen a scythe for many a year. Tonight the snow-caked cottage looked quaint but promised little comfort.

From the noisy green sports car emerged Toby Tremayne, like a bug from a protective larva case. He was tired after his drive, and couldn't wait to pour a very large gin and tonic into a very tall glass. He pulled out a heavy leather valise and lugged it up to the front door. That was the last time he would have to do this particular trip, he told himself gleefully. Goodbye Milan, hello again Banford.

The chilly interior of the cottage struck even colder than the air outside. Toby threw some logs and a firelighter into the ugly old brown stove and struck a match. It was surprisingly quick to catch, and began at once to take the mildewy chill off the place and spread some flickering light. He flipped on the mains electricity and opened the back door, pleased to see Terry Green had been round and cleared enough of a path for him to reach the woodpile. There were plenty of logs in the store, and some kind soul had also left him a pint of milk, a loaf and some eggs in a cardboard box where they wouldn't freeze. That was probably Terry too, he guessed. He must remember to thank him when he paid him in the morning.

Toby hooked open the outer shutters and retreated indoors. It was not long before he had unpacked his two suits, seven blue shirts, underwear and socks into the big chest of drawers and wobbly wardrobe. He flung some damp-spotted sheets and a grey army blanket onto the bed, made an omelette and opened a solitary bottle of wine he had forgotten about. There was nothing else at all in the food cupboard. The gin would have to wait until tomorrow when he went shopping. He banked up the fire and repaired to bed.

A few days later, thoroughly rested, he took a healthy winter walk across the common, through the woods and down Dutch Lane. He thought he would drop into the Mint for lunch, which was now not only a pub with grub, but also a hacking and boarding stables, or so he had been informed. He remembered the place had been a proper farm when he was a boy, with cows and a milking parlour.

"I say! Is that you, Tremayne?"

A voice he knew very well hailed him from over the wooden gates of Banford Place. He grinned, happily. He had been hoping to run into Gibb.

"Lady Longmont! How lovely! Yes, it's definitely me. Back again like a bad penny."

"You young rogue!" Toby was about fifty. "Don't tell me they finally kicked you out of Italy." Lady Longmont emerged from the shrubbery where she had been cutting back a yew.

"They didn't, actually, no. I'd had enough of teaching English to boring businessmen, so I'm back here for a spot of retirement and country living. How are you?" He hadn't seen her for several years and noted with delight that she was still as bizarrely dressed as ever. Today she sported a man's raincoat, wellington boots and a lumberjack's cap secured under the chin with a bow of orange ribbon.

"Come in and have a snifter," she cried, delighted to see him. Toby had been at prep school in the thirties with Erskine, her dead brother. He had drifted in and out of her social set from time to time ever since.

"No, you must come with me, I insist. I'm off to the Mint for a lunchtime pint of old and filthy. They could even be serving hot toddy on a day like this, who knows. Golly, but it's perishing! I must buy myself some gloves." Toby's hands were deep in his coat pockets.

"Hang on just a tick, then. Let me shut the mutts in and lock the back door. Can't be too careful these days you know," she galloped off and was back in a trice carrying a pair of rabbit-fur lined mittens.

"Erskine's," she said thrusting them Toby's way. "Bought them when he imagined he was going into the RAF. I've had them in the drawer for a while but they're still quite good. Here."

Toby pulled them on, fur moulting like a blizzard as he did so.

"Perfect. Thank you very much. Right, come on then. Belated Christmas drinkies – and you can tell me all about the jinks you've been getting up to. I demand to know everything."

They linked arms and set off for the pub, chattering away as happily and easily as only two old pals can.

A new appointment

"Yes, well, I think I've found someone who could take over your French lessons if you like," said Lady Longmont to Mrs Clark a few days later.

Skip and Chloe had almost given up trying to find anyone to teach French. Betty Nesbit had inherited the task from her kindergarten predecessor, but since September had been insisting she had reached the limit of her capabilities. Mrs Clark wanted to keep the subject on the curriculum, however, as she thought it gave Mayflower added sophistication.

"You have? Who?" asked Skip eagerly.

"Old school friend of my brother," Lady Longmont gabbled. "Lovely man. Taught English abroad in Italy and Paris until last year. Now retired to a cottage off the Fenchester road. Speaks about four European languages, I think. Says he might go barmy without a little part-time job. Qualifications and all that too, probably." She beamed at the ladies. It was nice to be the bearer of hopeful tidings. "Name's Toby Tremayne."

"What's his number?" Skip reached for the phone.

"No phone, sorry. Surprised he's actually got electricity, considering where he's living. I'll wander over and ask him to call, shall I?"

"Well, if you wouldn't mind. That would be lovely. Thank you, Gibb." Skipper grinned happily at Chloe. "See? Sometimes nice things happen," she added, then immediately wished she had kept her mouth shut.

Chloe smiled. "Let's hope he wants the job," she said. She was weary and wanted to get home to feed Cassius and not be anywhere she was required to talk.

Toby dropped by the school the very next day, bringing his credentials and a cheery smile with him. He turned out to be a highly-qualified language tutor, well-able to cope with Mayflower's needs. He also suggested he could fill in as a substitute classroom teacher, if needed, at the basic pay rate. This sealed the deal, as good supply teachers were rare and often costly items.

Skipper felt as if Santa Claus had dropped a belated sackful of much-needed gifts straight in her lap. She went home and told Dora.

"That's wonderful, dear," commented Dora. She glanced at Bick who was putting on her coat ready to go home. "Thank you, Bick. The house is lovely, as always. Do you know this Mr Tremayne?"

"I remember his uncle had that old cottage out near the racetrack. Dretful old place. I believe Mr Toby inherited it when his uncle died. He used to stay with the old man in the school 'olidays when his parents was abroad and he was at prep school with that Erskine, Lady Longmont's younger half-brother. They used to go fishing every summer. She were a good twenty years older than the boys, of course."

"Well that's a lot of background," smiled Dora. "Is this Mr Tremayne nice?"

"Oh yes, nice enough. Talks a bit Biggles, if you know what I mean." Bick had little to do with Toby's type now she no longer worked at the manor.

"Well I liked him," chipped in Skip. "I thought he was charming. He has a lovely deep voice."

"What's he look like?"

"Well, like a sort of eagle. Or a flamingo."

"That sounds very bird-like. I take it he has a big nose?" Dora was amused.

"Yes, beaky. Salt and pepper hair, blue eyes. Bushy eyebrows. Not much shoulder or chin. Six foot or so. Tweeds and flannels."

"Goodness. It sounds as if you took him in pretty thoroughly," laughed Dora. "Glasses?"

"No, don't think so. No. Not married, because I asked."

Dora groaned. "Not another charming Banford bachelor looking for a wife?"

Bick harrumphed. "Don't think he's the marrying sort," she commented, but her opinion was merely speculative. She had never been able to decide one way or the other about Toby Tremayne.

"He says he's OK with the paltry remuneration we're offering," continued Skipper. "Apparently he only needs it to beef up his foreign pension. I think he might also try to rustle up some extra hours at Dane Street or the prep school – they do French. And he mentioned something about compiling crossword puzzles for a national newspaper too."

"Well he must be brainy. What a bit of luck! I do hope he fits in." Dora yawned. "Ooh, is it that time? I must feed Nicky. Where's his bowl?"

She opened the back door and the cat shot straight in with a large live mouse in his jaws. He dived behind a chair holding the mouse down with a heavy paw while everyone yelled.

Nicky gazed at them smugly. That'll show them who's boss, he thought to himself.

Boat talk

The netball and soccer matches were cancelled that week, due to so many children being laid low with coughs and colds. Charlie, Mike and Ernest used the time to sit down in the staffroom with Reg to discuss their boat-building project.

"Skipper says we should look for one of those kit boats. We might be able to get one cheap, as it's January," said Mike.

The headmistress had been skeptical about the sailing idea but felt it would be too mean to stifle their eagerness completely, so she had offered to top up whatever sum they raised out of her own pockets. It was decent of her, the men thought. Today she was suffering from the sudden onset of a streaming cold herself and had gone home early.

"Don't need no ruddy kit-build," grunted Reg. "Don't need nothin' new in my opinion. Why not just buy a nice little second-hand boat? We can patch it up. Maybe buy a new set of sails if you're bound and determined to spend money." He felt like the only grown-up in the room sometimes.

The others sighed. Having their sights lowered to the level of second-hand wasn't what they had dreamed of, especially Mike. He so rarely yearned after anything, he had not realised the force of such a desire. He shook himself back to reality and nodded.

"Yes, Reg, you're right of course," he sighed. "What do you think, Ernest? Go for second-hand?"

Ernest had never owned anything second-hand in his life. "What if it was a piece of junk?"

"It wouldn't be," asserted Reg. "I'll give it a good check over before you pay out. Then all we gotta do is give it a lick of paint, re-rig it and make sure it's shipshape for the little-'uns to use." He was glad they were finally seeing some sense.

Charlie stood up. He had to be home before Tim got off the school bus, and it was already getting dark. "Well, I'm game," he said. "Count me in if you need an extra screwdriver. I've a ton of tools in storage and they'll all be unpacked come next Friday."

"A week today? Is that your moving day?"

"Yes, thank god. I can't wait for us to have our own home again and some space. Most of our stuff's been in storage in Portland for a couple of years, so unpacking should be really fun. Well, I'm off. See you Monday."

He hurried out into the frosty evening. I won't be turning left any more after Friday, he thought with pleasure, as he strode through the gates. I'll be turning right and be home a good deal sooner.

Sailboats were not top of Charlie's agenda right now.

French begins

The harsh weather did not let up. Deep snow shrouded the countryside, frozen pipes cracked in almost every home, and the children brought every cough and sneeze they developed into school, along with wet boots and damp clothes and irritable tempers. Peggy and Cathy thought they might buy shares in Kleenex, they went through so many boxes of paper tissues.

Classes were reduced and much subdued. Toby Tremayne could hardly believe the school was as quiet as it was the Tuesday he gave his first French lesson to Form 3. Charlie retired gratefully to the staffroom to complete some marking. He didn't want to take home any additional work this particular weekend.

"Brr! It's cold in here, kids," started Toby, looking around. The two radiators in the room were tepid to the touch and the windows were definitely draughty. "Come on, stand up and let's do some warm-ups in French."

Before long the children were flapping their arms and beginning to remember some of their French vocabulary. Mr Tremayne taught them so many new fun activities that by lunchtime even Tania Nichols, who hated French, was enjoying herself. She took Mr Tremayne in hand and kindly explained how to line everybody up correctly, ready for the descent to the hall for lunch.

"You have to tell them to go pee and wash their hands first," she added confidentially.

"Righty-o," said Toby, glad of the tip.

He was looking forward to lunch himself as he had heard Ivy's kitchen dished up some excellent fodder. His own cooking skills were broadly limited to toast, throwing things into the oven, and omelettes.

After his first school lunch of sausages beans and mash, he wandered into the staffroom where his new colleagues made space for him around the fire.

"Gosh, this is cosy," he commented.

"Do you smoke?" asked Heather. "Because if you do we're being banned to the terrace this year. Mrs Shaw says cigarettes are unhygienic. Now we have to shiver like banished Cain beyond redemption out in the Arctic wastes." She offered him a cigarette.

"No thanks. Though I do like the odd panatella of an evening. Never been much of a one for cigarettes," he said. "Is there any tea? Do we all chip into a kitty somewhere? Oh, this biscuit tin. Is that your domain, Mike?"

"It is at present. I pass the torch to Jean next term. We all get a turn at remembering to buy the necessaries. That drip coffee machine over there is a gift from our Mrs Shaw who prefers fresh beans ground in that little mill thing." Mike despised the fuss over coffee-making, though he did not object to the resulting cup.

"Oh, how splendid," said Toby. "And have I to do playground duty?"

"No. Not unless you want to come for a turn around the field with one of us in the summer. Skip will find you a whistle. It's quite pleasant out there unless some little pip falls over and breaks an arm. They do that occasionally," smiled Jean.

"I wonder how Jumbo is getting on," said Guy. "Kid broke his arm every five minutes last year. I miss that group of kids – they were fun."

"Are you interested in sailing at all?" enquired Ernest. He liked this newcomer and was eager to begin the sailing project.

"We're thinking of doing up a second-hand dinghy for the children to sail on Benning Water in the summer," explained Charlie, sipping tea.

"Oh, as an extra-curricular club?" asked Toby. "No, not really. I'm the clumsiest man alive. Can't hit a nail in straight and I wouldn't know a hand from a hacksaw. Hawk from a handsaw? No, don't ask me. Utterly useless. I'd fall over the binnacle and land in the scuppers. Complete duffer."

They all smiled kindly. Another Jumbo.

"Wouldn't you be better sailing your boat on the river?" Toby went on. "It would be much more convenient."

Mike shook his head.

"No, it's not really deep enough and you need a permit of some sort apparently. Wildlife – fish – something or other. I looked into that. Sailing needs stretches of open water."

"You could build one of those flat duck punts and pole it up and down the Wain like a gondola. Of course that would require tempting some additional romantically inclined ladies to romantically recline on cushions and eat peeled grapes of course." Toby suggested. "But you rustle up the ladies and I'll flog them the grapes. That would be a nice little earner for the school fund."

He looked across at May Fisher, who was busily knitting something fluffy, and winked.

A walk to Banford castle

The weather eased up sufficiently to allow the third and fourth forms to visit Banford Castle and its little museum. The castle was closed to the general public during the winter months but could be persuaded to open for a few small school groups.

It was a popular trip for Mayflower's children. Charlie and Mike made sure there were plenty of parent volunteers to accompany them.

"Sir, can we buy stuff at the museum shop?" asked Dean Underwood.

"Yes, but you're only allowed one pound pocket money, so spend it wisely." Mike could see the shopping aspect of the trip was a top priority for the lad.

Dean skipped off to stand beside his walking partner, Stanley. Stanley's mum was one of the helpers.

"Now then Susie, you all set?" asked Mr Tuttle pointedly.

She nodded to him. "Yes Sir. I been twice."

"Good girl. Right, all set here Mr Paton, lead on!" called Mr Tuttle.

Their walk took them down Fen Lane to the river, which they crossed using the familiar footpath known as Stokes' Steps. Their feet and voices echoed against the old flagstones. Below the arches of the long causeway the river ran high, swollen with melting snow-water. Its edges were lace-trimmed with ice and leaves and other debris. Dun-coloured sedges stood gripped by the ankles in freezing mud, and no birds flew in the colourless sky.

"Who was Stokes?" Stanley asked his mum. It was the first time he had really thought about the name, but there it was on a grubby-looking sign riveted to the balustrade.

"I think he had something to do with the castle," answered his mum. "But I'm not certain. We could ask the museum people."

At the castle entrance the children peered up at the portcullis in its groove of ancient stone, and Charlie took some photos the children could use later in their follow-up work. Within the curtain wall was a wide open area carpeted in snow, and a steep hill with the almost circular remains of the keep crowning its summit.

"Wow! I've never been in here before," cried Dean. "Great place to slide down."

"Don't even think about it," warned Mr Paton, and Dean grinned. Once, when he had been a new boy, he would have taken that remark as a reprimand, but now he knew he and Mr Paton were sharing a joke. His teacher smiled at him.

The little museum held many interesting treasures – Roman coins and pieces of helmet, medieval bowls, civil war pistols. Their guide was kept busy answering all their questions and quite relieved when they finally set about spending their pocket money in the little shop.

"Miss, why don't you put those proper roundabout gates in beside the portcullis and make people pay to come into the castle?" Keith Carter asked the guide. He thought the authorities were missing a trick not charging an entry fee into the bailey.

"Well now, I don't exactly know, my boy. I believe the council think the open space inside the walls should be left free for people to use as a park. The rest of the buildings are securely locked, like the museum for instance. Did you think someone might like to make a camp in here and claim squatters rights?"

Keith didn't not know what squatter's rights were but he could guess. He privately thought it was a distinct possibility in a place as sheltered from the wind and spacious as this.

"Please Miss, who was Stokes? The one the steps are named after?" Stanley suddenly remembered his earlier question.

"I believe he was once the priest of St Peter's church in the town. Father Stokes. The story goes that one day he wanted to cross the river to get to Oxthorpe. He was in a hurry, so to save having to go all the way up to the Yeoman's bridge, he took a running jump and skipped from one side to the other using the boats and barges that were tied up at the wharfside. Hop, hop, hop he went, like they were stepping stones! Left right, left right, all the way across to Latimer Island and then all the way over to the south bank. He never had so much as a wet toe! Ha ha! Father Stokes must have been a nimble old fellow."

Stanley was thrilled. He would write that historical nugget down when he got back to school for his history project and maybe paint a really good picture to go with it.

"Come on, sweetie," said his mum. "Time to make tracks."

Stanley grinned. Life was good. There was always something to look forward to.

The Tuttles move in

Charlie took his moving-in day off work. It was another chilly one but mercifully dry. He collected the old pick-up truck he had rented from Chandler's garage after breakfast, ready to take their belongings over to Well House. The vehicle was rickety but it served its purpose, and it was certainly cheap. Fiona had ridden her bike and opened the new place up before Charlie and Tim were even half loaded.

"There, that's the very last lot. Can you post this key through the landlord's door?" Charlie asked Tim. Tim had also been permitted a day off school and was very excited at being allowed to help with the move.

Tim duly pushed the door key of their rented house through the letter-box and climbed up into the cab alongside his father. "That's the end of that, Dad. Come on, let's go. I want to set my new bedroom up."

Tim had decided to take one of the bedrooms in the roof as his own. It was as far away from his parents as he could get – which would in theory, he reckoned, invite less scrutiny. He liked the idea of being high above the world at treetop level. Maybe he would lay out his electric train set again.

"Dad."

"Yeah? Lord, this bridge is trickier to drive across than I imagined."

"Will Mr Shaw's ghost haunt us?"

"What? No, of course not."

"But he's buried in the garden."

"No he isn't. Who told you that? His ashes were scattered in the garden, sure, under the willows down at the bottom end. It was a place he loved and had been his home for ever. He was a nice man, not the sort to come back and haunt anybody." The things kids imagine, thought Charlie.

"That's good. Can we get a dog?" Tim's fears and hopes were seamlessly intertwined.

Charlie chuckled. "Yeah, I expect so – but we'll have to clear it with your mother, of course. There's plenty of room and only a short walk to the common or heath. You could take him to see Twitch."

Twitch, Fiona's pony, was currently eating its head off in the Mint's stables.

"Those stables next door might get rather smelly in the Summer." Tim wrinkled his nose. He had better choose a bedroom on the opposite side of the house.

The truck turned into their new driveway and drew up outside the front door. Fiona's bike was leaning against the wall and there was already a mat outside for their dirty boots.

"I see Mum's ready for us," chuckled Charlie. "Oh, and here's Reg and Terry too. Well, now, aren't you the kind neighbours? Not much in this load, lads, but more to come later when we've collected the stored stuff from Portland."

Tim jumped out and ran in to find Fiona. She had brought the electric kettle, five mugs, a box of tea bags and a pint of milk in her bike basket and was making the first of many brews in her new kitchen.

"Go and ask your dad for that bucket of cleaning things, please Tim," she ordered. "And tell them all to wipe their boots. How many sugars does Terry take? I can't have snow and mud all over my nice wooden floors."

Tim knew the day was going to be one long string of orders, but he didn't care. It was all wonderful fun and soon they would be settled in this brilliant house and it was theirs – all theirs! They hadn't had a proper home of their own for two years and he couldn't wait to see all this old toys again. There was a yellow teddy bear he secretly longed for, his trains and his cars and a load of books. He was already planning a new shelf for them. He galloped upstairs two at a time to claim his new bedroom.

Charlie and Terry drove off after a quick cuppa to get the load of furniture and other belongings from storage, while Reg and Fiona threw down drop-sheets and prepared every room as well as they could. Then Reg perched on a stool and figured out the central heating boiler controls while Fiona and Tim yanked open one of the two garage doors across the front yard. They discovered both doors opened onto one large space.

"Oh, this is useful," cried Fiona. "We didn't even look at this before, did we? We could stack all the boxes in here and unpack slowly out of the weather. Now isn't that a good idea?"

"Yep," nodded Reg, limping in. "Boiler's on and the rads are heating up nicely now I've bled 'em."

"Oh wonderful, thanks Reg," cried Fiona.

She and Tim busied themselves back indoors while Reg picked up an old shovel of Max's and began methodically clearing snowy remnants from the front steps. Push chuck, sweep chuck. He threw down some salty grit from a plastic container and hoped the truck would arrive back soon. Fiona poked her head out of an upstairs window and urged him not to overdo it.

"Well, p'raps I better get orf back to school now," Reg finally called to her about noon when the truck still hadn't returned. "Be back later."

He stumped slowly up the street only to find everyone had managed perfectly well without him. The dinner tables and chairs were all neat and tidy, just the way he demanded. Basil and Leo from Form 6 looked very smug as he complimented them on a job well done. They knew he had once been in the navy and tried to live up to his exacting quarter-deck standards.

"We did the mats and the doors too, Mr Green," they informed him. Reg liked there to be mats beside the entrances so children could wipe their feet whatever the weather. The doors had to be hooked back until everyone was seated and then swiftly closed. No point letting precious heat out.

"Good boys," grunted Reg. "Now, 'ow about you find my long mop and that zinc bucket, and swab the bottom corridor for me after lunch?"

A reward indeed. Both lads grinned and nodded. It was excellent fun being a caretaker and no mistake. And Reg sat down a while to ease his leg, thinking how nice it was to be useful once more.

Cats, cheats and other recurring themes

On Saturday morning Reg Green bumped into Mrs Bicknell. She had been over to see Fiona Tuttle and ask whether she would like any cleaning done now she had moved house. Mrs Bicknell had a day to spare during the week and would be happy to spend it at the Tuttles, she said. Fiona had pounced on the notion. She worked shifts at the hospital and not having to clean her large new house would be a great relief.

"Morning, Mr Green," chirruped Bick. "How's the leg?"

They sheltered from the northerly wind beside the council allotment hedge and quietly exchanged neighbourhood notes.

"Doin' alright thanks, Mrs Bick. I could do with the weather turning warmer though. That Toby Tremayne's started work," he told her. "Fits right in."

"Hmph. All jolly hockey-sticks is it?" Bick hoped Mr Tremayne wasn't going to feature much in her future. "When's Sir Hugo back?"

"Dunno. Bunting don't know neither."

"Everything's died down a bit, ennit? Seems that when our side falls quiet, the Opposition does too," commented Mrs Bicknell. She did not usually voice an opinion about their covert surveillance operation and Reg was not especially keen for her to continue doing so. It didn't pay to speculate. Reg preferred facts, and so should Bick. They were the local watchers and being paid to note details. Others could deal with the bigger picture.

"I couldn't say, I'm sure. Now then, anythink else?"

"Brenda Kirk's still giving her paramour – Mr Perry up at the lodge – a bit too much of her time. Never seen Len in such a miserable mood, I haven't. Janey Birch next door to me has 'ad the electric cut off. Can't pay the bill. Somebody, probably kids, lit a bonfire on that island near Mint Pool. Kevin says there's more graffiti appeared on the station's crossing gates. Them Price boys 'as been talked-to by Pink a time or three. Dunno what was said."

Reg already knew about that. Pink was hot on the trail of the missing lead. "Anything else?"

"Someone's been borrowin' that old truck of Chandler's without permission. No harm done apparently, but it were reported to the police, as was a bloke up the quarry suspected of handling stolen goods. Someone else up Holly Hill Drive says their cat's been stole. Word is there's an old farmer shooting them and collecting the fur to make a rug." Mrs Bicknell liked cats, so this last news item had upset her. She was going to watch out specially for stray kitty-cats from now on. Couldn't have them being made into doormats.

Reg's patience ended. Cats for mats was a recurring rural topic in his experience and not to be credited as a helpful piece of intelligence. Still, the old lady was thorough, he had to give her that.

"Right. Nothing else? Talk to you soon, then, Mrs Bick." He touched his cap and went off to see about the blocked staff lavatory, which — like cat-mats and cheaters — seemed to be recurring themes in life.

* * *

12.

Steady as she goes

Mrs Clark stared at a page in the school's current account book that Peggy was showing her with familiar dismay.

"Where did it all go?" whined Skipper. Chloe was out sick again, and it was up to Skip to begin firming-up next year's budget details, whether she wanted to or not.

Peggy curbed an impatient response. If you took money out of the pot, the pot became empty. It was pretty straightforward. How many times had they been through this?

"Do you want me to explain it all again?" she asked, sighing over her hijacked afternoon.

Skipper nodded. She was feeling sorry for herself now the responsibility for the entire administration seemed to be squarely on her inadequate shoulders. Since the new year Chloe had almost entirely withdrawn from anything concerning Mayflower and could do little more than take the odd playground duty. Last year she had helped Skip through every tiny part of learning to be a school principal. How Mrs Clark wished she had knuckled down and really learned those lessons at the time. But no – she had been so busy flitting about with pipe-dreams of this and that she had not fully appreciated what hard graft running a school actually was. It was come-uppance time.

Peggy pulled up a chair and spent the next half-hour re-telling her boss how each school fund was allocated. When she finished she sat back and waited. Mrs Clark eyed her balefully. It wasn't so awful, she supposed. She still wanted everything on her own wish list, and she wanted it now, now, now, but it was no use saying that out loud – not to Peggy. Not to anyone ever again, really.

"Do you think we can keep out of the red?" asked Skip. "We haven't an inch of wiggle-room."

"Of course we can." Peggy counted things off on her fingers. "Running costs are covered, swimming's paid. Plumbers are paid. Terry Green will need money, as will the builders and decorators. We've paid the sweep, and the milk bill's not due. Jamal has agreed to a retainer. Mr Tremayne is our only additional cost and he's almost covered. If we draw our horns in and ask the parents for voluntary contributions along the way – for any trips out and so on – we should be fine. Everyone is working really hard, you know, especially Terry and his mate. I don't know what we'd do without them."

"I'd love to give everybody a pay bonus," sighed Skipper. "Everyone is so kind. Peggy, I'm really sorry to whine and moan, but all this extra hassle is such a huge responsibility."

"It is, I know. This is not a very straightforward school. Our trust funds are something of a minefield, and Sir Hugo not being around doesn't help. He's always been able to steer us through a bad patch up 'til now – and there were several when Miss Broadstock was in charge."

"Were there? I didn't know that." Skip felt slightly cheered by this news.

"Well, she went a bit dotty towards the end. For example, five years ago she blew the money I'd earmarked for the skylight replacement on booking an entire circus."

"No! A circus? With clowns and a tent and everything?"

"Yes, and an elephant and four white horses. It was great fun and the children loved it, but the big top collapsed at the end and there was a right old hoo-ha. Dr Granger had to treat fourteen people for cuts and bruises, one of the clowns swore at May Fisher, and the ringmaster sued us for endangering his livelihood. Didn't get anywhere with it of course, Sir Hugo saw to that."

"Well I never would have believed it. That makes me feel a bit better."

"I'll keep a close watch on the money, don't you worry, Mrs Clark. You just have to accept that some things will be accomplished a little later than you originally planned. But don't go dreaming up anything more, please, or booking a blessed circus." Peg was glad Skip had cheered up but could not resist ending on a note of caution. "I think by the end of *next* year we should be in the clear. You can probably afford your pay-bonuses then."

Mrs Bailey left her to it, feeling rather like someone encouraging a unicyclist to cross Niagara Falls on a wire. At least the boss is finally beginning to understand the benefits of taking things slowly, she thought. I just have to keep reassuring her. We'll get there.

Three good boys

May came home from school sneezing. She closed the front door and sneezed again.

Marigold looked shocked by the explosion, and stalked into the warm kitchen to await supper while May slowly took her coat and boots off. She hung her hat and gloves to dry on the hall radiator. If only the weather would warm up a bit.

Her face felt hot even though the rest of her body was shivering like a jelly. She put the kettle on and sat down, as her legs felt suddenly ridiculously wobbly.

"I don't *want* a cold," she informed the cat, out loud.

Marigold decided her mistress was being far too self-indulgent. She licked her lips and stared her straight in the eye. Come on – supper, she cried telepathically.

There was a knock at the front door. May groaned and got up to see who it was. Marigold departed in disgust through her cat-flap in the back door.

Rick Hodges, his brother Tom, and little Jimmy Birch stood there like three wise men. Jimmy held up May's handbag in two hands. It was damp from the drizzling rain.

"Oh," cried May. "Did I forget that? Where did I leave it?"

Jimmy handed it over. "In the front hall, Miss. By the picture of that man."

"Sir Garnet Broadstock," added Tom. "Mrs Clark thought you must have put it down when you were doing up your coat or something."

"She asked us to come and give it to you," added Rick. "We were heading home anyway." They lived next door.

"Well, I'm very – *atishoo*! Very grateful to you, boys." sneezed May. "Excuse me."

"You got the sneezes. Our mum puts us to bed with a hot water bottle when we get those," Rick informed her. "And rubs us with Vick on our chests."

Jimmy looked round-eyed at this idea. His mum was never there when he went to bed. She was usually out working, so he curled up on their mattress in the back bedroom where the blanket was and waited until he fell asleep. Today Jimmy had a runny nose too, and felt sort of scratchy. He would have liked his mum to tuck him into a soft warm bed and rub his chest.

Miss Fisher wanted to shut the door and keep out the draught, but the children had been very kind bringing her handbag to her.

"Would you like to come in and help me light the sitting room fire?" she asked. Tom and Rick politely shook their heads.

"No thank you," they said. "Our mum's expecting us for tea. Bye!"

They hurried away but Jimmy remained, staring hopefully at his teacher. No one was expecting him. May Fisher, tired as she was, knew there was only one thing to do.

"Come on, Jimmy. Come in for a little while and we'll find a nice big box of tissues for our poor sore noses. Hang your jacket on the banister to dry. Now then – how about we open a tin of tomato soup and make some toast for tea? Would that be alright?"

Jimmy felt the Christmas he had only ever imagined had unexpectedly twirled around and flown right back into his life. He prised off his shoes and placed them carefully beside Miss Fisher's little brown boots with their cosy fur tops and neat zipper. His own shoes were wet and had a hole in the bottom, but things had to be done properly. Miss Fisher was always insisting on correct procedures in class. He stood on a stool and washed his hands at the kitchen sink, wiped his nose, and helped her take the soup bowls to the kitchen table as carefully as any high-class restaurant waiter. She sat opposite him, her feet now clad in soft sheepskin slippers. His feet in their grubby wet socks dangled two inches above the floor as he sat on a fat cushion and sipped the soup of heaven. The fire crackled merrily and both diners finally stopped shivering. Despite their head-colds, neither lonely soul could have been more content.

Outside, it began to snow again.

A walk to the station

"Dean!" yelled Ryan across the wilderness. "Wanna go walk Mrs Hewitt's dog?"

"OK." Dean came bounding over, leaping over huge snow-covered mounds that were, in summer, box bushes. His wellington boot flew off and he landed with a giggle on his bottom.

It was the end of the school day and they knew both their mothers were still at work so there was at least an hour in which to play on their way home. They lived almost opposite each other in Ironwell, a village only a few miles from Banford. It lay further up the river on the way to the stone quarry where Ryan's dad worked. It was a pretty place, with a central green, an old forge and the watermill where Miss Winstanley the artist lived. To the north lay more houses but to the east was a wonderful open stretch of rough heathland where local children could run about and kick a ball or fly a kite in Summer. Or exercise their dogs.

Sweep was always ready for another walk, even if he had only just returned from one. Today he was raring to go as soon as he heard the boys opened the front gate.

"He saw you out of the front window, Ryan," smiled Mrs Hewitt when she opened the door. "Hello, Dean. Can you take his lead? I can't let go of his collar yet."

Sweep was duly clipped onto his lead and off the boys went.

"You do this for fun?" asked Dean.

"Yeah, every day if I can. He's a good old boy aren't you, Sweepie?" Ryan was happy as a lark.

"Can we call in at the station on the way down?"

"Why? That swan ent there no more. The vet took 'im." Ryan knew all about the swan.

"I know. But they got a new chocolate machine and Mum gimme 10p."

"That won't be enough will it?"

"Might be." Dean grew doubtful. It wasn't much.

They walked to the railway station and into the booking hall. Kevin Smith was talking to Mr Coker the stationmaster, and sounding decidedly hot under the collar.

"I've scrubbed it with hot *and* cold water, Mr Coker. It don't make no difference." Kevin was holding a bucket and a rag. "What do you two want?"

"Nothing. Chocolate machine?" Dean was wary of Kevin as he looked very annoyed. Ryan was holding Sweep tight. "I got money."

Mr Coker waved a hand. "Goo on, lad. Get yer KitKat. It's alright. You didn't paint graffiti on our wall did you?"

"No, Mr Coker," said Dean, stuffing cash into the chocolate machine.

"What's graffiti?" asked Ryan.

"Vandalism, son. Pure and simple. Damage to railway property. Oughta be horsewhipped."

That didn't sound very nice. Did people whip horses?

Kevin folded his arms. "You *sure* you didn't paint rubbish on our nice brick car park wall?" He might be going out with Iris, but he wouldn't put spray-painting past her perky little brother or this great lump of a lad.

"No, Kevin. I mean yes, I'm sure I didn't," protested Dean. "Ryan didn't neither. We're just dog-walking."

"Well, alright then. But keep an eye out, will ya? Look for anyone with a spray can of blue paint and a bad attitude. You tell me if you see him. I'll give 'im what for."

"Yes, Kevin. Thanks Mr Coker. Bye!" The two boys scurried back out into the snow and ran all the way down Latimer Street to the heath where they stopped and had half the Kit-Kat each.

"We should have made Sweep sniff round the station then track the criminal down," suggested Ryan. "Like a bloodhound."

"Mmm," said Dean. "Probably a bit late now. I expect whoever done it's long gone. Cor, that Kevin's in a right old mood, ent he? Never mind, Sweepie! Let's find you some frozen ducks, shall we? Come on boy!"

Pink sees blue

"Where is this latest graffiti then?" asked PC Pink wearily. He had arrived at the station yard where Kevin Smith was still fuming.

"Over here, Constable. Look, there. Bold as you like on the gates and the same on the car park wall. I tell you I've had enough of it, and so's my boss, Mr Coker."

"I know Hubert Coker," nodded Pink, taking out his notebook and slowly peeling through the pages. "He doesn't appreciate mess, that I do know. Now then, let's see if I've anything to match this pertickerler bit of 'orrible artwork." He always tried his best to copy graffiti scribbles into his notebook whenever he could, so as to maintain a record. Pink would have been a very happy policeman if he had been issued with a nice little camera to record such evidence.

"Blue. Last lot was blue too, wasn't it?"

"Yes dark blue. And it's the devil's own job trying to clean it off. I had to scrub my level crossing gate for half an hour with turps to get the first one of these stupid tags off."

"When was that?"

"Before Christmas. Which is when I thought I knew who had done it. Kid on a bike. Never seen him before." Kevin blew on his fingers against the cold. "'Course now I know he was one of those Price boys lives next door to me and my auntie. Ruddy yobs."

"Hmm. Is there just these two masterpieces?"

"Yes. I don't think this one's finished though. It's slightly different. Could be the Price boys, I dunno for sure. Looks like whoever did it got interrupted. Maybe a train come in and 'e fled the scene."

Pink grinned. He liked this lad Kevin. He was sharp, but did not jump to unfounded conclusions. "You'd make a good police officer, son," he commented. "Observation and deductive reasoning. You got both. Want my job?"

That made Kevin laugh. "Nah, not me," he chuckled. "I would 'ave, once. Now I like my nice little trains and helping Mr Coker. He's teaching me a lot. I've learned more since I come 'ere to Banford than ever I did in Finchley."

"London boy are you? So's that Dean Underwood down the school. So's Reg and Ivy Green for that matter. He's the school caretaker."

"I know them. Us cockneys like to escape the smoke."

Pink grinned. "Well, Banford's done that little Underwood kid a lot of good in my opinion. Right little surly monkey he were when he first come. Old Reg Green ran away to sea, you know, when he were a lad. Royal Navy, he told me – like Sir Hugo. Then Reg and Ivy come up here to work at the school together. You'll have to find yourself a nice young lady, Kevin, and settle down hereabouts. We could do with a few more Londoners like you."

"That's very kind of you to say so, Mr Pink. In fact I got a lady-friend. She's Dean Underwood's sister, Iris. We're going to the cinema in Portland next week, if the buses are back running after the latest freeze-up."

"Very nice too, I must say. I hope the weather cheers up for yer, so's you can do your Iris proud. Well, I'll let you know what I find out regarding this 'ere blue monstrosity. Hello, young man."

PC Pink looked up to see Joey Latimer cycling down the path towards him.

"Hello Mr Pink. Hello Kevin," said Joey. "You investigating something exciting?'

"More graffiti," said Kevin. "Vandalism. You ent got a blue spray can about your person? Cos if you do Mr Pink will arrest yer and shove you in jail."

"No. But I saw a spray can in a boy's pocket as he was riding his bike into school the other day. Might've been blue."

"Who was that, now?" asked Pink.

"Greg Price," answered Joey thoughtfully. "It was Greg Price."

Bag snatcher

Anna Lane loved school. She was in Mrs Hewitt's form and relished every minute of every day – from assembly to lunch to tidy-up time, it was all brilliant. Mrs Hewitt had handed her a prefect badge last September, which was the absolute icing on Anna's cake.

Every day, she and her sister walked through the town, over Stokes' Steps, and down Fen Lane to the school gate that led into the playground beside Mrs Bailey's office. Sometimes she and Naomi caught up with Mrs Duke, who also came that way, and they walked along together in a pleasant, chatty group. While admiring Mrs Duke's twin sets and pearls, Anna adored her own uniform – especially the green raincoat with its inbuilt purse on a strap for pocket money. Her prize possession, however, was the brown leather satchel that her dad polished every Sunday night when he cleaned the family's shoes. It always gleamed like a conker. And this winter, their grandma had knitted both girls some green woolly gloves, with actual fingers. Life, for Anna, could not get any better.

I'm ten, she said to herself. I love being ten. I always want to be ten. I know who I am and what I like and what I can do. I'm going to be ten in my head for ever and ever, no matter how old I grow on the outside.

"What are you grinning about?" asked Naomi.

"Just everything," answered Anna happily. "Hello, Mrs Duke. What's for lunch?"

"Morning, girls. It will be fish fingers today, because it's Friday. And apple crumble if I remember rightly." Cathy was used to being quizzed on menus.

"Ooh, that means chips. I love Mrs Green's chips," sighed Anna.

"You love everything," commented Naomi. "If Mayflower gave you a pile of slugs, you'd love that."

Mrs Duke laughed but Anna took umbrage.

"I'd put them down your collar," she cried. "Anyway, slugs are useful. There's a place for everything in Nature. Don't you remember *anything* Miss Fisher taught us?"

It was Naomi's turn to be miffed. "Of course I do. Shut up." She slipped her satchel off her shoulders and was about to swing it round and clip her sister a fourpenny-one, when it was snatched out of her hand by a boy on a bike.

"Greg!" yelled Mrs Duke. "Hey, give that back!"

Greg cycled away down the road, swinging the satchel round his head and laughing. Everybody called after him but he did not bring it back. Naomi was angry and upset and thwarted, all at the same time. Anna couldn't resist one final dig.

"Now you'll get in trouble with Daddy. You should look after your things, Naomi."

"Stop right there," shouted Mr Denny, seizing Greg's handlebars as he tried to cycle around him to the bike rack. The bike's handlebar caught Guy painfully on the thigh but he didn't let go.

"Get off me!" growled Greg, threateningly. He swung Naomi's satchel away from the teacher's grabby hand.

"You *don't* ride bicycles in the playground. How many more times?" Guy's temper was very short when it came to protecting the little ones from danger. "Whose bag have you got there?"

"Nobody's. Mine. I was riding round the stupid little kindergarten wet-bums, not into 'em, you pillock." Greg spat on the ground with anger.

"We ent wet-bums!" protested Jason Rother, a tall infant, walking past with his horrified mother.

"I asked whose bag is this? It certainly isn't yours," persisted Guy.

"Yeah, it is. I'm bringing it in for someone."

"No you're not, stop lying." Mr Denny undid the buckles and found Naomi's name inside.

Anna, Naomi and Mrs Duke arrived in a rush at that point. Cathy almost slipped on the icy ground, and Guy put out his hand to steady her. She was looking rattled, a rare phenomenon.

"There, I told you we'd get it back," she cried.

Greg scowled and slammed his bike into the bike rack. He had only meant to tease Anna, make her take notice him. Snatching her sister's satchel had been an unexpected bonus. He had wanted the girls to jump around and try to get it back, or plead with him. Stupid females. Girls *were* stupid. Serve them right if he was quicker and smarter than they were. He spat again.

"Stop doing that, you little…" Guy was livid. He handed Naomi her satchel and folded his arms, blocking the way. Greg actually quaked before this big angry man who seemed to be filling the playground. "This is not a good start to the day, Gregory. I will see you after school for detention when you will write me a three page essay on respecting other people's property. Count yourself lucky we no longer cane children."

Greg slouched off to annoy someone else before the whistle went. It didn't pay to get to school on time with all the rest of the wet-bums. You got into trouble for no reason and now he had detention.

The girls hurried off to find their friends, while Mrs Duke and Mr Denny continued to fume together over the incident. Naomi shared her outrage with her classmates, and Anna spent a completely miserable morning coming to terms with the fact that sometimes school was not very nice at all.

A welcome break

Mrs Clark had her 'Absolutely MUST Do' list pinned to a cork-board in her study. It was gratifying to see one or two items had already been crossed off. What she kept privately in her desk drawer was the far longer list of 'Wants and Would Likes'. Her mind ached from the constant pressure the first list represented. It was a mighty albatross that landed on her head every morning as soon as she woke up. She was swallowing an aspirin one afternoon when there came a tiny knock at the door.

"Come in."

"Excuse me, Mrs Clark, please may I sharpen my pencil?"

It was Mungo James, from kindergarten. His wild hair and scruffy look were suddenly very appealing to the overwrought headmistress. He sidled in with a blunt pencil stub in his grubby little hand. He didn't smell too good, his socks had fallen down, and his shoes were untied, but the headmistress knew angels could often appear in different disguises.

Mrs Clark had recently sharpened all the kindergarten's coloured pencils with her new electric pencil sharpener and Mungo had admired their long points immensely.

"Does Mrs Nesbit know where you are, Mungo?"

"Nearly. I just need this doing because of all the sky. It's wored out."

"I can see. Come on then – only next time, ask Mrs Nesbit or Mrs Moore before you leave the classroom, alright? Here, sit on my lap and push the pencil into the sharpener hard. Hold it there – that's right. Now then, is that sharp enough?"

Mungo turned and beamed at her. "It's lovely," he said. "I can do my sky now."

"You could add a few blue flowers on the ground too," suggested Skipper. "There's always room for flowers."

"Not on the moon." Mungo was doubtful, but then he had an idea. "Maybe my spaceman can have blue boots."

"Brilliant. Let's go back together so I can lend you a hand."

Jimmy takes the long way home

Jimmy Birch waved goodbye to his classmates, Annie and Ray, who had been told to hurry home together after school. He had tagged along with them as far as Dutch Lane, then decided that was far enough. His own home was miles away from Weston, although neither Annie nor Ray knew exactly where he lived. Jim always walked part-way with somebody from his class after school, he was never collected by a grown up. Usually, by the time anyone thought to look around for him, he had vanished. No one ever asked where he went.

Jimmy had found a hideout in the woods beyond Dr Legg's house and decided he would see if it was warm enough to sit in for a while. He wouldn't stay long, of course, just in case his mum came home early. Jimmy spent all his waking hours silently fretting about where Janey was and wondering what time she would be home, even though he understood perfectly well it was rarely sooner than midnight, after her barmaid shift finished. He roamed the woods and fields in all weathers, generally alone, until it was dark. Then he let himself in and watched for her out of the window.

The hideout was little more than a few branches stacked against a fallen log. When he reached it today, he found it pulled apart and the wood scattered. Maybe a fox had done it, or a badger. It certainly smelled rank. He kicked the pieces around then resumed walking through the damp and earthy wood. The snow was thin here in the beech hanger and tiny pink cyclamen were poking through the earth where it was patchy. Soon there would be primroses. He planned to gather two bunches, one for his mum and one for Miss Fisher, his angel. Maybe he should make one for Mrs Clark too. He liked her.

Jimmy cut back across Hendy's fields and searched the hedgerows in vain for fruit. The blackberries were long gone, and the sloes. January was a hard month for birds and squirrels and hungry children. He searched the hazel branches for cobnuts but could not reach the remaining few he found.

Emerging from the field-path opposite school, he crossed Mayflower Road and kicked along under the horse chestnut trees. All the conkers had been taken or trodden underfoot. He ran across the main road and met up with Miss Muggeridge, his Wag Lane neighbour, pushing her nineteen-twenties bicycle home along Church Road. It had a flat front tyre.

"Hello," she smiled. "Had a good day?"

"Oh yes, thank you very much," answered Jimmy. "We did sums and Miss let me use the counters. And it was rice pudding for dinner." He knew the things adults took an interest in.

"Oh, one of my favourites. I put a little jam on mine. Tastes lovely. Here, hold my hand over the road."

Jimmy complied. He was tired and his tummy hurt again. He was thirsty and wished it wasn't so long until midnight.

Eliza Muggeridge looked at him and sighed. What a skinny little waif, she thought. "How about I make you a drink of milk and a fish paste sandwich?" she offered. "Then you can go home at five o'clock and be all ready for your mum. I 'spect she won't be long."

"Thank you very much," replied Jimmy genuinely grateful. He knew the sandwich would make his tummy cramp even more but he didn't want to hurt Miss Muggeridge's feelings. She and Mrs Bicknell had often been kind to his mother, lending her a dab of marge or a spoonful of tea when theirs ran out. Not that they had ever come into their home or anything, but they were next-door neighbours.

He helped Miss Muggeridge put the bike away in her coal-shed and carefully removed his shoes before stepping into her rather dark house. Jimmy was glad to be out of the cold and damp.

* * *

13.

Stringer

Heart to heart

"Skipper, can we talk?" asked Chloe.

"Sure. Let's walk."

The two old friends wandered arm in arm down to the children's allotments where snowdrops lay thick and creamy. The latest dust of snow was melting where the morning's sunshine fell, and the quiet was broken only by the sound of bickering robins and dripping water. Skipper waited for her friend to start speaking, but the longer she waited the more an awful plunging fear gripped her.

"What's going on, Chloe? You're not sick again, are you?"

"No. Nothing like that."

Chloe opened her mouth but suddenly didn't know how to start. She had rehearsed this a hundred times in her mind, yet now…

Skipper stopped walking as her bucketing imagination clamped onto the worst of all possibilities.

"You're leaving us."

"Yes. I'm sorry – yes. I'm going home to the States."

"Oh my god! Chloe – you can't! You *can't*! Not for good?"

"Yes. I'm so sorry, Skip." Chloe clasped her hands together, her face grey with anguish. "I've tried, I've really tried, but I can't stay here any more. Not since Max. This isn't my home, Skip, and I just, I simply *cannot* be here any more. This was to be Max and my happy-ever-after – but now he's gone it never will be. I really need you to understand."

"But – but this is *our* school. I thought we were in this adventure together. I thought we'd agreed." Skip felt selfish tears leaping out of her eyes like individual drops of disbelief, denial, frustration, panic.

"Honey, I'm truly sorry." Chloe had feared this reaction. She knew how deeply Mayflower ran in Skip's veins. Hers too, once. Some of the carefully rehearsed phrases she had lain awake composing finally floated to her rescue. "You have to realise this isn't to do with you, or the school. It isn't personal. It's about me, and how I am to survive without him."

Skipper gulped. "I didn't… I don't… When do you... want to leave?"

"My flight is on the eleventh. The day after tomorrow."

"*What*? That's … Chloe! So soon?"

"I've been trying to tell you for weeks, I swear. I know it's sudden and I haven't given proper formal notice or anything but – well, I just have to get out of here."

"Where are you... where are you going?"

"Shane's meeting me in Boston and we'll fly on to Denver. I've been offered a principalship in New Mexico, starting – well now. It kinda came out of the blue. And they want me there as soon as possible. We'll drive down to Taos and find someplace to live."

So it was all done and dusted. Informing the headmistress had been the only remaining loose end, apparently. America wanted Chloe as soon as possible. She was expected. She was even prepared.

Like daylight slithering inexorably down into the crannies of the gaping Grand Canyon, the full extent of Chloe's point of view gradually dawned on Skip. Nothing, nobody here in England, mattered. No perfect little school world, no kind friends, no British colleagues. They were all expendable – and she, Skipper, the faithful old Lone Ranger, could do nothing but watch Tonto ride away over the horizon into the west.

"Why didn't you tell me, talk to me? Mayflower needs you. *I* need you."

"No, honey, you don't. All this English stuff isn't me. I have to go back where I know how to survive. I really need you to understand and be glad for me. I don't have a choice any more."

Skipper shook her head, trying to clear it. She stared at Chloe as if she were a stranger. An icy crust began to encase her heart and she shivered to try to expel its numbing effect. It was poor behaviour to throw a tantrum like a child. Her dear friend – her very best friend – was asking one final favour, her understanding. Like it or not, Chloe's future course was set. The time for discussion had passed. Her best pal was bailing out.

Skipper Clark mustered as much magnanimity as she could. "Do you need any help? Packing or something?" she croaked. "What can I do?"

Relief swept over Chloe like a wave. The worst was past. "No, no thank you. I'm not taking much with me. Thank you, thank you for understanding. I... let's go in."

They walked silently, separately, back into the school. Chloe went slowly upstairs to her study feeling as if a hamper of debris had suddenly been cut loose and she was finally able to swim up towards the light. Mrs Clark, however, drew her heavy curtains and sat silently in the dark study, feeling like a returned library book that had once been borrowed by mistake.

Dora cried. Chloe leaving was like losing a daughter. None of the staff believed her when Skip telephoned each of them at home that night to break the news.

Charlie Tuttle and Tim walked over to Church Road to collect Cassius the lurcher, and wish Chloe good luck. Charlie hadn't known her as long as the others, but he was very sad to see her go. Mrs Shaw was already packed, and sitting alone in the kitchen staring out at the garden where her little pond lay dormant.

It will be pretty when the daffodils came up, she thought. The kindergarteners would have loved to pond-dip in its oily depths. The Tuttles brought a card and a bottle of eau de cologne with them that Fiona hoped might be welcome on the long flight. Chloe showed Charlie a box of curtains and the Mexican rugs she was leaving behind in case they would like them for Well House. She was so relieved he had agreed to buy the place, she said, and that Cassius would be back in his own home once more. Cass had always been Max's dog, not hers. All the loose ends were tied up now. Chloe would be able to start over with a lighter heart knowing this terrible, fabulous, excruciating period of her life was finally finished.

On Tuesday morning Bunting honked the polite horn of Sir Hugo's Rolls Royce outside her front door at eight o'clock sharp. Skipper and Dora, Peggy, Cathy, Ernest, Rev Bill, June, Jean and May Fisher stood in the cold and waved a sad farewell. The dismal weather matched their mood. The car's exhaust vapour mixed with the mist making a halo around the tearstained face peering out through the rear window.

The Rolls rounded the turning, and was gone.

Chocs for Pru

"How old is she?"

"No idea. Forty? Fifty?" suggested Ivy vaguely. Pru Davidson was a hard one to judge. The school cleaner could be anywhere from forty to seventy in Ivy's view, she really hadn't thought about it.

"Anyway I got 'er a box of After Eights. That's alright, innit?"

"Very nice I'm sure," sniffed Ivy. "She's definitely older than eight. Valentine's the day after tomorrow. You adding a bunch of roses too?"

"Don't be daft." Reg had no time for Ivy's nonsense. "You watch out, or its a frying pan for your next birthday."

"Do you dare," laughed Ivy, her immense frontage shaking up and down. "Anyone who gives a woman a frying pan for a present deserves all he gets."

Reg took his stick and went to find Pru. She was clanking her bucket about upstairs, washing the lino where the children had left muddy tracks. Later on, she would pull out the big rotary buffing machine and do her best to put a shine on the surface, although it would never be as good as when Reg did it himself. Not long now, he told himself, and I'll be back to work full-time. He sat down on the chair outside the head's office to wait for Pru to descend. It gave him a chance for a bit of a think.

That Mrs Shaw was gone then, and Mr Tremayne was already working at the school. He hadn't wasted much time. Reg knew plenty about Toby. He thought he would ask him when they might expect Sir Hugo home permanently – he probably knew. Reg intensely disliked being half out of commission and felt at a distinct disadvantage since his hip operation. Forwarding intelligence was all very well, but he preferred to be hands on, out and about. It was lucky his op had coincided with a lull and Sir Hugo's protracted absence. He wondered if strings had been pulled somewhere.

Reg also mulled over the current local situation. PC Pink had kept Mayflower up to date on his stalled progress chasing the lead thieves. The police had expanded their enquires to the quarry and out as far as Ledgely, Fenchester and Portland. He brooded on how anyone could have moved the cumbersome haul so completely. They'd have to be bloody fit to scale the outside of such a tall building, prise it all off, and lower it down without anyone knowing, he thought. It made him mad, thinking about it. He and Pink and Stringer had been over Longmont with a fine tooth-comb but not come up with a single new clue. Of course the weather probably had a lot to answer for, covering tracks and limiting thc chances of any locals seeing anything. But somebody must know something – it was just a question of asking the right people.

"I say, are you on the naughty chair?" cried Lady Longmont, suddenly entering through the front door. She stamped her wellies on the mat sending showers of snow and wetness everywhere.

"Here – you'll have Pru after you, milady," commented Reg, not getting up.

"Who? Oh the cleaning person. Sorry. Just popped in on the off-chance of a word with Mrs Clark. She in? It's about Mrs Shaw fleeing the coop."

Reg nodded. "Gorn home to America you mean? Yes, she's left. There's an elementary school in New Mexico as needs 'er,

I'm told. She'll be missed around here. Knowledgeable lady was Mrs Shaw. Nice."

"Yes, she was" said Lady Longmont. She began unbuttoning her maxi coat, starting at the chin.

Pru came down the stairs and glowered at the wet floor and doormat. "Who done that? Oh, alright milady, I s'pose I'll see to it, never you mind. Dear, oh dear. Dear, oh dear. What a lot of mess there is in this school. Takes me twice as long to get round with you out of commission, Mr Green."

Reg suddenly remembered the reason he was there. "Here, 'appy birthday, Pru. Don't eat 'em all at once." He thrust the gift into her red raw hand. She couldn't have been more astonished.

Lady Longmont clapped her hands and grinned. "Oh splendid! Happy birthday and many returns and all that," she cried. "Chocs, eh? Jolly nice too."

Reg rose to his feet. "Arf-term next week, Pru. Terry'll be here doin' a few jobs, so don't worry about puttin' that rotary back. 'E'll do a proper buff-up when he's finished. You can give the lavs a good going over instead. And go 'ome early today, why don't you? It's yer birthday."

Conversation in a quiet corner

"Morning, Toby."

"Morning, Hugo. Officially back then?"

"No, just another flying visit I'm afraid. I'm due down at the American airbase later. Thought I'd pop by and see if you're settling in alright."

"Ah, thanks. Bit chillier here than I expected."

"It would be. Still."

"I've had a long chat with your bosun. He brought me up to speed. Nice bloke, seems efficient. A bit slower getting around these days of course."

"Why d'you say that?"

"New hip."

"Yes, I really must remember to enquire. You've spoken to Bunting too?"

"Briefly. He seems a competent sort. Both Buntings, in fact. He looks after your bus jolly well."

"He does, he does."

"Any tourist action for us on the horizon? Green says its been silent since the summer."

"He's right. We had to shut down our local B & Bs as you know."

"Headmistress getting too warm?"

"A little, but she soon saw the benefit of maintaining the status quo. Our chief concerns have been the other incidents. How the hell Moscow traced their defectors here and silenced two right under our noses we still don't know. I've had to perform quite a bit of fancy footwork to avoid Lambeth pulling the plug on us. They hate joint ops as you well know. As it is, we're on hold."

"Dutch Cottage?"

"No."

"Could you prepare an alternative B & B and bring it up to speed without too much trouble?"

"It's in hand, actually. I'm currently looking into the American's old place, next door to me. I'm obtaining the lease."

"Mmm. Excellent idea. Any intelligence from field operatives I should know about?"

"No. The boy, Jumbo, has gone. The old lady, Ada Bicknell, is currently our only feet on the ground. Surprisingly excellent, for an amateur, and unswervingly dedicated, but we could do with a couple more."

"Never underestimate an old woman, is my rule. Always sit next to them on trains or buses or at a party if you want to hear the most up-to-date gossip or tales of a lifetime full of sex, travel and intrigue. How about Ernest?"

"No. I've never recruited him. Not the right temperament."

"Another of the older kids? They're out to play all the time."

"Possibly. I'll leave that to you."

"Alright. When should we expect your public re-appearance?"

"A few weeks."

"I have one question."

"Fire away."

"The American. How did you arrange it?"

"I called in a favour and asked our cousins to find an irresistible little carrot, somewhere off the beaten track. She was ready, poor thing. Nice woman. Lovely woman, in fact. You've a clear run."

"Good. Well thank you, Hugo, I think that's everything I need for now."

"Yes. Well, I'll be off."

"Righty-ho. Toodle-oo."

Jimmy's Sunday

It was another Sunday – a boring, grey, foggy day halfway through February.

Ian, Weasel and Greg Price rode down Latimer Street leaping their Chopper bikes over the row of hump-backed bridges that spanned the island and the left and right forks of the river. Christmas had brought a windfall of cash into the Price household from their brother Malcolm's sale of the stolen lead to his contact up at the quarry. The boys did not share any of this bounty with brother Phil as he was not to be trusted. He also remained in the dark about who had borrowed his works' truck last month, which afforded them an additional source of private amusement.

The ice was melting like jagged slivers of silver in the sun which was struggling intermittently through the murk. The three bikes skidded in synchrony off the road and into the rougher part of the park where the boys had previously noted an old bench they intended to spend the morning setting light to. When they reached it, however, they discovered a funny little elfin child perched on it, peering through a green plastic telescope at a puffing steam engine making its way into Banford station on the far side of the river. Ian snatched the toy and threw it to Weasel.

"Hey!" yelled Jimmy. "Give that back."

"Come and get it, monkey-boy. Oooh, I'm scared!" Weasel flipped his bike around as Greg rammed the bench with his front wheel. Jimmy fell off onto the wet grass.

"That's a piece of junk," commented Ian as he caught the telescope again. He lobbed it far out into the river where it floated for a minute then sank.

"Hey!" cried Jimmy. He glared at the boys and put up his fists. "That's mine." He might be pint-sized but he wasn't scared of bullies.

"Butterfingers," scolded Weasel. "Poor old baby Long John Silver. Where's yer ickle parrot?"

Greg grew bored and rode off. Jimmy Birch wasn't worth taunting. His brothers dismounted and hopped around Jimmy calling on him to fight them, and laughing at his frustrated temper. Weasel took out a spray can of blue paint, shook it noisily and squirted a cloud in Jimmy's direction.

"Little boy blue! Is yer pussy down the well?"

The Prices tapped him and slapped him about. Ian delivered a hard punch to his left eye which sent him sprawling on the grass again. They finally rode off, glad to be rid of brother Greg and planning to spray their tags on the palings of the old well. Banford was simply asking for it.

Jimmy wiped his smeary face and sat up.

Sundays were hard. Mum liked to sleep in, and so he usually took himself off for one of his walkabouts. Today, as he had found the green telescope thrown into a bin near the swings, he played at being a pirate. It was nice in Latimer Park and he sometimes bumped into Mayflower kids who would share their sweets. He wandered the familiar heaths and commons most of the hours he was not in school as walking eased his constant griping belly-aches. Today he scuffed along the secluded perimeter path of the island, pausing to crouch in the bushes to do his business when the cramps became too bad.

The sun struggled out properly about noon, which cheered him up. He took the long route home, up through Roffett's Wood and back to the Fenchester road where he bumped into Mr Kirk, the pig farmer.

Len Kirk recognised Jimmy and called him over for a chat, wondering why a kid that small was out on his own.

"You look like you've been in the wars, you're black and blue. You got a black eye and what's them blue speckles all over yer? How'd that happen?" he asked. He had the worst hangover ever and he hadn't shaved in a week, but pigs still needed feeding. "Wanna come and feed the porkers with me? I daresay we can rustle up a cuppa tea after that. Come on, lad."

Jimmy went willingly.

They walked down the track to the sties and dished out the feed to the constantly hungry pigs. It was nice to see them gobble up everything with unashamed gusto. They enjoyed every moment of life, little knowing the abattoir van was their only future. Len lifted Jimmy up to scratch a few ears and heads, astonished at how light the child was.

"How old are you, Mr Birch?" he asked.

"Seven. I'm in Miss Fisher's."

Blimey, thought Len. My five year old's heavier than you. "Come on. Time for tea."

They took their shoes off in the lobby and went into the kitchen where it was warm and smelled of lunch-time roast beef. Brenda was feeding baby Rosamund in the parlour, with Jenny and Dale playing on the floor in front of the fire. Farmer Kirk shut the kitchen door and opened the bread bin. He cut a hefty slice of bread and buttered it thickly.

"Marmite or Bovril?" he asked.

Jimmy was unused to having choices but pointed to the Bovril as it had a nice red label. Mr Kirk handed the snack to the boy. He poured them some tea and searched under the sink for a bottle of turps.

"Where d'you live then?" he asked as he rubbed his turpsy rag over the worst of the blue paint specks in Jimmy's face and hair.

"Wag Lane. My mum has a sleep on Sundays so I go for a walk. We'll cook our dinner later," Jimmy explained as he licked and licked the butter and Bovril off the crusty bread. Len nodded.

"That's alright then. I expect that little walk's given you an appetite. When you're bigger you can come and help me with my pigs if you want a Saturday job. I used to have a Mayflower boy helping, but he's moved away now."

Jimmy thought that sounded like an interesting offer, then promptly forgot about it. The future had limited relevance for him and the past faded quickly. He lived in the moment.

"I better go. My mum might be calling me." He stood up and pulled his jacket back on. "Thank you for the tea." He had only sipped a little and left the slab of bread on the plate. It was thoroughly stripped of butter and Bovril.

Jimmy Birch hurried home. Maybe his mother had made them some soup and bought those Ritz crackers he liked. Maybe they would have a nice cuddle on the chair by the electric fire and listen to the wireless. Sunday nights were always *much* better than the days.

Old friends

One day during half term, May Fisher took a stroll round to see her good friend Dora York. They had many interests in common, not least of which were a love of gardening and a fondness for cats. May's cat, Marigold, was large and marmalade-coloured. She prowled endlessly through the gardens of Fen Lane, pausing only to rest on the top of a shed or fence like a tethered barrage balloon when the weather permitted. Today she watched May vanish at the end of the road, and took herself over to the fields in search of a few voles.

Dora was in her front garden concentrating hard on cutting back a massively overgrown hydrangea with her secateurs.

"Good morning, Dora," called May over the gate.

"Oh, gracious! Hello May, how are you?" Dora looked up. "Do come and tell me what you think of this brute. I've a good mind to ask Terry to dig it out."

May studied the offending plant. "I've always hated pompom hydrangeas," she agreed. "South coast bungalow plants, if you ask me. This one's looking horribly healthy, I must say, but it's far too big right here. You can hardly get through the gate. I'd cut it right back and then dig it out. Relocate it somewhere out of sight. What's beyond your compost heaps?"

"Good idea. Then I won't have the guilt of killing it will I? Well, I can't dig it up now, the ground's still frozen two inches down. Have you time for a coffee? I feel I need one after this wrestling match."

The kitchen was warm and cosy, as always. Dora put the kettle on.

"Skip's over at the school if you want her. I think the new sailing dinghy is being painted today in one of the stable-yard's sheds, so she's in the office minding the phone and doing paperwork. Mike and Charlie are very keen on this sailing club idea aren't they?"

"Yes, I'm not so sure about Ernest though. He's never been the outdoor type. But it's nice he has some friends to go out to play with these days."

Dora smiled. "Other than that awful Jack Murphy you mean? Yes, we all need friends. I'm still sad Chloe's gone back to America. Skip and she were very good buddies, you know, and she's really feeling abandoned I think. They went through a whole lot together in California – it wasn't at all easy at first. Funny how people move on, isn't it? One day you're the best of pals, next thing you know life has swept you off somewhere new and you never see them again. I never thought I'd leave Cornwall, myself, and not in a month of Sundays did I think I'd ever be involved with a primary school – yet here I am. And I met you and Jean, so it turned out splendidly for me."

"Yes, certainly for us, too. You must miss your Cornish chums, though," said May, smiling. She had moved house only twice in her life. Had she ever married and had a family, things might have been very different.

"Well, sometimes, yes. But I'm extremely happy here with my daughter. I have you and Jean and Ivy and dear Ernest. Not to mention Reg and Terry and everyone. Even Hugo, when he's around. Is he ever coming home again do you suppose?"

"Who knows. He's obviously very busy and doing some important lawyering somewhere abroad. I don't know why he doesn't resign as chairman of our governors, he's constantly being called away. But I hope he comes back soon, too. I'm sure Skip could do with his support just now."

"Yes. He'd certainly help calm down some of her blessed spending panics, wouldn't he?"

"Wasn't she a little keen on him, once?" asked May, archly.

"I think so. But I'm no longer as convinced as I was," said Dora.

They took their coffee into the lounge where Nicky was sprawled on his back fast asleep on the sofa, four legs up in the air. May tickled his tummy. He stretched and yawned and rubbed his head against her hand.

"There don't seem to be as many eligible men around the place as there were last year," sighed Dora.

"Like Max and Jack. Like Dr Granger, you mean? I rather miss his jolly presence," May said.

"Dr Legg's super, though, isn't she? She sorted out my earache in no time."

"That's good to know. I wonder if she's had any experience with psychological troubles," wondered May. "Guy Denny is still very anxious, and he bothers me. One day he's up, the next he's withdrawn and I think nearly in tears. He doesn't let on he's

274

miserable, of course, but you can see it. That Gregory Price boy is really stuck under his skin. Have you met him?"

"No, but I've heard. Little stinker. I saw him at the concert of course. I thought Charlie had worked a miracle by teaching him the guitar. He performed very well."

"He did, but he needs to behave better in general all the time – without the promise of some kind of reward. Good behaviour isn't a transaction." May shook her head firmly. Mayflower was stuck with Greg Price for another five months, and it wasn't a comfortable thought. "Well, I'd best be making tracks. Thank you for the coffee. I want to call into school and collect a cardigan I've left behind my classroom door and then do a little shopping in town this afternoon. Do you want to come too?"

"Oh yes. Lovely – that will make a nice treat. I could do with some warmer vests, if Coppen's has them in. Shall we catch the bus or walk?"

"Let's walk," smiled May. "It will do us good. But we can ride home on the bus if our shopping is successful can't we? See you later."

Eavesdropper

Greg spotted Miss Fisher leaving White Cottage and caught up with her as she was about to enter the school's front gates.

"Hello, Gregory," smiled the teacher. "That's a nice bicycle."

"It's a Chopper," answered Greg. "Got it for Christmas from my brother."

"Oh. Don't your parents buy you big things like bikes?"

"Nah. Our dad's on an oil rig in the North Sea. He don't come home much. Mum's working up the jam factory. Phil did the pools and won a load of money, so us three youngest got new bikes."

"Lovely," commented Miss Fisher. "You're a lucky boy. How's the guitar going?"

"Fine. I'm getting a new one soon. One of my own, like."

"Excellent. Well, I'm heading into my classroom to collect something. Bye-bye now – have a nice ride." Miss Fisher turned and was gone.

A nice ride. Like he was a little kid on a tricycle.

Greg rode off down the street and round the corner. He was bored with half-term. He took out a new spray-can from his pocket and shook it, liking the rattle it made. Maybe he'd go back into that old empty house and put his tag on a few of the doors. Or break a few windows.

It was easy to get inside Longmont's perimeter. He thrust his bike out of sight in some bushes where there was a piece of broken iron railing he could just wriggle past. As he did so cold dead leaves dripped water inside his collar, and he swore. Then he froze suddenly, hearing voices. Men's voices.

Greg silently wormed his way forward.

It was Mr Chivers, Mr Paton and Mr Tuttle. They sounded pretty happy.

Drunk probably, thought Greg. He found himself a good vantage point and settled silently into the shadows beside the stable-yard.

Ernest, Mike and Charlie were finishing off the last coat of marine varnish on the upturned boat's hull, which was a very pretty dark red.

"There, that has to be the last coat!" said Mike, flourishing the brush. "We're out of varnish, out of paint, and out of everything else. Can you see anywhere I've missed? You're the one with the PhD and the glasses."

"Nope," answered Ernest, peering at the dinghy. "Charlie?"

"Nope," echoed Charlie. "Looks bloody perfect to me. I've done all I can with this mast and this other thingummy-jig. Alright Captain, time to tidy up?"

"I think so. Oh – who's this?"

Guy Denny came trudging into the yard. He was wearing his hiking boots and had come over especially to see how the three were getting on and to lend a hand if need be. He didn't want them to think he didn't care about the sailing project.

"Hey, Guy. Nice of you to show up just when we've finished," called Charlie laughing.

"No, really? Well I'm sorry I've missed all the fun. Gosh that looks super-shiny. What a pretty red. Why's there a hole in the bottom?

"Centreboard," the others chorused.

"Oh, yes of course. When will you turn it right way up?"

"When it's completely dry. This weather isn't helping. Can't we plug a fan heater in somewhere?" asked Charlie, not for the first time. He stared vaguely up at the dangling light bulb.

"No safe socket," Mike reminded him. "We could maybe borrow one of Reg's paraffin heaters, only he says he can't buy more fuel until Friday week. It all takes cash."

Guy walked around the little dinghy. It looked brand new, gleaming and crisp as an apple. "Well I think it's brilliant. You've done a super job. What's next?"

"Turn it over the right way, tip in some water and see if it leaks," said Mike. "After we're sure it's watertight we step the mast, tighten the rigging, attach the sails and *then* we go a-sailing."

Guy congratulated them again. Their enthusiasm was infectious and he was glad now that he had dropped by. He had been feeling dismal at home. "I suppose when the weather improves you'll start selecting the kids who want to learn to sail, will you? Shouldn't be too hard with our lot, they're all eager little beavers. I wouldn't let the Price kid join, though. He'd sink it first day out, like as not." Greg had been weighing heavily on his mind. "Or worse. That one doesn't deserve to join in with decently behaved kids. When are the new sails arriving?"

"They're in that bag over there. Came yesterday. We thought we'd rig them in here first to make sure we've got things right. Sort of practise doing it so we don't look too much like landlubbers over at the reservoir. Cleats and all that," said Ernest. "Luckily the ceiling's just high enough."

"Yes, and so you can take a picture of it fully rigged for your little school magazine article," Mike reminded him. "You know you want to."

They all had a chuckle at Ernest's expense. He loved putting together the twice-termly school magazine and was happily immune to their teasing. This boat project had been fun, and anyway, he did want to write about it.

"Come on. I'll help you clear this mess up, then who's for a pint down the Yeoman? Right, that's what I thought." Guy suddenly felt much happier. It was surprising how good friends could perk you up. "Now, where is your rubbish bin?"

Greg watched them lock up and go, thinking all the while about his teacher's words.

* * *

14.

A pint

Tuttle and son help out

A steady thaw merged into days and days of nondescript mizzly rain. No one minded too much at first, because it was better than snowy blizzards, but it was not the kind of half-term weather to be out of doors, letting off a little steam. Constant dampness made people crotchety. Water coated everything and froze in the downpipes at night, causing Reg some fresh concerns for the school's Georgian brickwork.

He pottered about, still walking with a stick and still not completely perfectly, but his stamina was returning and the grinding pain in his hip had gone. He worked part-time with Terry's help, but then Terry caught the flu and was out of commission. Pru Davidson, grumbling all the while, took on some extra cleaning hours over the break but there was no one willing to volunteer to help with the rest of the sprucing-up that Mrs Clark said simply must be done over half-term. Not until Charlie Tuttle and Tim dropped by.

"Always ready to help a neighbour out, Mr Green. Tuttle and son signing in for duty," joked Charlie. The Tuttles had unearthed Reg and Stringer in the boiler room doing something complicated with a timer.

"Very good of you, I'm sure," grunted Reg. "Especially when you'd probably prefer to be doing a few jobs around yer own place. But there's only a few days left of 'alf term and I'm running behind. Now then, 'ow are yer with a bit of painting? I got walls, window frames, door frames, skirtin' boards, school kitchen. Or outside work."

"I'm very happy to paint whatever you say, but young Tim might not have the steadiest of hands."

"Hmm. How about 'e comes with me to knock a bit of sense into the bike shed roof then?" asked Reg. "If you tackle redecorating the school kitchen, Mr Tuttle, Ivy'll love you forever. She's 'ad it cleared and washed down for four days already, so it's all set. There's a mort of scrambling about to be done in there – ladders and such. I can't do it. Think you could?"

"Sure. Especially if Ivy sees fit to give me second helpings of jam roly-poly next week. OK Tim?"

Tim's eyes sparkled. Knocking some sense into the bike shed with Mr Green sounded much better fun than painting a dreary old kitchen. He liked hammering nails.

"Yes, please, Mr Green," he grinned.

Ivy came over with a cup of tea later to see how Charlie was getting on. He was standing on the newspaper-strewn kitchen worktop, white paint frosting his frizzy hair.

"Is it alright, Ivy? I haven't dripped too much have I?"

"No, that's looking lovely, ducky. I'm just 'appy to have it done before next week. Sally and me always scrub it down proper, but it's always a struggle, this kitchen. Them snoopy inspectors turned their noses up at my blotchy walls when they come in, and I wasn't best pleased about that, I can tell you. What's Reg up to?"

"Tim and he are knocking seven bells out of the bike shed. I think the snow finally got the better of its roof so they're nailing a new one on."

"Oh well then," said Ivy. She perched on a tall stool. "You settled in alright to your new house? Mrs Tuttle happy, is she?"

"Yes, thanks. We love it. It's huge after our rented place."

"Ah, it's a big old place is that. But I'm glad you're all settled down. You'd better watch yer step though. You know what they say, Mr Tuttle. New house, new baby," Ivy chuckled.

Charlie grinned at her over his mug of tea. "Now there's a thought. But I don't mind if I do, Ivy. I really don't mind if I do!"

Making progress

Dora watched her daughter staring at the steam rising from her afternoon cup of tea. Skipper had been very withdrawn since Chloe's departure.

"Penny for them," she offered.

"I was just wondering what Joe Granger's doing," Skip murmured.

"Who? Oh the doctor. He's in Edinburgh isn't he?" Dora thought Skip's recent head-cold was probably adding to her current fit of the blues. The inspection, Max, Chloe, money. No Hugo. That blessed Price boy.

"Yes. I thought I might ask Dr Legg, or possibly Hilary Presley, if there's any news."

"Are you expecting news?" asked her mother.

"No."

This was ridiculous.

"How's that new Mr Tremayne fitting in?" asked Dora conversationally.

"Oh fine. He's very nice and the kids love him. His French lessons are a lot livelier than Betty's or Molly's. I suppose he has a more modern teaching style."

"Well, change is good, isn't it?"

"Not all. No, definitely not all," answered Skipper wistfully. "I don't think I approve of change any more."

"What piffle. How's the little boat coming along? Could we have a walk over and take a look at it?" asked Dora, thoroughly exasperated with her daughter's constant ennui. "Come along, Susan. Put your hat and coat on."

They clomped down the damp street, arm in arm. It did them both good to stretch their legs a little and take the footpath to the main road and around the corner to Longmont's main gates. Dora peered hopefully through the railings at the Donkey Field for signs of spring bulbs, but could see none. The playing field itself was currently a shallow brown lake of rainwater, with dirty drifts of old snow lurking in the corners the sun had not reached. One of the goal posts had fallen over.

"If we'd had a snow-plough this winter we'd have made a fortune," commented Skipper, still thinking about money. "People never expect snow in this country, and it *always* snows."

"You've no money to buy anything so daft," Dora reminded her, crisply. Silly remarks like that get you nowhere, she thought. Where on earth did I go wrong?

Unlocking the little wicket gate, they stepped through onto Longmont's weedy driveway. Skipper made sure to lock it behind them, mindful of the need for increased security. They picked their way around to the stable yard where Mrs Clark flipped an outside switch and a dim light flickered on. It illuminated the familiar cobbled square like a film set. There was Reg's mower repair room, there his old desk storage area, there the sports equipment lock-up, there the steps to the Lodge's back door. It all looked quiet and tidy. Skip shuddered, remembering how sinister the empty building was inside. She walked over to the far side of the yard and unbolted yet more double doors and pulled them open, switching the interior light on at the same time.

The jaunty little red dinghy was resting upright on its trestles, with its varnish now completely dry. It had a mast and rigging and only needed the sails to be raised. It looked very spruce in this dreary old shed.

"Oh I say, what a lovely little boat," cried Dora. She hadn't expected anything so professional-looking, or as finished. "Is it ready to go in the water?"

"Yes, so they tell me. When the weather is better, of course."

"How will you select which children to take?"

"Don't know. I'll leave all that to Mike and Ernest and Charlie. They have a plan, so they say. I must admit I honestly didn't think this little second-hand dinghy would ever turn out as well as this. They bought it from that fellow over in Ledgely, you know. Reg has been overseeing the restoration project even though he hasn't been able to help much."

"So you said. Well, I think it looks…" Dora stopped at the sound of a voice and the scampering of a dog.

"Hi!" shouted a man. "You there! What are you up to?"

Mrs Clark and Dora turned in surprise. Charlie Tuttle came puffing up the wilderness path with Stringer galloping ahead of him and Cassius pulling on his lead. Stringer was thrilled to see his old chums and even Cass started wagging his tail.

"Oh, it's you, Mrs Clark! Hallo, Mrs York. Sorry, sorry, I didn't mean to startle you. Well, I did, but only if you were thieves or cut-throats you know. Taking a look at our little project are you?" puffed Charlie. "What do you think, Dora?"

Dora and Skipper calmed down. It was only Charlie and the dogs.

"Hi. Yes, we came out for a walk. Sorry if we looked like burglars. We just wanted to see how your boat is doing," smiled Skipper. "Are you walking everybody's dogs now too?"

"On patrol," corrected Charlie, importantly. "I'm helping out while Reg's hip is still a bit tender. Said I'd do evenings and weekends. I gotta take Cassie out anyway, so it's no bother. I'm like Wee Willie Winkie, I am. I try the locks, check the bolts and rattle the doorhandles and so on. I wondered why Stringer didn't bark just now. There's a good boy, well done."

Stringer wagged his tail then went off to growl at something in the bushes. He dragged back a pair of dirty old gym shoes tied together by their laces, which he then sat staring at in a meaningful way.

"Think she'll float?" asked Dora, meaning the dinghy.

"Oh yes. We've filled her with water and there's no leaks," enthused Charlie. It should be fine. We're just now waiting to bend the mainsail, raise the jib and try the spinnaker."

"I've a couple of old bed sheets you can have as spares," said Dora with a twinkle.

"They sound perfect, I'll let Mike know. A couple of bed sheets and a pillowcase and we'll be all set. I expect Ernest will have them clewed up like Nelson's Victory in no time, he's been reading that many Hornblower books. Come on now, why don't I close this shed up and walk you home around the block? Stringer, come on lad, leave those nasty old things alone, do. Oh, he's gone. Probably home by now, warming his paws in front of Ivy's kitchen fire. Now then ladies, let's lock these doors."

Charlie scooped up the old shoes and took them along, as it wouldn't do to leave rubbish lying around Reg's nice tidy yard. He would dump them in the lost property box, then nip home for a nice hot bath and some of Fiona's best shampoo. See if he couldn't get a little more of the white paint out of his hair.

Alternatives

After half-term yet another vicious northerly snowstorm blew in, much to everyone's disappointment. The temperature plunged back to below zero, causing everybody to long for the olden days when each classroom had been allowed a fire to keep it cosy.

Skipper had been forced to cancel the Animal Man's visit, an annual event everybody had been looking forward to. Dr Giles usually delivered a fascinating educational talk to the entire school in February, bringing several live animals, birds, a reptile or an amphibian, in special carry-boxes. He would carefully take each one out describing their habits and life cycles to a silently enraptured assembly. He was very popular. By way of modest compensation, Mrs Clark showed the children a film about Africa in the gym hall. The projector was a touch temperamental but overall the afternoon treat was a success.

"Miss Clark," began Mungo James as he exited the hall with the rest of the kindergarten.

"Mrs Clark. Yes, Mungo?"

"Has your sister gone to Africa?"

"You mean Mrs Shaw?"

"Yes. Has she gone to Africa?"

"America. She's gone to live in America."

"Doesn't she like us any more?"

"I'm sure she still likes us very much. Why?"

"She never said goodbye. Maybe she'll come home again soon." He was an optimistic child.

"I'm sorry she didn't say goodbye, Mungo. Maybe we could write her a letter and see how she's doing, what do you say? I think she'd love one of your paintings of an African zebra too, if you can spare one."

Mungo thought back to the afternoon's film. "Yes please, thank you very much. Only I'm going to do her a big fat anocerous, not a zebber. They got horns on their noses. I won't do his legs because he'll be standing in the water."

"Ah, I see," said Mrs Clark, nodding. "Good idea."

Mungo was pleased he'd thought of the water. He wasn't very good at legs yet. He grinned at her. "See you tomorrow, Miss."

"Mrs. See you, Mungo."

Reg calls in for a pint

Reg continued to recover very well. Ivy told everyone who asked that he had always been a quick healer. He exercised, he rested, he plugged on. He returned his walking stick to the back of the hall cupboard.

Thankfully, the latest snowfall did not stay long. The wind backed round to the southwest and in a few days everywhere was once again dripping with melt-water. Reg walked to the police station in the market place with the pair of mystery training shoes Stringer had found in the bushes near the lodge.

"Mmm, these are interesting, Reg," said Sergeant Drysdale, who was on the desk. "We've some shoe-print plaster casts and some unidentified fingerprints from your lead theft we're still checking. These could well be a match for the shoes. They say people who climb things favour certain types of footwear. Dunno if that means 'cos they're lucky ones or just good grippers. I'll send them over to Portland CID. Mind you, they can be a bit slow, Portland."

"Probably bein' thorough," commented Reg. "Anything else?"

"We've a bloke in Ledgely scrapyard sayin' nowt but looking right shifty. He's the brother of a fellow up the quarry driving around in a truck that don't belong to him. You know about Chandler reporting his old jalopy being taken out and then brought back one night? Them Price boys is top o' my list o' suspects, though that Phil as works there don't seem to be involved. He's like the odd one out in that family. I believe the younger buggers nicked the lead, transported it in the borrowed truck to the quarry bloke, who then fenced it to Ledgely. I seen three of 'em little oiks cycling around on new Chopper bikes, which is itself suspicious, as their mother only works down the jam factory. Pink maintains they're likely our graffiti yobbos too. You got the youngest Price kid at your school, ent yer? Graffiti never started till they moved in. I think they're likely our entire crime-wave. They'd have known about that truck from their brother Phil, and thought it amusing to borrow the thing from right under his nose. However – proof's in short supply. We just need a little more solid evidence." He patted the shoes, hopefully.

"Impressive," said Reg, who had long ago arrived at similar conclusions. It was only too obvious to one of a suspicious nature, like him. He thought about the clasp-knife in his pocket, and what he'd like to do to the Price boys if he caught them.

"No other lead missing, though, which is good," said Drysdale. "I've had a man go round and check all the church roofs and anywhere else that might've had some lifted. Hall Manor, for instance. You'd be surprised how much of it there still is in these old buildings. I'll let you know anything new, Mr Green, soon as."

Reg felt a pick-me-up was in order after this conversation so he called into the Yeoman on his way home. The huge dark interior was warm and smelled of beer and woodsmoke. He took his pint over to a corner away from the massive hearth, only to discover Len Kirk already slumped on a settle nursing a half.

"Bit early for you, innit Len?"

"Never too early," grunted Len, coming-to. He lit a cigarette, flipping the spent match across the room into the fire. "Not when your old lady's giving her attentions elsewhere."

"That still going on? Not exactly keeping it secret are yer?"

"Maybe I'll publicly shame him out, Reg, get the little bastard on the run. That'd shake Brenda up and bring her to her senses. She should be thinking of me and the kids not screwing around with some scooter-riding twerp. What she sees in that little runt I don't know – and she's not saying. Thought you was in hospital."

'I was. Now I'm 'ere, a rejuvenated man. I've had a new 'ip and an 'ooray so to speak," Reg was darned if Len Kirk was going to spoil his day. He took a pull on his beer and wiped his moustache. "You should have your missis clip your toenails more often, Len. That's where you're goin' wrong."

"What's toenails to do with marital infidelity?"

"I get my old lady to cut mine, reg'lar. Well I've 'ad to, not being flexible enough to do it meself recently. She don't object. Then she sits quiet while I do hers. And you can varnish women's toenails, you know. Very intimate, that is. Very nice. It's them little acts of mutual kindness you gotta work on." Reg set about filling his pipe.

"Kindness? Trimming *your* great thick hooves?" said Len shaking his head. But he grinned too, which had been the whole point. Reg watched as his friend sat up a bit straighter and rubbed his stubbly chin.

"Maybe I should have her give me a shave and a hair cut too," suggested Len. "Or maybe muck out the pigs with me every Saturday evening."

"Now, you're talking, old son. Little acts of togetherness, little deeds of kindness. They keep a wife's concentration where it oughta be, if you ask me."

Greg gets the blues

It was no good. He couldn't wash it off and it was fast-drying. Ian Price stared at his hands in irritation, and finally resorted to wiping the streaks of paint on the lining of his brother's coat where Greg would probably never notice it. Ian pulled some gloves on and went to school, throwing the empty spray can into next-door's dustbin.

A short while later Greg also put his coat on and set off for school. He was walking today, not wishing to ride his recently cleaned bike on the muddy streets. He was getting to like things clean.

Today Greg aimed to finish his jungle painting. It was coming on well and he hoped Mr Denny would select it for the next art show. And he was to have another guitar lesson with Mr Tuttle. Greg was enjoying the lessons very much and could now even read music. It helped that Mr T was a good accompanist. Mr T was brilliant. He could play any instrument you handed him, remembered Greg, admiringly. He had brought a tenor banjo into school last week. It had been in storage, he'd said, and he was eager to give it a whirl again. Greg had strummed along on the acoustic guitar and the sound the two instruments made together was very satisfying. He had even let Greg have a try.

Greg generally disliked tramping to school on foot, as everyone else had a group of friends to walk with. Today he kicked along on his own through the slush in his wellingtons, resenting them all.

"Hey Greg," called Dean Underwood. He was with Ryan Hale as usual. Ryan liked Dean because he was lively, and pointed things out that Ryan had never noticed before. "Wanna walk with us?"

"OK," shrugged Greg, pretending not to be pleased. "How's it going, Ryan?" he added, making an effort to be affable.

"Er, pretty well, thanks. Dean and me's been walking dogs. We got a pound saved up between us."

"Dog walking?" Greg had never thought of that as a way to acquire decent money. He hadn't ever considered actually *earning* money at all. "A pound ent much. Whose dogs?"

"Mrs Hewitt. Mr Tuttle. And there's a woman with two Chinese dogs in Portland Street."

"And a fluffy white thing that belongs to Mr Jenkins down the shop in Weston," added Dean. "We take them up the heath usually."

"Nice. And they pay you." said Greg. "How much a walk? Show me."

Dean held out his palm with a several coins in it. "We don't ask for it. They offer."

"Give me that and I won't kick your head in," hissed Greg, venomously, suddenly switching from pleasant to threatening. He grabbed Dean's hand and twisted the money out of it into his own before laughing and booting puddle-water at the astonished pair. His coat flared open as he continued to aim kicks at them. Dean noticed Greg's fingernails and the inside of the coat were smeared with blue paint, but he was too shocked to say anything. Greg would find out soon enough when he took it off and discovered more had transferred itself onto his school jumper and shorts.

Ryan and Dean finished walking to school on the other side of the street, while Greg jingled coins in his pocket, delighted his day had started so profitably.

But when he went to hang his coat up he saw the paint stains inside, and on his grey sweater. He swore at his brother, knowing immediately who was responsible. He draped his coat carefully before the other children saw, then stripped off his jumper and stuffed it down behind the new lockers where no one would look. Still cursing under his breath, he hurried down to the office where he told Mrs Duke his mother had forgotten to provide him with a warm woolly today. It was so cold, he whined. Please could he borrow an old one nobody wanted out of the lost property? Kind-hearted Cathy found him one, which he wore all day, pulling it down constantly to cover any tell-tale blue on his shorts. He was very angry indeed.

He took all his pent up fury out on his frustrated teacher and miserable classmates. When it was time to finish his art work, he screwed the jungle painting up and threw it in the waste-paper basket. He was banished to Mrs Clark instead of making music with Mr Tuttle, and had to write two hundred lines during lunch-playtime.

Mutual agreement

Since Chloe's departure, Mrs Clark's workload had increased dramatically.

"Why don't you ask Mr Tremayne to help out a bit more?" suggested Peggy, anxious her current boss didn't end up as dotty as Miss Broadstock. "He's always around and he may appreciate an extra hour here and there."

It was worth considering. Mrs Clark went upstairs to sit in Chloe's old room and think. Its empty desk and abandoned files looked as forsaken as the headmistress felt. A Navajo rug still lay on the back of a leather chair and Chloe's pretty yellow curtains hung at the windows. The space resonated with her friend's personality – it was hard not to imagine she had merely stepped outside for a moment. Skip expected to hear her voice and see that wide white grin when she turned her head. It was sweet that Nicky had taken to stretching out on the top of the sunlit desk whenever he could, but even he didn't fully compensate. Mrs Clark pulled open the filing cabinet to search for a folder.

Toby Tremayne poked his head round the door.

"What ho. Oh, *you're* rather nice," he said, picking up Nicky and ruffling his ears. Skipper had briefly thought Mr Tremayne was referring to her. She chuckled.

"A black cat. Is he lucky?" asked Toby.

"No, he's Nicky," quipped Skip.

The cat struggled free, deeply affronted at having his ears messed about with.

"Glad I caught you, Mrs Clark. Now then, I'm teaching here most of the week, one way or another."

"Except Thursdays."

"Except Thursdays, indeed. So I'm going to be mighty cheeky and ask the most tremendous favour." Toby clasped his hands together in what he hoped was an appealing manner.

Uh-oh, thought Skip. What now? She looked at him enquiringly.

"I wondered whether I might possibly beg the use of a spare desk somewhere, during the times I'm not teaching. The attics, say, or over in that lodge place. Just a desk and a chair. I'd be quiet as a mouse and not drop fag ends or anything, I promise."

Skipper was amused despite herself. "Why?"

"Well, I've picked up a couple of hours extra at the Priory until the end of term. The prep school, you know. Just a couple of Latin periods with the oldest lads. And it would be wonderful not to have to cart books backwards and forwards."

"So you'd want a bookcase too?"

"Well, that would be terrific. I could do my marking and compose my monthly crossword in peace. Of course I'd be around to help you out too. You must be a little shorthanded with Mrs Shaw gone."

You've had this all planned, Skip suddenly realised. I might have imagined such a request as serendipitous once upon a time, but not any more. I've grown suspicious. She remained silent, looking at him and wondering whether he and Peggy were in cahoots.

"Well, I don't see why not," she said, cautiously. Where was the possible harm? If he was willing to help out with a little administration here and there, it certainly solved her immediate problem. "You can take this room, if you like. You can even light the fire." She grew happier as she spoke. Another decision made, a problem apparently solved.

"Oh I say, might I? Are you sure? Thanks awfully."

Skipper smiled, feeling rather like Lady Bountiful. "Sure. To be honest, I was going to ask you to think about possibly joining us full-time after Easter anyway, to help out with some of my administration. Only if that wouldn't interfere with your other commitments, of course. Now Chloe's gone, I could really do with the extra help."

Toby appeared to consider this.

"Mmm, well, I'll think about it. I must say I like your little school – everyone's so jolly friendly. And the money helps of course. Yes, why not? French and some admin? Can I still have time to devise my crosswords? Alright yes. I think I should like it here very much."

Skip grinned at him with relief.

"Wonderful! Thank you Toby. Just tell Peggy, and she'll fix you up with a 'Do Not Disturb I am Compiling a Crossword' sign. I'll let Pru know – she's our rather cantankerous cleaner. You'll want your desk dusted I assume?"

"Indeed," said Toby. "Thank you very much, Mrs Clark."

"Call me Skipper, like everyone else, why don't you?"

"Aye-aye Skipper," grinned Toby. He saluted as she walked out and back down the stairs to her own domain. He brushed a few cat hairs off the desk and sat down in the swivel chair with a satisfied smile.

This was a very agreeable study. Nice view over the main entrance, clean and light. Right at the heart of things too. He picked up the phone and asked Peggy for an outside line.

Spring floods

The cold land had thoroughly thawed by the end of the month. One morning the straggling little River Wain was stuck fast to its banks by anchors of solid ice, and the next the windy air was warm and the channels between the islands were running free once again. The brown fields, the swales, the fens, all unlocked themselves and melded into a liquid milk chocolate sludge that moved and slithered with ever-increasing speed and weight eastwards, the fullness edging sideways over the sodden commons and reedy boglands. Marshes, heaths and levels crackled into delicate lacy patterns, then dissolved and oozed in clumsy new directions, tumbling solid bergs of muddy flotsam and jetsam as they swelled, blocking ditches, dykes and drains. The waters at the centre of the main river could be heard whispering, then rumbling deeper and deeper and more menacingly as the hours wore on. People gathered in groups on bridges and high ground to watch the blobs of ice and muck roll and rotate with the flow. The meltwater added so much volume the river soon spread like a shallow sea from Ironwell to Weston. Latimer Island lay like a half-submerged shipwreck beside Banford's ancient castle walls, and the roar of the high-water past the man-narrowed wharves in the town filled those who lived nearby with alarm. Up and up the walls the water climbed, to within inches of the street. Beyond the main road-bridge, where the filthy liquid frothed and flooded deep into the Yeoman's cellars, the river swept distractedly eastwards again, spilling far and wide, where its dirt finally settled in fat ridges across the levels, under a wind-blown surface of criss-crossing ripples. The ruins of the ancient Greyfriars monastery loomed above the new ocean like some abandoned lighthouse.

"I had to go all the way into town and over the bridge to get to school today," complained Heather Jackson, who lived in Ironwell. "Did they say when they think these horrible floods will go down again? It's most inconvenient."

Charlie commiserated. "No, not on the wireless anyway. My guess is it will get worse before it gets better." He was worried himself, as his new garden was almost completely submerged.

The two of them were sorting through the sheet music in the multi-use room. There was an awful lot of it and Ernest had asked them to chuck out what they didn't require before he started cataloguing the rest. Sunshine was pouring in through the little window, making the dust rise.

"I forgot to say happy birthday," remembered Charlie. "I hope you saved me a piece of that coffee cake."

Heather laughed. "I did. My mum's recipe, so I know it's good."

"Will you be going to see her soon?" Charlie knew Heather's mother was in a home somewhere for patients with dementia. Christmas had been a difficult time for Heather.

"No. Not till the Easter holidays now. She doesn't recognise me anymore anyway – which makes me sad." Heather looked forlorn. "To be honest, I feel very unsettled."

"I can understand that," nodded Charlie. "But you've a good job and a nice house here haven't you?"

"Yes, I know I'm very lucky. But – oh, I don't know – I've had the fidgets ever since Chloe left."

"Spring fever, I expect. D'you know, the floodwater was up to that line of willows at the bottom of our garden yesterday morning and now it's ten feet from the back door. The railway track is the only thing above the floods for miles. I thought I'd woken up in the Mississippi delta this morning."

"You had better get that boat of yours launched *tout de suite*. It sounds as if we'll be needing it," chuckled Heather.

"Yes. I could row over and fetch you each morning," offered Charlie. "And you can pay me in coffee cake."

*　　*　　*

15.

Fire

Trying hard

Eleven plus exams were scheduled in early March for Guy's form. He sent Greg to take the test papers in Skipper's study in order to allow the others their best chance of concentrating. All the children worked diligently during the three pressurised mornings and by Wednesday afternoon were almost fit to explode. They ran outside and hurtled around the muddy Donkey Field like demented chickens. It was windy and sunny and Spring was in the air. They were free – no more tests! They breathed in the warm air and stretched themselves.

Everywhere the noxious tide of floodwater was receding at last, allowing the low sodden fields to begin to dry out. Through the dirt and grime pushed the welcome green noses of Spring flower bulbs. Willow and hazel catkins waved their soft fat paws and wagged their wiggly tails cheerily in the breeze. Everything young was reaching up towards the blue sky once more, and dancing.

Ryan had done his level best with the difficult tests and wanted Mr Denny to know he had honestly given them his best shot. His reading had now improved to the point at which he could manage most questions, but Mrs Raina had helped him decipher a few troublesome words.

"Will it matter that she helped me with some of the words?" he asked his teacher anxiously.

"I'm sure it doesn't, Ryan," answered Guy. "Did she help you spell or write anything? Or explain?"

"No Sir. I done all that myself."

"Good boy. I'm very pleased you gave it a real go. Now scoot along and play with Leo. He'll teach you all about baseball."

"Baseball? Do we play that here?"

"We do. Well we did before Mrs Shaw left. I think we'll try it again this summer. It's a grand game."

Ryan bounded off obediently and left his teacher feeling very pleased with the rapid progress the lad had made. He seriously doubted Ryan's exam effort would qualify him for the grammar school, but the child had tried, which was the main thing. Maybe by the summer, when he finally left primary school, Ryan would have caught up even more. At least Portland Secondary would now have a solid foundation of literacy and numeracy upon which to build the rest of his education.

Greg came slouching over.

"I done that exam. It was stupid."

"Right. So you didn't try very hard then?"

"I finished that last paper in half an hour. Piece of piss."

"Half an hour? Seriously?"

"Piece of piss," repeated Greg. "I don't want to go to no grammar school anyway. I want to go where my brothers are."

"The place where they are always in trouble?"

"Yeah. Ian got sent home for a fortnight after Christmas because he set fire to a rubbish bin and all the alarms went off. The whole building had to evacuate into the snow. Brilliant."

"Oh. Your brothers don't seem to be making the most of their educational opportunities do they?" Even to his own ears Guy sounded pompous. "I heard they are now heading off to borstal."

"School's stupid."

"Thanks."

Smirking, Greg sauntered off a short way. He would never tell Mr Denny he had in fact tried extremely hard with the test papers and had secretly enjoyed their challenging questions. Or that he had used every moment of the time allowance to review and correct his work, just as his teacher had advised.

Mr Denny sighed and shook his head once again over the boy. He turned to watch Reg Green walk in through the playground gate. Guy was glad to see him, but wondered where Stringer was. The terrier usually followed his master like a shadow.

"Mornin'," Reg greeted him.

"Morning," answered Guy. "Where's Stringer?"

"Throwing up. Vet says he'd eaten something bad and wants to watch 'im for forty-eight hours. 'Ow's that boat comin' on? Sailed it on the mighty floods yet? Proper little Noah's Ark."

"Ha! I think it's all shipshape. Mike did suggest sailing it over to the pub, but as the water's finally going down it's back to Plan A again. They're waiting to hear from the Benning Yacht Club about launching it, apparently. Len Kirk's been kind enough to lend us a trailer. You've seen the sails up, haven't you? All it wants now is a name painted on the side and an anchor, I think. Mayflower One?"

"Mr Paton going to build a fleet then? One, two three and four?"

"I wouldn't put it past him," laughed Guy. "We're all pretty chuffed with how it's turned out."

Mr Green continued to the wood store to find some logs to cart indoors. It was chilly outside and he knew Mrs Clark would have worked her way through her last bucketful already. He looked around for Stringer, forgetting the dog was out of action.

Greg heard them talking. He thought it was odd too, the dog not being there.

Stringer

Mr Quincy, the local veterinary surgeon, was very worried indeed about Stringer. He had kept him in overnight and asked his wife to check on the little dog from time to time while he was out on a farm visit. When he returned she reported no change. The white-haired terrier hadn't moved. He lay in his crate on a soft blanket, his head down and his tongue out. His eyes flicked open if someone walked by, but left alone the dog lay quite still with his eyes shut.

Ivy had rushed him into the surgery, having found the dog slumped in the bushes in a puddle of mud and vomit the day before. Stringer had been icy cold and was wringing wet as if he had fallen into some floodwater. He was missing a tooth, had a blood-frothed muzzle, and had bitten his tongue through. Mr Quincy suspected someone had poisoned him, then beaten and tried to drown him. He sent off samples to Fenchester to find out what toxin might be responsible, but the results had been inconclusive. The vet sighed, put the animal on a drip, swabbed his mouth and gave him an injection. He stroked Stringer's poor head, hoping Mother Nature and good care would suffice. Reg telephoned four times.

"Stringer don't usually scavenge," said Reg, beside himself with worry. "Likes the odd marrow bone, and always finishes his own food. Gets a few titbits from time to time from the kids, but nothink likely to upset 'im – a bit of sausage or a pennyworth of 'am from the missis, if she's in the mood. 'E don't beg neither. No one I can think of would smash 'is face in or chuck 'im in the river. I can't understand it."

"Nor I, Mr Green. But he's been beaten and half-drowned and picked something up – or been fed something laced with poison. Would he take anything from a stranger?"

"Maybe. But not if it smelled orf, 'e's too smart. Maybe he found a dead poisoned rat down by the floods. Or in the wilderness, even. It smacks of deliberate attempted murder, to my way of brooding."

"Well, I don't know, Mr Green, I really don't. I'll call you again later and give you an update." Mr Quincy had to get on. "Your Stringer's a fighter, so let's keep our fingers crossed he pulls through."

Reg put the phone down and wiped his face with his blue duster. It was obviously touch and go.

Shipwreck

That Thursday Mike unlocked the boat-shed's doors and realised at once something was badly wrong. Ribbons of new sail fabric were flapping in the breeze. He turned on the light and stared in dismay.

The pretty little red sailing boat they had spent so much time on had been brutally shoved off its trestle supports and was lying wrecked against the far wall. Its gaily painted plywood hull was completely broken – a splintered hole the size of a wheelbarrow in it. The ropes and fittings were destroyed, the centreboard housing kicked apart. The half-empty paint tins Mike had so carefully stacked together in the corner had all been prised open and their remaining contents wildly splashed around the place – on the ground, up the walls, on the floor – everywhere.

Mike froze.

"No!" he cried. He had never felt more like swearing in his life. All their hard work! All their pleasure in renovating a perfect little boat only to see it now reduced to matchwood.

"Whatever's the matter? Oh, my *god*!" cried Ernest, arriving a minute later. He stood transfixed.

"Who the… who could have done such a terrible thing?" cried Mike. He held out a warning hand as Ernest went to step forward. "Wait. We shouldn't disturb anything. We have to report this. It's criminal damage."

Ernest was horrified. He pushed up his glasses and rubbed his face hard because he felt like howling. All their effort and all their plans! Their lovely little boat was smashed beyond salvage, even he could see that.

Half an hour later Sergeant Drysdale arrived to view the scene. He had left Pink to man the desk as the constable needed to make some phone calls, and this latest Mayflower outrage was obviously a serious case of breaking, entering and criminal damage.

This here school is becoming a repeat target, thought the sergeant, as he stood staring at the disaster before him.

"Well, it's a particularly vicious sort of mind that's done this, and no mistake," he said, sucking his teeth. "Somebody's really angry, I'd say. Do you know of any disgruntled neighbours? Parents? Kids? Delivery men?"

"No. I don't think so," answered Mrs Clark, who was standing beside him. She couldn't get over the smashed-up dinghy. Why would anyone want to hurt them all so much?

"You say this shed's kept locked? Who knew where you put the key? When did you last check the boat? Well, well. You'd best leave me to it, Mrs Clark. I've got a fingerprint man coming down from Portland directly, if someone'd be kind enough to show him over when he arrives. I'll drop by your office before I leave, for another chat. Is Reg Green about?"

"Yes. He'll be back in a minute."

Sergeant Drysdale grunted. "And where's his clever little dog? He ought to be given a sniff about. Best detective in Banford, Reg's dog."

"He's been under the weather, I'm afraid. The vet, Mr Quincy, brought him back home just before lunch. He'd taken a beating, and eaten something – some poison or other. He's much better now but it was touch and go yesterday, they said."

"Poison? Deliberate? Do they know what?"

"No. And he might have been thrown in the river too, he was soaking wet when Ivy found him. But he's on the mend now, thanks to Mr Quincy. Stringer's a tough little chap."

"Stringer, that's right. Like in those Miss Marple films. Poor little fellow. We could do with a few more good sleuthing noses in this business, I can tell you."

"Well, I'll leave you to your work, Sergeant. Will you have Reg lock up after you please? I'll see you before you go." Skipper nodded her head as if to reassure herself. All this mayhem had to end sometime, didn't it?

"Righty-o, Miss," nodded the policeman.

Greg loses his temper

"You what?" shouted Greg Price. His brother was grinning nastily over his cod and chips. "Why would you do that?"

"Obvious ennit?" Malcolm said with his mouth full. "Bloody dog's a nightmare. We didn't want it barking or biting us did we?"

Ian and Weasel grinned, enjoying their little brother's genuine upset.

"Oughta shot it, really," commented Ian conversationally. He liked guns and had earmarked some of his lead money for a new shotgun. His old air pistol was only good for small animals, like local cats.

Greg punched him round the face and sent him sprawling onto the floor.

"Hey! Calm down, you dipshit! Lay off," cried Weasel.

Greg didn't stop pounding on his brother as he sat on his chest. The other two pulled them apart and threw Greg bodily onto the sofa. He was crying and furiously angry.

"Stringer's a nice little dog! He didn't deserve no rat poison. I thought you was just going to tie him up somewhere. Not poison him and kick his head in, you fuckin' bastards," sobbed Greg. "He might've died!"

"We don't care," shrugged Malcolm. He shoved Greg's head down and thumped him on the ear, making it bleed. "It were your idea to smash up the teachers' poxy little boat. We didn't want the stupid dog sniffing around like it did that time we nicked the lead. We tried tying him up then, and he still got free. Like bloody Houdini. I swear he found my trainers too –

305

the good ones I like to climb drainpipes in. So while you was dealing with the key we give him a bit of old mince Ian'd laced, and then chucked 'im off the bridge. I thought he'd go right under but he must've swum back and crawled home."

Malcolm was growing tired of the subject. "Go and practise your stupid guitar, baby boy. Or set fire to something – that usually takes your mind off shit. Anyway, the stupid dog's still alive. I'll kick its head in better next time."

He and his brothers laughed as they threw their plates in the sink ready for their mother to wash when she returned home from work later. They piled into the other room to watch the football.

Greg wiped his eyes and forced his rage down, down into an icy resolve. He'd show Malcolm and Ian and Weasel. They didn't care about nice little dogs or about anything to do with the things he was beginning to appreciate. Such as school. Or music. Or keeping things clean. Phil was the only one who ever gave a toss – except he was never around now he'd hitched up with Mr Green's daughter. Up until now Greg had managed to show he didn't care about the things his brothers despised. He had fended for himself ever since he could remember, after all. He was well-used to their opinions.

Only now things were suddenly different.

His mind traced back over recent exploits. Greg himself was the one who had done all the groundwork. It was he who had watched and learned the best time to steal the old water-pipes and when best to strip Longmont's roofing. It was he who suggested they 'borrow' Phil's employer's truck in which to shift the stuff. Those little escapades had netted a massive amount of money, just in time for a Christmas share-out. Creeping around school property during half-term, it was Greg who had overheard Mr Denny telling his friends not to invite him to join the poxy little sailing club, which angered Greg so much he had persuaded his brothers to smash the precious dinghy to smithereens. That had been a right laugh at the time, especially as they hung the door keys back in place again like nothing happened. It had been sweet revenge to trash the teachers' boat.

But that was also when Stringer had been half-killed. That particularly vindictive act Greg had known nothing about. Hurting an innocent animal was a step too far in Greg's book and confirmed his revised opinion of his three older brothers. They were nothing but heartless thugs. They were the stupid ones, the losers, the sickoes, not him. They would never have had that lead money if it hadn't been for him, and been content to spend their lives spraying stupid graffiti tags everywhere, ripping branches off newly-planted trees or joy-riding in stolen cars. They were just heavy-handed ruffians with no imagination, no style. No finesse. No ambition. Nobody liked them. No wonder the cops had them squarely in their sights. They might as well have sprayed blue paint all over their jackets, and written 'Whatever it was, I did it. Arrest me' on their own backs. They were beneath contempt.

True to his resentful nature, Greg sat and stewed over various revenge options. He had already blacked both Ian's eyes for wiping paint all over his school uniform, and filched seven quid out of Malcolm's pocket to slide secretly into his mother's handbag, knowing she never had enough money for cigarettes. Tomorrow, in town, when they rode their bikes to the cinema, Greg decided he would sneak out during the intermission and slash Ian's tyres, or throw his bike bodily into the river. That would be some payback for poor old Stringer. Greg genuinely liked the little white dog, and he liked Mr Green too, who always treated him fairly – as if he were a proper bloke, not just some silly kid. School – Mayflower school – was actually alright. He intended to start acting a little less disagreeably and maybe give it more of a chance.

He took out his box of matches and lit one, wondering what his brothers owned that might burn really well.

A tale of Little Boy Blue

"Is it Antibes again for you this year?" Mike asked Ernest when they stopped for a swig of water on their cycle ride. They were high on a ridge ten miles west of the town and could see for miles over the Spring countryside. Vast white clouds scudded across the pale turquoise sky and the air was crystal clear. It was still chilly but now the local floods had disappeared the world looked far more promising. Green stalks furred the corduroy fields and shoals of birds swam on heavenly thermals.

"No, I don't think so. I'd like to explore the British Isles a bit more. Maybe give Cornwall a try. Dora says it's gorgeous."

Mike said, "In parts. The coast is amazing. She seems to have settled into Banford well, doesn't she?"

"A sweet lady," nodded Ernest. "Like Glenda."

"My mum's getting dottier by the day, I'm sorry to say," sighed Mike. Glenda had recently taken to pouring sugar into the washing machine, believing it was soap powder. She had also started to wander about the house at night, which worried Mike immensely.

"Glenda's just old, not batty," comforted Ernest, not knowing the first thing about either women or the elderly. "Heather copes with *her* mum OK, and she's down in Bristol or somewhere."

"Keeping a roof over their heads is one thing. Managing their daily living is a bit more of a challenge," sighed Mike. What would he do when Glenda needed a female carer to tend her? When she needed someone around twenty-four hours a day? What was he to do then? "I suppose there's a home somewhere she could go into. But she'd hate it."

This conversation was all about the topic he was trying to forget for a while, so Mike changed the subject. "How about we take a cycling holiday together next summer, based here in Banford? We could go out every day in a different direction, then sleep in our own beds each night. What do you say?"

Ernest looked at Mike's open smiling face. He looked decidedly windswept, nut brown and lean in his bright yellow nylon cycle-shirt. He knew Mike rode slower than he preferred so that Ernest, in his expensive new gear and on his state-of-the-art bike, could keep up. He also understood Mike's constant worries about his mum and reluctance to be away from home for too long. And he also knew Mike and he could both do with a little fun and relaxation to look forward to after the miserable experience of the boat wreck.

"OK," he agreed, stowing away the possibility of visiting Shane Owen in America for another year. "If you are *that* determined I should get fit, who am I to stand in your way? A local cycling holiday it is. Come on! It's perishing cold but I've got my second wind. Race you home."

They were almost back at Weston when they encountered PC Pink, biking ponderously along the lane from the quarry. They slowed down and pedalled beside him.

"Any news?"

"Well yerse, as a matter of fact," said the policeman, stopping and taking off his helmet to let the breeze flip his sparse hair about. "I was going to call in on your Mrs Clark on my way home and tell her the news. We've made an arrest."

"No!"

"Yerse.

"Is it the boat smashers?"

"Nope. Try again."

"Lead nickers?"

"Coo, they sound uncomfortable. Nope. It's Little Boy Blue. I nabbed the lad what's been tagging the station gates and every other blank wall in the district. Caught him yesterday blue-handed, so to speak." Pink chuckled at his own wit.

Mike and Ernest were enthralled. "What happened? Who is it?"

"One of them Price boys – Ian. Just as I suspected. Sheer chance I nabbed him, though. I was having a go at that shifty creep Barry Gribbins up at the quarry about the truck 'e's riding around in and don't own. Anyway, I'm talking to him yesterday when I spot someone spraying one of these here tags on one of those special stone-moving ve-hickles they have up there. In blue paint. An intruder, bold as you like. It were a gloomy evening so it were sheer luck I spotted the varmint at all. The lad himself were so busy being hartistic he didn't hear me come up behind him. I hooked him by the collar and 'ad him cuffed before he knew what 'it him. Classic it were!" Mr Pink was grinning like a Cheshire cat. "Classic."

Ernest and Mike heartily congratulated the policeman on his quick actions.

"I bet Kevin Smith'll be pleased. He's had to repaint those level crossing gates down at the station twice, he told me. And the others at Weston Station three times."

"Is that right? Well, there's all sorts going on with that Price family now. Social workers, probation service and the like. It's the mother I feel sorry for. Got four juvenile delinquent boys to cope with on 'er own, poor woman. Still, numbers ent any

310

excuse. My mother had seven of us and I turned out a copper, so there you are."

"Indeed. Well, we had better leave you to it, constable. Congratulations again. Good night."

Ernest and Mike rode off, laughing and talking about Pink's story. It was excellent news. Perhaps things would start looking up from now on.

Fire!

Toby saw the smoke miles before he reached his turn off. It billowed upwards with the horrible energy of a rick fire, and for a moment he felt sorry for whoever was trying to contain it. Then, with a jolt, he realised it was coming from his own cottage.

"Oh my god," he cried.

The little MG accelerated, swerved, then slithered to a juddering stop just as the Banford fire engine roared in from the opposite direction, its bell clanging urgently.

"Yours Sir? Anyone inside? Pets? Hydrant anywhere? Well? Pond?"

"Yes, no. A well round the back. That might have something..."

"Don't think our tanks will make much difference to this, Sir, I'm afraid. Looks like it's already taken a good grip. There's no other water source nearby? We'll do our best, but those huge roof timbers have really took a-hold. Take more than this appliance to make a difference now, I'm afraid. Stand well back, please. These old places go up like bloody rockets. Any valuables inside?"

"No. Nothing I can't replace." His various undercover passports, his shirts and suits, his best Borsalino hat. Dammit, that was an expensive hat. Toby stood and watched in misery as the three-hundred-year-old house disintegrated piece by piece with terrible roars and groans, its ancient wood writhing and howling in the conflagration.

"Did you leave anything turned on? Could an ember have spat out onto the carpet?"

"No. Everything was turned off. I had to be in Fenchester for the day, so I made sure I left nothing on. I locked up. I laid the fire after breakfast but I didn't light it."

"Well, I hope you're properly insured. Do you have anywhere you can go tonight, Mr Tremayne? A neighbour?"

Several locals were standing watching in horrified groups on the edge of the common opposite. A tall figure struggling with the leads of two frightened dogs came striding over and tapped him on the arm. It was Gibb Longmont.

"Toby – this is awful. I'm so sorry. Are you hurt?"

He dragged his eyes away from the glare and shook his head. "No, no. I'm fine. I was in Fenchester. Saw the fire as I drove. That's everything I own going up in smoke."

"I'm so sorry. Look, you can come and stay with me for a bit if you like. There's plenty of room."

"I couldn't. You're too kind. Are you sure? I can't think where else to go." He could have gone to the Yeoman or a bed and breakfast, but an old friend taking him in was much more comforting. Much more convenient.

"That's settled then. You come home to my place. We're old pals after all, aren't we? Good that's settled. When you've, er, finished here – rescued what you can, and whatnot. I'll leave the light on."

Toby stood with the firemen and watched for an hour or more. Finally, he climbed back into the MG and trundled slowly down the hill through Oxthorpe and drew up outside Banford

Place. The porch light was glowing a dim welcome and the dogs met him with wagging tails. Dazed and disconsolate he rang the bell. Gibb opened the door and ushered him in.

His cottage continued to smoulder for three days before a heavy rainstorm finally quenched it completely. A fire officer investigated the cause of the blaze and discovered decayed electrics and tinder-dry timbers riddled by worm and vermin, but no evidence of human foul play. The police issued a report which ruled out arson, but even so the insurance company refused Toby's claim on the grounds that he had not maintained the property sufficiently over the years.

New digs

"Look, we must talk about rent. I'll pay you monthly for Erskine's rooms. That's if you are still absolutely sure I won't be in the way."

"No, I've told you – I like having you here," said Lady Longmont firmly. "Erskine's rooms are only sitting empty in the east wing, all closed up. A little rent money, though – if you're quite sure – would be very welcome. I already have a modest amount coming in from Dutch Cottage of course, but having you as a PG would honestly make a huge difference. We get along alright don't we? It will work out fine, don't-you-know. We can be quite separate, but if you want we can meet up for meals. You say you like cooking, I hate it. You don't garden, I do. Although you do claim to know one end of a lawnmower from the other, which is the brute I always have trouble with, so perhaps you could help with that from time to time? Only if you want to, mind. The odd-job man deals with any other major tasks about the place, as and when. I think your living here would suit us both very well."

She forbore saying 'a match made in heaven' as that bordered on the suggestive. Her Paying Guest was what she would call him, if anyone asked. Or if Vern Petty the odd-job man raised one of his hairy eyebrows. She was growing suspicious of Tremayne and wanted to know if her instinct was correct. Keep your enemies close, she reminded herself.

In less than no time Toby quite settled himself into Erskine's old rooms – after all he had no possessions to move. His new domain comprised a first-floor bedroom, sitting room, and a large bathroom all to himself. He had a key to the East Wing's outside door and the MG could be kept under cover in a large lean-to woodshed. The loss of the Holt remained a severe blow, but moving in with Gibb Longmont was a real stroke of luck. She had been on MI5s radar for quite a while.

And Sir Hugo Chivers would be sincerely grateful.

What the police said

Gibb Longmont hadn't been presented with a birthday cake since she was a little girl, her mama not having sanctioned such frivolity after she and her step-brothers had turned six. She was sharing this one with Guy Denny, whose birthday was tomorrow, and she was enjoying herself immensely. Toby had brought her to school in the bumpy little MG to spend the whole afternoon helping out here and there. She had joined in with the Knit Club, taken a small group of first formers to the library, read a story to the kindergarten, buttoned them into their coats at the end of their day, and even chatted with some of the mothers who arrived to collect the little characters at home-time. It was all very safe, very organised, comfortably familiar and huge fun. There was also the return ride home to look forward to. And this orange drizzle cake was simply delicious. Lady Longmont sat in the staffroom feeling happy and content.

"Are you coming to our next bazaar?" enquired May.

"When is that?"

"Tuesday week, lord help us," Jean chipped in. "I'm on the white elephant and I'm looking for a strong volunteer to fend off the hordes."

"Here, I was about to ask her to help me on the cake stall," cried May.

"And I wanted to ask her to help me on the tombola. All those numbers won't stick themselves on things, you know," grumbled Toby. "I'm all thumbs."

"Are you sure you want to help at all, Toby? It's only been a little while since the fire," said Skipper, licking sticky icing off her finger.

"Of course," he answered. "Life goes on, don't-you-know. Gibb has very kindly provided me with a roof over my grizzled head, and I still have a job, thanks to Mayflower. Anyway, there's nothing I like better than a bizarre bazaar."

"I say, how exciting," said Gibb, delighted to be part of it all. "Alright, first I will tape numbers onto things, then I'll help sell unwanted heirlooms on the white elephant. Sorry May – but I'll do cakes next time. Is that alright?"

Everyone agreed, and Gibb thought how pleasant it was to be made to feel part of a real family. They all wanted her and valued her help – they were very sweet. She hadn't been this much in demand since before the war, when her social world had been entirely different.

Guy and Charlie arrived discussing some information on a piece of paper.

"What's that?" enquired May. She budged over as Guy sank down onto the sofa next to her and Charlie found them some refreshment.

"Drysdale's notes. Well, a preliminary report on the boat smash. Comments on what they found, really," explained Guy.

"It says they found a load of fingerprints in all that splashed paint and varnish and on the handle of some old axe that was thrown away in the wilderness bushes. Which is good. And footprints matching those trainers Stringer found. It says it's all to be verified but they believe they will make an early arrest," said Charlie handing Guy some cake. "He's optimistic, that Drysdale."

"What baffles me is how anyone got in there. That boat shed was locked and the only key was on the secret hook," said Heather. "They *must* have known where it was kept."

"Drysdale thinks someone has been watching, saw where we hid the key, did the deed, and then locked up and returned it to the hook, cool as you like. Very calculating, if you ask me," said Charlie.

"Who would do such a thing? It has to be an insider, surely. A child? Not one of Mayflower's," said Ernest, not for the first time.

"Must be. Has to be. Or more than one."

Reg and Stringer came in at that point. Heather vacated her upright chair to let the caretaker sit down more comfortably.

"Hi, boy! Tummy feeling better now?" May scratched Stringer's ears fondly. He wagged his tail and sniffed around the room. He had not checked it over for a while.

"He's fine now. Bit wary of eating anything that isn't kosher and 'anded to him directly by the missis or meself. You'd think he knew someone had slipped him a load of rotgut," said Reg.

"Poor boy," crooned May. "You stick to Doggibix. You don't think he picked up rat poison over at the allotments or somewhere, do you? They say there's somebody killing cats off in the district – for their fur." She was worried about Marigold.

"I wonder if the boat vandals poisoned him," suggested Guy, as the idea occurred to him. "What if they knew he'd be running about the place – an efficient little guard dog – and did it to get him out of their way."

Everyone stared at Stringer who pushed his face into May's skirt to avoid their scrutiny. Reg felt the hair bristling on the back of his neck.

"Devil they did!" he hissed angrily. He couldn't think why he had not linked the two events before. That wasn't like him. He was usually much more astute.

"You know, I bet they did," cried Mike. "Oh poor old Stringer – they could have *killed* him. Attempted dog murder. None of our kids would do that though, surely? God, I want these people brought to justice!" He grew hot and angry again as the idea took root. Taking revenge on the school by smashing a boat was one thing. Trying to kill the school dog was quite another.

Toby Tremayne and Lady Longmont watched the group intently. These people, thought Toby, exhibit the solidarity of a clan under pressure. They were quite unlike his previous teaching colleagues who had had little to do with each other outside work. He saw what Hugo meant about them always rallying round each other.

"I think we had better do our own little investigation into this business," said Mrs Clark meaningfully. "I'm going to have another word with Gregory Price."

Everybody nodded. Greg remained their chief suspect. Probably the police's too.

"First thing Monday morning," suggested Mike.

"First thing," echoed Ernest. "And while you're at it, check his hands for blue paint too."

*   *   *

16.

Longmont Lodge

Greg gets quizzed

"So you know nothing about how Stringer was poisoned, or how the blue paint found its way onto your clothes, or how the school dinghy got smashed? You don't know anything about our missing lead, or Mr Chandler's borrowed truck?" Mrs Clark glared at Greg Price as he stood opposite her. PC Pink sat on an uncomfortable chair to one side, writing in his notebook.

"No."

"No, Mrs Clark," corrected the headmistress, sharply. "I find that very difficult to believe, Gregory. Several people have seen you with a can of blue spray paint."

"Loads of people have that. I ent done nothing. People pick on me and my brothers."

I can't think why, thought Skipper. "Mr Pink says your brother's training shoes were those found by Stringer in the bushes near the Lodge, and their fingerprints were identified as those on the vandalised boat. What have you to say? Did *you* let them in? Did you know where the key was kept?"

Greg shrugged. "Not me," he lied. He was glad now he had worn gloves.

Pink was tired of this pointless procedure. He had quite enough solid evidence to add to the older Prices' charge sheets, without this one's testimony. The three teenagers wouldn't be home in Banford any time soon, thanks to yesterday's court hearing. Malcolm was already back inside and the two others had been sent to two separate juvenile detention centres – where they would be staying for a considerable amount of time. It was only this slippery little perisher Pink couldn't pin anything on. Maybe he had better talk to the mother again. Or go and see if the older boys were willing to rat out the lad. It was a long shot, he knew, as he'd tried this approach before and the Price brothers had always clammed up. Was that 'honour among thieves'? Pink got to his feet, irritated this little eel was going to wriggle free when he was obviously in it up to his neck.

"Well, stay out of trouble from now on," he growled. "Because you got no more chances left, see? You knuckle down and just do your school work because folks is watching you. Me, I'm watching you like an 'awk, Gregory Price. You give me cause to come and find you, you'll also be in borstal before you can say Jack Robinson. Juvenile detention centre. And the judge won't be kind, neither, like Mrs Clark and this 'ere school. You won't be getting no more chances offered you. You'll be far, far away where nobody cares one iota about you. And being locked-up definitely ent where you wanna be, son. You're a smart lad and could have a much sunnier future than your delinquent brothers if you took a bit more effort, so I suggest you start turning yourself around right now, you hear me?"

"Yeah."

"Yes Constable Pink!" he barked, making Mrs Clark and Greg both jump.

"Yes Constable Pink," echoed Greg. Blimey, the old boy was in a right old two-and-eight. But he had a point, even if Greg didn't want to hear it.

St Patrick's Day

"Well everything was green," laughed Skipper. "Everyone was dressed in green too. It was by far the best fun of the year." She was describing St Patrick's Day in America to Jean and May. May thought privately that it all sounded rather brash and vulgar.

"I expect the children enjoyed it," she said. Jean nodded.

"Oh, they did. The teachers too. There were green cookies and leprechaun tricks and jokes. I made sure they knew who St Patrick actually was, of course."

"Of course. Did you mention any other saints?" asked Jean.

"No. It wasn't exactly an Anglo-Saxon community. No one was of Welsh or English heritage. Or Scottish. I suppose a few would learn about saints in church of course." Skipper was a little hazy what American Sunday schools taught. She made a mental note to ask the vicar to mention a few memorable saints next time he took assembly. Children came from everywhere nowadays and families followed all sorts of religions. It would never do to upset anyone or let them feel left out. Perhaps he could bring in a little more about other types of worship too – broaden their horizons.

Miss Fisher and Mrs Hewitt returned to class, and the headmistress drifted back to her study. Electricians needed phoning, and Paul Moore the builder wanted to know when he could come and fix the cracked flat roofs. There were a hundred jobs she should be getting on with, but instead, Mrs Clark watched the last of the children troop in from playtime and went to stand outside on the playground steps in the sunshine.

It was a lovely morning, a perfect Spring day.

Reg had gone for a check up at Dr Legg's. Ivy was clanking pans in the kitchen getting ready for lunch. Everyone was busy. Everyone was elsewhere.

Skipper crossed the blacktop to the iron gate which was swinging in the breeze. Instead of closing it, as she had intended, she treated herself to a short walk down the track and into the wilderness where she and Chloe had once felt like excited explorers. Already there were flowers blooming and sheaves of leaves swaying on fresh green shoots. She inhaled deeply and felt the regenerative power of nature strengthen her. After Apple Alley, she turned deeper into the jungle – up and down the rough ground where once a wartime bomb had landed, and thence to the more open aspect of the low hill topped by a small group of pines and firs. An immensely tall sequoia grew to one side and at its base she was surprised to find Greg Price sitting, his arms round Stringer the school dog. He was sobbing and did not hear her approach.

Stringer wagged his tail at the headmistress. Greg raised his wet face from the dog's neck fur and scowled at her. She sat down beside them and stoked the dog, saying nothing.

After a while Greg sniffed, and brought himself back under control.

"I didn't know Ian and Malcolm fed him mince with poison in it," he croaked. "Honest, I didn't. I give 'em a good bashing for doing it. Poor old Stringer, poor old boy. He was just being a good dog." Tears tumbled down his face again and he was sobbing hard despite his aching ribs and stinging cuts and bruises.

Skip was astonished. She had never expected Greg to display any kind of emotion at all, let alone sob his heart out in front of her. Perhaps there was some genuine empathy under the bravado after all. It didn't do to write a kid off too soon. Or anyone else, she told herself.

"He's fine now, though, aren't you boy? It was a horribly cruel way to treat an animal, you know that. But it wasn't you, Greg, and your brothers are gone away now, aren't they? You'll make it up to Stringer I'm sure. He never holds a grudge. Why don't we walk him back to school and I'll show you the bottom drawer of my cabinet where he and Nicky like to cuddle up together in the Winter. No one else knows about it. I've put a piece of blanket in there you might be able to arrange a bit better for him. I'm not much good at making beds. It's the cutest thing, seeing them snuggled up together."

Greg looked at her, puzzled. She hadn't said a word about him missing lessons, or not coming when the whistle went, or crying, or apologising or anything. She hadn't told him off. She hadn't even been horrified at him admitting he had a hand in Stringer's attempted killing. She was once again reaching out to him.

He smiled a perfectly pleasant smile at her and ruffled the dog's ears as Stringer trotted along beside him on the walk back.

"It's funny, a dog and a cat liking each other," he commented.

"It is, you're right. But I suppose friends come in different disguises."

This was not something Greg had ever thought about. He didn't have any proper friends, not outside Ian and Weasel anyway. "I could maybe take that blanket out and give it a shake for you if you want," he said. "It could probably do with a fluff up."

"Thank you, that would be great. Mmm, I wonder what's for lunch?"

Back again

Sir Hugo stepped off the Banford train. Bunting was there to meet him again for the short drive home. Bunting nodded to Kevin the porter, who swung Sir Hugo's suitcases into the boot of the Rolls. Paper money changed hands.

"Your latest signal was somewhat confusing," said Hugo mildly to his driver as he settled himself into the passenger seat. "What did you mean by it?"

Bunting shifted slightly as he drove.

"Possible snooper, Sir. I discussed it with Mr Tremayne and Green."

"Where?"

"Dutch Cottage. The outhouse we used. I noticed someone had been through the wet grass beside the driveway last week, so I took a quiet look. The padlock on the door was turned around the wrong way and I had the distinct impression the room had been turned over."

Bunting's instincts were sound and Hugo trusted them. If he said someone had been there, they had.

"Could it have been the new renter? That Dr Legg woman? Did the dog find anything?"

"Dog wasn't available to investigate. No, it wasn't the doctor. She's not the least curious in outbuildings, I'm pleased to say, and always off working somewhere."

"So the dog was out of action?"

"Yes. I sent what I knew in that signal. Very unfortunate for us, the dog being taken sick. Nothing else noted by Bick or Mr Tremayne that I could see. Nothing further to report, Sir."

"I'll take a gander myself later on. I'm back for the rest of the year, now."

"Yes Sir." Bunting changed gear. "That's a relief to us all."

"General news?"

"Mr Tremayne's well-embedded, full-time at the school and moved in with her ladyship. Mr Green's much better, pretty-much up to speed I'd say. Milady seems to be behaving – we maintain a joint watch on her, as instructed. School's still struggling financially with the cost of renovations. Three young hooligans have been sent away to reform school. No new local watchers have been recruited as yet."

"Hmm, that's a pity. Is my son aware I'm coming home today?"

"No Sir. I thought you might like to surprise him."

"Hmm," Hugo sighed.

Here he was, home again, picking up the familiar Banford reins. Once more becoming retired local gentry, the eminent lawyer, the chairman of the school governors. The traveller, the sophisticate. Here he was, the keeper of secrets – the man in charge.

Matches

For once in a very long while, Mayflower was winning. Mrs Elbridge, from Dane Street Primary, was exasperated with her girls.

"Why on earth did you pass that to Jenny?" she shrieked at Paula. "Couldn't you see she was covered?"

Paula burst into tears. Her team mates threw their arms around her and whispered malign opinions of their headmistress to each other.

"Oh come on, girls. Now that's time up! Alright, well never mind. Over here, please."

Jean Hewitt kept quiet, but she felt rather smug. It wasn't often Mayflower came out on top. She gathered her netball team together too.

"Well done, everybody!" she cried. "Time to go in. Three cheers for Dane Street!"

The girls trooped into the cloakroom known as the Great Aunt to change out of their games kit while the boys finished off their football and clomped slowly in from the field in their soccer boots. Their match had been a draw, which satisfied both sides.

Mr Denny had suggested to Greg Price that he come and help him referee the game that afternoon. The boy had been at home for a couple of days nursing the bruised ribs and other wounds his heavy-handed brothers had recently left him with. His mum had stayed two days off work too, which had been an unexpected treat for Greg. But he was able to return to school on Friday, when Guy had welcomed the lad's much subdued behaviour with relief. They had made it through an entire schoolday without a head-to-head, which Guy hoped was the shape of things to come, and was why he had made the refereeing offer.

Greg was more delighted to be asked to help than he let on. He was not willing to publicly articulate his current feelings of remorse over Stringer's poisoning, but he did now feel genuinely sorry about his part in the boat smash-up, and the lead theft.

He was glad to be back at school – an emotion that surprised him. Home, without his brothers, wasn't all that much fun as now the spotlight fell only on him. Once his mother had recovered from her shock and rage at Malcom, Ian and Weasel being carted away for good, she had grudgingly agreed to take Greg to the surgery for a check-over. The doctor explained that Ian's fists had split something in Greg's ear, a rib was cracked, and there was an actual shoe-print on her son's left arm. His mum had feigned horror, although in truth she had seen it all before and done nothing. She bought him chicken and chips on the way home and made him tell her everything, from the very beginning. She was upset with all her boys, Greg could see that, but strangely she seemed just as cross about him having to stay home a few days as about the police coming round. She sent him straight off to bed, declaring she wanted some peace and quiet. There were never any cuddles or soothing words of comfort in the Price household, so Greg wasn't surprised. It had always been hard to figure out what really mattered to his mother. Home was probably just as boring to her as it was to him. At least Mr Denny was trying to be nice.

He always starts every day being nice, remembered Greg. It's me that mucks it up.

He did his best to help referee the game properly, although running up and down rapidly grew very painful. Mr Denny smiled and nodded at him when the match ended and they were walking in. He came over and asked how he felt.

"I'm alright. A bit tired."

"Well, try to stay out of mischief and get some rest this weekend, OK? You did well today. You didn't give up even though it was hard. Maybe next match, if you're fit, we might let you play. What do you think?"

"Really?" Greg hardly knew whether to trust this offer. "If I don't fu… mess up again, you mean?"

"Yeah. If you don't mess up. I bet you're pretty quick midfield."

Changes afoot

At the regular Monday staff meeting Skip brought up a matter she had been brooding on for some time. It wasn't on her 'Absolutely Totally Must Do Without Fail' list, but it was important.

"How do you feel about fazing out some of our uniform requirements next year?" she asked tentatively.

Silence met that question, then Betty nodded her head.

"Well, I think that's a brilliant idea. Get rid of some of those wretched buttons. My babies have so much trouble with buttons and laces and toggles and zippers."

"Well, I wasn't just thinking buttons. I've been looking at our uniform list and comparing what our kids wear with other schools. We're a bit outdated."

"Still be green and gold, though?" asked Charlie. He liked the current uniform immensely and did not want the Mayflower kids to dress the same as every other school. He believed the children liked their school colours, and took pride in how they looked.

"Oh yes. Bottle green, gold and the neutral grey, stays. But I was hoping we need no longer insist on blazers and caps and panamas. No one wears those things anymore. Times have changed. Shorts are shorter – hemlines are too."

"But you don't want mini skirts do you?"

"No, maybe not. But a little bit shorter wouldn't hurt. Then the girls could wear tights with their pinafores in winter. Not trousers, obviously, but maybe their ties could go. Duffle coats and parkas are cheaper than school outfitters' specialised raincoats. The kids don't really need blazers do they? What do you think – in principle?" Skip had that zealot light in her eye they knew so well.

"Mmm. Can we have some time to take a look at your lists and make suggestions?" asked Jean cautiously. "Then talk about it a little more?" It was as well not to jump in with a downright No when it came to Skipper and her ideas.

"Sure," said Skip, a little grumpily. They didn't like the idea at all, she could see that.

"Jolly good," said Toby. Let's move rapidly on, he thought. "Now then, if there's nothing else, I'd like to propose a toast to Guy Denny for making it through to last Friday and all day today without sending Greg Price out of the classroom once. Here's to you, Guy!"

Forces of nature

Mrs Elbows was a formidable woman at any jumble sale, even when she wasn't fighting her way through a mob of Mayflower mothers. There was nothing she liked better than to intimidate stall-holders into giving her a bargain. She was over six foot tall and made use of every angled bone in her body to work her way determinedly forwards. She would have made a good commando. At the school's Easter bazaar she had seed potatoes on her mind.

Reg saw her coming and was prepared. He had bagged up some chitted potatoes for sale, and had kept the largest to one side for her.

"Spuds?" he offered loudly, temptingly wagging the bag up and down.

"How much?" growled Mrs Elbows.

"20p take 'em or leave 'em. I ent arguing."

"Daylight robbery. Give you ten."

Reg held the bag up higher and called out, "Chitted spuds, only 25p," in a loud voice. "Biggest bag o' the afternoon."

Right on cue, Charlie and Toby made as if to jostle for the privilege of buying them, digging in their pockets for cash. Mrs Elbows hurriedly grabbed the bag and forked over her 20p. She barged Toby and Charlie roughly aside in her hasty escape, grinning with the glee of one who has scooped the best deal of the day.

The three men couldn't help laughing.

"Just like you said, Reg," Charlie chuckled. "She's a force of nature!"

"Couldn't resist, could she?" said Toby, wiping his eyes.

"Oh, that were good," sighed Reg. "Best laugh all year. And she'll 'ave a good main crop of King Edwards too, come summer."

May and her band of helpers were very proud of their knitting stall. Not only were there plenty of woolly items for sale but also several boxes of oddments kindly supplied by a local haberdasher's shop that was closing down. Fiona Tuttle had brought them in. She and May were soon selling ribbons and lace as fast as they could measure and cut each length.

Dora and Jean rapidly sold out of homemade cakes, as usual. These always disappeared in the first half-hour, so the ladies were soon free to spend their way around the rest of the bazaar and thoroughly enjoy themselves. Jean had found a walking guide to Amsterdam she was pleased with, as next summer she would be flying over to attend John and Lisa's wedding. Dora's treasure was a little stool she could use in her garden. It could be knelt comfortably on one way, or sat on when turned upside down. It was going to make weeding so much easier.

Mrs Clark looked at the pennies rolling in and was guiltily pleased the room was so busy. This will help with our petty cash situation, she thought. Maybe we will even be able to afford that theatre group again after all.

Stringer, sitting in a quiet corner of the stage away from the hustle and bustle, didn't budge when Greg slid down onto the floor beside him.

"Hello, mate," whispered Greg. The dog lay his head on Greg's leg and licked his hand a little. Greg thought he was going to burst, he was so grateful Stringer wasn't holding a grudge.

"He likes you," commented Jimmy Birch, sitting down beside them. Miss Fisher had bought him a piece of flapjack, which Jimmy now carefully split into three. He handed Greg one piece. Stringer gulped his portion and wagged his tail.

"Thanks, Shrimp," said Greg. He was making a real effort not to say the first sarcastic thing that came into his head.

"I wish Miss Fisher was my real grandma," continued Jimmy on a familiar theme. "She give me this. It's what grandmas do."

Greg wouldn't know. His relatives didn't go around handing out cake or anything else for free. They would expect something in return. He studied Jimmy's dormouse face with its big eyes and decided the kid was tougher than he looked.

"Yeah, I 'spec' so." He stroked Stringer's head and patted funny little Jim on the back. No need to say any more was there? Life wasn't so bad, some days.

Breaking up for Easter

Rev Bill had gone to the trouble of having Mayflower's usual end of term hymns and prayers printed on individual service sheets this year. By so doing he hoped there might be less wear and tear on St Andrew's elderly hymn books. The sheets would be considerably cheaper to replace and much more modern-looking. He was already planning further miscellanies for baptisms, Christmas and Harvest Festival. He smiled to himself, feeling up-to-date and efficient. 'There is a Green Hill', 'Ride On! Ride On in Majesty', 'Praise to the Holiest in the Height'. The Mayflower School song. 'God be in my Head'. The vicar had included all the school favourites for today's service. June and he had spent all yesterday afternoon folding and stapling the pages into pamphlets.

The vicar watched the children troop in quietly for their end of term service, and let his mind dart around. It was lovely to have such a full church choir now, he thought, especially as Mr Chivers was also on hand as a baritone and kept the choristers in order. Mayflower was doing St Andrew's proud. Mr Tuttle was a very accomplished organist and a jolly sort of man to have about. He wished Mr Paton would also agree to join the choir and add a little more depth to the men's side, but he had so far refused all entreaties. Maybe that new Mr Tremayne would turn out to be a singer. Glancing down the nave, Bill noticed Sir Hugo had returned and was sitting beside Mrs Clark. They were a pleasantly reliable pair of church-goers. It was such a pity poor Mrs Shaw was no longer living in Banford. Losing both Max and Chloe had come as a real blow. However, the recent arrival of splendid Dr Legg, today in a very colourful outfit, was certainly a bonus. She was a wonderfully uninhibited singer. Maybe she could be prevailed upon to give a solo in that majestic alto of hers one day. Bill hoped the narrow pew would accommodate her generous proportions – his sermon had better be brief.

June gave her husband a nudge and he stood up.

The new service papers were a hit. Lizzie Timms and chubby little Zoe Smith sang 'Amazing Grace' together in harmony, causing Dora York to rummage in her handbag for a handkerchief. Today no one had to be hurried out to the vestry toilet and nobody dropped marbles down the heating-pipe grating. It all went perfectly well.

"Your birthday is on Easter Day, isn't it Reg?" said Rev Bill, as the crowd dispersed afterwards.

"Fancy you remembering that," chuckled Ivy.

"It's because I look like a flippin' egg these days," Reg suggested, patting his tummy. "You feed me too well, old lady."

"Actually, I think of you as risen again, Reg, since that hip replacement," Bill replied. "I say – he's risen again, Doctor!"

"Hallelujah, Vicar!" Dr Legg called back with a grin. "But miracles gotta be worked at, don't they Mr Green? Maintenance isn't easy, you know. It takes diligence."

It certainly does, thought Mrs Clark, overhearing. Maintaining what you'd fought long and hard for was a huge part of everyday happiness whichever way you looked at it, and it could be quite costly.

A Sunday stroll

On Easter Sunday – his birthday morning – Reg took the dog for a walk around the block, and thought about all that had happened since his last birthday. It was sad that one part of his skeleton hadn't made it through, but he was more than thankful for his new metal hip replacement. He felt rejuvenated, like the vicar said, and he promised himself he would maintain this new found flexibility.

I'm doing alright, he told himself. Still got the missis. The kids are grown up and working, the dog's pulled through. Got a roof over me head, and enough money to stay afloat. Still doing me best for the Firm, and me cover's not blown. Still got me wits. Yes, life's alright.

There had been setbacks, of course. The school's peace and calm seemed to have vanished ever since Mr Shaw died – as if some lucky charm had been snatched away. Since then, there had been that horrible inspection business, the vandalism, poisoning, money issues, and desertion. Snow, floods and fires. Even his mate Len was going through the mill this year.

Reg looked up at the blue sky shining through the trees. Well, at least the weather was finally improving.

"Hello there, Mr Green," said the cheery voice of Toby Tremayne.

"Good morning, Sir," he answered. "Come for a decko at the primroses?"

"What's that? Oh yes. Very nice. Funny how Nature decides everything should first be yellow and blue, then pink and purple. I've often wondered about it." Toby looked as if he had never thought about any such thing until that exact moment, but Reg let it pass.

"Hello, Stringer. How are you feeling today? No after effects? Such a good boy." Toby patted Stringer. He liked dogs and this one was particularly appealing.

"You all settled in with her ladyship?"

"I am. I knew her and her brother back in the day, you know, so its quite easy to fit back in again. I have Erskine's old quarters, which are proving unexpectedly interesting. I don't think she's been in there much since he passed away in 1945. Didn't want to disturb his memory, or something. I'm giving the place a very thorough going over, as you can imagine. I have already found a couple of items Sir Hugo will be interested in."

Aha, thought Reg. That's good.

"Relevant to our current concerns, do you think?"

"I think so, yes."

The two unlikely secret agents strolled along together as the Easter church bells began their joyful peals. New life, resurrection, joy and forgiveness, they announced. Salvation is today in the competent hands of MI5 and MI6.

"How's our latest bed and breakfast coming along?" asked Toby.

"Doin' alright. Bunting's gettin' it ship-shape. I've finished installing the mikes."

"And the automatic recorders?"

"In the sealed part of the back bedroom's built-in wardrobe. The strongest mike's hidden in the light fitting in the sitting room directly below. I'll finish off the customers' secure bedroom this art'noon. You'll never know the whole place is bugged."

"Well it looks very nice and ordinary from the outside. Secluded. Are you intending to keep the front lawn cut? Are there lights on time-switches?" Toby approved of Reg Green. He was a solidly reliable fellow and wasn't likely to skimp details, even if he was working for the foreign branch of the service.

"Bunting's seeing to the timers as we speak, Sir. It'll be better, 'avin' him so 'andy next door to this place. The kitchen window of his flat overlooks the front, a nice and discreet little observation post. Sir Hugo says he's quite satisfied."

"Good, good." Toby nodded. He looked up at the treetops bursting with tiny fresh green leaves.

"Lovely morning, isn't it? Well, I'll leave you to it. A very happy Easter to you and Mrs Green. I'd better toddle off home or milady will have overcooked the roast lamb."

He raised his new Borsalino hat and strode off.

"Come on, dog," Reg said. "Take yer 'ead out of that perishing mole 'ill and let's go find Ivy, shall we? Terry's coming for lunch – and Pat and her feller – so we'd better make sure you've washed yer paws and brushed yer 'air or there'll be trouble. And we've had quite enough trouble for now, ent we?"

* * *

17.

Playtime

Pinch, punch

Reg's hope of better times unfortunately went unheard by Fate.

"Pinch punch, white rabbits, happy birthday!" cried Ben Nesbit, as he brought his wife, Betty, her breakfast in bed. He snuggled in beside her and helped himself to a piece of the toast and marmalade he had made.

"Mmmm, lovely. Thank you darling." She gave him a sticky kiss on the cheek. "I thought you might have April Fooled me with no breakfast at all."

"No, that's lunch," Ben said.

She tapped him on the head with her egg spoon. Hades, the Jack Russell, jumped on the bed hoping for a few tasty titbits. Bess, the eldest of their three sheepdogs, also ambled in and sat grinning beside Ben. He scratched her ears affectionately.

"What time are the girls arriving?" he asked.

"Mary and Jill said about three, and Carolyn, with her new fellow Nigel, about four." The Nesbit's three girls were coming for tea as usual on their mum's birthday. Only the youngest had a man in tow today, which meant more cake for Ben, the way he looked at it.

"Did you feed Binky?" Binky was the cat. She mostly slept in the woodshed, preferring the outdoor life to a domesticity that included several annoying dogs.

"She hasn't touched her food again. I chucked the last lot out and put some more down for her. I haven't seen her for ages." This was unusual, as Binky was a creature of habit.

Betty searched for the tabby later on, but still couldn't find her. Maybe Binky had her eye on a mouse-hole somewhere, but she didn't respond to calling her name or tapping her bowl. Maybe she had got locked in someone's shed. Maybe she was caught in a trap somewhere. It was a very worrying mystery.

The afternoon tea party was a big success. Mary and Jill brought plants for Betty's garden and Carolyn some fancy chocolates. Nigel, the new boyfriend, was a little overwhelmed by the family hen coop. Ben could see him watching the women round-eyed as they chattered about this and that. He finally took pity on the lad and suggested a short walk over the fields to check his fences. It was a beautiful evening, cold and fresh but clear. Bess, Fly, Hades and Luther – the four dogs – loped along in a pack beside the men, happy to be scaring small furry wild creatures out of their complacency.

"Fly! Go down on the lower path," Ben instructed the smartest dog. Paths ran parallel above and below one of the thickets and Ben didn't want to get in too much of a muddy mess this evening. Hades sprang off too, his little person bouncing like a rubber ball through the brushwood. Nigel picked his way carefully. The countryside seemed terribly damp and dirty.

There was a sudden commotion as Fly returned with her mouth full. She dropped a muddy, furry lump at Ben's feet. Nigel recoiled in horror.

"Oh no! It's Binky!" cried Ben in dismay. He turned the stiff little corpse over gently with his boot. The cat had been dead for quite some time. It was stiff and maggot-ridden. The cat had obviously been shot by an airgun. Nigel felt his stomach flip over when he saw the sightless eyes.

Ben pulled out his handkerchief and wrapped the little body up as best he could, and carried their pet home. Betty and the girls sobbed and cried over it before burying their furry friend in a quiet place near the hornbeam hedge where she had once lain in wait for birds.

It was a horrible birthday.

"Who would do such a beastly thing?" sobbed Betty. "Binky never could catch another living thing. She just liked to watch and prowl around the place."

Ben returned to the scene of the cat-murder the next day on his way to his pheasant pens. He poked carefully about, peering at this and that. He was about to jump back into his jeep when he saw PC Pink walking by on the high road. The constable was pushing his bicycle, as it had another flat tyre. Ben offered to fix it for him.

"So, your moggie's another one been shot, has it?" Pink was grateful for the bike help. He listened closely to Ben's tale of woe.

"Yeah. She was a dear old thing – couldn't catch a mouse, of course. Must have been quite a while ago, I'd say. I think it must have been a poacher mistook her for vermin or some kid taking pot-shots with an air gun. They probably saw a furry target and pretended to be on a tiger hunt. I'd like to catch the little bastard."

Pink nodded sympathetically, watching Ben as he mended his puncture. Pets brought out the best, and the worst, in people. "Several other cats have been shot at recently. Dogs too. You heard about Reg Cook's dog Stringer getting poisoned? Len Kirk's eldest 'ad two white rabbits in a cage taken out and killed – shot, same as yours. They never heard a thing. Upset the kiddie."

"It would."

"I'm on my way out to Christmas Farm. Dawkins says he thinks his ewes are being worried. He dunno what by. Could be a rogue dog, could be a tramp. I think your cat was most likely shot by one of those older Price kids, before they were finally locked up, you know. One of them was airgun mad."

The Nesbits' South Lodge, the Kirks' Abbey Farm, and the Dawkins' Christmas Farm were all part of Lord Dexter's estate and bordered his extensive parkland. Ben thought about the sheep worrying. That was a serious business, as ewes could abort their lambs when harassed by dogs. His own animals were well-trained and obedient, but it only took one to run amok and the flock would be ruined. And he couldn't have his birds disturbed. He would increase his patrols.

"Chief Constable's going to have to get me one of them panda cars, or a moped if he wants Banford's crime rate to fall, you know. Getting around on this heavy old bicycle ent the speediest or most efficient mode of transport. This year it's been ruddy ridiculous."

Ben handed back the bike. "There you are, Mr Pink. All done. Look, I'll double my patrols around here, and take all the dogs with me. I daresay we'll catch any sheep worriers or cat killers pretty soon."

Pink nodded, although he was not convinced. He swung his leg over the crossbar. "Much obliged to you, Ben. Give me a bell if there's anything else you think I should know about, won't you? But if you call and get that twerpy new cadet of ours on the blower, make sure he writes any message down. Rememberin' important information ent one of his strengths. And tek extra care around your fields and woods when you're out. If there's trespassers with loaded guns knocking about we don't want any more corpses on our hands."

Toby and Hugo discuss operations

Toby's rooms at Banford Place were spacious, but still contained all Erskine's boyhood and wartime clutter. There were too many chairs and too many little tables for Tremayne's taste, which (had anyone asked) inclined more towards whitewashed walls and Persian rugs. However, the large bed was comfortable enough and there was a wide desk under the window next to a good reading chair and a standard lamp. The bookshelves held 'boy's own' authors – Marryat, Johns, Buchan, Wells, Haggard and Henty, but also disturbing evidence of a strong interest in fascism.

Toby meticulously examined everything. He took down each book and pamphlet and inspected it from cover to cover, then checked the space it had occupied before returning it with precision. He also examined the writing desk and every stick of the ugly furniture, running his sensitive fingers over the surfaces seeking anomalies in the mouldings that might signify hidden cavities. He took apart lamps and light fittings checking for hiding places, pushed at the panelling, unscrewed taps, shone lights into cobwebby crevices and up the chimney. Being thorough, professional, and perfectly patient, this all took a long time, but by the end he had discovered several interesting items of historical relevance. A box of letters from a known Nazi sympathiser, and another from a British government minister. There were ten postcards from Holland, and two well-thumbed notebooks full of diagrams and strings of letters. There was a whole page of notes recorded after a private meeting with three royal personages. His most important discovery was a children's book on animals which contained various underlined words and phrases. He was convinced this would have been used as a code book, a cipher key, meant to unlock enemy communications. It had been 'A gift from her mother to Edwardia Lambert in 1915 on the occasion of her tenth birthday'.

When he could discover no more, Toby phoned Sir Hugo who strolled round for a chat.

"You've done well," Hugo congratulated him on the treasure trove.

Toby smiled and nodded. "Quite a haul isn't it? Erskine ought to have destroyed all this immediately he realised the game was up, silly fool. I don't think Gibb has any idea such sensitive items were still in here or she would never have let me have the rooms. Do you want to look things over or shall I take them directly to the archives?" He referred to a section of the registry that stored such material.

"Mmm, no, I will. I'd like to wave a few under the old girl's nose first, before they disappear, if you don't mind," Hugo said. "Remind her of one or two home truths. Keep her focused."

"Do you think that's still necessary? She seems to me to understand her position well enough. She's genuinely enjoying the school and, as far as I can ascertain, is not in touch with any undesirables. She hasn't quite made the connection between the two of us yet of course, although she will figure it out soon, I'm sure. Something of a shock for her when she finally twigs. But she was the one who suggested I move in."

"You're being a little generous. Gibb Longmont's never done anything without a hidden motive since the day she was born. She's a crusted-over cesspit, in my view," grunted Hugo, waxing lyrical. "I don't trust her an inch. Time and tide mean nothing to her. She revolves in a circle, coming back and back to whatever went before. I'd lay good money on those youthful ideals she and her benighted brother espoused being still very much alive underneath that dotty old aristocratic façade she affects. A traitor stays a traitor, Toby. Erskine Lambert turned out to be an especially nasty little fascist shit, and I certainly don't trust his horse-faced sister now. She was always twice as underhanded as he was and twice as smart. Emotional bloody creatures, women – always have love as their bottom line."

Toby considered that generalisation as inaccurate as it was misogynistic, but he was more interested in other things, so he didn't argue. It was not as if Gibb would have her matrimonial eye set on him. As requested and required, he was watching her closely to ensure she did nothing to imperil important future covert activities. Toby saw himself as Banford's guard dog, constantly sniffing around like Stringer, checking potential weak spots and only getting more involved if he had to.

"You're nicely ensconced in the deputy's office at school, I hear," Hugo continued. "Quick work."

"Yes. That's going rather well. I can remain on site in the deputy's study and help out as needed. I've dropped teaching at the other school now, so I'm full-time. Mrs Clark has been finding this year jolly tough you know, especially without you or the American there to help."

"It was unfortunate I hadn't had to disappear for half of it. Still, I'm back now."

"I'd say everything's pretty much on track."

"But treading water. My team took a hell of a pasting in the Summer, as you are aware. Your – our – suspected red sleeper, damn him, more than proved his ability to evade us, but whether he's still actively live we won't know until we dangle a little fresh bait. We need to pick him up, fast, Toby. Who knows how long he's been here, lying like some pike in a millpond awaiting his chance. Head office hasn't come up with any helpful new information on him, which I find worrying. They have a couple of possible suspects but nothing definite." Hugo frowned with irritation.

"What do you want to do?"

"Well once our traffic resumes, and with your help, we'll flush him out and nab the bastard."

"And if he calls in a shooter, like he did before?"

Hugo thought that question did not require an answer.

"He's good, I'll give him that," added Toby.

That peeved Sir Hugo. "You don't have to rub it in – I know. Don't forget that even *with* him around we've managed to hand several guests on successfully, in both directions. Only now our impatient American cousins are breathing down our necks and threatening to pull the plug if they don't receive everything they're paying for pretty soon. The clock's ticking."

Toby re-crossed his legs and tilted his head. This was going well. "How did the opposition pinpoint Banford originally do you suppose?" he asked mildly. "I mean, it's a bit off the beaten track."

Hugo scowled. "Well if I knew that…"

"Best guess?"

"Three possibilities, as I see it. A high-up insider came across our plan in Whitehall and tracked it to here. Or Moscow's spotted where I had 'retired' to and followed me, running across

344

the op by chance. Or some home-grown sympathiser, such as milady here, tipped them off. My money's on the latter. This country has lamentable levels of rural scrutiny."

Toby nodded. His branch. He was not deluded about its responsibility in all this. "And so they slid their sleeper in."

"Yes."

This was Toby's conclusion too. "We need to redouble our efforts to find and eliminate this sleeper, if our joint op is to start up again and stand any chance of success. Matter of urgency."

"Yes, indeed. Time's pressing," Hugo said. So were the Yanks.

"I'd say we'd do well to acquire fresh watchers, as a matter of urgency. This is a tricky rural patch with plenty of places to hide. Your team know how to manage the house, and have it prepared. We can start things rolling slowly again. But as we still don't know precisely where the local danger lies, we must cover a huge amount of ground. If the opposition send in another shooter to silence their defector before he can be of any use to us, we're both screwed."

Hugo nodded again. He was well-aware of the situation and had had quite enough of being cross-examined. He didn't appreciate Tremayne explaining the finer points of egg-sucking. "I know. Plenty of open land and far too many unused out-buildings round here. I say we keep your landlady tied up with a bag over her head for now and increase surveillance to the maximum. Let's let it be known we have re-opened for business and see what transpires."

Toby stood up and stretched. Outside the sun was shining.

"Between the two of us, and Reg and the Buntings, we should be able to flush your sleeper out quick enough now, old man. Try not to worry. I'll recruit the lookouts, leave that to me. Oh, and do we completely trust the headmistress?"

Hugo put on his coat. "You'd have a job fitting Susan Clark up as our sleeper."

"D'you think so? She's an odd one, but I like her. Not as straightforward as she looks if you ask me. We have a great deal in common. Maybe I'll propose wedlock."

Hugo ignored this nonsense and rubbed his sleeve along his hat brim.

"Church Road is ready," he said. "Green and Bunting are just tidying up." He peered around the room they were standing in, and grinned. "Bunting took care of this place too, one afternoon while milady was at some school knitting club or other. Did you know? Well, tell me how you get on recruiting your snoops. Run them past the team first so we can add our four-penny-worth on suitability, if you would." Hugo picked up the innocuous plastic supermarket bag full of Toby's treasure. "I'll see this reaches the archives. Catch you at the Yeoman one evening."

Toby saw him out. He stood watching as Hugo strode away down the lane, then went to chat with Lady Edwardia Longmont, who was endeavouring to tie back a very wayward jasmine on the side terrace.

Fight! Fight!

Len Kirk bumped slap-bang into his rival Dick Perry coming out of the Post Office in Oxthorpe the Saturday after Easter. Len had taken a walk into the village with Jenny and Dale, his two oldest children, to buy ice cream. Brenda was at home with the baby, Rosamund. Before he could stop himself, Len shoved Dick to the ground.

"You swine!" he yelled, scaring the children. "Leave my bloody wife alone, you little… "

"Daddy!" cried Jenny.

Dale began wailing. He didn't like his dad being cross and making another grown-up fall over. There was blood on the man's face where Daddy had hit him. He clutched Len's trouser leg and hung on for dear life.

Dick Perry twisted away and stood up. He was a small, wiry man with a white pointed beard who favoured flat caps and corduroy jackets. He picked up his fallen shopping bag and snarled at Len. A horrified passer-by shook her fist at the attacker and called Len a bully. Out came the postmaster who pushed Len back against the doorpost and held him there while Dick scuttled away.

"Don't come here manhandling my customers, Leonard Kirk. You sober up and keep yer hands to yerself. You've made your little 'uns cry, so you have. For shame! They shouldn't have to witness you tekking out your bad temper on anyone. Be off home 'fore I phone the police," he cried.

Jenny and Dale gripped each other's hands and did not know what to do. They had been hoping for a nice walk with their dad, but all they got was him swearing and making a scene. Both children wished they had stayed at home.

"Come on," growled Len. "Stop that noise. I ent coming to this shop again. Nothing but bloody nosey parkers. Get out of my way, old woman."

Len grabbed the children's wrists and barged past Mrs Bicknell, who had been passing by after having tea with a friend in Oxthorpe. She was outraged at the violence and upset for the children. She nodded to Jenny and whispered, "Go on now, lovey. Take your dad 'ome."

Jenny took the hint and tugged Len's hand, leading him back up the lane the way they had come. Whatever would mum say?

Summer Term begins

"I like the Summer term best," commented Heather as she hurried in and sat down. She was fidgety, worried about her mother who wasn't doing at all well in her old people's home. Parents were such a responsibility.

The teachers were meeting after the Easter break in the gym hall around a block of lunch tables positioned so as to catch the afternoon sunlight. Reg had opened the french doors to encourage some fresh air to waft in and dispel the lingering odour of spam fritters. They sat discussing Skipper's brief agenda. Cash-flow still seemed to be her top concern, closely followed by yet another imperative brought up by the inspection – in-service teacher training.

"Why do we need more training?" Heather grumbled. "We've all got teaching certificates or degrees. They're acceptable in any school, aren't they?"

"I haven't," Miss Fisher reminded her. "I have a diploma, although I have absolutely no notion as to where I might actually have put it."

Skipper reassured them. "All your basic credentials are fine. But the inspectors say I ought to offer you the chance to attend some short courses to update your knowledge on, say, modern reading techniques or mathematics teaching, or something else. Modern science, say. But I can't find any suitable courses being run anywhere nearer than the next county. Our LEA doesn't offer any. I suppose I could look at the university offerings in Fenchester if anyone wanted to travel down there to night school once a week after work. Or do they call it evening classes nowadays? They wouldn't be free, of course."

"Would attendance give us extra certification?"

"No."

"Or give us credit towards a higher degree?"

"No."

"Or a higher salary?"

"No."

"Then why bother?"

"Fair point. I personally don't see that any of you need any additional training in order to continue the great job you're doing anyway."

Sandi had been quietly thinking about all of this. She rarely spoke at staff meetings but something occurred to her today.

"I suppose we couldn't offer to *run* some classes, could we? People could come here and might even pay us." She looked around.

"What – design and run something in the holidays, you mean? Well, that's a thought." Mike nodded. It was a bright idea. "We could even host a visiting expert, couldn't we?"

"Maybe. After school, or on a Saturday might work. We could easily run a class on helping struggling readers, for example," Sandi said.

"I could give advice on getting the most from your school library," offered Ernest, quickly seeing the benefits in the idea. "Mr Alexander over at the Priory might help me."

"How about a course on music teaching? Or gardening? Or improving PE skills with the five year olds?" Charlie was also eager to begin.

"Hey, steady on!" laughed Mrs Clark. She beamed at them, amused that they were the eager beavers for once and she the one trying to put the brakes on. "I'll have to have a think and sit down with Peggy to go through the possible costings. I don't want to turn us into a teacher training college."

May Fisher glanced at Jean, whose chin was tucked back in a rather Victorian way.

"We could possibly try *one* short course first, and see how that goes, couldn't we?" she suggested cautiously.

Charlie took the hint. It was no good getting carried away.

"That's right. No use starting something we can't sustain or that would need too much time spending on it, is there? Maybe other local schools might like the chance to run courses too. We could form a – a sort of co-operative group. Then they would have that training box ticked too, if *they* ever got hit by an inspection."

"Now that *is* sensible," said Jean, approvingly. "You could sound them out at the next heads' meeting, Skipper."

They moved on to talk about Summer games, the women sitting back and letting the menfolk have their moment of fun. Guy was back on form with plans for the swimming gala and cricket season. Mike was happy organising tennis and rounders. They all agreed to keep the fourth of July as baseball day in honour of Chloe. The children had loved their game against the staff last year, but this time Skipper suggested they hold a straightforward kids' match – Lions versus Tigers.

"Oh thank heaven," cried Mike. "It was humiliating last year. Yes, let the boys and girls slog it out. Couldn't we do the same with tennis? Maybe next year other schools might like to join in and we could hold a tournament."

Guy grinned. "That's a great idea. No need for us crumblies to be embarrassed."

Reg harrumphed and stood up. Time he was off. Time they all were. These overblown plans were irritating as they usually involved a whole lot of mess he had to clear up. He clicked his tongue to Stringer who stretched all four legs one after the other and trotted out into the garden. Summer was here at last. It was time to be on the move.

Charlie walked May home.

"How's Fiona?" she asked.

"Well, to be honest, I'm a bit worried about her." Charlie was grateful May had brought it up. "She's loving the house, and Tim is happier than he's ever been, but she's suddenly very anxious and I can't make out why."

May was sorry to hear this. "Have you tried talking to her?"

Charlie stopped and dug his hands into his jacket pockets. "No. No, I haven't."

"Why-ever not?" asked May. Honestly, men.

"I don't know. It might be me. It might be she's ill. Maybe she's hoping I'll guess what it is."

May patted his arm. "No use being scared of an answer. If you really can't guess, then ask straight out. Secrets are no good."

"You're right, as always. Thank goodness I've got you around to put me straight, May!" Charlie kissed her cheek and opened her front gate for her. "I know where to come if I don't know how to cope with the answer. Or if she kicks me out."

May turned and smiled at him. "That's right, my dear, you do. Now off you go."

Charlie hurried home and had Tim's supper ready by the time he arrived off the school bus, as Fiona was working the late shift this week at the hospital. It was a homework night, so father and son sat together finishing off some elementary algebra together before Tim decided to plant the seed of an idea in his dad's brain.

"Dad," he asked.

"Yes Tim?"

"Do you like spending time with me?"

"Funny question. Of course I do."

"Well, you know our river?"

"Yes. Can't hardly miss it."

"Well, I was wondering."

"If it's a gold plated sailing yacht, forget it."

"No. But it would be a waste of the river if we didn't, sort of, use it – wouldn't it?"

"How d'you mean?" This was getting serious, so Charlie was all attention. "Use it for what – baptisms, bridge construction, hydro-electricity?"

Tim smiled. "No, fishing."

"Fishing? What, like, trawlers and that?"

"No," laughed Tim, knowing when his leg was being pulled. "No, angling. With a rod and line. Do you suppose we'd catch anything?"

Charlie rubbed his chin and thought it over. "Probably be trout in there. Or minnows or something. It's deep in parts and clear as a bell so I suppose it has a fish population. I daresay there's someone we could ask. Is this about what you want for your birthday?"

"Yes. I'd like a fishing rod, please. With a little wheel thing you turn. And maybe a net so I can land a big monster fish. I've seen it on telly."

"Oh, on telly was it? Well, let's see what your mum says tomorrow morning, OK? Now hop into bed, boyo, and go to sleep. You can dream about catching our supper. Night-night now."

"You could have one too, Dad, with a little wheel thing. Yeah, yeah, I know. Goodnight."

A fishing rod, so that was it. It was rather a good idea of Tim's, and a hobby they could both enjoy. He hoped the subject wouldn't add to Fiona's reasons for being out of sorts with them both. He tidied up and went to bed himself, brooding on when would be the best moment to talk to her.

Fiona has news

Tim waited for his dad to make an appearance at breakfast before launching into the birthday request for a fishing rod. His tired mother smiled and wiped her hands on a tea-towel.

"I think we might run to one," she said. "Don't you, love? As long as he promises not to fall in the river while he's hauling in Moby Dick or something."

"Exactly." Charlie poured out his cornflakes and sat down beside his son. "We don't want him towed out to sea by some giant squid. It would play havoc with his hairdo."

"Dad!" grinned Tim. He loved his parents. He loved this house and this new life where he had his own bedroom. He loved being nearly twelve. It was great to contemplate the up-coming summer holidays.

"I've got something to tell you both before you vanish for the day," said Fiona.

Charlie looked up in alarm. Oh god, she *was* ill. Had she been sacked?

The two male members of the Tuttle family stared at her, round-eyed.

"I'm…" she took a deep breath. "I'm pregnant. I'm going to have a baby."

The two breakfasters stared in astonishment.

No! thought Tim, horrified.

Yes, thought Charlie. I *knew* it!

"Darling! Oh my goodness, that's wonderful!" Charlie rushed over and hugged her. He was almost weeping with joy.

Tim continued to look aghast as the full horror of her words engulfed him. That meant his parents had had sex! That was disgusting. And a baby would change everything. Their family would be ruined. The Summer would be full of prams and ooing and gooing over bibs and duckies and baby-grows. There would be no money to buy him a fishing rod now. There would be toys and sick everywhere. His mum would look like a balloon and she wouldn't be just his and dad's any more. He didn't want a crying, smelly, ugly *baby*. He threw down his cereal spoon and picked up his satchel.

"Aren't you going to say anything, Tim?" smiled Fiona.

"Not really," Tim answered. "I'll be late for the bus."

He vanished, but his parents were too absorbed in the good news to mind very much about Tim's mood.

*   *   *

18.

canoe

Skip's birthday

"Oh you shouldn't have! Thank you Toby," cried Mrs Clark. The box contained the fanciest chocolates she had ever seen. He grinned cheerfully at her delight.

"And a trip to either Portland or Fenchester to see the film of your choice. How about it?" he asked. "Any day."

"In your little car?"

"Bit windy I know, or we could go in yours. I'll drive."

"You don't trust my driving."

"I do, but your car's a tad on the damp side isn't it?" Toby disliked the smell of mouldering carpet in Skip's Morris. "We'll go in mine. You can put a headscarf on and I'll tuck a rug round you. You'd look like Princess Margaret. Have you a mink coat?"

Skip laughed. "Not until next birthday," she said regretfully.

The following Saturday evening they roared off in a cloud of exhaust to Fenchester where Toby bought her an early dinner and their chosen movie. Skip couldn't remember when she had enjoyed a night out more. Toby even offered to take her to a night club in town afterwards, but she decided that was a step too far. She felt like a giddy teenager again as she put her key into the front door and hung her coat back in the hall cupboard.

Dora was still up and waiting eagerly for information. Disappointingly, there was little of a romantic nature to relate. Toby didn't seem to be offering her daughter that kind of relationship. He was entertaining Skip said, attentive, fun. Dora couldn't decide from that remark whether Toby was honestly uninterested in romance or was merely playing a long game. It was confusing. In magazine stories couples met and married, simple. Maybe she was hoping for too much too soon. The pair obviously had heaps in common and there was no reason to hurry.

Skip, surprisingly happy and uncharacteristically relaxed, felt nothing but contentment as she snuggled down and turned off the bedside light. From out of the blue, a very pleasant male companion had appeared, like some long-lost brother. He was the ideal work-colleague and a pleasant playmate and for once in her life she yearned for nothing more. Toby Tremayne was the best birthday present she had had for a long time.

Dr Granger returns

Joe Granger pulled his overworked old car to a stop outside the school's Mellow Lane gate. He straightened his back on emerging and swore to himself he was going to trade the Singer in tomorrow for a modern vehicle before his spine grew irreparably bent by its springless seats and neuralgia-inducing draughts. It was alright for cutting a dash around Banford but on a long drive, such as he had just undertaken, it was dreadful.

"Home again, then Doc?"

Joe swung round to see Reg Green, as always sweeping the playground. Stringer bounded up to him, tail wagging. The doctor bent down to stroke his bobbing head.

"Hello! Hello, Mr Green. How's it going?"

"Not so bad now," commented Reg, ambling over and shaking hands. It was nice to see the fellow again. "Me 'ip's fixed. Like a spring lamb, I am. You back permanent?"

"Oh, I'm pleased to hear about that leg. Yes, my adventures north of the border are over. I'm a little sorry, as I enjoyed it up there, but it's time to come home and pick up the reins."

"Your nurse'll be pleased," said Reg, meaning Nurse Presley. "School too. Dr Legg ent too bad, mind. Quite took to her, some of the parents have."

The doctor found Skipper in her study. She was delighted he was back too, and brought him up to date on Mayflower's arrivals and departures, chattering happily until she noticed his stricken face.

Joe Granger was staring at Mrs Clark as if she had suddenly grown two heads.

"Gone? Gone where?"

"Chloe? Back to the States, Joe." She was surprised at his obvious shock. Did he have something dreadful to talk to her about? Had Chloe been suffering from some terminal illness and not told them?

"The *States*?" It might have been the moon. "When?"

"February. Just before half term. I'm sorry Joe – I didn't think to tell you."

"No. Why would you?"

Joe quickly sat down as his head was spinning and he felt sick. Skipper came round the desk and patted his shoulder.

"It was all a bit sudden," she explained, hoping to comfort him. She liked Joe and enjoyed the fact that other people often linked them romantically together. However, that little mirage was fast evaporating. She watched the doctor's reaction to the news of Chloe Shaw's recent departure with sudden understanding.

"Let me get you a drink of water. Or a slug of red-eye would probably be better."

She pulled open the bottom drawer of her filing cabinet and took out a bottle of rye whiskey, poured him a shot, handed it over and was relieved to see his colour begin to return.

"Thanks." He gave her back the empty glass. "Wow, sorry. That was a shock. No, I was – I was just hoping to catch her, that's all."

Skipper wasn't about to have the wool pulled back over her eyes. After all, if you hit her over the head often enough she finally got the message.

"You're fond of her, are you?"

Joe nodded miserably. "Yup. Have been since, well, forever really. Since the first time I met her. She's very special."

Deja vu, thought Skip glumly. Chloe had this electro-magnetic effect on men, so why should Joe Granger be any exception?

"And she was scooped up by Max Shaw right under your nose."

Joe nodded again.

"And, being chivalrous, you did nothing. Said nothing."

"Nothing. Not a thing. Max was her choice. She never even knew I cared. But I did – I do. I always will."

Skipper sighed inwardly and tried to see it from his lovelorn point of view. "Is that why you went to Scotland?"

"Yep. I applied for the posting the day they got engaged. I had to get out or fall apart. But then he died – poor old Max. I thought… and I hoped... god, I'm so mixed up."

Skip's perception of the romantic relationships of the past year-and-a-half shifted and resettled like a kaleidoscope – same pieces, new pattern. Joe had never been interested in Skipper at all. All that nonsense, all that flirting, had been pure camouflage. So much for my irresistible allure, she thought bitterly.

They sat in silence while she poured them both another whiskey.

"Chloe said she couldn't stay here any more, Joe. It all became too alien and painful. Take it from me, she has no idea about you. She was offered a principalship in New Mexico – somewhere near Taos. It all just came out of the blue." Skip ended lamely "Taos is lovely."

"Oh." Joe roused himself. "Where is that exactly?"

"South from Denver. Denver's about in the middle of the continent."

"There's an airport?"

"Of course. Why?" She stared at him with foreboding.

Dr Granger stood up. "Thanks for the whiskey, I needed that." He put the glass down on the desk.

"You're not flying out there."

"Yep. Yes I am. I'm going to America. I don't know what the outcome will be, but I have to go. I have to see her, talk to her – if only to know she's alright." He nodded his head vigorously. "I don't expect anything, Skip – but I need to know whether there might one day, possibly, be any hope."

Skipper was so astonished she could say nothing at all.

Dr Granger hurried away, fortified with strong liquor and invigorated by a new purpose in life. This was his second chance.

He had been a fool and left it too late once before. He wasn't about to make the same mistake twice.

Mrs Clark went swiftly to the office and told Peggy all about it. Cathy had gone to the bank so the room was quiet.

"Well, I'll be darned." Peggy was as amazed as Skip had been. "He kept that very dark. Not that I'm surprised, when I really think about it. What about the medical practice?"

"He didn't say anything about work, or about anything else for that matter. Oh lor, what will Nurse Presley do?"

Peggy raised her eyebrows and pursed her lips. "What she always does. Take it out on the rest of us."

Skipper went to wash up the whiskey glasses in the staffroom sink. Oh Chloe, she thought exasperatedly. Romantic attachments were really best avoided. They had horrible ripple effects that often caused the lives of others to implode. It was far better to remain on pleasantly platonic terms with members of the opposite sex, and not get tangled up, however attractive they might be.

She smiled smugly to herself. Like Toby and me, she thought.

Paddling

"Just drop your end," called Mike. Charlie dropped his end. The two-man canoe smacked down into the slow-moving river and swung round. Mike stood back and looked at it with satisfaction. "There. What did I tell you? Floats like a cork."

"I still don't think I'll fit in. I've developed a bit of a corporation these days." Charlie's waistline had expanded a little in recent years but he was blowed if he was going on any kind of diet.

Mike eyed him critically. "Try. I'll keep her still. You've got your shorts on."

"Yes, and bloody cold that water looks too. Alright. Hold her steady – here goes."

Charlie stepped nimbly into the front seat and settled himself down. His knees took a bit of folding up but he managed not to flip the thing over. "Come on. Your turn. I'll hold the paddles."

The canoe stabilised and they set off on their first venture out into the wide, slow waters of the Wain. Charlie had come across the canoe in Well House's old boathouse, lodged in the rafters where Max must have stowed it years before. He had cleaned it up and Mike had come over to help launch it. It would be an extra birthday surprise for Tim, in June. Tim was currently having a week at camp with his school, so it was an ideal opportunity to try the two-seater out.

It was a beautiful morning. The clear river gleamed in the sun and tiny specks of light drifted like fairies across the surface and shimmered down to its sandy bed. All manner of busy bird life dipped and dabbled, catching breakfast or preening plumage. Willows shivered along the banks and lines of lofty elms and oaks stood further back, like parents watching the waterside scene from a distance. The two men felt the sun on the top of their balding heads and laughed.

Greg Price was watching the teachers from his camp on the end of Ironwell Eye and wishing his brother hadn't thrown Jimmy's telescope into the river. He would have liked to spy on them. It looked fun out there and much easier than sailing the red dinghy would have been. Greg wanted a turn in that canoe. He could imagine himself as a wild trapper living in the Canadian forests, hunting bear and beaver and taking the pelts to be traded for tobacco and food at a rendezvous. He would buy Anna a gold chain and some turquoise bracelets and they would live in a log cabin somewhere high in the mountains. He would steer the canoe expertly over the white river rapids and paddle downstream to hunt ducks and shoot turkeys. Or maybe they would even take it to the ocean, where they could lie in the hot soft sand and become beachcombers.

The little canoe disappeared round a clump of trees.

Greg rolled over on his stomach and fell to lighting matches and flicking them into the river, still dreaming about the canoe.

St George's Day

St George's Day at Mayflower was taken up with the usual mummers' play. The morning went with its usual swashbuckling verve and the rain held off until it was all over, for which everyone was heartily thankful. The vicar and his new curate, Mr Wichelow, applauded extra loudly at the end. Theodore Wichelow had never seen anything like it before.

"Oh wasn't that splendid?" he gushed. "I must say I do *like* these old traditional celebrations being revived."

Rev Bill nodded. "Not so much revived as never left, in some places," he said. "You should put a note in your diary to come here on May Day morning. You'll enjoy that too."

"Oh I shall, I shall."

Mrs Clark held up her hands for the applause to cease and beamed around the playground at everyone. There was a good audience today of loyal parents, relatives and friends.

"Thank you. And thank you girls and boys for a splendid reminder of our English heritage. Needless to say our other British patron saints will all be celebrated in their turn. Now visitors, I'm sure you remember we don't charge an entry fee to these little Mayflower performances, but we do give you the opportunity to contribute on the way out! And this year, if you can give generously in aid of our school funds, we will be particularly grateful. There have been many unforeseen expenses at school lately and however much you can afford to contribute today will be so *very* – so – very welcome." Skip faltered to a stop, choked by a sudden surge of emotion. Tears streamed down her face.

People looked at each other, then began delving in their pockets, embarrassed. Dora and Mr Wichelow hurried over to Skip and escorted her indoors, where she apologised repeatedly into a large handkerchief.

"I don't know why I'm being so silly," she hiccupped. "It's just – it's been very *hard*, lately."

Theo decided he would be more use outdoors and beat a hasty retreat, while Dora sat and offered her daughter a little quiet reassurance. She had not fully realised how big a worry the school's lack of cash this year was to Skipper, nor how rapidly her anxiety could undermine her outward composure. She was like quicksand. Tears in public were appalling. Whatever happened to keeping a stiff upper lip?

Peggy bustled in with a red plastic bucket almost full of loose change.

"Look," she cried. "This'll cheer you up. Cathy and I are going to count it after lunch. I'll bet there's close on fifty pounds here."

Dora beamed. "You see? People only have to know the school needs a little extra help. You have to give folks the opportunity to be kind – I keep telling you. See here? Now buck up, do. I'm going home to my greenhouse and you should probably be heading into the hall for lunch, am I right, Peggy? I thought so. Now off you toddle."

Peggy and Dora edged Mrs Clark back out into the wide world and closed the study door firmly behind her.

"Well," muttered Dora. "What a to-do. Does that sort of thing happen much?"

"No," answered Peg. "It's been an overwhelming year, though. I don't entirely blame her. Things will get easier, I'm sure."

Dora wasn't completely reassured, but she trusted Peggy and knew she would help all she could. Peg, meanwhile, was fervently praying that good St George was hard at work fighting Mayflower's dragons somewhere behind the scenes. It didn't do for people to have to see an over-emotional headmistress, whatever the justification. She must have a word with Sir Hugo.

Toby finds a couple of likely lads

The school wilderness was fully open for playtimes once again. Mrs Clark had forbidden anyone to enter its jungly depths during the snow and gales and floods of Winter, but now Terry and Olly had slashed, scythed and mown open some of the tangled trackways, and nudged aside the worst of the fallen branches and other hazards in order that the little ones could resume their adventures. It was becoming popular to walk in there again. The new curate had begged to set two beehives deep in the heart of its acreage and created a neat little pathway of his own to reach them. Mrs Clark forbade the children to go near the wooden hives, but as the bees caused no bother at all everyone soon forgot they were even there. The honeybees droned away in peace in the warm shelter of ceanothus, thistles and nettles.

The sun pulled life upwards through each tiny dry twig and rough branch, swelling them with fresh sap. They brought forth miniature leaves of more shades of green than even Robin Hood could have identified. Narcissi and windflowers carpeted the ground. Everywhere nature uncurled little hands and stretched them out towards the light of the sun. The dead matted jungle grew rich and beautiful once again.

Dean Underwood had been thinking about the colour green. He was convinced Robin and his Merry Men must have known every shade on the planet – hadn't they invented Lincoln green? Dean's new big black paintbox had many colours listed in tiny writing on the inside where you put the paintbrush. The written layout matched the little shiny blocks of paint so you knew which was which. He had all the names by heart, and in the green section was written viridian, lime, mint, celadon, apple, emerald, jade, moss, grass, olive, hunter, and forest. Dean had never in his life expected there to be so many, all with such poetic names. He adored his new paintbox.

"Shall we play by the big oak or up on the knoll?" asked Ryan grinning happily, as the oddly-matched two jogged out to play one lunchtime. He pulled his sweater off over his head, forgetting he now wore glasses. They flew off his nose and into an overgrown privet bush. When he retrieved them they had little round leaves stuck to the greasy discs of glass. The boys tied their sweaters round their waists and resumed their canter up the low rise with its crown of fir trees, commonly known as the knoll. It was the highest point of the wilderness and commanded a view down to the river and over the town one way, the higgeldy-piggeldy roofs of Longmont Lodge in another, and the main school building in another.

"Hello boys," called Mr Tremayne from the top. The boys greeted him eagerly.

"Hello, Sir. You playing up here too?"

"No, not so much playing as taking a walk and looking at the view. Nice day isn't it? This is a splendid wilderness. I should have liked to play cowboys here when I was younger."

"You can play Robin Hood with us if you want," offered Ryan kindly.

Dean nodded. "Yeah. Ryan's Little John – you could be the Sheriff of Nottingham. Cowboys have sheriffs too, so you'll know what to do."

Toby laughed. "It's a tempting proposition, but I'll pass this time. Thank you for the suggestion though. Come and see me later and I'll show you how to make a Robin Hood hat out of paper. I might have another little project for you as well." He waved and left them to it.

Toby wandered back along the grassy paths picking a posy of semi-wild flowers as he went. Violas, primulas, aubretia, jonquil and grape hyacinth looked lovely together.

He knocked on the open kitchen door and presented his posy to Ivy, whose birthday it happened to be. She was up to her elbows in soapy water washing the dinner dishes while Sally cleaned the stove-top. Mrs Green pulled her hands out of the sink and wiped them down her apron.

"Oh my! Are those for me? Here, Sally, bring me one of them beakers over. Now look. Ent they a picture? Thank you Mr Tremayne. That's very kind of you."

Toby was pleased Ivy was pleased. She worked hard and he appreciated her tasty dinners. He chatted for a bit, then went to find Peggy Bailey – another woman he was finding invaluable.

"Any messages, Peg?"

"Yes." Peggy consulted the notepad she kept beside her four-line switchboard. "Er – Mrs Petherbridge rang asking whether you were going to run a French club after school.

Apparently Veronica is really enjoying French now and wants to do more. She's in Form 6. Then a rep from the bookseller you talked to last week called again. And a Mr Arnold phoned and asked if you would call him back. You have his number."

"When did he call?"

"Half-past twelve. It didn't sound urgent." Peggy flipped the notepad shut.

"Righty-o, thanks Peggy," said Toby, and went upstairs two at a time to the deputy's study and closed the door.

He pressed a switch for an outside line and dialled Arnold's phone number.

Nicky spots a rat

Nicky had been sitting in the wilderness for hours. He and Stringer had discovered some abandoned pieces of carpet that had been thrown over the fence by some irresponsible human which had become a home to a nest of brown rats. Keeping his local territory patrolled and free from a surfeit of vermin was, Nick felt, his *raison d'être*. So when Stringer ran home for lunch, Nicky remained patiently in wait throughout the long afternoon. It was hot and he was glad of the shade. His black coat blended into the darkest under-plant places. Even if a rat did emerge for a sun-bathe Nick would not be noticeable. And he was downwind – a basic rule in the world of successful hunting. He had learned a great deal of predator wisdom in his short life. In fact, Nicky's general education was coming along very nicely. He knew that humans disliked mice left on their doorsteps, even if they were half-eaten. He knew where the driest places were for a nap. He could chase fat pigeons off the vegetables growing in the children's allotments, but had not yet managed to catch one. He knew how to glue dead frogs to the kitchen floor. He could climb tall trees – and descend. He could work a cat-flap, and was familiar with those houses nearby that possessed one. He knew where Skipper worked and how to wangle entry. He was currently learning when it was acceptable to play with Dora's knitting wool and when it was not. Nicky licked his paw as he waited and semi-dozed, a hunter of vigilance and sophistication.

A person he did not recognise approached.

Nicky watched through slitted eyes. The man was unusual because he made no sound. The cat kept stone still and followed the person's slow and careful progress through the undergrowth, recognising the practised look of a fellow prowler. The man's eyes darted here and there while each step was as calculatedly cautious as Nick's own. When the man spotted the old carpet he paused and sniffed before continuing.

Unseen, Nicky slid silently away without disturbing a single leaf.

The stranger eventually arrived at the corner of the wilderness where the old abandoned wellhouse stood. Beneath its roof and weather vane the square structure was built like a wooden cage surrounding the padlocked iron grille that covered the shaft. A strong fence, nettles, brambles, and thick clumps of underbrush grew head-high all around. The well shaft could only be reached by someone very determined. The stranger apparently was such a single-minded investigator. He crouched down and crept between clumps of elder and bramble trying to avoid the tender early bluebell foliage. He jerked out three of the wooden bars of the cage and edged inside where the darkness discouraged all but the meanest vegetation. He lay in the small space beside the shaft's lip, catching his breath. His fingers felt for a particular stone around which he had previously tied a thin string. Pulling on the string, he brought up out of the depths a waterproof bag from a ledge five feet down. He opened the bag and into it slid a small notebook, a miniature telescope, two passports, a pistol and a flick-knife. Then he re-hid the bag.

The man slowly reversed his way out, leaving few visible traces of his presence. He paused, checked there were no passers-by, then slid through a gap in the palings to the public street and strolled along his way. It was a pleasant afternoon for the short walk home

Homework for two

Dean called for Jimmy one Saturday morning. He had walked all the way from his home in Ironwell in the west, to Wag Lane in the east where his mate Jimmy Birch lived. They had become firm friends last year when Mr Denny was teaching them to swim and, although they differed in age by two years, they had a lot in common. Neither had a dad, both their mums went out to work all day, and both needed to get their homework finished.

"You got a pencil?" asked Dean as Jimmy pulled opened the front door.

Jimmy shrugged his bony shoulders. "Dunno. I'll look."

No pencil could be found, so the boys decided to call at the newsagent's in the market square to buy one. They had 20p between them. Jimmy closed the front door, making sure it was locked. Both boys had keys on strings around their necks and knew the correct procedure.

"Hello you two," called Mrs Bicknell, who lived next door to Jimmy. She closed her front gate and smiled at the little boys.

"Good morning, Mrs Bicknell," they said in unison. They liked her as she always spoke to them and sometimes offered them a fruit gum.

"You off somewhere nice?" she asked.

"Homework."

"Homework? Where you goin' then, the library?"

"Nope. I gotta draw the castle and Jim's filling in an I-spy Banford sheet. It's part of a Banford project Miss Fisher set them."

"Really? What's a project when it's at 'ome?"

"Like a... I have to find different things in the town and give 'em a tick on here when I see 'em," Jimmy explained.

"Sometimes he has to add a word or something so he can't just tick 'em and pretend. We're going to buy a pencil to share at Maynard's because we ent got one," added Dean.

Bick smiled. "I expect I can help you there. I've a couple I keep in my Ringo Starr mug." She went and found two sharp yellow pencils and presented them to the boys.

"Cor, thanks Mrs Bicknell."

"Thanks, Miss. That's brilliant. We'll bring them back. Can we get you any shopping or anything?"

Bick was touched by their gratitude. "No, thank you. I done a bit while I was out. You can keep the pencils 'til tomorrow. Go on, orf you pop. Mind how you cross that road, and don't go gettin' into any mischief."

The boys waved and loped off.

"What the 'eck is a Ringo Starr mug?"

Jimmy had no idea. "Don't know, don't care," he said. "But now we can spend that 20p in Maynard's on sherbet."

That was a far more interesting topic of conversation. It kept them occupied all the way into town.

"Hello, Mr Tremayne," called Dean as they exited Maynard's with a small bag of sugary sweeties. The sherbet dabs had unfortunately all gone. "Want one?" He generously held out the bag.

"What you again?" grinned Toby. He had been to the Post Office and was on his way home for lunch. Saturdays were busy in Banford and he was eager to get away from the crowded town. Queueing to post an airmail letter was a major bore. "No, no thanks. Trying to think about my figure, don't you know."

The boys looked baffled.

"We're doing our homework," Jimmy informed him, a little self-righteously.

"Jolly good for you. What's the brief? Need any help?" He took a look at the I-Spy quiz sheet. Jimmy had already done pretty well for a seven year old, he thought. He was an odd lad, big in the belly and skinny in the limbs. Toby wondered if there was something medical the matter with him.

"Miss Bicknell give us a lend of two pencils," said Dean. "We said thank you."

"She did? That was kind of her. Is she at home now, do you suppose? Right, well, I might just pop round and see if she wants to give me a cup of tea. Cheerio then."

"She'll probably give him tea in that Ringo Starr mug," joked Dean. The boys scampered through the town, pausing only to check off spied items on Jimmy's sheet. Even if they were having to do homework it was turning out to be a fun day after all.

*　*　*

371

19.

Toby gains another fan

Mrs Clark had never felt more embarrassed than she had on St George's Day. She had openly wept in public, and begged for money. She went hot and cold all over every time she thought about it. However, by the time May Day dawned a week later she had calmed down a little. She knew everybody around her was doing their best to help her precious school. She wouldn't keep anyone's respect if she had too many wobbles like that.

No one was proving more helpful and supportive than Mr Tremayne. In only a few months Toby's cheerful presence had already started to re-align Skip's perspective at work. He dropped by White Cottage for supper quite often, which pleased Dora. Now and again he suggested a walk or a trip to Portland or Fenchester for some shopping. He was a good steady influence, entertaining, erudite and companionable. His brotherly attention was helping Skip to remember she had a lighter side and other interests beside school. He encouraged her to move forward.

Toby brought a fancy camera to the May Day celebrations and took snaps of the May Queen and her entourage through various expensive lenses. The inevitable cake sale, held after the crowning of the May Queen, was a short-lived event this year as it was sold out in the space of half an hour – a testament to the quality of the baked offerings supplied by the Nosh Club and other helpers.

Mrs Raina and Mr Tremayne stood together by the hall doors watching Mrs Elbows leave with a bag of delicious bargains. Toby ventured a quick snap. His long-range candid-camera shots often turned out to be highly revealing.

"Who's she?" he asked. Sandi filled him in on Mrs Egan and a few more of the locals visiting that morning.

"This town seems to foster some unusual characters," she smiled.

"So I've noticed. I like them though. Your doctor is rather fun."

"Dr Legg? She's terrific – colourful too. Dr Granger was nice, of course, but he seems to have disappeared."

"New Mexico, so I heard. Gone to pay a house call on Mrs Shaw, Skip told me. Is he coming back?" Toby clicked away, grabbing shots here and there.

"Yes of course. I suppose so. One day." Sandi did not sound very certain.

"Good lord! Who-ever's that?" Toby stopped astonished. A woman with wild hair escaping from a hard helmet, and wearing rainbow shades of attire, had brushed past them heading determinedly for Mrs Clark. She left a waft of lemon verbena in her wake. From her patchwork bag she pulled an old box Brownie camera.

This apparition amused Sandi considerably. "Oh, that's our local artist, Miss Winstanley. I wonder what she wants." She filled Toby in on all she knew about the woman. "And she has a gypsy caravan in her front garden."

"Heavens above!" Toby was agog. "Did she drive it here today, do you suppose?"

Sandi laughed. "I don't think even she would be that eccentric. No, she has a motorbike."

Miss Winstanley peered around the room through her horn-rimmed glasses, and grinned toothily. Several children had come up to her and asked if she was going to work with them today.

"I want to take a few snaps of the May Queen," she twittered. "Is she around?"

Toby and Sandi stepped forward. Toby introduced himself and Sandi explained that the May Queen, Trudy Hilder, was just about to go for lunch. Why did Miss Winstanley not stay too, and then take her photographs afterwards on the playing field, if Mrs Clark granted permission.

"Oh I already have full clearance from your headmistress. I say, lunch would be most welcome, thank you. Will there be enough? I could sit beside you, Mr Tremayne, and talk cameras," chattered the artist, grabbing Toby's arm and gazing into his face with sudden adoration.

Sandi beat a retreat to alert Ivy for the need of a few extra slices of ham, while Toby sauntered outside for a walk through the playground and down to the school field with his new fan. She went on and on about taking photographs for The Press, which Toby surmised was probably the local newspaper. She also confided she was at daggers drawn with Mr Simms, the local professional photographer, regarding some event or other they had both attended in the belief that their pictures would be an exclusive double-page spread in the Banford Chronicle. Toby bore it all with admirable fortitude.

Miss Winstanley suddenly demanded if he owned a donkey by any chance.

"A donkey? No – can't say I've ever really had call for one."

"Pity. I thought coming from Italy you might have adopted one of those poor creatures they so cruelly abuse."

Toby had never witnessed any such inhumane behaviour and felt this was rather a slight on his Italian friends. "No. All the donkeys I ever saw there were fat as barrels and as happy as larry. Why do you ask?"

"Transport," she explained. "Inexpensive solution to the occasional need to get from A to B. Need to acquire one, what with petrol for the bike going up the way it is."

Toby gravely promised to look out for a suitable burro in his travels, although he couldn't promise her anything. This seemed to satisfy her. "Well, shall we head back for lunch now? I believe it's cold roast donkey leg today," he said conversationally.

Miss Winstanley belatedly twigged he was joking. "Oh gosh, Mr Tremayne, you are a caution!" She grinned girlishly and skipped happily along beside him.

Saturday cricket

The Mayflower cricket team was fielding against a formidable side from Fenchester on Banford Town's sports ground, Blake's Field. It was a hot Saturday afternoon and there were plenty of spectators for once. Terry Green was pleased his girl Vivienne had come along to watch their first proper match of the season and hoped she was admiring his new white shirt, fashionably turned back to the elbows to show off his tanned arms. Phil Price was batting, hoping that his girl, Pat (Terry's sister), was admiring his fresh white ducks too. Phil had volunteered to make up the numbers for the Fenchester eleven today, and dreaded Terry bowling him out first ball. The two girlfriends were sitting together and no doubt discussing them.

Ivy Green had brought along what she considered to be a small picnic, and she and Reg were perched on some aluminium chairs in the shade of the pavilion. Deck chairs would have been a bit too low-slung for Reg and his new hip, so Ivy was pleased they had invested in these more up-to-date seats. They were a bit skimpy for her bulk, but much more stylish than the old-fashioned wooden things. She looked across at Reg who was sipping his tea and knotting the corners of a hanky which he then placed delicately on top of his perspiring head.

"Dad – you can *not* put that on yer head! Take it off, do. Everyone's looking. *Mum*!" Pat was scandalised by her father's titfer. She whipped it off his head and thrust it into his empty hand.

" 'Ere, 'old on," cried Reg. "Why d'you do that?"

Viv and Ivy burst out laughing.

"Oh, Mr Green! Men are s'posed to wear a proper panama hat these days," explained Viv, who knew all about fashion. "It's *cricket*, not Blackpool sands."

Ivy folded her arms and nodded. "These girls are quite right, Reg. I've told you before. Good job I brung your sun hat along or you'd have showed us all up. Can't have that now, can we, girls?"

She handed it to him from out of her picnic bag. It was a little scrunched up, which made Reg cross. He whacked it grumpily before placing it down over his forehead.

"My 'ead'll make this all sweaty," he grumbled, and patted his face with his hanky. Dammit, your life wasn't your own.

Len Kirk, who should have been playing today on the Mayflower team, came wandering past. He was leaning slightly, as if on the deck of a heeling ship. His little son, Dale, was with him kicking along on the grass, far enough away so as not to get tripped over by his preoccupied parent.

"'Art'noon Len," called Reg. "Come to watch?"

"Yeah. I brought the boy. This'll do, Dale, sit down here." Len flopped down on the picnic rug and took a can of beer out of his pocket. Dale edged closer to Ivy who handed him a biscuit. The child looked very miserable, his face was streaked with tears.

"Where's your mummy?" Ivy asked the four-year-old.

"Home," said Dale. "Jenny and baby Roz and Mum's playing in the garden in the paddling pool."

Ivy handed him another biscuit. Poor little mite. Dale would obviously much rather be at home too, than sitting watching a boring cricket match with his drunken father.

"How's your pigs doing, Len? Still enjoying our left-overs?" she asked the farmer, quite sharply.

"What? Yes, o'course they are."

"You found another lad to 'elp yer yet?" asked Reg. "That Jumbo was a good kid."

"No, more's the pity. Moved up to Portland." Len took another swig. "I liked old Jumbo. Make a decent farmer someday."

"Probably learning a lot of agricultural theory at that model farm set-up they 'ave at the secondary school, I shouldn't wonder," Reg said. He squinted at the umpire who was signalling. "Looks like your fancy-man's out," he called to Pat with a good deal of satisfaction. "Where's Iris this afternoon?"

"Her and Kevin's gone to Portland. They're engaged now and I think Saturday's the only time they can do any shopping together for their new place."

"Ooh, where they going to live then?" asked Ivy.

"Trafalgar Road. They're taking over his auntie's place. She's moving to Milton Keynes to live with her sister."

"Oh that *is* nice." Ivy was pleased. "What about Olly? Ent 'e got a girl?"

"Olly Hobbs? I think he's happy playing the field, Mrs Green. Who's his unlucky latest, Pat?" asked Viv.

"Pammy Finn. Pamela. My money's on her. If anyone can knock some sense into Olly it's Pammy." Pat laughed.

"What, that Pam Finn you had a ding-dong with when you was at school? Over some cake tin or other?" chortled Ivy.

The women went on jabbering while Reg did his best to ignore them. So much for a peaceful afternoon watching the cricket, he thought. Len had dropped off and was snoring, Dale was picking daisy heads and weeping silently. The women seemed set for a very long gossip.

Reg heaved himself to his feet. He took Dale's grubby little hand in his.

"Come on," he said. "Let's see if that sweetie shop on the corner's got any ice creams left shall we? They might even 'ave a bit of left-over old bread they don't want, for us to take down to the river and feed the ducks. Might even 'ave a smart sun hat like mine in your size, you never know. Or a bit o' sun-cream for them red arms. Come on, young Dale, look lively."

"I vote we take her for a paddle in the canoe," said Charlie. "She'd love that."

"Have you gone quite mad?"

"Just a joke. How about a café somewhere for tea?"

"Now you're talking. Fenchester? She can't get there very much these days." Fiona and Charlie were trying to tidy the garage while discussing Miss Fisher's upcoming birthday.

"Well, Thursday is Ascension Day so it's a half-holiday. We could go then, unless you're on duty," suggested Charlie.

"No, I'm not. That would work."

Charlie wished she would pack in nursing altogether, but knew any comment from him would go down like a lead balloon. He said he would check with May and book a table at the posh place near the cathedral. He would ask Jean too, as the two friends loved spending time together. The Tuttles finished their last bit of sweeping and went to sit in the garden.

"We'll be busy this summer, preparing for our baby," said Charlie. "I worry that Tim will miss not having a proper holiday."

Fiona agreed. "Well, you're going to take him canoeing aren't you?" she said. "Maybe we could help him set up a camp in the garden and invite a couple of his school friends round to stay for a couple of nights.?"

Charlie thought he could manage that. "Yeah, he'll like that. He's a good lad. He's been pretty adaptable, hasn't he, what with all our house moves and so on. Oooh! Look at all those bees."

A swarm of honey bees was gathering on the trunk of a nearby apple tree, buzzing and seething in a brown mass. Charlie jumped up.

"Where's Tim?"

"At Barry's until five. What's it doing?" Fiona was watching the swarm fearfully and edging herself towards the french windows.

"Look – you go indoors and phone the curate while I keep an eye on this, OK? Yes, the curate. He knows about bees. You'll have to phone the vicar first though, to get his number. Where the hell have they come from? It can't be very far."

Fiona hurried off to her task while Charlie watched, fascinated, as the lump of live insects grew and writhed around the apple tree. Why did they do that? Where had they come from? He didn't think Fred Unwin, the landlord of the Mint next door kept honey bees, nor Fred's daughter who ran the boarding stables. The Unwins wouldn't appreciate a bunch of stingers buzzing around their customers. Next door the other way lived a couple whose manicured garden had probably never even had a real bee in it. That only left the raggle-taggle bottom end of Lady Longmont's property across the other side of the road as a possible source. Yes, hers was the likeliest place this swarm had come from, he decided. Charlie retreated a little further and kept watch over the mesmerising insects from the patio.

Fiona called out of the dining room window that the curate was on his way and to open the gate open for him. In ten minutes Theo Wichelow arrived wearing full protective gear, and collected the shimmering mass into a special bee box. He was thrilled with his new swarm and headed straight over to Mayflower's wilderness to find them a permanent, pleasant and peaceful hive.

Theo thought that, all things considered, Banford was turning out to be a very agreeable place indeed.

Progress

"Greg passed? You are *kidding*!" Guy couldn't have been more astonished.

The eleven plus exam results were out and Greg Price was on the list of those children accepted for Fenchester Grammar School.

"Now he'll be swearing in Latin," said Mike, equally amazed. The rest of the staff chuckled.

"Well, he's quite brainy isn't he?" said Jean, defensively. She was honestly pleased to hear the news as she had got on well with the boy during the Christmas pantomimes. "I think it might be the making of him."

"Do you? Or will it herald the demise of Fenchester Grammar?" joked Heather. "Who else passed?"

Mrs Clark looked down the list. "The usual suspects," she said. "Annie, Lizzie Timms, Baz, Martin, Tom, and Peter."

"Oh I'm pleased about Lizzie Timms," said May. "She's a nice little girl. She's done well, seeing she has only been here five minutes."

"It will please Greg his singing partner is going to the grammar with him," commented Charlie wryly. "I wonder if he'll surprise us all and manage to hack it, or whether he'll play up so much they chuck him out within the first month."

"Don't be so pessimistic. I have high hopes," said Jean, firmly.

"It's all very well for you to talk, you don't have to deal with his constant attention-seeking every day," sighed Guy. "You give that kid an inch and he takes a mile. Yesterday I let him hand out the geography books and he slung them across the room like Frisbees. Nearly knocked poor old Ryan's teeth out."

"There's a boy who has improved in leaps and bounds," nodded May.

"I agree. Now he can hear and see and talk and read and isn't constantly crashing into things, he's a different lad," smiled Skip. "I can't think how Sandi has made him literate in only a few months, but he's honestly doing really well. She says he's almost at age-level expectations. He's never going to shake the universe, but he's turning out OK, that one."

Jean had also grown fond of Ryan who, with his chum Dean, faithfully turned up every weekend to walk Sweep for her. "Yes, he's a good boy," she agreed. Why did she always end up liking the most challenging children? It was a mystery.

Sandi came into the staffroom. "Whistle's going in three minutes," she informed them, sitting down. It had been a very long morning.

"Well, here's a birthday surprise for you, Sandi. Greg's been selected for Fenchester Grammar. What do you think of that?" said Mike.

"No! Really? Wow, what will they make of him there, I wonder?" Sandi was astonished.

"It will probably do him the world of good. He'll start afresh and stretch his brain," said Jean, firmly. "He strikes me as very intelligent and was really useful during the Christmas plays. Will his mum have been notified?"

"She should have the letter this morning. I think we had better watch out for some difficult queries from the other parents, though, once word gets out. Not everyone will be thrilled about him making it to Fenchester."

"Hmm. Especially Lizzie's mum."

"Lizzie can handle Greg fine," stated Charlie. "She's got him round her little finger."

That was interesting. Maybe the love of a good woman was all the boy needed.

On the heath

Ryan and Dean collected Sweep as usual on Saturday morning and took him for a long walk across Latimer Island to the heath on the far side of the river. There he could roam around, scaring up the odd duck while the boys played cowboys or spies or Robin Hood to their hearts content.

His new mate Dean, story books, and TV programmes were all opening up Ryan's imagination in a giant wave of discovery and he was always ready now to join in the playtime games his friend suggested. Sometimes Ryan became a little too exuberant, as when he kicked Dean's ball up onto the roof, but for the most part he had learned to deal carefully with those smaller and weaker than himself. Ryan was turning into a gentle giant, eager to please and happy to join in. He admired Dean immensely and adored his teachers. Life was fun.

Today the lads were playing soldiers and creeping on their bellies through tussocky clumps of grass as they sneaked up on a couple of skewbald ponies tethered on long chains near the riverside.

"Shh, men," hissed Captain Underwood. "The foes are sleeping yonder. Now is the hour we snatch their four-legged transportation."

"Yes Sir," responded stalwart Sergeant Hale. "Want me to disable the guard?"

The boys wormed their way forward with Sweep snuffling happily in their wake. He loved this kind of morning and was keen to join in. They came up to the two ponies who had spotted them long ago. The boys stood up and ferreted in their pockets for treats, stroking the horses' silky noses and patting their necks. They snorted and huffed at the dog which sat watching from a respectful distance. Suddenly Sweep turned and growled at a rough-looking lad who was approaching.

" 'Ere, don't touch them ponies! My dad'll wring your bloody necks," he warned.

Dean and Ryan jumped back as the ponies tossed their shaggy manes. "We weren't going to hurt them. We just wanted to…" stammered Dean.

"Well don't. Them's ours, bought and paid for. Piss off." The boy started waving his arms belligerently, unintimidated by Ryan's hefty bulk.

Ryan was about to push the boy over when they were hailed from the path. It was not often frequented, so all three boys turned to see who was calling.

"I say! Hello there! Is that you Ryan? Oh hello Sweep old boy. Out for a walk again, Dean? That's a nice couple of little ponies." Mr Tremayne was heading homewards from the town and had taken the long route through Ironwell and Weston as it was such a lovely day. He trod carefully over the tussocks to where the group stood, and chattered on, defusing the horse-owner's threatening mood by sheer bonhomie.

"Splendid day for a stroll, isn't it? I've been into the Post Office in town again, you know. Wish I hadn't bothered, mind you. Hate queuing for anything and it's Saturday morning so all the world and his wife's cashing postal orders or something. It took positive ages, so I rewarded myself by coming home this way. I expect you're all playing something fun, eh?"

The rough-looking lad stood and watched as the three from Mayflower School returned to the beaten path. Toby waved to him, clicking his fingers to Sweep who loped along in their wake.

It wouldn't do for his little innocents to get tangled up with travellers and their ponies. Then he had a thought and turned back.

"I say there, young man!" he called. "You wouldn't happen to know of anyone who has a donkey to sell would you? No? Well if you do come across one, would you let me know? Drop by Mayflower School and leave a message for Tremayne? I'd be most awfully obliged. Toodle-oo."

"Did you say donkey, Sir?" asked Dean once they were safely out of earshot.

"I did. Miss Winstanley down at the old watermill wants one. The artist woman."

"Oh her," said Ryan. "She's got a wagon-thing in her front yard."

"Indeed she does. Maybe she wants the wagon drawn by the donkey. Or maybe she wants to draw the donkey? Ha ha! We could say good-morning to her on our way past if you like. That's if you're going my way."

"That heavy old wagon would be tough for one little donkey to pull on its own," commented Dean, feeling anxious for the non-existent animal. Mr Tremayne patted him kindly on the back.

"Don't you worry, old son. We won't let her be unkind to anything. If it's that heavy she could always buy two donkeys." He squinted at these mismatched human specimens and decided they were exactly what he needed. "You could keep an eye on her – and on anyone else around the place, couldn't you? You could be cadets in the new Tremayne Observer Corps if you like. All you'd have to do is keep me informed of what happens in and around the neighbourhood. Fill me in on what folks are doing as you walk around the countryside. Tell me about everybody's comings and goings – especially strangers."

"Like spies, Sir?" asked Dean, thrilled.

"Yes, like that. Report who goes where and when. You too, Ryan. Want the job?"

"Yes, Sir!" cried both lads eagerly.

"Right-o then. There'll be a little pocket money in it for you from time to time. Keep me up to date every few days – report to my office at school. And we'll keep this little arrangement secret for now, I think. Mum's the word. We don't want any deadly foes to know you're my private observer corps, now do we?"

Toby Tremayne strolled along, congratulating himself on a successful recruitment. The boys were ideal. They were here, there and everywhere all the time. With Bick, that made three efficient amateur observers. They would do well enough.

He turned up Dutch Lane and in at the gate of Banford Place feeling he really deserved his lunch, while the two boys scampered on over Hendy's Fields to take Sweep home.

Bunting gets more than he bargains for

Mrs Bunting handed her husband a plastic tray. On it was a frugal meal of bread, ham and onion and a bottle of beer. She had put a cloth over the top to deter flies.

Mr Bunting took the tray out into the garden, down the side path and around a straggly clump of bushes to an artfully hidden gate. This he opened and closed without a sound. Then he let himself into the kitchen of Chloe's old house. Bushes and plants had grown up vigorously since her departure, so his quick journey was unobserved. Night was falling.

The dark house might have appeared empty, but a new guest was inside, waiting in a bedroom on the most comfortable mattress he had lain on in a very long while. Even though the windows were ajar to dispel his cigarette smoke, the place was stuffy. He lay against the wall, nervous and excited, trying to think straight – rehearsing his backstory. He ran his hand over the stubble on his chin and wished a razor had been provided and some water. He breathed hard and tried to ignore the panic that rose in his chest whenever his mind returned to the loved ones he had left behind.

The key in the bedroom door clicked, and Bunting entered with the tray of food. He set it down and pulled the blackout curtains more tightly across the window before switching on a low-wattage lamp.

The two men spoke in a foreign tongue for a while as the newcomer ate. Bunting took an electric razor out of his pocket and showed the fellow how to use it, while he explained additional plans for the coming days. The man focused hard on memorising what he was being told while noting all he could about Bunting – every detail.

Halfway through one of Bunting's explanations the man suddenly delivered a swift and savage uppercut to his chin and laid him out cold. He snarled with pleasure at the success of this surprise attack. He ripped the bed sheet into strips and trussed Bunting up like a turkey. The man switched off the light, exited the bedroom and locked it behind him. Unaware his movements were being recorded on the latest in covert surveillance systems, he cautiously exited the safe house, looked up and down the street, then walked briskly across Church Road and into St Andrew's churchyard where he paused to collect something hidden beneath a funerary vase of plastic flowers. He slid into the shadows and waited.

The church clock struck midnight. All was quiet. The man crossed the main road quickly and found his way through some undergrowth to a gap in the fence of Longmont Lodge. As silently as he could he found his way around to the stable-yard and up the stone steps to the back door. He tapped on it. It opened immediately. He stood inside, breathing hard, while the person who had let him in welcomed and congratulated him.

Dawn patrol

Reg stepped energetically along the grassy paths of the wilderness with Stringer forging ahead. On these fresh spring mornings they were both eager to be up and about before dawn – before Ivy could find them something to do. Before the kids arrived at school. The birds were calling and the air was filling with light. Along Apple Alley the blossom was already tumbling like snow onto the crunchy old cinder walk. The little garden squares, so beloved by the schoolchildren, had been dug and planted with everything from cucumbers to Dinky cars and were glittering with dew. The earth smelled sweet. Spiderweb gossamer floated from leaf to leaf and a clatter of pigeons swung back and forth in the pale sky, warming up for the day's work. Even snails, fat with a night-time feast of tender green plant-tops, waved their horns energetically as the twosome trotted past. It was far too magical an hour to lie in bed.

Stringer paused at a fork in the path. Reg flicked a finger forward and the dog scampered straight on towards the pedestrian gate beside the main road instead of heading for the old lodge. No doubt they were opening up early today, Stringer assumed. But Reg did not stop, as expected, at the perimeter gate. He closed it behind them, crossed the street, and kept walking.

The caretaker knocked quietly at the back door of Sir Hugo's rambling old home and was admitted immediately by Mrs Bunting. Anxiety had prompted her to phone Mr Green this early.

"He took the dinner over, Reg, but he hasn't come back. I know enough not to go over there in any circumstances myself, but Sir Hugo's at his club until tomorrow and I need to know what's happened."

"What time did he go over?"

"About quarter-past eleven last night. I didn't realise he hadn't come back 'til I woke up this morning." Mrs Bunting was pale and frightened. Nothing like this had happened before.

Reg looked at his watch and nodded. He clicked his fingers to the dog and they hurried next door. Reg had his own sets of keys and picklocks. He let himself in, posting Stringer on guard outside.

As soon as he entered the kitchen of the safe house he knew something was wrong. He tried the locked front door, looked up at the positions of the hidden cameras and moved cautiously up the stairs, an automatic pistol gripped in his left hand. The guest's bedroom door was locked and the key was missing. Reg listened hard and thought he heard someone breathing. Peering through the keyhole he saw the lock was empty, so he found and used his own master key.

Bunting lay semi-conscious beside the old fireplace. His chin was swollen and bruised and he had hit the back of his head on the fender. Reg saw his eyes fluttering and decided the best thing was to take him over to his wife and call an ambulance. He swung the heavy man over his shoulder like a rolled carpet.

Mrs Bunting gasped at the sight of her husband, even though she was a seasoned field agent and was well-aware of the potential dangers. No need for the hospital, she told Reg. Leave Bunting to her.

Reg was helping to put her husband to bed when Sir Hugo himself walked in, having caught the milk train up from London a day earlier than expected. Reg was very relieved to see him. After explaining, he and Stringer returned next door to secure the safe-house and retrieve the security camera footage.

Later that morning Hugo, Toby Tremayne and Reg studied the footage together and listened to the tape-recordings. It was obvious what had happened.

"He's no genuine defector, that's for sure. He's a plant. Bugger caught Bunting completely by surprise," growled Reg. "He give 'im an 'efty wallop, although I don't suppose 'e realised he'd bashed his 'ead on that fender."

"No," agreed Sir Hugo. "But now we have to track the rogue bastard down. Damn and blast the man. I can't leave this place for a minute." He glared at the other two. "Have your observers seen anything, Toby? Has anyone reported anything?"

"No. He'll be lying low somewhere, I'd say, if he hasn't already left the area. None of our cameras show us an outside view, so we don't know which direction he took after he left. He could well have been on the first down-train to London this morning."

"Passed me coming the other way, you mean? God damn the blighter! Alright, start your search at the station while I contact Arnold again. Reg, have Stringer take a good sniff up and down the road. This is not going to look good at HQ. We're being made a laughing stock." Hugo almost ground his teeth in fury. "And be especially vigilant, please Mr Bosun. We don't want any more bodies littering the neighbourhood."

Café society

Dr Legg and Mrs Clark were enjoying a coffee late one afternoon at the Italian café in town that overlooked the Market Square. For once Skip had enjoyed a peaceful day at work, so while her mother was busy in the greenhouse she took herself into Banford to browse around the bookshop. Finding several items she wanted she retreated to wait for the bus in the café, where she found Afra Legg sipping a shallow cupful of froth. It was lovely to catch up with her and discover a little more about this exotic personality. Afra told her there was nothing she enjoyed more than watching the world go by from a comfy vantage point like this one. Not that she ever seemed to have much chance these days. It was better than going to the pictures.

"Well *there's* a story for you, going by right now," Skip pointed out. Jo Winton, Mayflower's ex-classroom assistant, was beetling across the square as if crabs were nipping at her heels.

"Really?" cried Afra all agog. "That doesn't seem likely."

So Skipper filled the doctor in on the way Jo Winton had intimidated poor Miss Fisher into believing she was too old and outdated for her job and that the school didn't want her any more.

Afra was appalled. "That little shrimpy person said all that? I'm glad you sent her packin'."

Mrs Winton had stopped to put up a rather awkward folding umbrella and was being helped by an equally shrimpy-looking man in a scooter helmet who had been pushing a Lambretta in the opposite direction. They were both giggling flirtatiously.

"That *woman*. She's awful."

"But you gave her her cards, right?"

"I did. It was a nasty business, but I did." Skip was still proud of herself and the way she had risen to her first serious professional challenge. She hadn't handled it perfectly, she knew, but she had certainly sent the message that Mayflower valued experienced teachers, no matter what their age. She was heartily glad Jo and Molly had resigned and that Sandi and Betty had taken their places. Jo was now working at one of the town's playgroups for the under-fives.

"Looks like those two are on the road to a little romance," commented Dr Legg, nodding at the pair. Dick Perry had his arm round Jo and had obviously whispered something suggestive in her ear.

Skipper suddenly came over all puritanical. "Well I do hope not," she stated firmly. "Bill Winton is a perfectly nice man. He doesn't deserve to be two-timed."

"No," sighed the doctor, who had some experience in that area. "No, no one ever does. Spoonin' in public is not acceptable. Now then, Mrs Clark, have you time for another coffee?"

*　*　*

20.

In the pool

Parachute

Three days later, Dean and Ryan discovered a discarded pile of parachute silk stuffed under some bushes at the back of Mr Kirk's pigsties. It was a thrilling discovery for the two intrepid amateur spies but as they had been trespassing they did not immediately relay the information to Mr Tremayne, fearing a telling-off. When he did finally hear about it (from Greg Price who had been sent to finish a history essay in Toby's study) he made sure he collared the two next playtime.

"Where was it exactly?"

"Back of the pig house. In the trees by that stinky mud pit. We sometimes hunt for fossils between the roots of the trees," said Dean. "Sorry we didn't say earlier."

"Never mind." Mr Tremayne frowned. Little wretches. "Where is it now?"

"We took it over the back of Dutch Cottage… in the woods. We were going to make a camp," Ryan informed him, doubtful now whether they would be permitted this joy. We haven't done our duty properly, he thought. We might get the sack and we've only just begun. "We're very sorry, Mr Tremayne," he said. "Can we still keep it?"

"Greg told me you found it yesterday afternoon. Is that right?"

The boys nodded.

"Did you see anyone else? Anywhere? No man, on his own, walking? No strangers around the neighbourhood anywhere? "

"No Sir. No one."

"Well, I'd like to see this 'chute. After I've had a look at it I'll decide whether you can keep it or not. Can you take me to where it is after school?"

"Yes, Sir. Of course." It felt like the least they could do to make up for their dereliction of duty. The thing was obviously important. It didn't seem as if Mr Tremayne was merely playing a game.

Taking to the water

"Go on, mate! I done it. Try!" yelled Dean in encouragement.

Nervously Ryan leaned forward and pushed his foot back against the wall of the pool. The cool water ran over his shoulders and over his head as he shot forward. Never had he been so scared – not even when he had been in hospital. He opened his eyes and discovered an underwater world full of wavy light and muffled gurglings. It was beautiful. His head came up and he turned to look back at how far he had come.

"Gor!" he spluttered as he stood up. "That were great!"

"Good lad!" called Guy Denny, really pleased with the boy. "Now then try again and see if you can do that doggy paddle thing like Basil. Show him, Bazza."

Basil, the Darwin team captain, was a good coach and it didn't take long before Ryan was actually doggie paddling up and down the full length of the Lido pool. Guy and Jean and all the children from their two classes applauded as Ryan finally reached the end of his third length. Here was a boy who previously had been overweight and as clumsy as could be, and had never even been to a swimming pool before. Yet now – in a single session – here he was afloat and able to swim. Ryan could hardly believe it himself. He stood up, puffing and blowing like a grampus and grinning like a cat. Basil and the rest of the boys were delighted. There was no way Ryan would let their team down now at the swimming gala.

"That lad's a natural," laughed Jean. "Big and strong and undoubtedly born with webbed feet."

Dick has work to do

A small donkey grazed beside the road near Greyfriars, tied with a length of rope she had not yet managed to chew through. The boy clicked his tongue softly and went up to her. She flicked her ears as he stroked her neck.

"There-there, ool gal. You gonna coomalonga me, 'smornin'." He whispered as he looped the rope expertly into a halter and led her away. Her little feet pattered on the road surface as she followed in the hope of few treats.

It was a beautiful May morning, ideal for the long walk to Ironwell Mill on the far side of town where he was to deliver the animal. His travelling family was camped in the river's

Eastern Levels where the ruins of the old monastery stood in the long meadow grasses. The lad whistled as he strolled along, noting a dark-clad man lying half-hidden in the gorse bushes opposite the main entrance to Hall Manor. The fellow had a rifle-case on his back and some field glasses around his neck. Had the boy not been particularly sharp-eyed it was unlikely the man would have been seen. He spat in the fellow's general direction.

"Won't pot many this side o' the road, mate. Best poaching's yonder, on 'is lordship's land."

The man gave no acknowledgement, so the boy carried on his way with the donkey plodding patiently beside him.

After a few minutes Dick Perry scowled, stood up, scuttled swiftly across the empty street and jumped over the wall into Lord Dexter's estate, acreage he was very familiar with. Crouching low, he scanned the distant manor house through his binoculars and decided to start his hunt for the abandoned parachute at the estate's furthest point, miles away opposite Castor Cottage. It meant an initial long hike, then a slow walk home inspecting every copse and farm building. He had to find the 'chute and get rid of it before anyone else came across it. He had already wasted time scouring the remote Eastern Levels – up until now the preferred landing site. The travellers family might well have already filched it, of course. He couldn't be sure. He must keep searching. He must find it. Blast the incompetent arrival who hadn't disposed of his landing gear in the proscribed way. Blast the wretched travellers and their camp. Blast all farmers, game-keepers, dog-walkers and bird-watchers. The latest arrival had obviously been poorly trained. He was sloppy, lax, a maverick who probably thought procedures were for other people. And he had most likely already quit the local area. Perry was infuriated he was having to clean up the man's mess like some insignificant caretaker.

Perry scanned the heavens. He would have to make sure to look for tell-tale rags of canopy silk and strings up in the branches too. He hitched up his rifle and set off on a very long day's hunt.

Slurry

Len Kirk was a little hung-over but not currently completely drunk. He trundled his swill-bin trolley down the track to the pigs' building and forked out the school-kitchen's remains into their enclosure. The hogs snuffled and gobbled it up, loving their weekly treat, blissfully ignorant of Len's febrile state of mind. Usually the pigs were fed in the morning but today the evening was the earliest Len had been able to get around to the deeply unappealing task. He had fallen asleep at dawn and was only now starting his day's chores. He wished more than ever that Jumbo were still there. Jumbo had never minded unpleasant or heavy tasks. Len loaded the empty bins back onto his trolley and took a minute to scratch the shoulders of his favourite porker, a sow named Ethel, who grunted happily to be near him. She did him good. Len still felt deeply depressed and touchy but, because he wasn't currently brimful of alcohol, less confused.

Brenda and he lived separate domestic lives these days – she in the sitting room and he in the kitchen. The kids had become very quiet, except for the baby which did nothing but yell. Len could only speak to his wife in tones of scathing disgust and all she could do was scream and cry and sulk. The pair were long past communicating rationally. The will to revive their relationship was long dead, yet neither had found a way to move on. They were stuck.

Kirk lifted his gaze to the familiar line of the horizon. The sun was dipping already and twilight shadows stretched before him across the pigs' slurry pit, its putrid crust lying like something on a year-old steak and kidney pudding. As he turned back towards the farmhouse a slight flicker caught the corner of his eye. A movement, a hint of – what?

Suspicious, Len continued his plod back up to the yard then abruptly nipped over a stile and circled back down a shrubby path in the general direction of the slurry pit. If some animal had become caught in one of his barbed wire fences he would have to release it before it struggled itself to death. If it was some dozy lost hiker he would give him a lecture on private property before showing him where the bridle path was. If it was another bloody poacher he would give him a damn good thrashing. The last one he had caught – a sneering teenage boy with an air gun and a catapult – had wriggled free and legged it before Len had even managed to clip his ear.

There! What was that?

"Hey!" yelled Len Kirk.

At first whoever it was remained frozen, then – realising he had been spotted – reluctantly stood up.

"*You*!" Len snarled in astonishment.

All Kirk's murderous wrath rose like a tidal wave. He charged faster than a bull around the scummy, stinking pond of ordure. Before Dick Perry could even swing his rifle off his shoulder, Len struck him. The gathering dusk and dreamy evening were suddenly made ugly with a sickening thwack as Len's lowered head collided with Dick's chest. Birds flew up in alarm and the pigs set up a terrified shrieking. Dick's gun spun away into the bushes in one direction, his binoculars in another.

The two men writhed together like unequal wrestlers, shoving and swinging their fists, knees, elbows, grabbing clothing, grabbing at anything. Perry was a well-trained fighter, and for a small wiry fellow he was remarkably strong – but Kirk had the bulk and tenacity of a berserk bear. He whacked the smaller man backwards and forwards again and again, holding onto him with one hand while delivering hammer-blows with the other.

"You piece of…! Hold still, you little *fuck*!"

Brenda, hearing the ruckus from the house, rushed down the track to the pigsties where she saw the terrible beating her husband was giving her lover. She screamed, but neither man heard her. She called and sobbed and watched in horror as Len finally caught Dick up by the shirt front and slung him, body and boots, high into the air – out into the middle of the slurry pit.

There was an awful pause of suspended reality as the surface held the spreadeagled man. Then it quaked, cracked and sucked him under.

"Oh my god! Len, Len!" screamed Brenda. "Stop! Get him out!"

Len panted, his teeth clamped and grinning as he watched his enemy's boot disappear beneath the filthy carapace. Green and brown slime bubbled up and slithered back together.

"See how you like that!" yelled Len, sweating and steaming. "Count yerself lucky you ent on my *pigs*' menu tonight!" He wiped his hands together and started up to where Brenda was. She cowered as he stalked past her, his eyes mad and bloodshot. She could feel his steaming hot rage and knew better than to get in his way. The pigs were still screaming knowing something terrifying was happening.

Brenda grabbed an ancient pitchfork from a hook on the pigsty wall and ran to the edge of the pit. She thrust the thing in as far she could, calling Dick's name and sobbing. But there was nothing to be seen, nothing to feel. She could not reach the centre of the mire at all. A few slimy green puddles lay on the thick scabby layer where her pitchfork penetrated, but there was no sign of any object within.

"Oh my god, you've killed him! Dick, Dick! Here, catch hold!"

Brenda kept thrusting the pitchfork into the thick quaking sludge in a panic. The stench was appalling. If she had encountered Perry's body she would have likely skewered him in her frenzy and never been able to pull him out, but there was nothing. She encountered nothing, retrieved no one. There was no body. Dick Perry had vanished beneath the excrement.

After a while, Brenda collapsed and sat on the ground howling and wailing, overcome with fear and grief and horror and fumes.

The darkness began to deepen. The pigs grew quiet.

Len returned down the track, and yanked Brenda to her feet. Now he smelled of whisky again, but she had nothing to say about that. Nothing to say about anything – she was too numb. He dragged her back to the farmhouse kitchen and sat her down on a chair at the table where he poured her a glass of whisky. She drank it and stared at him, still shaking.

Who was he? Why had he done such a terrible thing? And what, oh what, were they to do now?

Len is given a lift

Toby Tremayne had spent the day alone in Fenchester and was driving home in the pleasant evening light. It had been a long day, so he decided to treat himself to a pie-and-a-pint supper at the Yeoman. As he drew near the Lido he noticed Len Kirk trudging heavily alongside the carriageway, seemingly in a bit of a daze. Although they had hitherto only held brief conversations at school mostly about pigs, Kirk struck him as a decent bloke. This evening he didn't appear too well, so Toby slowed down and hailed him.

"Hello there! Going my way? Need a lift?"

Len lifted his buffalo-like head and tried to remember who this was. That's right – the new French teacher.

"No. No thanks."

It didn't take a genius to see something was terribly wrong. Len was covered in muck and blood. One eye was puffed and there was a nasty cut on his nose, his work-shirt was soaked in sweat and you could smell the man a mile away. This wasn't somebody off to spend a convivial Saturday evening in the fleshpots of Banford.

"Get in," ordered Toby in quite a different tone of voice. Len got in.

Toby drove to the next corner and pulled across the road into the Dutch Lane turning. It was absolutely deserted, so he stopped the car abruptly. A half-dollar moon started to gleam silver in the southern skies and a barn owl glided away over the desolation of Hendy's Fields. He turned off the engine and swung round to look at Len.

"Now then, old man, I suggest you tell me what you've been up to. If you don't mind my saying so, you don't look or smell acceptable enough for polite company tonight." Toby wound down his window.

Len lowered his head. Now he had stopped moving he felt as if he was going to fall to pieces. All resolution drained out of him and he desperately wanted to talk. He began his story haltingly, then as anger rekindled his emotions, he jabbered on and on, ending in a brief description of the terrible events at the slurry pit.

"So where is your wife now?" asked Mr Tremayne calmly.

"Home. I left her home."

"Why didn't you phone the police?"

Len stared. That had not occurred to him, but he could not think why it hadn't.

"I want to hand meself in. In person, like. I'm going to find Pink. Pink'll know what to do." He got abruptly out of the car and was sick into the bushes.

Toby sat and thought rapidly. Dick Perry's name had come up before and Toby began to feel increasingly certain that he was their elusive sleeper agent. Perry had a rifle and a large pair of binoculars. He'd been caught snooping near where the parachute had been found. He was a loner, and had only ever come to anyone's notice because of his ill-advised philandering. The more Toby quizzed Len about the fellow, the more convinced he became.

And if that really was the case, this news that Perry had been drowned in a slurry pit – by a civilian, no less – was an incredible stroke of luck. If Dick hadn't managed to crawl away under his own steam, Len Kirk had unwittingly done queen and country an enormous service tonight.

Sir Hugo should be informed at once.

"Feeling better, old man? I'm not surprised you came over a bit queer after all that. Nasty business, yes indeed. Now then Kirk, you listen to me."

Len sat back heavily in the passenger seat, feeling light-headed, freezing cold and boiling hot all at the same time. He did his best to pay attention, only too relieved someone else was now taking charge.

Toby explained they were going round to see Sir Hugo Chivers. He was a top-notch lawyer and would know the correct procedure in this situation. After that, if Sir Hugo advised it, they would head straight for the police station. How did that sound?

Len's brain could only absorb two items of information at a time by that point, so he simply nodded and grunted. If Mr Tremayne had said steal a boat and sail to Australia, he would have done it. Nothing felt real. Everything tonight was as if it was happening in somebody else's bad dream. Len slumped down and closed his eyes.

By the time the car drew up in front of Sir Hugo's gate and flashed its headlamps for admittance, Len Kirk had fallen into a deep, dark sleep.

More trouble

An hour later, Toby Tremayne returned Len to his empty house, where he tucked the farmer round with a blanket on the sofa to sleep. Of Brenda, the only trace was a note lying on the kitchen table saying she had taken the children and the car and would be at her sister's in Portland.

Tremayne made a note of her address, then found a torch and did his best to search the farm's slurry pit area for any indication Dick Perry might still be alive or was, indeed, definitely dead, but the farm dogs barked and snarled so madly on the end of their chains he feared they would rouse the next county. Doing anything tonight was impossible. Better leave a full investigation to Reg Green in the morning. There seemed nothing immediately obvious to be tidied away. Toby did, by pure chance, find the pair of binoculars beside the path and pocketed them. He returned to his car and climbed wearily back in. There was nothing more to be done. A short ride and he'd be home. He could hear the distant sound of St Andrew's clock striking two.

Avoiding the deeply rutted, pitch dark short cut down Dutch Lane he accelerated to Mayflower Road and turned along beside the school. It was a beautiful quiet night, bright with moonlight and a million stars.

Suddenly, for the second time that evening, Toby spotted something amiss. He slammed to a halt. This time it wasn't a staggering pedestrian – it looked more like a heap of discarded clothing lying across the footpath and grass verge. Except there was a naked leg and foot sticking out.

Someone was lying there. Some woman. Toby grabbed the torch again and clambered out.

The body of a young lady lay unconscious and twisted in the weeds. She had the appearance of a discarded shop-window manikin clad in a cheap coat – disjointed, vulnerable. Toby bent and touched her soft throat, seeking a pulse. His fingers came away covered in a sticky mess of warm blood.

Where was the nearest telephone? Toby thought fast as he stripped off his jacket and covered her upper body and bundled up his sweater to pillow her poor broken head. The closest phone would be back at White Cottage, Skip's home. There were never any coppers on night patrol in these rustic places – in fact nobody about at all. It was too early for a milkman, or even the railway men. Time was critical, that much was obvious. How long the girl had been lying there he could not tell, but possibly a few hours as her clothes were damp with dew.

Hit and run, he guessed. He racked his brains trying to remember where the cottage hospital was. He glanced at the moon and made up his mind. He scooped the limp body into his arms as gently as he could, and laid it beside him in the passenger seat, risking further injury in favour of speed. The girl was as light as a feather. Blood dripped from her face, and her shoulder hung awkwardly against his arm. He grabbed her handbag from the grass, cast his eyes quickly over the scene for anything else and accelerated for the hospital.

At the door they were met with well-practised efficiency by emergency staff, and Tremayne finally managed to get a clear look at the young woman's face under full electric light. It may have been pretty once. It was heartbreakingly young.

"You know, I think – I *think* – she's the barmaid, or the cleaner possibly, from the Mint public house," he told the staff on duty, handing over the handbag. A nurse flipped it open and found her name, Jane Birch.

Jimmy's mother.

"Ah, alright, thank you. One of our people will ring the police and let them know. Please go over to the desk there, and give the nurse as many details as you can. Did you hit her with your car?"

"No, no, of course not. Not me. I just came across her on my way home. I've no idea how long she may have been lying there." Toby was far more upset about this hit-and-run than he had been about Dick Perry's murder. "Please help her. She's the mother of one of our Mayflower boys."

While the nurse called the police station, Toby used the public phone booth to ring Skipper Clark, no longer caring what the time was. When the headmistress finally answered he rapidly explained the second part of his night's adventures, begging her to either wake a neighbour and have them call round and check on seven-year-old Jimmy Birch, or go there herself. Toby hated to think of the kid waiting in vain for his mother to come home from work, and spending the night alone. Or having a policeman knock on the door and tell him his mother was half dead in the hospital.

Skip immediately dressed, explained to her sleepy mother what was happening, and returned to the hall just as Police Cadet Nichols rang her front doorbell. He had been dispatched hot-foot by the night sergeant, who currently had no-one else closer than Portland to send. Nichols didn't mind. He quite enjoyed night duty he told Skip, as she hurried him into her car and drove round to Jimmy's house in Wag Lane.

Awakened by the car and the insistent knocking on the door of No 1 by a policeman and the head of Mayflower school no less, Mrs Bicknell peered out of her bedroom window next door. Trouble, she said to herself, and hurriedly tied her dressing gown cord and put her slippers on.

"Whatever's the matter?" she called just as Jimmy heaved open his front door, eyes wide with terror.

Mrs Clark held the child's hand and took him into the kitchen to explain what had happened. Once he understood, he burst into tears and sobbed in her arms. Cadet Nichols gave him a cup of water, then Skipper took the boy upstairs to get dressed, while Nichols spoke with Bick in the front room. He made a few notes about Miss Birch's usual comings and goings just as the sky began to lighten and the birds awoke. All around them the natural world looked forward to another day of sunlight and hope.

A kindly woman from the social services arrived after a while, and took Jimmy off to his aunt's in Portland. Bick took charge of Janey's house, locking doors and closing windows. Cadet Nichols asked Skipper if she would be kind enough to drop him back at the police station where he could start writing up his report. Exhausted by the crisis, Mrs Clark did so.

Then she went home for a jolly good cry.

406

A thorough search.

Reg Green and Stringer were given a lift down to Abbey Farm by Bunting in his second-hand Ford runabout an hour or two after dawn.

Reg quickly fed the animals, then joined his inquisitive canine friend who was searching the area around the slurry pit. Reg tied his handkerchief over his nose like a robber in a Western in order to lessen the noxious stench, but there wasn't much he could do against the already madly buzzing flies. He wished farmers had better ways of disposing of animal muck instead of filling up old ponds with it. He did not poke about in the slurry long. There was no safe way to thoroughly search the ordure and he had no wish to end up in hospital again. The vile crust lay still. No one had crawled out from under it, as far as Reg could tell. He turned his attention to the hedgerows, tracks and ditches, ferreting about in the undergrowth and turning over anything interesting with a stick. There was nothing that led him to believe Dick had survived. Reg glanced over at Stringer who was yapping and staring up into a holly bush where the butt of Perry's hunting rifle could be seen poking out.

"Aha!" cried Reg. "Good dog."

The two continued combing the scene for a while but found nothing more. No footprints, no pieces of clothing, no blood. They headed back to the farmhouse kitchen to see how Bunting was getting on with the traumatised pig-farmer.

While Len took a bath, Bunting was striving hard to clean up the chaotic kitchen. He made Reg a coffee then returned to his rubber-gloved task. They had orders not to linger too long, but Bunting was pathologically incapable of ignoring so much disorder and dirt. He poured all the whisky down the sink and scoured the place clean. He needed to prove he was back on form and fully functional again.

Reg sat and examined the rifle. It was the usual type of countryman's piece – quite powerful and accurate, but not a professional assassin's weapon.

Len emerged from the bathroom and Bunting fed him scrambled eggs and bacon. He gave the farmer strict orders about what indoor chores required immediate attention and why he must make the bed, tend the animals and stay off the booze until they came back to check on him this evening. Kirk nodded and said he would do it all. He was as docile as a child, and only too relieved to have someone else take charge.

Last night he had told Sir Hugo everything. Len then accepted his advice without demur. Keep quiet about the fight, Hugo had said, leave the police to him. He and his colleagues would deal with anything relating to Dick Perry from now on, Len could forget about the man. He must stay sober and carry on farming as normal. If anyone asked, Brenda and the kids had simply gone on a little family visit. Len absorbed these directions like a sponge. He asked no questions. Sir Hugo knew best.

Bunting pinned a list of chores onto Len's fridge door and left him to it.

He and Mr Green and the little white dog next drove to the top of Long Drive, the western entrance to Hall Manor. Either side of the impressive iron gates stood neat Victorian lodges with diamond-leaded windows and yew trees in their gardens. Manor Lodge was currently rented from his lordship by Dick Perry.

They approached the locked front door together, boldly ringing the bell and calling through the letterbox. There was no response. They found their way around to the back door which was also locked, so Reg used his set of picklocks and soon had it open. Inside, all was silence, except for a slowly ticking clock. The three searched the place thoroughly, making sure Stringer gave every corner of the house and yard a thorough sniff round. No one had been there recently.

Glued to the underside of a desk drawer they discovered some small cheap notebooks, similar to (but separated by decades from) those Erskine Lambert had once owned. Codebooks. Reg slid them into his pocket. Bunting discovered some female garments in the only bedroom, presumably Brenda Kirk's. There was a wad of cash in the tea caddy and a box of bullets in the pantry, but little else to interest the spy-catchers. Perry knew his business, Bunting grudgingly admitted. He would return tomorrow and clear the place out properly.

They drove back to Sir Hugo and Toby Tremayne, who sat waiting, like spiders in their black webs.

Heather makes a decision

Heather Jackson handed Mrs Clark an envelope on the Friday morning before half term.

"What's this?" smiled Mrs Clark, expecting nothing more than a funny greeting card. "Oh!" She read the short text through twice before it dawned on her this was Heather's leaving notice. "Oh Heather. Is it because of your mum?"

"I'm afraid so," sniffed Miss Jackson miserably. "I can't go on driving down there every weekend and coping with this job too. I'm so sorry, Skip. I love my job but Mum has to come first. She just isn't likely to get any better."

"Of course she must come first, my dear. And of course I understand, I really do. If it were my mother, I'd want to spend every precious day with her. What will you do? Work as a supply teacher until you find a permanent post?"

"Yes. It's the most flexible option."

"Yes. A new permanent post would be a killer challenge," Skip wished she hadn't said killer, Heather's mother was so very weak and poorly. Why did such words pop out at inopportune moments?

"Yes." Heather seemed not to have noticed. "I think that job will free me up enough time to concentrate on Mum and let me live reasonably. I'll miss you all terribly." She hung her head and sniffed louder.

The rest of the staff took the news as a dreadful blow, which made Heather cry all over again. None of them wanted her to leave.

"When will you go?" asked Guy. He had privately imagined he would be the one most likely to be handing in his notice this year, but had recently been feeling much less negative. Greg Price's attitude had altered sufficiently for the whole class to rub along much better. Perhaps it was a little of Mayflower's magic returning.

"I'm going down to look for somewhere to live over half-term next week. I've put my cottage up for sale."

"My dear," sympathised Jean. "We will all be so sorry to see you go. Mayflower won't be the same at all without your wonderful musical talent."

They all felt incredibly sad.

Heather finally smiled. "Oh, Jean, of course it will. You have Charlie. He'll keep the flag flying, even if it has a Welsh dragon in it."

Charlie gave her an unexpected hug. "I'll do my best, I promise. But Jean's right, you'll be sorely missed, Heather. And the kids certainly won't appreciate all the Celtic songs I make them learn, I can tell you that."

*   *   *

21.

comfort

In the hospital

Sgt Drysdale was feeling rather bucked. With the three vandalising Price boys sent away, the town's criminal activity had definitely calmed down. Graffiti, lead nicking, dead cats, boat-wrecking, car thefts and general hooliganism had all, thankfully, ceased. The Banford constabulary's local arrest and conviction record was looking very good – the only serious incident left on their books being the recent hit-and-run. In this buoyant mood Drysdale splashed out and bought the police station kitchenette an electric kettle, some new tyres for Pink's bike and informed Cadet Nichols he was probably trainable after all. He also bought everyone a ginger beer and a sandwich for Friday lunch at the Wheatsheaf.

Janey Birch continued to be in and out of a coma and the doctors grew pessimistic about her recovery. They explained they could set the broken limbs and treat the wounds, but the girl's underlying constitution had been ravaged by childhood infections, malnourishment and general neglect. She was little more than skin and bone. Long days cleaning pubs hadn't helped, neither had a lifetime of smoking. She may have been knocked-about by a boyfriend, it was hard to be sure, but there were bruises under her bruises and old scarring beneath the accident damage. Who knew what she got up to when she wasn't cleaning pubs?

Pink visited every day and shook his head sadly at the sight of the young woman lying swathed in soft bandages and shiny plaster. It was pitiful. The ward sister sighed and told him she would certainly not survive a move to the County General. Someone had been very rough with Janey before the hit-and-run, she thought. Lying there she looked as fragile as a baby bird.

The social worker, Mrs Harris, brought Jimmy to see his mother as soon as ever she could. He was staying with Janey's step-sister, Ann, in Portland for the time being, but Auntie Ann had eight children of her own, with another on the way. She lived in a tiny little house and she was very unhappy about being asked to find food and a bed-space for nephew Jimmy.

As soon as she collected him, Mrs Harris saw Jimmy was not faring well. He was listless, compliant, dirty and silent. It did not look as if he had washed or eaten in days. He smelled pretty unpleasant and his thin hair was matted with something brown. He had a freshly bruised eye and an obvious belly-ache. Mrs Harris gritted her teeth. She had better seek a foster placement fast – except all her current resources were full and she agonised about where to put such a vulnerable child.

The day after she had first taken him to see his mother, Mrs Harris called by the Banford doctors' surgery to see if they could think of a more suitable placement.

Dr Legg and Nurse Presley squeezed half-an-hour out of their tight schedule for her. The nurse ran briefly through

Jimmy's childhood history, describing his failure to gain weight and height during the few years she had known him. He was willing enough to eat, and joined in with most games at school. He learned to swim a little last year. But even with the Nosh Club motivating him and Ivy Green's excellently balanced daily meals, he made only limited physical growth. His bloated belly ached, he was sick, he was ravenous, he had diarrhoea, he was constipated. He had headaches. He wasn't learning as fast as the others. He was constantly anxious about his mother, according to his teachers – where she was, when she would be home, what they might eat that night. Janey's accident would be a terrible extra worry for the child, particularly at half-term when there was no school to distract his mind or kind teachers to watch over him. Having to stay with that awful aunt, in Nurse Presley's not so humble opinion, was utterly ridiculous. It was well-known the woman was hard and feckless, and could not look after her own children properly.

Dr Legg and Mrs Harris listened to her, shocked and appalled. The doctor suggested she examine the lad immediately herself, and draft an up-to-date medical report to add to the Children's Services' case-notes. Mrs Harris readily agreed, and Nurse Presley nodded her head fiercely, pleased to have finally been listened to. Dr Legg hurried out to talk to their ferocious receptionist, Mrs Drysdale, with whom she brooked no argument about rearranging her appointments. She would examine Jimmy tomorrow afternoon in a consulting room at the Cottage Hospital, and that was that.

Mrs Harris collected Jimmy the next day, thinking that at least she had made a good start. She drove him to the hospital in silence. They walked in just as PC Pink was leaving Janey's bedside. He shook his head at Mrs Harris.

Janey was in a small side room, lying comatose and hooked up to machines, barely breathing. Sunlight filtered through the dusty window and a bunch of wildflowers wilted in a little vase beside her.

"Mum!" whispered Jimmy. He let go of Mrs Harris's hand and went to the bedside. He put his hand out to stroke his mother's face, then rested his head on her arm, his fingers twisting between hers. The patient did not move. The machines clicked and purred steadily on.

"Doc says it won't be long now," Pink muttered quietly to the social worker. She felt tears begin to spill down her face. What a dreadful, horrible tragedy. This poor young woman. This poor little boy. She stood with the policeman for a while, gaining comfort from his solid presence and wiping her tears with his big white hanky.

"Are you any closer to finding the car that hit her?" she sniffed.

"No. You could almost match the shape of the bumper to her injuries, mind you, she was walloped that 'ard, poor kid. Only twenty-two, yer know. Must-a had Jim there when she were just a bairn herself. He ent got no dad listed. Janey's no parents neither. Not much of a life was it?"

"No, but she *gave* him life and she *kept* him. That has to count for something, doesn't it? She must have been tough to do that. She did the best she could, Mr Pink. Life isn't easy for some girls. They don't stand a chance from day one. Probably did what she had to – we shouldn't judge her. And she didn't go having eight kids like her step-sister either, did she? Just this one little lad. Look, I'll make sure he finds a better home, you see if I don't." Mrs Harris felt freshly motivated.

PC Pink patted her shoulder. He recognised that determined look and admired it.

Dr Legg examined Jimmy Birch from head to toe that afternoon, while Mrs Harris sat watching from a chair by the door. The doctor had an interesting collection of sweeties and toys and storybooks on her desk to chat about. She was gentle and soft-spoken with him and, compliant as ever, Jimmy allowed her to prod and poke to her professional heart's delight. She made three pages of notes and assessed everything she could think of. From hair follicles to toenails, she told Mrs Harris. Shyly, bravely, Jimmy stood in his grubby vest and pants and bore it all.

"And who knows you best, do you think? Who do you like most?"

"Friends?" asked Jimmy.

"No, grown-ups. Who in all the world, after your mum, do you like spending time with?"

There was no hesitation. "Oh, my teacher. She's lovely. I love her."

Dr Legg feigned surprise. "You *do*? Well that's wonderful, Jimmy. And what is her name?"

"Miss May Fisher," Jimmy gravely informed her, as he pulled on his smelly socks and did up his sandal buckles. He stood like Oliver Twist before the large doctor in her colourful clothes, eyeing the rings and bangles with which she was adorned. "Thank you for having me today," he said politely, and shook her hand. "I think you are very beautiful."

Never had Dr Legg felt more complimented. She handed Mrs Harris some sweeties for their return journey to Portland and hurried off to the hospital's little lab which had promised to process Jimmy's various samples post-haste.

By the following morning, the doctor had some answers from her medical evaluations. Health-wise, she now knew how to help the little boy. Feeling bucked, she reached for the telephone. Poor Mrs Harris would have to cope with everything else.

The joy of friendship

Miss Fay Winstanley was delighted with her new donkey. She wanted it primarily to look picturesque standing on her front grass next to the gypsy van, secondly to keep the grass short, thirdly for the manure, and fourthly as an occasional carrier of cumbersome objects. She had bought two antique wicker panniers and had the donkey's hooves properly trimmed in anticipation. One day there might be enough cash to purchase a harness so the creature could pull the little caravan – but not yet. That was still a dream. Miss Winstanley realised her priorities for daily living were unlike those of her neighbours, but their opinions never bothered her very much. She believed in individual style.

Tim Tuttle had been for a bike ride into town to buy an Airfix kit, and was taking a long detour home through Ironwell as it was such a beautiful morning. He had called for his friend Barry to see if he wanted to come over to play, but Barry was out, so he stopped at the war memorial in the centre of the Platt where four Mayflower kids were sitting on the steps eating home-made ice lollies. They knew him, even though he did not go to their school, and offered him their last lolly.

"Oh thanks," he said gratefully. "It's hot today."

Ryan and Baz agreed. "Too hot to go for a ride," they said.

"Unless you ride a donkey, like Miss Winstanley," joked Olive. Her friend Yulissa nodded.

"She's bought a little donkey. It would be lovely riding that. Have you seen it?" Yulissa was darkly beautiful with hair flowing like a midnight waterfall almost to the hem of her skirt. Tim couldn't take his eyes off her.

"Er, no," he admitted, hurriedly licking the icy orange dribble off his hand and wiping his mouth. "Where is it?"

"Come on, we'll show you," said Baz. "It's just round the corner."

They walked down to the old watermill where Miss Winstanley lived. It had a large front yard, which was now full of grass and weeds, on which stood the yellow gypsy caravan. It had been re-painted by its owner with roses and bluebells and sprigs of greenery in highly ornate swirls.

The donkey, recently christened Persephone, was grazing in the shade of a large mulberry tree. She gave them a long-suffering look. Persephone was today modelling a blue felt collar with her name embroidered on it, a small Robin Hood straw hat with a pheasant's feather, and a lace tablecloth draped across her back. Fresh flowers had been fastened through some of the tablecloth's little holes. The children stroked the donkey's neck and fussed with her ears, which she liked. Tim offered Yulissa some grass with which to feed the animal, and the girl rewarded him with a dazzling smile.

"This is one posh donkey," Tim said in admiration.

Olive agreed. "I'm going to ask if I can take a picture of it. We sometimes have art shows at our school and you can enter photos."

That sounded much more interesting than Tim's school. He wished he could have gone to Mayflower.

"Baz, are you coming to Portland Secondary next year?"

"Nope. I'm off to learn Latin in Fenchester Grammar, worse luck. I don't want to, but Dad says its best." Basil looked fed up at being reminded. He wanted to stay with his mates and lark around on the bus, not have to catch a train with a bunch of toffee-nosed swots. He glanced at Yulissa. There would be no girls at his new school either. Ryan noticed his friend was growing sad so he punched him on the arm.

"We'll still be here," he comforted him. "Tim and me. And Dean and the girls and the rest. 'Less you're too stuck up with playing chess and rugger to come and feed this 'ere donkey with us. Oy! Per-Stephanie, giddada my pocket!"

Persephone's tongue was snaking its way into Ryan's shirt pocket where he kept a roll of Polo mints. She he-hawed at his big flapping hands and turned her back in disgust when her visitors capered off, laughing.

A tidal wave of exuberance overwhelmed the children, making them suddenly yell and leap and gallop. Everything today was young and fresh and healthy and bright. Everywhere was filled with colour and bursting with joy. Each tiny blade of grass, the deep crystal river full of foamy bubbles and the high blue sky blended together in a newly invented cocktail meant only for them. School didn't matter! Life was now.

Dealing with Jimmy

Jimmy Birch's mother died on Saturday morning, at the end of half-term. Janey's exhausted and broken body gave up its struggle in the wee small hours when no one she loved, no one who loved her, was around.

Mrs Harris fetched Jimmy the next day. How she wished there was someone more suitable to comfort and protect him now – but there wasn't. There was no one, apart from his Aunt Ann who actively disliked him. She complained he smelled, he messed up the lavatory, he wet his bed, he wouldn't eat. She did not want him back. Her children did not get along with him. He wasn't welcome.

Fortunately Mrs Harris was made of stern stuff and had finally secured an emergency one-night placement at a busy children's home in Ledgely, so she scooped up Jimmy's little backpack and bade the sour-faced aunt a final farewell. Anywhere has to be better than here, she told herself, looking angrily at the state of the child as he climbed into the back seat of her car. Do I take him to Ledgely or arrange his immediate admittance to the cottage hospital, fretted Mrs Harris. The child's physical condition was shocking, his mental state could only be guessed at. He hadn't made a sound.

Her day continued terrible and ended beyond miserable. Tough as she was, poor Mrs Harris went home and cried into her pillow that night, thinking of Jimmy in his borrowed pyjamas trying to sleep in yet another strange place. No wonder he wet the bed. No wonder he could not eat. If only he would scream or throw things or howl and sob she would know there was some fight left in the child, but this stoicism, this drifting silent passivity terrified her. When she finally fell asleep she dreamed Jimmy was transparent, fading to nothing like a departing Tardis.

Mrs Harris hurried in to talk to Mrs Clark at nine o'clock the morning school re-opened. While Mr Tremayne took assembly, they put their heads together to find a solution to Jimmy's immediate accommodation problem.

"I don't want to have to lose this child to another school," cried Mrs Clark. She was adamant. Jimmy belonged at Mayflower and nowhere else in her view. "Could we ask his teacher to come in on this discussion? And Mrs Bailey or Mrs Duke? They all care about him very much, and they know the local families."

"By all means," agreed Mrs Harris." Let's ask anyone you can think of."

Sandi Raina took May's class while she, Carol Moore, Peggy, Cathy Duke, Skipper and Mrs Harris put their heads together. It was dreadful to think of Jimmy's life becoming even more blighted, and each kind heart was desperate to find a solution. They churned over a few possibilities, but while everyone cudgelled their collective brains it slowly began to dawn on May Fisher that the only solution that made any real sense was that she herself should take him. If the authorities agreed, of course.

"What? May, you can't."

"Yes I can, Mrs Clark. It's the best answer. I'm not so dreadfully old yet, no older than a grandmother might be anyway, and I have steady work with good money coming in. I have savings. I have a house with a spare room. Jimmy knows me and I am very fond of him. We have a bond, I think. But I *am* unmarried, which may be a drawback in the law's eyes." She stared at Mrs Harris with eyes dark with determination.

"But – someone else's child is an awful responsibility, Miss Fisher. And Jimmy Birch is currently quite a sick little boy. He's grieving for his mother. He's … He'd be a terrible tie. You love your solitude and your freedom, don't you?"

"Yes, I do. But I would also love a family. I have no people of my own left, you see." May did not say whether she had ever yearned to marry and have children – that was not the point. They did not need to know how lonely she often was, nor how she secretly dreaded the rapidly approaching end of an active career filled with little children. What they *did* need to be told was that now, suddenly out of the blue, she saw her chance of a new future. She was fit, she was able – and she wanted Jimmy. No one else, just Jimmy. May felt a sudden overwhelming tug on her maternal heartstrings and a shockingly visceral surge of primitive protective instinct. She could have killed a tiger with her bare teeth at that moment, but instead she continued rationalising.

"I would welcome him, and undergo any scrutiny the authorities require. It would be no different for me to cope with Jimmy and his troubles than for any other working parent, would it? I am in a better position than most. Being a lone carer, I can devote myself to his welfare. I can offer him a proper loving home with all the care and stability he needs. Of course I could foster Jimmy at first, Mrs Harris – while the authorities decide whether I am suitable to adopt him. Of course, he may not wish to come to me, and I would have to respect his choice, but I do know him better than anyone else, I think, and I believe he will agree. I may not be able to offer him a father or any siblings, but Jimmy and I would constitute our own little family. We both need a proper family."

The more she spoke the more May's heart filled. She couldn't – she *wouldn't* – let this opportunity of a new future pass without fighting hard for it.

They all turned towards Mrs Harris who looked as if a lone life-boat had finally emerged through the Atlantic fog and was heading her way.

"I know I will need help. Lots of help," May smiled and nodded at her Mayflower colleagues with tears running down her cheeks. "And more than a little advice. But it would be a start wouldn't it?"

"Are you quite sure? Boys can be a handful."

"Quite sure. I'm used to children. I'm not exactly a starry-eyed beginner." She gazed at Mrs Harris imploringly. "You may come and inspect my home at any time, Mrs Harris. I do so hope you will remain Jimmy's social worker."

Mrs Harris looked about ready to kiss her.

"Well, I … Thank you *very* much indeed, Miss Fisher. Placement would only be temporary fostering to begin with of course. You understand that? There are procedures, protocols. We'll have to see how it goes."

The women stared at May whose heart was beating so hard she felt as if she had run a mile. Mrs Harris was smiling and nodding, trying to be cautious and composed but not succeeding at all.

"Well then," said May sitting up very straight. "Thank you, Mrs Harris. I will put my offer of a permanent home for Jimmy in writing later. Will Dr Legg be overseeing Jimmy's future medical needs?"

"Yes, she has already agreed to that as long as he lives within the Banford area. Mrs Duke and Mrs Bailey say they are happy to administer Jimmy's new medicines during the school day, isn't that right?"

"It is. He's a dear little boy, and we all love him," cried Cathy, ready to weep with happiness. "Oh Miss Fisher, thank you! You're wonderful."

"He will be alright, Mrs Harris, never fear," promised Mrs Clark. "Mayflower will care for Jimmy Birch now."

Mrs Harris put on her coat feeling like new woman. There would be no horrid dreams to haunt her tonight.

Miss Fisher was given the rest of the day off. She and Mrs Harris hurried around to No 2 Fen Lane where Marigold the cat was shocked at seeing her mistress return so soon after having left for work. The social worker inspected the back bedroom and other living arrangements but everywhere looked spick and span, and there were all the modern conveniences on her list of essentials. She thanked the teacher from the bottom of her heart again before hurrying back to her office.

Dr Legg and Mrs Drysdale the dragon-like receptionist, meanwhile, had moved heaven and earth to arrange an emergency appointment at the County Children's Hospital with two eminent specialists. The doctor collected the boy from Ledgely and drove Jimmy there herself. The specialists scanned her assessments and test results, then peered long and hard at Jimmy. They agreed his physical state was critical, and their confirmation of Dr Legg's diagnosis was rapid. They scrutinised the child over their glasses like a textbook specimen as he stood before them in scratchy new underclothes.

He was bruised, tired and stressed, his inner organs bloated. Dry yellow skin moved over his bird-like chest and boney buttocks like crêpe. He could have been a child from a famine poster. Since starting school, records showed Jimmy had suffered ringworm, scabies, lice and other parasites associated with poor hygiene and general ignorance. He'd had nits, infected blisters and a burst eardrum. Janey, though doing her best, had had little understanding of what a growing child required, and until Jimmy himself had learned about healthy foods at school their diet had mainly consisted of shop-bought chips and the occasional sausage. Janey's own physical and mental health had always been poor, her labour with Jimmy long, difficult and unattended. Her own schooling had been sporadic at best. She was barely fourteen when Jimmy was born. Fortunately, the experts agreed, with better care, a good diet and appropriate consistent medication, a stable home with less anxiety, the road to better health for Jimmy was promising. He might still have a childhood. He might live to see his eighth birthday in November.

By the time they finally ushered Dr Legg and her diminutive charge out, they were confident they had caught the child just in time, and were already wondering whether they could write Jimmy's case up as an article for the Lancet.

Afra Legg, tired but now much more confident, took Jimmy to Treve's for some lunch before driving back to Ledgely. On the way upstairs to the restaurant they walked through the toy department, and she bought him a colouring book and some wax crayons. He was amazed at this gift and kept stroking the packet of crayons as he sipped his soup. However, before he had finished eating he fell fast asleep. The doctor, large and exotic, swept him up in her arms and carried the little mite all the way back to the car. Feeling his lightness and fragility in her strong arms, she wept every step of the way, much to the surprise of other shoppers. Afra settled him gently in the rear seat and tried to pull herself together.

She stopped the car once on the way to make a phone call, and left the red phone box a much happier woman. She had discovered that that tireless warrior, Mrs Harris, had worked magic and gained permission for Jimmy Birch to be taken directly to May Fisher's house in Fen Lane that very evening. She would be expecting him.

"God Bless These Marvellous People," sang the doctor all the way to Banford, to the tune of 'The Church's One Foundation'.

Afra carried Jimmy into No 3 Fen Lane at teatime. It was a modest home, filled with sunlight and peace. May Fisher stood there in a cross-over pinny – stout, sensible, and prepared for anything.

The ladies tucked him into his new bed and retired to the sitting room where Dr Legg handed May the bag of medicine and instructions she had brought from the pharmacy at the hospital. They sat and drank tea and discussed Jimmy's medical needs.

"I don't expect he'll wake till morning," said Afra. "He's been through so much these last few days, the poor thing is exhausted."

May agreed. "I have everything ready to care for him, Doctor. Mrs Clark has kindly agreed to my taking this entire week off so we can settle in together properly. Will you call by tomorrow?"

"Yes, of course. Wild horses wouldn't stop me. Now don't you go spoilin' him, Miss Fisher," smiled Dr Legg. She took a long look at the old lady and decided May Fisher was the perfect auntie for this sickly child. "He's a very lucky boy to have found you, you know. Just don't go overdoin' it yourself."

May closed the door and returned to Jimmy's bedside.

About seven o'clock, he woke up and saw her knitting.

"Is it socks again, Miss?" he asked sleepily.

"It is. I could knit you some if you like, though I don't think these fluffy ones would be quite right for school, do you?" She sat down on his bed and showed him the brown angora wool.

"Mum likes pink," he told her. "But she's been knocked down by a car."

"I know," murmured Miss Fisher.

"She's died." His eyes suddenly opened large and brown. "She died, didn't she?"

"Yes, she did, Jimmy. Now she's not hurting any more. And you're going to stay here with me."

That was all the child needed to hear, all he could take in. He sat up and clutched her as tightly as his arms could hold. He cried and sobbed and hiccupped into May's bosom as if he would never stop, his skinny frame shuddering fit to fall apart. The old lady stroked his hair and let him cry, knowing these were the first unrestrained tears he had shed in a long, long, long while.

When the storm subsided she kissed his forehead and wiped his face. She settled him back gently on the big white pillow, gave him a drink of water and tucked him tightly around with sheets and blankets. She held his hand until he fell back asleep.

When Jimmy awoke the following morning, the first thing he saw lying on his pillow were the angora socks newly transformed into a little fluffy brown teddy bear. It fitted perfectly into his hand and felt soft – very, very soft – against his lips. As soft as his mum's kiss.

He struggled out of bed and found his way to the bathroom just as Miss Fisher emerged from the other bedroom, clad in a blue dressing gown and sheepskin slippers. Her white hair was in a plait over her shoulder.

"Good morning," she said. "And how did you sleep?"

"Very well, thank you," replied her guest shyly. "I never wetted your nice bed."

"I see you found Brown Bear. That's good. Now, what do you suppose he might like for his breakfast?"

Breakfast for a toy? Jimmy had to think. He had never owned a teddy bear before and imagining what one might eat took an effort.

"I suppose it ought to be honey, as he's a bear."

This was a good sign. Miss Fisher nodded gravely. "Well, we do have honey. How about we spread some of that on some rice crackers? Then later on we can pick strawberries from the garden and see if he likes pink milk. What do you say?"

"Yes please, Miss."

Afra has news

Skipper was astonished to hear Joe Granger had not only returned from New Mexico but was now engaged to be married. Dr Legg filled her in on the details when she called into White Cottage to update her on Jimmy Birch.

"Engaged? To Chloe?"

"Chloe? No. He won't really talk about the American visit. I think it is far too painful for him."

"Not Hilary Presley then, don't tell me that!" Skipper's idiotic hopes and fears were up and down like a yoyo.

Dr Legg opened her eyes wide and grinned. "No," she chortled. "Not poor Hilary. That one's destined for life's romantic disappointments."

She and I both, thought Skipper bitterly. We are delusional types. "Who then?"

"Someone he's had an on-off relationship with for years, apparently. She's a nurse at the hospital. Elaine Hill. You've got her little brother Billy in Mr Paton's class."

"Have we? I can't say I've ever met her. What's she like?" If Joe wasn't marrying Chloe or herself Skipper at least wanted to think the doctor had selected someone interesting. "It's a bit rushed isn't it?"

"Is it? Why? Was he going with someone else?"

"Not exactly." Skip didn't feel like explaining. "Well, I hope he'll be very happy. Is he back at the practice permanently or heading for the frozen north again?"

"He says they're staying here. Buying some house out in one of the villages, I think. There's more than enough work for the two of us at the surgery now Dr Jenkins is finally retiring, so Joe and I are going into partnership We should be able to cover most of this half of town and some of the hamlets round about between us."

"Oh, that's wonderful. Mum will be so thrilled. She loves you both. Now, fill me in a little more on Jimmy's progress. I went round on Thursday to see them and everything looked OK to me. You'd never think May had been living alone for sixty years."

"Yes, duck to water, that one. She's one of nature's natural aunties – straight in, no messin'. She has Jimmy on sensible daily routines and gives him plenty o' time and rest. Love is all most kids require."

"I think it's all most lonely old ladies require too," smiled Skip. She told her about the little scene she had witnessed when she called in. Jimmy was sitting at the kitchen table colouring in his new book with Marigold stretched on the rag rug at his feet. May was preparing a bowl of strawberries for their supper. It was as if the pair had always been together.

"He's taking these new pills to help his stomach retain some goodness," went on Dr Legg. "And he's getting plenty of vegetables, and protein and so forth. Now he's off bread and biscuits he's in a lot less discomfort. May says his favourite supper is cheesy potato cakes and ham."

Skip chuckled. "That's wonderful. She knitted him a little teddy bear, you know. I don't think he's ever had anything like that before."

"Yes. He must have missed out on a whole lot. You should have seen his face when we went through that toy department the other day," remembered the doctor. She wished now she had bought him something other than a colouring book, but never mind, he seemed to like it. "I'd say he can start back at school next week, if he takes it gently. You'll keep a close eye on them both?"

"Of course," answered Mrs Clark firmly. She would pop into May's classroom whenever she could and make sure Carol was there as much as possible too. "Don't worry. Cathy or Peg will see he takes his lunchtime medicine and Ivy already has his dietary list pinned up on her noticeboard in the kitchen. She knows about snacks and milk and not overloading his tummy."

"That's it – little and often, and no bread or cake or biscuits. Well, not yet."

Dr Legg decided her workday had better finish now and her personal life begin. She stood up. "Well, I'm off to Ledgely to see my ex-husband for lunch. Thanks for the coffee." She went out to the car and waved to Dora who was gardening.

Dora hurried over from her rose bushes, hands stained from squashing greenfly. "You off, Afra? Sorry I was otherwise engaged. Do pop in – any time, I'm always in the garden."

"Yes, when you're not runnin' the WI or helpin' out at school," laughed Afra. She was beginning to know Dora and her busy-ness.

Dora smiled. "Well this little town is full of life now summer's come, isn't it? I don't want to miss out." She grew suddenly serious as she remembered something. "When is that poor girl's funeral? Jimmy's mother? What a tragedy."

"Yes, a tragedy indeed. Next Tuesday at St Andrew's. Not that she was a church-goer, but Rev Bill is a generous soul. Eleven o'clock. Miss Fisher will bring the boy if she thinks he's up to it. The vicar says he will keep it short."

"Quite right. Jimmy ought to be there. Do you think May will want to adopt Jimmy one day?"

"It's early days yet," commented Afra as she squeezed herself back into her driving seat. "But I hope so, Dora, I really do. I think once those two settle down and get used to their new life together it could be the makin' of both of them."

She beeped the horn and scrunched out of the drive. Dora closed the gate and returned to her never-ending war with the aphids, feeling confident that finally things might be starting to go right again for the people of Mayflower School.

*   *   *

22.

Funeral

Dust

Ted Jolly was the painter and decorator Mrs Clark had engaged to freshen up the interior of the school. He proceeded as slowly as molasses over ice, but he was cheap. Although she would have preferred the work to be done in the summer holidays Ted was available now, so she agreed to let him start while the children were still in school. After all, she reasoned, it was June and they would probably spend most days out of doors. Lessons on the grass under the chestnut trees were fun and there were all sorts of sports to be getting on with too. Without the children around, Mr Jolly would be able to make steady progress.

Peggy Bailey wasn't so sure. She knew Ted of old and told Cathy she thought he'd spin out the job until Christmas, given half a chance. Paul Moore's men would have taken a fraction of the time. She glared at Mr Jolly with his sandpaper and drop-cloths and wished him further. The endless scratch-scratch of his scraping got on her nerves. Everywhere was covered in thick dust.

Jolly got on Reg's nerves too. Stringer couldn't stop sneezing and every day there was extra work for him and Pru Davidson. Pru herself grew rapidly mutinous.

"Gawd knows I done this top landing twice already this week," she complained bitterly. "Why I have to come up 'ere and polish it a third ruddy time beats me."

She stumped off to fetch a bucket of water and a clean rag, with her daughter Shelley trailing gloomily behind.

It was no fun having to stay at school until six o'clock when everyone else had gone home, just because your mother was the cleaner. Of course it meant Shelley always had her homework completed, but she would far rather be watching telly or playing outside like other children.

Mr Jolly carried on, deaf to criticism and oblivious to any need for speed. He put his cloths down and rubbed and scratched and filled and finally painted every square foot of the downstairs corridor before moving slowly upstairs, stair by stair.

Randel Bay treats for all

Despite Mrs Clark's empty coffers, the youngest children had their annual day-trip to Randel Bay after all. Most parents had been only too happy to help with the modest cost, knowing how much the little ones looked forward to it, and that times were apparently hard for the school. It was sad that Miss Fisher could not attend, but Mrs Moore and the supply teacher Mrs Wheatley had both been able to go, so everyone ended up satisfied.

The visit felt like a week away to some participants. Riding there and back on a coach was an adventure in itself. Thankfully, only one child was travel-sick. The weather was wonderful and the children ran about and screamed to their hearts' content on the wide empty beach, dabbling in the water, clambering over rocks, eating sandwiches and sipping orange squash out of unfamiliar picnic cups. Even the dribbly ice creams purchased from a colourful van were magical. The children went splashing in the salty water and built wonderful castles with moats, then long-jumped down the soft, warm, thick sand of the dunes. Everyone came home hugging pails full of seaweed and trailing sand, while their sleepy teachers and mums dozed happily down the winding country roads.

Mr Nesbit, that staunch supporter of all things kindergarten, had come along too, and told everyone the day constituted his entire summer holiday. It was he who thoughtfully purchased two cotton sun-hats at the new kiosk near the car park and took them back to school. One was for Jimmy and one for Miss Fisher.

"If they couldn't visit the seaside this time, the seaside must come to them," he explained.

Rick Hodges and Lulu Diaz helped him quietly arrange the hats, a bucket of sandy seaweed, a spade, and a few shells on Miss Fisher's doorstep for her to discover next time she put her milk bottles out.

A sad morning

The interment of Jane Birch's ashes was not a lengthy business. More people turned out than expected, however, which pleased Rev Bill Williams. June Williams carried the urn to the place in the graveyard where Dora, Mr Unwin from the Mint public house, Mrs Dawkins from the Yeoman, Mrs Bicknell and Miss Muggeridge stood waiting.

As he began to speak, May Fisher appeared, holding Jimmy's hand. The child looked as grey as his new school jumper and shorts. In his other hand he held tightly to a small knitted teddy bear. He looked more like a four-year-old than a lad of seven. He stood quietly while Rev Bill spoke, then Miss Fisher handed him a bunch of pink roses from her basket to place on the ground. Then the pair turned and left, stepping slowly and carefully – an odd couple of ducks, thought June Williams, wiping her eye. Old souls.

Miss Muggeridge and Ada Bicknell walked home together, talking about Jimmy and all that had happened recently.

"If only I'd been a better neighbour," sighed Miss Muggeridge regretfully. "I could have given Jimmy his dinner sometimes. I could have offered to mind him a bit more."

"He could have come and sat with me of an evening, too," added Ada. "But she never asked, now, did she? Never asked for nothing."

"No, she never did, poor Janey. Only twenty-one the vicar said. Must've bin hard having a nipper when you were only fourteen and not wed. Fourteen! Most likely took advantage of, you ask me. Ent decent, is it?"

"No. Still, Janey done right by the boy, as far as she could. I can't say as much for that blessed sister of hers – that so-called auntie he went to stay with first-off. Piece of work, she is. But he'll be alright now. May Fisher'll give him a good home, if they let him stay. Always was a kind lady. Bit strick, mind, but a real lady, you ask me," said Bick firmly.

"That she is," agreed Eliza Muggeridge. "Old school. He's got some new fancy medicine too, did you hear? That'll help his everlasting belly-ache. He'll be alright now."

"I wonder who we'll get livin' at No 1," Bick went on. "Ooever it is I hope they give it a proper scrub-through first. Not that Janey didn't try, but I've seen more than a few cockroaches on that back step lately."

The ladies hurried on discussing the merits of various pesteliminating products, a subject close to both their hearts.

At a loose end

Greg Price still couldn't decide if he was happy or sad, pleased or angry. All his brothers had been taken away, except for Phil, which meant it was loads quieter and a lot less confrontational at home. Having Phil about was alright, especially when he stumped up the occasional fiver as pocket money. But Phil was often round at Pat's, which meant Greg had his mum's undivided attention far more often than he liked. For a start she was thrilled about him winning a grammar school place and couldn't stop talking about it. For another she was set on moving house to Fenchester, just when he was beginning to like Banford. But she expected him to do chores around the house, all the grocery shopping, and inspected his homework too. Greg was guiltily relieved when she went to work and left him to his own devices.

He finished washing the dishes and made himself a glass of orange squash. He took it outside where he was trying to grow some sunflowers and peppers in the weed-patch that passed for a back garden. They were coming along as nicely as those he was growing in his square allotment at school. He sipped his drink and felt quietly proud. It was the first time he had ever managed to grow anything without his brothers trampling on it.

Greg wondered where Phil and Pat Green would live when they shacked-up together next month. Nowhere posh, that was certain. Chandlers didn't pay all that much in wages, but Phil said he was saving and had plans. Maybe one day Chandler would give him extra responsibility, like running a taxi service or something. He and Pat were determined to get married and have kids one day. Greg had been thinking about the pair often lately, and realised he was envious of Phil and his modest hopes. Steady, honest money was looking to be a much better bet than shoplifting or stealing lead off roofs. The trouble with thieving was someone always dobbed you in in the end, and then where were you? Borstal or Ledgely prison, that's where. Somewhere without a future.

Greg scooped up his swimming bag and locked up the house. He decided he would ride his bike over to the Lido for a dip as it was going to be a long boring Saturday on his own.

It was peaceful, cycling down the heath's dusty trails. He crossed over the two forks of the Wain that ran either side of Latimer Eye and came to the railway station where his next-door neighbour, Kevin Smith, was sweeping the platform. Kevin had always been one of the Price's principal targets for pranks, but today Greg stopped and said hello – which considerably surprised the porter.

"How's that little lad getting on, do you know?" asked Kevin. Everyone locally knew about Jimmy Birch's troubles.

"Alright, I think. Gone to live with his teacher."

"No. Really? That's a bit weird innit?" Kevin had never heard of such a thing.

Greg shrugged. He hadn't thought about it long enough to form an opinion. "She's alright. A bit old. All them old women like fussing round little babies."

Kevin laughed. "I expect they do. Still, where's the harm eh? Might be good for him. Get a bit of decent grub and some attention."

"See yer," said Greg, thinking what a boring conversation this was. He cut through the hedge at the back of the railway car park, across a field full of grazing bullocks, and up the grass alleyway that ran beside Miss Fisher's house and garden, to Fen Lane. He paused and stood up on his pedals to see over her privet hedge. What was the kid doing?

"Hey Jimmy," he called.

Jimmy was surprised at being addressed by a body-less head, but he got up from where he was playing by the cold frame with a little blue toy lorry and went over. "Hello," he said.

"How's it going with old Fish-face?"

"Auntie May is kind to me. We had red jelly yesterday for tea. And egg salad."

Instead of sneering Greg nodded and let it go. "That was nice. I'm going for a swim down the Lido. See yer."

"See yer," echoed Jimmy. This unexpected conversation with a boy from school had suddenly helped him feel a little more back-to-normal, more able to think about that part of his life again. He went to sit beside Marigold on a cushion on the sunny doorstep to show her his lorry. This afternoon he would be going round to see Grandma Dora, a lady he knew very well from school, while Auntie May went shopping with Mrs Hewitt in her car to Fenchester.

In a minute, he thought, I'll go inside and pull out that shopping bag from under the stairs for her.

Lady Longmont reappraises her paying guest

Lady Longmont had quickly grown used to having Toby Tremayne around her home. Mostly he kept himself to himself, but they usually met for a meal or a drink on the terrace at the weekend. He seemed to have chummed up with the headmistress with whom he was often seen racing around the lanes in his little car. Gibb did not envy them that experience very much – the MG was a devil to get in and out of and almost blew one's ears off when the top was down. Mrs Clark could have it. Although he was a prompt enough payer, and a quiet enough house guest, Toby had proved absolutely no help at all with any jobs about the place. In fact he was a liability, as he often managed to break whatever he set his hand to. Still, she mused, just having a man about again was pleasant. Tremayne could hold an intelligent conversation on almost any subject, and was a good listener – for a man, she added patronisingly. In her experience men usually only wanted to talk about themselves and changed the subject when it came to your turn. But Toby actually seemed genuinely interested in other people. He asked questions, he commented. He helped you notice details or motivations you might have previously overlooked. Yes, he was articulate and interesting alright. She had to remind herself every day to be extremely guarded whenever they chatted, because now she was aware he was best pals with the rat Hugo Chivers.

Toby Tremayne was definitely a cuckoo in her nest – he was there to keep an eye on her. A fixture. There was no doubt he was either MI5 or MI6, she couldn't decide which. Gibb knew he had searched her house, the ungrateful snake in the grass. It annoyed Gibb intensely that she had not suspected him from the very beginning and she was doubly annoyed with herself for suggesting he come to stay in the first place. Her guard had been down that night his house caught fire. She had felt sorry for him. She wouldn't be making that mistake twice. The more she pondered the more she fumed at having dropped her guard. She had been seduced by the rediscovery of a charming long-lost acquaintance. She must be much more vigilant in the future.

Gibb wiped the little blue teapot she had been washing up and placed it back on the high mantle-shelf above the range. Before popping its lid back on, she pulled out a couple of keys from the pocket of her gardening smock and slipped them inside the pot. It would be very unfortunate if her nosey jailer discovered these, she thought to herself, smiling grimly.

Back in business

An outward-bound guest arrived at the safe house. She was a sight for sore eyes, in Bunting's view, being quite young and attractive. What her assignment was he did not know, but she also delivered some new surveillance equipment from the technical department for him to install – four little American TV cameras, a screen, a miniature tape recorder, four tiny microphones and all the wiring associated with them in a shoebox-sized unit. Bunting had never seen such items before, but he quickly figured out how they worked. The only question was where to place them for optimal monitoring.

Sir Hugo puffed on a cigar and also brooded the question. Their range wasn't huge, so best situate them in the most obvious hotspots. He had Bunting unscrew and investigate each individual piece of the new equipment to see whether the bugs themselves were bugged, and grudgingly admitted they were not. He did not trust American spyware any more than British.

The en-route agent also brought the information that up until a month ago Moscow had continued to believe the old brick work-shed at Dutch Cottage was still being used as their safe house. To Hugo this suggested their informant was not able to update his – or her – masters very promptly, which was satisfactory, as it afforded them a little flexibility.

Bunting quickly installed the new equipment at No 2 Church Road, and spent the following two days re-installing all their original listening devices back in Longmont Lodge. Mr Tremayne had convinced Hugo that the empty mansion was well-worth recommissioning as no one would suspect the place to be reactivated. If No 2 was likely to be compromised soon, a back-up was vital. They were under pressure. So Bunting and Reg Green drilled and screwed and camouflaged lengths of wire and the boxy old recorders back into the lodge's walls and ceilings once more. The basement and most of the ground floor could now be monitored from a small bedroom two floors above. The whole extensive system was motion-triggered and silent. Satisfied, they locked the place carefully back up and breathed a cautious sigh of relief.

Hugo himself updated the headmistress of the change in the lodge's status. She took the news better than he had expected, not appreciating the fact she now privately welcomed the involvement of the secret service, as it could provide protection from the interfering local authority who might seek to compulsorily purchase it one day. Turning a blind-eye, like Nelson, seemed to her now a reasonable price to pay.

As for the parachute canopy, which had been so well-hidden behind the pigsties at Abbey Farm and found by the two schoolboys, it was quickly verified as genuine. Hugo's team scoured the surrounding area, but could find no other trace of the sloppy agent who should have hidden it properly, and who had so unprofessionally abandoned this task. They found no trace of him, though they searched for several miles all around. He, like his predecessor, could now be anywhere in the kingdom. Hugo was glad he was MI5's problem now.

Bunting went back to gardening, Mrs Bunting to housekeeping and Reg to his school caretaking. Sir Hugo resumed his local interest in all things related to the school, and slotted back into his old Banford lifestyle. Toby Tremayne composed cryptic crosswords, taught French, and kept a weather eye on the world from his new study. He allowed the two boys to keep the yards and yards of dark parachute nylon, which they happily carted off to Weston Common where it became a wonderful tent to play in after school.

Photo day

"Bit of a wet one this morning, Mr Green," called Mr Simms the photographer, as he unloaded his cameras, bags and tripods from his car. It was late June, and he was at school to take photos of groups of children, and the annual panoramic one he found so profitable. "How are you keeping? Had your hip done last Christmas I heard?"

"Morning," grunted Reg. He took his cap off and whacked it against his leg in an effort to dry it. "Yerse. Like a young gazelle I am now. Wonderful what they can do these days."

"It certainly is. Now, where am I today? Oh the gym hall, fine. If you'll just be good enough to grab that bag for me I'll try to finished by – when was it again?"

"Lunch is 12.15 as usual. So if you can be done by noon I'll 'ave my boys set up quick-sharp so Ivy don't give me an earful later on." He liked to pretend Ivy nagged him. "I'm to remind you that the staff is to 'ave a formal group picture."

"Oh, right. I have that down on my list, yes. Now then, there we are. I'll just nip back to the car for my backdrop screen. Those polished wooden wall-bars are nice but parents prefer a softer image these days. You got a boy can help me? Or a girl? I usually have a runner."

Reg sent him Annie White, one of the Form 6 prefects. She brought Mr Simms a cup of coffee from the staffroom, thrilled she had been chosen to help. Everyone was revising for the end of term exams this morning which made her more than usually anxious. She told herself she would revise quietly over the weekend, in her own bedroom instead of in class. Mr Simms kept her employed fetching various groups of children and bringing him cups of tea. Annie loved it.

At breaktime the weather cleared. Three volunteer parents and all the prefects took outdoor duty, watching the children play on the damp field while the staff stood in an embarrassed cluster in the hall, waiting for Mr Simms to click his shutter. Luckily he didn't take too long.

"Well, that's one for the News of the World," he quipped. "Or maybe the rogues gallery. Now then, how about I take one of all your school pets?" He knew this school had various cats and dogs so was calculating this too could be a nice little earner.

"What a splendid idea," said Skipper, constantly glad of ways in which she could make money for the school coffers. "Perhaps we could make it into a Christmas calendar."

Glenda

Like Heather Jackson, Mike was worried about his mother. Glenda was so forgetful these days, it was hard to leave her alone for long. He talked about her latest near-miss as he and Ernest sat in the library marking exam papers.

"I've asked Dr Legg to take another look at her," he said.

Ernest nodded sympathetically. He was desperately sorry for his friend. It must be awful seeing your mother fading away before your very eyes. He could barely remember his own but felt the want of her presence every day. "That's sensible," he said.

"It was a good thing Mr Watson happened to call in when he did. He managed to turn the gas off and open all the windows. She was fast asleep in the front room with the telly on."

Mr Watson was the postman who often called into Mike's isolated cottage when he had a letter or even a tedious piece of advertising matter to deliver, as there was always a cup of tea ready for him. It was a long bike ride out their way. Yesterday he had discovered the gas turned on but unlit. He had saved the day and called the ambulance people, then waited until Mike hurried home.

"She could have been blown to kingdom come. What on earth will you do?" asked Ernest.

"I don't know. I'm hoping the doc may have some ideas. Mum's eighty, you know. Should I be thinking of an old people's home somewhere?"

"Like Heather arranged for her mother, you mean?"

"Well yes. It seems an awful thing, but I can't keep her safe when I'm at work, can I?" Mike looked so forlorn, it hurt

Ernest's kind heart. The man was grey from exhaustion and thinner than ever.

"Well, why don't I help you find out about the best local places? We can have some brochures sent, then at least you'll be able to choose wisely." Researching the available literature was all Ernest could think to do. "I'll come with you and visit those you think might do, you know I will."

Mike smiled. "Practical as ever, Ernest. Alright, thank you. I'll take you up on that. And yes, after the doc has properly assessed her I'll be able to make a better decision. She's stopping by tomorrow morning so I won't be in until later. Skip knows."

"Good. Now then, where d'you want this pile of essays?"

Dora swings into action

Jimmy Birch knocked on the front door of White Cottage. There was no answer so he trotted round the back where he found Mrs York tying back some wayward rose fronds.

"Hello, Grandma Dora," he called. "It's me."

"Oh my goodness, is it that time already?" Dora smiled and kissed the top of his head. His hair should surely thicken up a bit soon, she hoped. "I'm so pleased you're here. Now we can have some tea."

They went indoors and put the kettle on. From a tin Dora took out some rice crackers she had bought at the local Chinese restaurant. Jimmy usually came round after school nowadays so that Miss Fisher could tidy up her classroom in peace for half an hour, and he had some playtime away from her. Dora had been only too happy to offer to have him. She was very fond of the little boy.

"How was school today?"

This was a question he had not often been asked before. He had to think about what had happened and whether he liked it, an answer requiring him to remember two things.

"It was exams. You get questions and have to write answers," he explained.

"Was it difficult?"

"No, not really. Miss helps you if you don't know how to write some words. Gillian Davy lent me her pencil sharpener."

"That was nice of her. So it was a tough day. Now then, here's your milk. Try the crackers. They're new."

Dora set a Snoopy mug down in front of him. It was his mug, she had told him when they bought it together at the jumble sale, his alone. They would keep it at Grandma Dora's house and he could drink out of it every time visited. He nibbled a cracker and decided it was excellent, especially with some peanut butter on top.

They were happily munching when Dr Legg knocked at the door. Jimmy hurried to let her in. She was his great pal now. Dora could hear them laughing in the hall as she slid the kettle back on the Aga top.

"Well now, good afternoon Mrs York! Jimmy's telling me there's Chinese crackers for tea. How wonderful – I love Chinese food." So saying she plonked herself down on a creaky chair and mopped her forehead. It was a warm afternoon.

"How's it goin', Jimmy?" she enquired.

He knew she meant at Auntie May's house and whether he was feeling happy living there. He smiled indulgently. People always asked the same things nowadays.

"I'm fine, thank you," he said. "I call her Auntie at home and Miss Fisher at school. I ent wet the bed at all and I eat my eggs up in the morning. And I do responsibilities. That means jobs. I feed Hannibal and Marigold and I put the letters on the table. I lock the front door every night too." That was a recent honour. He was glad he remembered to tell her that, as it was impressive.

"And who, pray tell, is Hannibal?"

"He's a tortoise. He's got a little cage thing on the back lawn so he can eat down the grass. If he didn't have that he'd be off down the street again."

The ladies laughed.

"He must be a very energetic tortoise," said the doctor. "Now, Grandma Dora tells me you have a scooter here in her shed. Would you like to go and play on it while we ladies have a chat?"

"OK," he said and went obediently off. His scooter had also come from the jumble sale and it was great. It was red and, now that Mr Green had oiled its blue wheels, it ran really well.

"Dora, I'm concerned about Glenda Paton out there at Caster Cottage. She's not doing well at all."

"Oh dear, I'm very sorry to hear that." Glenda was one of Dora's Women's Institute pals although she had not seen her for a few months. "What's the problem. Something I can help with?"

"Bless you, always it's the busy people that offer to help," smiled the doctor. "I think it's just *anno domini* with her. She has developed some quite severe memory problems and almost blew the house up recently, leaving the gas on. She's had three falls, one of which really messed her chin up. She's incontinent, and wanders about at night. Her son does his best, but he's at work all day poor man, and worried sick about her. I wondered whether you could recommend anyone who might possibly be able to go and sit with her sometimes? Mike says he'll pay. It wouldn't be everyone's cuppa tea I know, but, well…"

Dora's organiser's brain clicked rapidly into gear. "Leave it with me," she said. "I'll try and organise a rota or something with the WI. Glenda has plenty of chums there. I'm sure I can work something out. And I'll liaise with Mike too. Jean or Skip wouldn't mind running her into the clinic for any appointments, if you needed to see her. Yes, leave it with me."

"You're a wonderful woman, Mrs York, and you make a lovely cuppa tea. Thank you. Yes, thank you very much."

* * *

23.

Ernest

Mr Tremayne delivers a lesson

After school one day, Jimmy's friend Carl asked Miss Fisher if he and Jim could go 'down the rec' and play on the swings. She had no objections as long as they did not fall in the river or get into any other kind of trouble. Carl smiled at her, knowing when his leg was being pulled.

"And he's to be home no later than half-past-four, please Carl. Does your mother know where you will be?"

"Yes, Miss Fisher. She's given me 50p for a lolly each. Is he allergic?"

"No, not to ice-lollies. It's only biscuits and cakes and bread he mustn't have. He knows." They had visited the consultant at the hospital a couple of days before for more test results, and Miss Fisher now had an even firmer grasp of her foster-child's specific dietary needs. "Thank you for being such a good friend, Carl."

Carl went off to find Jimmy, who was waiting by the school's front gate. As they left for the recreation ground, the two school inspectors – who had upset so many people last October – marched into the building. They ignored the front door bell, bypassed the secretary's office and walked straight into the headmistress's study without knocking.

Mrs Clark had been deep in conversation with Mr Tremayne over the end-of-term exam results. They looked up from their piles of papers in surprise.

"May we help you?" asked Toby in a deeply chilling voice. He loomed very tall with his back to the window.

Mrs Busterd and Mr Phillips, unabashed, stood their ground. They enjoyed their reputation as harbingers of turbulence. A thoroughly good shake-up was what these complacent old institutions and their outdated teachers needed.

Emboldened by Toby's obvious anger and commanding presence, Mrs Clark rapidly recovered her composure. She discovered, to her surprise, that she had evolved from the pusillanimous panicker of last October. With Toby beside her she felt much more confident.

"Mr Tremayne," she said calmly, "May I introduce Mrs Busterd and Mr Phillips. They inspected our school earlier in the year. Mr Tremayne is my new deputy headmaster."

Phillips held out a hand but Toby pointedly crossed his arms and stared at the intrusive pair. He discounted the man immediately, narrowly focusing his attention on the expensively attired and flawlessly made-up female. He had met her type before. Self-serving know-alls who enjoyed using their sexuality to intimidate others.

"We have called in to discover what progress you are making," stated Alicia Busterd, pulling off her beautiful blue gloves in a gesture Skip remembered very well. "We trust by now your school is showing substantial improvements."

Toby touched Skip's arm, signalling that he would deal with this.

"Well now, with Mrs Clark's permission" he said. He walked around the desk and leaned his backside against it, shielding Skipper and the confidential paperwork. He did not ask the visitors to sit down.

"As it so happens, the headmistress and I were just going through the children's examination results, and other quantitative indicators of the effectiveness of our school's teaching. If you would like a copy of the full annual report we shall be drafting for our board of governors, we will be happy to supply you with a copy at the end of the academic year. Only with their permission, of course, and only in response to a formal written request from the Chief Education Officer himself. At that time you may also like to see the eleven plus results, PE performance ratings, parental comments, a budget distribution forecast and a separate report on the quality of our learning support department, an outstandingly excellent area of our educational provision I noticed you lamentably failed to visit while you were here. You will discover that this school compares very favourably indeed with other similar-sized local primaries." This last information was a wild guess, but the inspectors weren't to know that.

With a glazed stare, Mrs Busterd made a grab for one of the papers on the desk. "I will take this with me now," she stated loudly.

Toby pressed his hand firmly down on the paper she sought.

"No, that will not be possible. These data are currently strictly confidential, as I'm quite sure you understand." He wasn't having this. "Mayflower School does not release confidential information to any old Tom, Dick or Harry who happens to waltz into a private office unannounced and uninvited."

His eyes glittered blue sparks at the woman's seething countenance. Mrs Busterd should be scared, thought Skipper, in awe. Mr Phillips obviously was. Alicia Busterd tilted her head and narrowed her gaze, as if sizing Tremayne up for a coffin. Phillips cleared his throat nervously.

Toby rode majestically on. "Any further follow-up enquiries you might wish to pursue should be addressed to Mrs Clark respectfully and in writing. As far as this afternoon's visit is concerned, we will undertake to record its date and time in our visitors' register, as a matter of professional courtesy. And now, as we are both very busy, Mrs Clark and I will bid you good afternoon."

The two inspectors left without another word, leaving the doors wide open behind them.

Skipper grinned at Toby who puffed out his cheeks and wiped his hands together.

"That's the way to do it," he told her. "Pinch-punch and no returns."

America Day

It was America Day again, July 4th. This year, as Mrs Shaw was no longer around, the day might have lacked relevance had not Mrs Clark made a particular effort. She was keen to maintain links with the New World, the land she still loved. After all, she reasoned, the Mayflower was the Pilgrim Fathers' little ship, which was as good a symbol of learning as any. She did not want to press the analogy too far, however, as the pilgrims had apparently not been the best equipped group in history to embark on a new life in a strange land. She aimed to send her little travellers off much better prepared.

The Lions and Tigers softball teams had been practising after school each week under Mike's eagle eye and were able to provide a very enjoyable demonstration match during the afternoon. All the children were encouraged to come into school in tee shirts and jeans or shorts, for once. There was an American lunch of burgers and fries, followed by ice cream. Mr Tremayne took assembly and made it memorable by giving a potted version of the history of the continent, complete with a slideshow. Everyone had a chance to paint or draw a picture of anything American, such as a cowboy or a skyscraper or flag or a buffalo, and Mr Tuttle helped the whole school learn to sing 'She'll Be Coming Round the Mountain'. The yippie-ayes raised the roof. By four o'clock, when the building was finally empty, the staff sank down exhausted in the staffroom for a very welcome, sedate, cup of very English tea.

Just as a collective sigh of relief had been breathed out, there was a knock on the door and Dr Granger entered, shyly holding the hand of a red-haired young woman he introduced as Elaine, his fiancée. Everyone was delighted to meet her at long last.

"You're a dark horse," smiled Guy. "Lovely to meet you, Elaine. I hear you're a nurse."

"I'm a midwife. I worked with Mrs Tuttle for a while." Elaine was a pleasant girl with a wide smile and countless freckles. She accepted the inevitable cup of tea happily.

"Oh did you?" said Charlie, pleased. "Don't let her go overdoing it now, will you, Elaine? She's expecting you know."

"I know," laughed Elaine. "Don't worry, I'll keep an eye on her. If I can, that is. She's a little stubborn."

"Really?" smiled Charlie. "I hadn't noticed."

"When's the wedding day?" asked Jean. Weddings were on her mind.

"Hopefully this Autumn," answered Joe. "We're on our way to see Rev Bill for a chat about dates. Don't fill us up with too much tea, Skip, you know what June is like. There'll be gallons of the stuff and an entire seed-cake to get through later."

"And where are you going to live?" asked Dora, who had spent the day in school.

"We've bought a place out at Kirk Torby. It's about three miles west, off Scotch Road."

"It's gorgeous," enthused Elaine. "You cross a little stream to get to the house. There's a paddock at the back and I'm trying to persuade Joe to let me buy a horse. I've always wanted one of my own." She gazed at him with adoration. She had waited a long time for Joe Granger and knew how to be patient.

"Well, let's wait and see about that, shall we?" he grinned. "You never know your luck."

Indeed you do not, thought Skipper to herself. She raised her teacup. "All the every best to you both," she toasted them.

Joe smiled again and ventured a kiss on top of his betrothed's bouncy head of hair, grateful Skipper Clark was of a generous and forgiving nature.

Towards the end of term

Mr Tuttle was in charge of the end-of-year concert and decided that this time it should be held well before the manic final week. He wanted the audience to fully appreciate the children's musical talents without the distraction of the swimming gala or prize day or various other sporting fixtures.

As Mayflower had not entered the local music festival this year, and Heather Jackson would be moving away, he wanted this concert to be especially memorable. His wife despaired of him ever settling on a final choice of pieces as Charlie sat up long into the night deliberating, running over tunes on the piano.

Having trawled through every music book and every TV and schools' radio broadcast pamphlet, he did eventually settle the programme and began rehearsing the choir and the ever-expanding orchestra. He really wanted Heather to relax and be part of the audience this time, but she insisted on conducting one complicated piece with all the children. As he couldn't deny her that last pleasure, he worked around it, highlighting the talents of each class in turn and several individual performers. The finale, he decided, should follow a similar pattern to the Christmas concert and be led by Lizzie and Greg. Greg was delighted, even if Lizzie was slightly more reserved about the honour.

Greg was trying his utmost to be agreeable these days. Once he made up his mind not to make sport of every remark a classmate uttered he found himself enjoying his final days at school. He began to comply with his teacher's requests, put more pride into every task and to stop harassing the other kids. He discovered he got on well with Basil Russell and one day asked if he could sit next to him in class. Mr Denny reluctantly agreed, and was secretly delighted with the outcome. The boy buckled down and worked even harder than before. He seemed a lot happier and relaxed. Guy rewarded Greg with small additional responsibilities, which improved his attitude still further – and incidentally helped Lizzie Timms relax and enjoy singing with her musical partner.

The hall was packed for the six o'clock show. Mr Green and his team had every chair in the place set out. The governors graced the centrally located mishmash of upholstered seats at the front, while parents and friends settled on the less comfortable green canvas and tubular metal variety. Mrs Hewitt, assisted by Ryan, hauled back the heavy old curtains and the musicians shuffled shyly on stage, the singers in white tee shirts, the orchestra in green.

Lady Longmont sat next to Julia Scott and prattled on about music being the best way to teach everything from mathematics to art to geography. Teach history through music, teach science through music, she advised. It was an educational philosophy she had adopted from a diplomat at an embassy party long ago, who had found such notions amusing ice-breakers. Julia privately thought the same could be claimed for any school subject but knew her opinion was not required. She let the old lady chatter on.

"Ladies and gentlemen, boys and girls," announced Mrs Clark in a loud voice. "Welcome to our final concert of the year."

The youngest singers stood up and sang 'The Ink is Black' and the final concert was off to a flying start. Rounds, choruses, solos all followed. There were instrumentals and a wonderful sing-along with the audience of 'She'll be Coming Round the Mountain' and a grand finale of 'Waltzing Matilda' for no other reason than that it was a great song. Greg and Lizzie led the event like professionals and took their bows together, hand in hand. Heather was in tears as she received a massive bouquet of flowers and Charlie was surprised and delighted to be given a bottle of champagne.

"What a wonderful thing music is," shouted Dora to Miss Muggeridge who was sitting next to her. They clapped and cheered with everyone else before gathering up their bags and heading out into the late evening sunshine where the prefects were rattling collecting buckets in the hope of generous donations.

"They're going to miss that Miss Jackson," commented Miss Muggeridge.

"Yes they are. But Mr Tuttle is very good, you know. They have been lucky with their music teachers."

Miss Muggeridge agreed. "This school's been lucky with all its teachers if you ask me," she added. "Ever since you and your daughter took the place over this school's been looking up. It was a good day for Banford when you arrived."

Dora was so astonished at this kind observation she could only stand and stare as Miss Muggeridge edged her way out through the crowd. What a lovely thing to say, Dora thought. After all the nasty and difficult events that had happened that year, it was like a parting of the clouds. Dora hurried off to find Skip and tell her.

A visit to the dentist

Miss Fisher had been advised to take Jimmy to the dentist as a matter of some urgency. His teeth had been an on-going worry for the school dentist, Mr Andrewartha, since the child had first started kindergarten. He had sent notes and even driven round to Wag Lane twice to talk to Janey about the lad, but to no avail. Now at last, Miss Fisher brought him to the newly-built surgery in Paisley Road where the dentist had created a very modern set-up with children in mind. She filled him in on Jimmy's complicated health background before he started, which went a long way to explaining the decay he saw.

Jimmy was very nervous about the visit. He had listened to all the tales of horror about drills and needles from his classmates and was in two minds whether to run out of the door and down the road and never be seen again. But then he caught sight of Miss Fisher's anxious face and gave in. If she was worried it was for a good reason. He never, ever, wanted to be a cause of anxiety to his angel – she took such good care of him. He would sit in the big chair and open his mouth like a hippo.

The dentist was surprisingly gentle. He chatted away and tutted and poked and counted Jimmy's teeth, then sat back and pressed a button to make the chair return to its upright position. Jimmy rinsed and spat some pink pepperminty liquid into a basin and was rewarded with a tiny tube of toothpaste and a sticker for his shirt front. He held Auntie's hand all the way out.

She sat down on a seat at the bus stop and made him stand in front of her.

"You were a very brave boy, back there. I know you were scared, but you didn't cry. I am so proud of you," she whispered.

He tried to smile but found the corners of his mouth turning down instead of up.

"How about we nip into Woolworth's and buy Marigold a tin of pilchards? She loves those. And maybe a better comb for her fur. Her purple one is falling to pieces."

"Like my teeth," suggested Jimmy, miserably.

Miss Fisher smiled. "Your baby teeth are not very good, Mr Andrewartha says, but they will soon fall out naturally and some strong new ones will come through. If we brush those properly twice a day, and you keep on eating well, they'll be alright. I think one of your baby teeth has already fallen out, hasn't it?"

The boy nodded. "The comb might grow new teeth too – will it? No. That's silly." Jimmy felt much brighter. "Can we get her a pink one, because Marigold's a girl?"

Tired and strung-out from the tension of the previous hour, May Fisher allowed herself to be pulled into Woolworth's where Jimmy chose a small tin of pilchards, a lurid orange comb and a toy bird on a stick for the cat to play with.

There would be many future trips to the dentist, but now that Jimmy knew what to expect he accepted them as another inevitable part of his new life. It wasn't so bad. Buying Marigold a tasty treat each time would be an extra reward.

Glenda needs a helping hand.

Open Afternoon and Evening was next on the school calendar. It was the last chance that year for parents to visit their children's teacher and discuss their progress. Now it really began to feel like the end of term to everyone. For the occasion, all the classrooms were tidied up and new displays pinned to the display boards. Parents milled about, chatting noisily.

Mrs Lara, this year's parent governor who owned the cake shop in town, arrived after lunch with a van full of cakes and buns she had donated to boost the afternoon's cake sales. All the locals tried to pop into the hall to buy something as her offerings were famously delicious. There was also a splendid exhibition of art to admire.

"Gosh, is that Mike's mum?" whispered Betty to her husband, pointing down the path. She had paused her conference schedule to snatch a quick drink with him outdoors by the front shrubbery. "She really doesn't look very well."

"Pretty brave of her to turn out, if you ask me," answered Ben, slipping both dogs he had brought with him a sneaky piece of bun. "She's leaning hard on that walking frame thing. I don't suppose she gets out much nowadays."

"No. Who brought her, do you suppose? Mike will be up to his ears in parents."

"Maybe the district nurse? She's over there too. Look, I'll go and help get her into the hall and onto a chair. Oh…! "

Ben dropped the dogs' leads and hopped quickly over to Glenda who had missed a step and had fallen heavily into a large bush. Gently, Ben manoeuvred her into a sitting position and with others help raise her slowly to her feet. Glenda was smiling and muddled and looking around for her glasses. Betty found them and brought them to her as she sat in the hall on a nice safe solid chair with Ben's sheepdog and Hades the Jack Russell at her side. Peggy dabbed Germolene on her scratched hand while Ben picked leaves out of her cardigan.

Nurse Presley, who had been purchasing a cake when Glenda tumbled over, came and checked the old lady carefully.

"Och, no need for an ambulance, thank you Mrs Bailey. But I'll take Mrs Paton home in my wee car as I think she's maybe had enough excitement for one day. Perhaps you'd not mind explaining to her son? He asked me to bring her along, you know, as a little treat. Now then let's put this Victoria sandwich you wanted in my bag, dearie, and head home shall we? You can leave that cup of nasty stewed tea. Mine's very lukewarm. Much better if I make you a fresh cup in your own kitchen."

Betty left Ben to help, as she had to get back to class. What a worry elderly parents were, she thought, especially when they tip over into bushes in public places. She hoped Glenda wasn't too shaken up and that she would rest properly once she was home.

As she welcomed her next set of parents into the kindergarten classroom and sat them on the tiny chairs to hear all about the academic gains their little darlings had made that year, Betty promised herself a trip over to Caster Cottage the next morning to check on the old lady for herself.

Ernest

July was turning out to be a month of rain and sunshine, mimicking April.

"So now, how have you been coping with yon Birch laddie?" asked Nurse Presley, as she and May Fisher walked together over the bridge into town one showery afternoon.

May had asked Ernest Chivers to mind Jimmy for an hour while she went to pick up some wool she had ordered. It was nice to stretch her legs after being in school all day.

"Oh, I think we're settling in together well-enough, thank you Hilary," answered May, cautiously.

"It's not too much for you, having a wee sick laddie to care for after those long years alone then?"

May rather resented that but she let it pass. "No, I'm fine thank you. We jog along. He seems to be coping and I can hardly remember when I was without him."

"Really? Well isn't that lovely. Young boys can quite a handful so don't go overdoing it now," warned the nurse. She was well aware Jimmy Birch wasn't very much of a handful, but he did require particular attention. "Have you the right medicines for him? Is he missing his mother?"

"Oh, I make sure he receives his medicines correctly," May assured the nurse. "And yes, I'm sure he misses her. But all things considered, he seems to have settled down alright. It's not like we're strangers."

"I'm sure he couldn't have found a better home," said Hilary making it sound as if she were talking about a puppy. "He's lucky to have you."

"And I him," agreed May Fisher firmly. She appreciated the uncharacteristically kind remark.

As directed, Jimmy had gone to the library after school. Mr Chivers wasn't there when he arrived so he sat on a bean bag and looked at picture books. He liked these books but rarely picked one to borrow when his class visited the library as they were meant for the babies, not big boys of seven.

Sunlight was sifting through the lofty stained glass windows above him making flickering patterns on the floor. He could hear the huge grandfather clock by the door ticking heavily – tick…tock… tick… as if it were alive. Far away a bird chirped. The sun went in and rain began to patter and tap at the windows.

Jimmy allowed himself think about his mother. He did not hear Mr Chivers return, he was too busy sobbing his heart out.

Ernest could not at first decided where the sound was coming from, but then he spotted the child curled up in a ball on the beanbag. He squatted down and stoked Jimmy's shoulder, then gathered him up in his arms and took him over to the big armchair he called his story chair. He sat down with Jimmy on his lap, and let him cry for a while without saying anything. The child eventually hiccupped and rubbed his snotty face on the inside of his elbow. Ernest dug out his own handkerchief and wiped away a little more.

"What's up?" he asked gently.

"I miss my mum. I want my mum. But she don't come home no more."

Mr Chivers' kind heart was wrung with sorrow for the little scrap.

"No, she can't, that's right."

"My mum died. I put flowers on her but she's not there."

Jimmy rested his aching head back against the librarian's shirt front as he didn't seem to mind. He felt hot and angry and sad and all muddled up about school and home and who was who.

They sat in silence for a while.

"You know, I don't have a mum either," confided Ernest.

That was interesting. "Why not?" asked Jimmy.

"She died when I was a little boy," said Ernest. "I can remember exactly how I felt then. It still really hurts that she's not here any more."

Jimmy turned and studied Mr Chivers' face.

"Did you cry?"

"I did."

"Did a car hit her too?"

"No. She was very, very ill though. And like your mum she really, really wanted to stay and be with me – but she was just too poorly. I didn't want her to be in pain and worrying about me. So I had to let her go."

"You let her go?" whispered Jimmy. "My mum's pretty. I don't want her to go."

"I know. Mine was pretty too. You know, things can't go back to how they were before, but you can go forwards a little bit at a time. That's what mums want you to do. And you can take her memory with you – inside. Here, in your heart. You can tell her things every day and she'll hear you."

"Do you still tell your mum things?"

"I do. But that's a secret between you and me."

Jimmy felt calmer, lying against Mr. Chivers' shirt. He felt safe. He could hear the man's heart beating like the clock. This was what a dad might be like, he guessed.

"Shall we walk round and find Miss Fisher in a bit? I expect she might make us a cup of tea. What do you think? Or shall we sit here and have a story first?"

"Please may we have a story?"

"Which one would you like?"

Jimmy knew it was babyish but there was only one he really, truly wanted. "Can we have the one about Winnie the Pooh and the blue balloon?"

Mr Chivers never made any judgement about anyone's choice of story. It was one of the other nicest things about him. He simply opened the book you wanted and started reading.

Mike

"Home again, home again!" called Mike, as he always did. Hopping, to pull off his bicycle clips, he heard no familiar response. His heart flipped.

"Mum?" he called, hurrying into the sitting room.

Glenda lay asleep in her chair. Tiddles was stretched on the hearthrug.

"Mum?" asked Mike. "Mum!" He pushed her white hair back off her face.

"Mmm," mumbled his mother. She came-to and opened her eyes. Words would not form in her mouth for some reason so she had no way to ask where she was.

Mike was terrified, but he and the nurse had had more than one long conversation about Glenda's deteriorating condition. He had spoken at length to Dr Granger only the other day when he took her for a check-up after the tumble she'd taken. Joe Granger had carefully explained how very fragile Glenda was becoming.

"It's just old age, Mike. She's not exactly sick, but everything's wearing out. Worn out. You must expect her to fade pretty fast from now on, I'm afraid."

"I was thinking maybe an old people's home would help her, where she'd have round-the-clock care and people to talk to."

Dr Granger shrugged. "Is she too much for you?"

"Never," Mike began. Then he faltered. "But I'm at work all day. I can't tend to her personal hygiene as a proper nurse might. As it is I'm up all night."

Dr Granger knew only too well the stresses and strains of caring for the elderly. Mike was looking far from well himself.

"Look," said Joe. "Go and see that place you like out at Sorburn. It's well run and has places available. Miss Muggeridge can watch Glenda for an hour or so. I'll pop in to see her again tomorrow."

Mike nodded. It would have to do. The days of being together as mother and son were coming to an end, and all he wanted now was to see she was properly cared for. To see her dignity respected. He wanted to walk beside her for one final mile and let her know she was safe and loved.

"It's only a few days now until you break up," Dr Granger reminded him.

So here he was carrying Glenda upstairs again and putting her to bed. He phoned for the doctor who arrived within the hour.

"She's had another little stroke," Dr Granger explained. "Just tend her carefully, Mike. Check that monitor I've given you and let her rest."

"She'd like to see the lavender bushes come out in the garden," Mike said forlornly. "They're always such a picture."

Joe nodded. "I know, I know. Call me or Dr Legg if there's any change, old man. Or the ambulance if you need to."

Mike saw the doctor out. He noted Joe's smart new car thinking how sad it was the old blue Singer had finally been pensioned off. It disappeared in a spat of gravel down the Drove. He went back upstairs to his mother's little bedroom under the roof. She had slept there since she was a bride and her future had looked so rosy.

Glenda lay dozing against the pillows. She opened her eyes and said quite clearly, "Oh there you are."

"What's your favourite flower, Mum?"

His mother drifted off for a while. Mike held her hand and watched her breathing, in and out.

After about twenty minutes she opened her eyes again and muttered, "Roses."

"What colour?"

Another half hour went by before she stirred again.

"Pink."

Mike sat and watched, holding her warm hand in his.

*   *   *

24.

Stokes' steps

Summer comes

"It's never our birthdays again, is it?" asked Peggy, remembering her and Cathy's fancifully iced cakes of the year before. Today the offerings were less ornate but nonetheless welcome. Peggy and Cathy's birthdays fell so close together the staff combined them into one joint celebration. The invaluable duo shuffled shyly into the staffroom where everyone was gathered around the table admiring the huge chocolate tray-bake that lay in one of Mrs Lara's largest boxes.

"Ooh, how gorgeous," cried Peggy.

"I've already put you some in a bag to take home for Albert, Gary and Trudy – and some for Jim and Simon," fussed Jean. She didn't want anyone to miss out. "Heather, are you having some?"

"Yes please," she said. "Oh I'm going to miss all this!" She couldn't believe she was actually leaving and was already saying to herself, 'This is the last time I ..'. It was making her sad.

Peggy sat with her plate and a mug of tea on the squishy old sofa next to Charlie Tuttle.

"How's Fiona keeping?" she asked.

"Doing well, thank you Peggy," he replied. He was far more impatient for this baby to be born than his wife, and was making the most of the run-up to its arrival by re-learning everything he had known about when Tim was born. "We have four months left apparently, so I'm decorating like mad."

"Is she still working?"

"Yes but packing up in a month, thank heaven, or so she says. Fortunately she's been very well this time around, I'm glad to say." Charlie hated Fiona working so much. Any nurse's life was hard on the feet and legs and Fiona was no longer twenty-one.

Cathy Duke and Jean took their plates outside into the sunshine and perched on the low wall that ran beside the path. Through the shrubs they could see the Donkey Field with its margin of shady chestnut trees, now lacking their splendid candelabra display of pink and white blossoms. It was all very peaceful at this time of day.

"I don't suppose you see so much of May these days," commented Cathy.

"Because of Jimmy, you mean?" asked Jean. "Well I can't say I've noticed much tailing off. He trots around with her like a shadow. They come for lunch on a Sunday and I help him with his homework sometimes."

"Is he very far behind?"

"No, not as much as I thought he might be. He has Sandi during the day and – with a little extra explanation here and there – he's beginning to cope with most of what you'd expect a seven year old to be doing. The gap may widen more when he's older, of course. He had such a rough start and his nutrition issues mean he is going to have to be very careful for a long time. I do hope he grows out of it. It must be a hereditary thing, don't you think? It can't just be neglect."

Jimmy had been preying on Cathy's mind. "You know I always tried to make sure Jimmy was on the doctor's list whenever he or the nurse visited," she said. "I always added him to the dentist's too. He's always been a concern to me."

"I know. We *all* know, Cathy. But his impetigo and whatnot didn't start in school. It was actually school that flagged him up from the very beginning. That's you and Peggy. It was our Nosh Club that helped him find things to eat that didn't upset his insides, and Ivy and his classmates who always made sure he didn't starve. Mayflower's been Jimmy's saviour – and you more than any of us helped keep him going. Please don't think you've failed him in any way. You and Peggy have been marvellous."

Cathy sniffed. It was kind of Jean to reassure her and horrible to think they had actually been quite close to losing the little lad, according to Dr Legg. "His poor mother," she said. "How she coped when he was a baby I can't think."

Janey was a sad memory on a birthday afternoon.

"I know. But honestly, Cathy, Janey Birch was very damaged herself. She undoubtedly did her best but – well I'm sorry to say it – maybe now the situation is different Jimmy will finally get what his little body's always needed. I think Janey would be pleased May has him. I had my reservations as you know, but now I sincerely hope she's allowed to keep him. If anyone can help him grow up big and strong, May Fisher can."

"I heard there was a court hearing coming up with a mountain of documents to sign," said Cathy. Everything was so complicated these days.

"Oh you wouldn't believe how many," answered Jean nodding. She had already accompanied May once to the children's court. Thankfully the judge had had no concerns over May Fisher's age, suitability, willingness or ability to raise a child on her own but, as everyone knew, in light of several recent adoption cases that had gone dreadfully wrong, the authorities had to be extremely cautious when placing a particularly vulnerable child.

"Listen," Jean reminded her, patting Cathy's hand in reassurance. "Jimmy's a Mayflower lad. Between the lot of us I think we can raise him right."

Mrs Duke smiled. Jean was right. Mayflower was the best place for little Jimmy Birch, to be sure.

Promotion

An official letter from the Local Education Office lay on Toby Tremayne's desk blotter one morning. He picked it up with a sigh and tore it open. More red tape? More pointless scrutiny?

No. It was formally confirming his appointment as Mayflower's deputy headmaster and stating his salary and contract details.

"About bloody time. Yippee and yeehar!" he cried as he galloped into Skipper's office waving the paper at her.

"Oh that's come through has it? Well done, Toby, I'm so glad. We all are. I'll ring the governors and let them know." Mrs Clark could not feel more relieved. Finally, at the end of two very stressful terms without Chloe, she now had a permanent deputy. One she trusted to be strong and supportive. She had been feeling like Matt Dillon without Chester for so long it was a huge relief to finally have someone reliable onboard.

Toby was genuinely delighted too. He was formally established as an integral part of the school, and right where he wanted to be to oversee the intelligence operation. He even dwelt where he could keep old Lady Longmont under his eye. This deputy headship was perfect legitimate cover all round. Long may it last.

Peg and Cathy each received a kiss on the cheek from Mr Tremayne when he told them the news.

"Now you'll have to get me an outside line a bit sharper," he said spikily.

"When did I ever not?" remonstrated Peg, affronted. "You're just *always* demanding outside lines. I don't know why you don't have your own direct one installed, Mr High and Mighty Deputy. Save me the bother of dropping what I'm doing every five minutes."

"I might just do that," answered Toby. Not a bad idea, actually. He would ask Skip while she was in a good mood. Maybe MI5 would pay to upgrade the whole telephone system.

A new game for Sports Day

"Out you go then," Miss Fisher instructed her eager class. "Pick that up Rick, and put it in the bin please. Alan – shoelaces. Jimmy Birch I'd like you and Carl to carry this umbrella and my shopping bag for me, please. Who could manage their chairs as well as their own? Thank you, Peter. Thank you Lulu."

Jimmy grasped his angel's umbrella while Carl took the heavy shopping bag full of who knew what. Carl – a quiet, kind boy – was only too pleased to be chosen to help out. He cast a fleeting look at Jim and decided his friend was looking much better. The whole school knew about his mum being run-over and how their teacher had taken him to live with her. Carl wondered whether she would do the same for any one of them if they were suddenly orphaned. He would ask his dad about it tonight.

They trooped out to the field, doing their best not to bump the walls with their chair legs. Mr Green was watching everyone closely, as usual. He was not a fan of chair-carrying from the upper floors. He and Stringer were setting up two sun umbrellas over the table where the announcer would sit. Today this was Mr Tremayne's job, which freed Mrs Clark for more general duties.

"Oy, mind that electric wire," Reg shouted at Dawn Lennox who was jabbering fifteen to the dozen with her classmate Philly, and not looking where she was going. "Push yer chairs back much further than that, you girls. No, *further*. You can't sit right on the line like that, it ent safe."

Lady Longmont hurried over with a neat wicker lunch hamper. She wanted to share this with Mrs Clark as they had the previous year, but the weather did not look quite so reliable today. She grasped her sunhat to her head and peered around for the headmistress.

"Ah, tally-ho!" she cried, and set off for the long-jump pit where Mrs Clark was overseeing Kenny as he raked the sand into a neat flat pancake.

"And chase him away if he looks like he's going to do his business in it again," Skip was telling the boy. He was a sensible lad, not easily flustered by a little dog poo.

"Yes, Miss."

"Oh hello, Gibb," said Mrs Clark. "What a splendid hamper. Shall we leave it in my study while the races are on?"

"Righty-o. The BBC said the weather might hold off if we're lucky. Shall I nip in through the staff-room?"

"Yes, good idea. Kenny, thank you for doing that. Leave the rake beside the pavilion please, as we'll need it again between competitors.

"Yes, Miss."

Mrs Clark hurried off importantly, looking for more things to oversee while Lady Longmont strode off to deposit the lunch basket. She almost collided with Toby whom she had not seen since last Sunday.

"Morning!" he said cheerfully. "I hope there's strawberries and cream in that basket."

"Ha!" scoffed Lady Longmont. "Have you a spare whistle? There's usually one in a drawer somewhere."

Fully equipped with a whistle, she was the day's official starter. She set the runners off in very efficient style with a loud "Ready, steady!"

After the usual bean bags and slow cycle rides, one brand new race was announced. It had only been invented this year, and was called 'Stokes's Steps'. Four teams had to leap from one point to another using hoops laid on the ground as stepping stones, left right, left right. It was third-former Keith Carter's idea. Keith was highly delighted when Darwin, his own house, won.

In fact, Darwin won the entire Sports Day by nineteen points – a first for them. Ryan Hale was so thrilled at the announcement, he picked Jimmy up like a mascot and set him on his shoulders for the lap of honour, while the spectators clapped and cheered. May and Jean stood together under the umbrella, too exhausted to speak, while Greg Price – who was watching Jonah Webb perform cartwheels – whistled and applauded and waved, a nice normal, genuinely happy smile on his sharp-featured face for once.

Gala day

After Sports Day came the Swimming Gala at the Lido across the road from school.

Ryan was raring to go. He had on some new black trunks and was rubbing his arms in order to warm up his muscles. It wasn't the hottest of summer days, but it would be alright once they were in the water. He couldn't wait. He had been terrible at running and jumping the day before, but had redeemed himself a little in the ball-throwing contests where his height and strength sent the cricket ball almost to the hedge. Today would be when he came into his own, he felt sure. In the water it didn't matter if you were slightly big and clumsy.

Since finding out he could swim, Ryan had been practising every day after school on the way home, taking a covert dip in the river at Mint Pool. He would go from bank to bank, up stream and down, trying to get his arms and legs to pull and push him through the cold water like he had seen athletes do on TV. He taught himself to put his face in the water and breathe to one side. He even taught himself to float on his back. By gala day he was as ready as he could be.

Team colours were handed out in the form of little ribbons and a safety pin to be attached to each swimmer's costume. Everybody was in one race or another, even the youngest kindergartener. There were lines of chairs for spectators and towels spread on the grass or on the benches around the side of the cold-water pool. It was a colourful sight, and those parents who could attend brought their cameras along to record the scene. Sweep was there with Jean, but Nicky was busy hunting mice in the wilderness well away from the nasty water he had jumped into last year. Stringer trotted round with Reg, accepting pats on the head and watching in case anyone wished

474

to share a treat. Not that he would have eaten it – he had learned his lesson. Ivy supplied jugs of orange squash that stood under tea-towels on a side table. Peggy and Cathy took turns throughout the morning to mind the office phone and trot across the road to watch a little of the fun. All the governors except Sir Hugo were there, dressed in their summer hats. The excitement was palpable.

"Just do yer best," Mrs Davidson told Shelley, who stood as still as she could while her mother forced a white rubber swimming helmet over her long hair.

"Ow!"

"Stop that. There, now 'old still while I do the snapper. Drat the thing. There, that's done it." The rim of the hat pushed Shelley's eyebrows down as if she were frowning. It was quite a bit too large and covered with rubber daisies that flapped in the breeze. She pushed it up a bit.

"Nice hat," remarked Ryan.

"Don't be cheeky, you great galumph," replied Mrs Davidson.

Ryan was surprised. He thought the hat was rather pretty, not plain like everyone else's. He went off to see if Mr Denny wanted any extra help setting up. Shelley soon escaped and found her way after him. She smiled at the boy with her rather large teeth. He grinned back.

"Good luck," she said.

Guy and Mike always organised the gala and over the years had refined the event to run like clockwork. At one point, the heavens opened and the rain came down in torrents, but that only set everything back by ten minutes or so. It didn't really matter.

Eventually the last and longest race was announced. It was the one Ryan had been waiting for. He and Trudy were the green team, Martin and Naomi the blues, Kit and Veronica the reds, Greg and Emily the yellows. One of each colour swam up and back the length of the pool then tagged their team member. It was a race to complete as many lengths as they could in four minutes.

Side by side, the four girls stood waiting for the off.

"Ready, set…" Mr Denny blew his whistle.

They dived together and swam up and back, then the boys dived in. Ryan used his legs like an engine, pushing himself on and on. His arms felt more like wings than ever before – it was as if he were flying. Down, turn, push, glide, and start pounding back. Trudy again. She swam like a quick little fish. The crowd cheered louder as the time ticked down. The boys dived one last time. Greg and Ryan swam neck and neck leaving Kit and Martin far behind.

"My goodness, look at Ryan go!" shrieked Mrs Clark to Sandi Raina.

"He's wonderful!" cried Sandi. "Come on Ryan!"

Greg caught the mood. He glanced at his classmate and realised that at last Ryan had found something he could win at. Greg eased off, just a little.

"I think Greg is tiring," commented Sandi. "Come on Greg!"

The boy smiled inwardly. It was nice that Mrs Raina was encouraging him too. He liked teachers when they treated you fairly. Ryan touched the wall just before the whistle sounded time was up, and just ahead of Greg. They grinned at each other.

"And the winners are – Darwin!" announced Mr Tremayne.

"Well done, Trudy. Well done Ryan." called Mrs Clark. "That was quite a swim!"

The two happy green team members beamed around in delight, as everybody leapt into the pool and congratulated them.

"Nice one, mate," Greg said to Ryan as they eventually towelled themselves dry. "At least you won't smell of pee all day now."

Ryan burst out laughing and crashed his large hand heavily down onto Greg's shoulder.

"That's true. Thanks though. I really enjoyed finally beating you at something."

The end of a difficult year

Founder's Day was also Prize Day. Mrs Clark had delegated much of its organisation to Mr Tremayne this year as she was still burrowing her way through piles of budgets and paperwork that had continued to grow like a reef around her since Easter. She sorely missed Chloe's sunny disposition and sensible advice but Toby was helping enormously, and he was very good at formal events.

Skipper felt exhausted as she tied ribbons onto the trophies this July morning. Last year Chloe and Max had been with her to hand out these awards and everybody had been happy and hopeful, looking forward to their upcoming nuptials. The winds of change had certainly blown hard against everyone ever since that day, and the headmistress felt more than a little weatherbeaten.

Sir Hugo Chivers found his way to her side about eight o'clock and actually lent a hand with the ribbons. She started telling him again about the year.

"You've had a challenging time," he commiserated, wishing she would desist.

"Indeed we have. After Max died, things went from bad to worse somehow. It's as if we were ill-wished."

Hugo had no patience with such piffle, but he did agree the school had had quite enough setbacks. It was no use commiserating too much with her, though. She would only get maudlin – a gloomy state of mind that might mean she let slip information he would rather she kept silent about. He mulled over ways of jollying her up. Should he tell her about Chloe's new school or that Len Kirk might be a bit less morose from now on? He tied another ribbon onto another trophy as he thought. Fortunately, there would be no new house guests arriving any time soon – not until after he returned from Yorkshire anyway. What if he suggested a holiday? That might be enough to keep her on track.

Soon the hall was full of excited children, teachers and parents, all eager to know who was collecting which prize. Skip had set the portrait of Sir Garnet Broadstock on an easel at the side of the stage so that even the smallest children could visualise who their founder was. A bowl full of Dora's best roses stood beside it. On the stage sat Lady Longmont, the vicar and Sir Hugo, while Heather graced the piano stool for the last time. They began with 'He-who' – otherwise known as 'To Be a Pilgrim' – the children's favourite end of term hymn.

Mrs Clark, resplendent in cap and hooded gown and looking very important, welcomed everyone in her most queenly tones. She gave her usual speech acknowledging the hard work of the entire school community and its wide network of supporters. The time to reward and celebrate the year's achievements had finally arrived, she said grandly, and sat down.

Stringer trotted onto the stage with a little silver handbell in his mouth. He stood at the front and shook it like he was shaking a rat. The children sat up straighter and laughed out loud. This was better.

Mr Tremayne, also robed and mortar-boarded, stood up and walked over to the lectern.

"Bonjour, mes enfants," he cried.

"*Bonjour, monsieur,*" returned the children.

"Now then, I believe we have some silverware to hand out. Mrs Duke has carefully polished everything, thank you Mrs Duke. Mrs Bailey has counted it's all there and has not been stolen by pirates, thank you Mrs Bailey. And Mrs Clark has tied all the pretty ribbons on, so we're all set. Once this treasure has been distributed, Mrs Clark and I will take it back from you and lock it back in the cabinet for everyone to see and admire for another whole year. Does that sound like a good plan? Right, then let's make a start."

Cup by cup, trophy by trophy, the pieces were gradually handed over by Sir Hugo and Lady Longmont. Hugo looked elegant in his Savile Row suit, Gibb was spectacular in a shimmering wine coloured two-piece, a small iridescent feathered hat and coral coloured shoes and gloves. It was as if Hollywood had come to Banford. The occasion moved swiftly along, excitement and pride reflected in the parents' faces as each child in turn gripped a hard-won prize. Everybody was applauded and some were even cheered. Greg was thrilled to the marrow with his music prize and Ryan was cheered to the rafters to receive the Founder's Cup for Merit and Character. Dean made his hands ache from applauding his friend. He remembered winning this trophy himself last year. It was a real achievement, he knew.

"Rad, man" he called as Ryan went past on his way to sit down again at the back of the hall. The big lad was grinning from ear and his glasses were fogged up. His mother, perched on the end of a line of parents looked fit to burst.

The house prize went to Darwin, as everyone knew it would. Baz and Trudy – the green team captains –went up to accept the rose bowl, then turned to face the photographer from the local newspaper. It was hard to imagine a more thrilling moment ever happening again in their lives.

The photographer stayed for lunch then attended the Summer Fete in the afternoon, much to Miss Winstanley's disgruntlement. The weather was overcast but dry, which was a distinct blessing in Mrs Clark's view. The children had set out their stalls and raffles with great care, and voted to deck themselves in preposterous hats as a gimmick. Dean was a pirate, Ryan a cowboy. Trudy's sunbonnet was trimmed with wildflowers and Shelley Davidson had her floral rubber swimming hat on. Greg Price tried a few unkind comments about the others at first, but as no one took much notice, he twisted his baseball cap around and joined in the fun.

Reg and Stringer were everywhere at once, on the field, in the hall, out the front where two parents were arguing about where to park. Mr Tremayne, still in his mortar-board, joined the caretaker in explaining that the front gravel and lawn were not strictly meant to double as a car park.

"This school could really do with a bit more parking, Mr Green," commented Toby.

"Indeed it could Sir," replied Reg, holding his temper in.

Toby went to see if the cake stall had run out of chocolate do-dahs. As it had, he wandered off to the Donkey Field where Miss Winstanley was supervising Persephone, who was walking up and down giving rides. Miss Winstanley had offered this treat in return for her animal being allowed the freedom of the grassy field during the long summer holidays. Fay said Persephone would keep the grass down, although Reg did not think one little donkey would eat that much grass in a month of Sundays.

Stringer was currently leading the animal up and down as if they were a circus act. All the kindergarteners had each had one ride already and couldn't wait for a second turn. The photographer clicked away with his camera, knowing the next edition of the paper would sell well.

"Is it true we don't have to wear blazers next term?" Joe Latimer asked Anna Lane as they worked together on the roll-a-penny stall nearby. "My mum says we don't."

"Yes," said Anna. "It was in the last newsletter. Don't you ever read it?"

Joey shook his head. He usually forgot he had it in his bag at all. His mum normally only unearthed it when searching for his lost PE kit or snack bags, by which time it was always out of date. His satchel was an area Joe preferred to ignore.

"Us girls can have a cardy instead of a blazer. We can have a grey pinafore too, 'stead of green, which is good because my mum says it's easier to find grey in the shops. And it's white or green shirts for us. You boys can just wear a jumper."

"But we gotta keep our grey shirts and ties, right?" Joe's tie had gone missing. He was going to look in lost property for it later with his mum. The uniform changes didn't seem to amount to much in Joey's opinion. He would prefer to wear long trousers, but that didn't seem to be on the cards at all. He sighed. It would be different at secondary school, he comforted himself.

The roll-a-penny was popular, and at the end Joe and Anna took the heavy cash box over to Mrs Bailey who was busy counting and re-counting tins full of change and bagging it up.

"We've done really well," Peg commented to Mrs Duke who sat beside her. "There may be enough after the charity donation to pay that blessed man to go away."

"What blessed man? Oh, Mr Jolly you mean? He hasn't finished yet, has he? I think he must be related to a sloth or something. Miss Fisher's tortoise moves faster," smiled Cathy.

Peggy grunted. Ted Jolly was still the bane of her life. Reg Green was no fan of the man either. They both thanked heaven that tomorrow was the last day of term and after that, for a whole month, they need have nothing to do with Mr Jolly and his dusty clutter.

Greg has a big surprise

"These are to go straight into your bags and given to your parents directly you get home," commanded Mr Denny sternly. Every other teacher was saying much the same thing in their classes.

End of year reports were a serious business. To Ryan a good one might mean he would get the bike he had his heart set on. To Lizzie Timms it could mean a new pair of roller skates. To Greg Price however, a report represented little more than the written evidence of his year's delinquency, and was therefore only fit to be ripped open at the school gates and then chucked in the nearest bin. School reports were nothing but rubbish – their mother didn't want to see them. After having a laugh at the pompous comments, the Price boys always screwed the papers up and chucked them away. Or set light to them. Greg didn't care.

Except – this time – he found he did. Maybe he would rip his report open on the way home then toss it away carelessly into the kitchen bin, from where his mother might retrieve it. That way he would still have acted like a bad boy, but she would find it, read it, and know he had tried his best this year.

Mr Denny was saying the reports were being given out now, before church dismissal. It was a departure from tradition.

Greg stuffed his into his inside blazer pocket and put his chair up on the desk like everyone else. He would decide later whether to show it to his mum.

It's the last time I'll see this stupid classroom, he thought. He smiled at Trudy, who had suffered so much, and put her chair up for her. She wasn't so bad.

The whole school walked in a crocodile over to St Andrew's one last time. Form 6 were the soberest on this occasion as it dawned on them all that today was their last ever as Mayflower pupils. They gazed around at the adults and friends who had helped them along their educational journey. Most children had started in the kindergarten, and were ending seven-year careers. It was their first big parting of the ways, and they were aware they might never see some familiar faces again. Most were prepared and eager to move forward. A few were dreading it.

Greg was surprised to find himself sorry that he had not spent longer at this funny little school. It dawned on him, as he sat in church folding the service paper into a paper aeroplane, that his earlier years might have been different if he had been there longer. He looked at the adults crowding around the church door, parents and teachers, helpers and one or two animals. He finally remembered to remove his cap.

"Hey, Greg," hissed his brother Phil tapping him on the shoulder. Greg turned in astonishment.

His mum was there, standing between his brother and Pat Green.

"Hello, love. Thought we'd come along as it's a nice day," she smiled. Greg's heart flipped.

"You bunkin' off work, Mum?"

She chuckled and nodded, and Greg thought he was going to cry.

Rev Bill stood up and delivered his usual homilies and reminders before the choir and congregation sang a final rendition of the Mayflower school song. It was a spirited piece with words designed to encourage even the most faint-hearted of life's voyagers. Everyone sang the final chorus with gusto as they joined together in its simple message of togetherness and hope. And by the time the final note had been played, even Greg Price knew that although you could not know what was coming, it was family – brothers, sister, parents, school – that gave you strength to go forward.

After the end

The schoolchildren, except for Shelley and Jimmy who were playing with Nicky outside in the shade, were long gone. Gone too were Mike and Ernest who had cycled home to check on Glenda. Ernest was halfway through buying his first motor car, as he felt he was growing slightly too old to be cycling everywhere. He would collect it next week, which was timely, as Glenda had an appointment at Fenchester hospital on Thursday, and they could hardly take her there on their bikes. Toby had hurried off to catch the London train. Betty and May were in the office with Peggy and Cathy. Heather had departed amid a welter of tears and good wishes, leaving the hamster for Skip to deal with. Guy and Jean were supervising Sweep and Stringer on a lazy wander through the wilderness.

Sir Hugo sat alone with Skipper in the staffroom where the french window was propped open to admit the afternoon breeze. The headmistress had provided sandwiches and cold drinks for anyone who wanted to stay on and tidy their classrooms. It was nice to unwind together after three such hectic terms.

"So, how are the finances looking?" asked Hugo.

"Better, thank you. Yes, much better," answered Skipper. "Peggy says we will be back in the black by Christmas. I've had a bit of a tussle with the county office over Mr Jolly's bill but it's alright now."

"Toby says you've had to shelve a few of your other projects."

"Unfortunately yes. The central heating upgrade, the new lino, the playground equipment and the greenhouse. The little minibus will have to wait too. But on the plus side, the rewiring should be finished by September. There's a man coming to look at the skylight. It's going to be busy this Summer holiday, I think, but I'll be here to oversee it." Skip sighed. Even with the rest of the school on vacation, she somehow never was.

Hugo looked at her and noted a few more grey hairs catching the light. He had had a long, private word with the chief education officer during the week and convinced him Mayflower was not worth too much official scrutiny in future.

"Once the major fixes are done I think the LEA will be satisfied," she added hopefully.

"Good. So that's all that matters, then surely? Now then, I was wondering whether you might spare me a couple of days for a run up to Harrogate next week? A friend of mine has a flat there we can use. I have a small amount of business to do up that way, but it won't take very long. Reg can manage here, I'm sure. What do you say?"

Skipper was speechless. Go away with *Hugo* somewhere? Just the two of them? And stay in a *flat*? Her insides suddenly woke up and jumped for joy.

"Do you think Dora would mind being left behind just this once?" Hugo smiled.

"No – er, no. Yes, that would be lovely, thank you." Skipper felt hot all over and got up to fetch some more blackcurrant juice.

"Splendid. I'd like to drop into Whitby, too. Have you ever been? It's delightful. You wouldn't mind?" Hugo rose, ready to leave.

"No, not at all. Well, thank you very much. When do you want to go?" Skipper was sincerely hoping she had time for a shopping trip to Fenchester before the off.

Jean drifted in from the field just as they were finalising their plans, and was very surprised to see the headmistress's flushed face and unaccountably sunny mood. She was even more amazed when Hugo leaned down and kissed Skip on the cheek.

It looked like Mrs Clark was back on form.

* * *

25.

Cheers

Toby Tremayne and Gibb Longmont were sitting in the magnificent garden of Banford Hall enjoying a convivial moment of truce, when Sir Hugo appeared unannounced. Bunting had dropped him off on his way over to Castor Cottage.

Hugo sank down beside Gibb on the swing seat that stood in the cool shade of a vast cedar tree.

"Mike Paton's mother passed away overnight," he announced. "It's all very sad. I've sent Bunting over to help."

"Oh dear," cried Lady Longmont. "How absolutely rotten for Mr Paton. But not unexpected I think?" She turned towards Toby.

"No indeed. Glenda was a doughty old lady by all accounts. Must have been ninety if she was a day, though, and not at all well latterly. Mike will be pretty cut-up, poor man."

"Ernest's there," said Hugo. He thought back to when Eleanor had died – not a memory he often cared to dwell on.

Ernest had been away at school, and Hugo had managed everything alone.

"Well Ernest will be a great comfort and help, I'm sure," said Toby. He sipped his martini. "They've grown close, those two."

Hugo stirred himself. "Yes," he said. "It's nice for Ernest to have finally found a decent friend." By 'decent' he meant acceptable. "He hasn't always chosen wisely before."

"That odious Murphy character, you mean?" recalled Lady Longmont sagaciously. "No, but one can't choose one's children's friends and associates, can one?" She assumed this must be true. It had been true of brothers.

"At least he and Mike are discreet," remarked Hugo, not wishing to discuss Ernest any further. "I'm off up north next week for a few days. I'm taking the headmistress with me for a little break. If there's a funeral, would you be kind enough to stand in for us, Toby?"

"Of course, happy to. Flowers?"

"Yes please."

Lady Longmont closed her eyes and sighed as she felt suddenly very weary thinking about everything that had happened since last summer. Trouble had found them all, one way or another.

"It's been one long sausage-string of problems for that school this year, hasn't it?" she remarked. "Ever since the Shaws got married. He died, she left. There was that awful inspection, the lead being taken and those dreadfully difficult children to deal with. Money worries, your fire. It all takes a toll on people, you know. Not to mention little whatsisname Jimmy something and his poor mother. Plus the weather's been *absolutely* abysmal."

Toby Tremayne acknowledged life had certainly been a little rough since he arrived, knowing Gibb counted him as yet another of her unwelcome sausages.

He lay back in his old-fashioned deck-chair and stared through the random tangle of branches at the clear blue sky far, far away. Tomorrow looks slightly more hopeful though, he thought. Yes, tomorrow things will surely start improving.

* * *

The Mayflower Trilogy

Printed in Great Britain
by Amazon

79326375R00284